A Graduate Education

Phoebe Thorpe

ISBN: 9798479147616

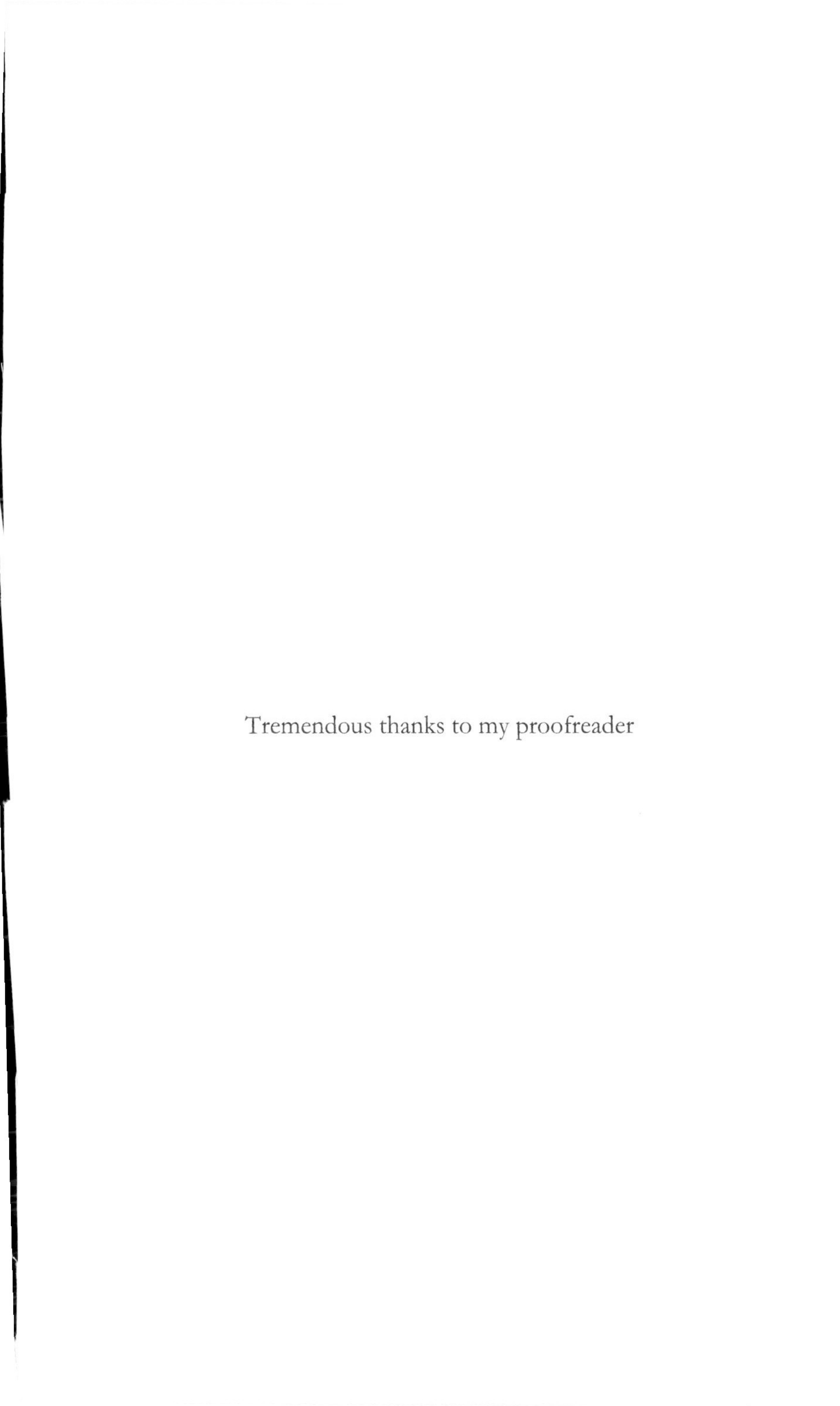

Tremendous thanks to my proofreader

CHAPTER 1

Mia James sighs and pushes back a long stray blonde hair that escaped from her messy bun. She hunches over her textbook at her desk and rubs her face, trying to work some energy into her body. It's only ten in the morning, but she finds herself already exhausted by the work she had completed and what lays ahead of her. As a third year psychology graduate student at Earl University, she is trying to balance her course load with her master's thesis research, and the end of the first semester is quickly coming to a close. Also as a twenty-five year old, she is trying to balance having a social life with academic and professional goals and obligations. Which meant that while it is only ten am, she also had not gone to bed until two in the morning and woke up at seven in order to beat the undergraduates to the gym. Mia would have chosen to skip that morning and sleep a little more before starting to read for her classes, but she had promised Leigh Black, her closest friend at school, that they could be accountability buddies at the gym. That promise stung a little when Leigh texted Mia right as Mia got to the gym to say that she's sleeping in and will make it up to her later. Mia was eager to see Leigh and tell her about the latest date she went on last night. He was cute and tall, but slow on understanding her sarcasm. Mia was out with him until midnight at a downtown bar and leaned heavily into her drinks the further into her date to make up for the lack of chemistry. When she finally went home she read an email from her advisor and spent over an hour skimming her advisor's latest notes on her most recent thesis draft. The notes were only mostly unpleasant this time, instead of entirely. Finally, Mia dragged herself away from the brutal commentary and went to sleep knowing at least she could tell Leigh about it all the next day.

Instead Mia found herself running alone on the treadmill, quickly followed by a smoothie for breakfast and back to her apartment to shower and get some work done. As her feet pounded on the treadmill she pushed away the thoughts that came with reviewing her advisor's notes and focused on her playlist. She even kept it together during her smoothie that she drank on her drive back home. It was only once she was in the shower that she let herself cry just a little bit over the cutting phrases. However, she made her plan for the day to tackle her reading and get back to the thesis draft after the other work was done.

Mia is tired, physically and emotionally by ten am and ready for a break. She pushes herself back from her desk and the chair rolls with some effort over the carpet. She reaches her tan arms over her head and stretches. Once she's out of her chair Mia rolls her shoulders to loosen the tension she created by hunching over in the first place. She looks around her sparsely decorated office. Her apartment was technically a two bedroom, but the second bedroom was too tiny for someone to comfortably live in, so it perfectly fit her desk, a chair, and a bookcase. By the window is an empty cardboard box that Renly, her tuxedo cat, preferred over the cat bed that came in it. Mia had hung her undergraduate diploma on the wall over her desk, along with a whiteboard, currently listing her academic to dos, but otherwise the walls were bare. She steps out of her office into the main space of her apartment, which housed the living room, eating nook, and kitchen. Mia decorated the main living space to be bright and welcoming, with lots of pops of color, and her bedroom to be a place of serenity, reflecting the one time she went to a spa, with mostly whites and tame blues. Right now she heads straight for her refrigerator and pulls out a can of soda, pops the tab and takes a big swig.

The caffeine will totally do the trick, she thinks to herself almost jokingly, knowing that her preference for soda has made her practically immune to its caffeinated contents. Mia reaches for her cellphone, which had been plugged in to charge in the kitchen so as to prevent herself from being distracted by it in the office, and leans onto the counter as she taps in her code to unlock it. One obnoxious, sneaky ex led her to keep her phone locked with a keypad. It wasn't that she did or usually intends to do anything wrong, it's the overall lack of trust and snoopiness of it all that irked her. She swipes to her text messages and pulls up Leigh's last text.

so sorry gonna cancel too tired for this ish. lunch?

Mia looks at the clock and begins keying in her answer back: **brunch?**

She pulls open Instagram and scrolls through the latest posts as Leigh's response quickly comes in.

duh. 11? Eastern's?

Mia sends back her yes response and glances at the clock again. There is enough time to read through at least one article for her Cognitive Development class and write up her response before she would get ready and head over to one of her favorite diners. Mia puts her phone back down on the counter and walks back into the office, where she shuffles through several folders on her desk and pulls out the one labeled CogDev as she sits down. She takes out the article on top, grabs a highlighter from the mug on her desk, pops off the top, and begins highlighting as she reads. She rolls her eyes a few times at methods she just could not agree with and begins typing her response at her computer. It takes a great deal of effort to stop herself from writing "junk science" or "this was dumb" in her response, knowing that her professor would not find it humorous.

After finishing her response Mia goes back to her bedroom to change out of the sweatpants she had settled into earlier in the morning. She switches into curve-hugging jeans and an oversized black sweater. She puts on sneakers and then makes her way across the hall to the bathroom. Mia examines herself in the mirror. Her long blonde hair is still in a messy bun from when she dried it after her shower. When she wears it down, it cascades past her shoulders and lays at the top of her breasts. She grabs some concealer and carefully applies a light amount of makeup: concealer, blush, and lip gloss.

Just the right amount, she thinks to herself, as she weighs applying eyeliner around her warm brown eyes. She smacks her lips together and does a pose in the mirror, hand on the hip, head cocked to the side and then shoots finger guns at her reflection

"Pew-pew!" She whispers and giggles. While she wasn't making herself up to impress Leigh, there was always the chance of a cute grad student or a cute anyone at the diner on Saturday morning. Earl University's location in a middle-sized town in the southeast was gentrifying quickly, pulling in young professionals. The opportunity to meet others was high, and since last night's tall, cute, and slow on the uptake was not likely to have a second date, Mia wanted to look nice enough but not like she was trying too hard. Mia spins out of the bathroom, and makes her way out of the apartment, grabbing her purse and keys on the way out the door.

CHAPTER 2

Mia pulls into Eastern's Diner characteristically a few minutes past eleven and bounds into the bustling restaurant to find that Leigh is already seated and staring at a menu. Mia gently snakes her way through the crowd waiting to be seated excusing herself along the way and scoots into the seat across from Leigh.

"I don't know why you even bother looking at the menu, you always get the same thing," Mia quips at Leigh as she picks up her own menu. The smell from the open kitchens wafts towards Mia practically causing her stomach to growl.

Leigh finally looks up, not paying attention to when Mia sat down, and smiles as she lays her menu down. "You never know, I might one day wake up adventurous and try something new." Leigh's short brown hair swings as she tosses her head and her green eyes fill with the same warmth as her smile. "And I'm so sorry about this morning. I really meant to come, I set my alarm and everything. But Jake texted and came over at two, so…" Leigh's voice trails off as her eyes trail off to the side where a lanky young man in an Eastern's t-shirt and serving apron is weaving between tables with a loaded tray.

"Ah, is that why you are already seated despite the wait?" Mia teases Leigh. Leigh shrugs and smiles down at her lap before laughing with Mia.

"The undergrad owed me."

"Yeah, he owes you a lot. How many first dibs on seats at Eastern's do you get for reaaaaally lenient grading?" Mia says with a wink, letting her friend know it was all in fun.

"He earned that B, we didn't hook up until after the semester ended and I wasn't his TA anymore, and he's not even a psychology major." Leigh sighs with some irritation at what felt like an already dead joke.

Mia picks up on the tone and quickly changes the subject, "Okay well, I had the date last night with finance guy." Leigh raises her eyebrows, encouraging Mia to continue. "He looked the same as his pictures, so cute, and didn't lie about his height, but I swear to god Leigh, someone else wrote his profile because he was not funny in person."

"So no second date?" Leigh asks as a waitress comes up

to the table.

"Are you ready to order?" The girl with the notepad watches Mia and Leigh expectantly.

"Yes, I'll have the breakfast burrito, and please bring hot sauce, and also a refill on my coffee." Leigh says.

Mia looks over the menu once more, "Um, I guess I'll do the Eastern's combo."

"Protein?" asks the waitress.

"Bacon, definitely bacon," Mia answers, eyeing a generous portion of bacon that was just delivered to the table behind Leigh.

"And drink?"

"Just the water is fine," Mia says as she points to her glass.

Leigh raises an eyebrow, "No soda?"

Mia shrugs, "I already had my breakfast soda, and I'll probably have second lunch after this, so nah."

Leigh nods, "Right, so back to the date, not great but you're gonna give him a second chance? Gunning for a free meal? Trying to bone?"

Mia laughs, "Another free meal?" Leigh gives a knowing nod and smiles. Graduate school stipends don't pay a lot, and a date with a meal is one less meal to purchase or make. Mia shakes her head, “Nah, it’s not worth being that bored. For food or sex.” Mia’s last relationship was with a chemistry graduate student, one that she took more seriously than him, and then he broke it off to have a more serious relationship with someone else at the end of the spring semester, which seemed to be the pattern for Mia. Mia quietly sighs out as she thinks about her last relationship that apparently was not one.

“Any way, I made some Wolf of Wall Street joke and he just stared blankly and it was kind of downhill from there.” Mia takes a sip of her water.

“Just cause he’s in finance doesn’t mean he’s a movie buff,” Leigh counters.

“Fair, but if there’s no spark, there’s no spark,” Mia responds.

“So no spark, but fuckable?” Leigh pushes.

“No mental spark, but maybe physically I’m down.” Mia says with a smile, thinking of how he’d be a nice break from her classwork. “Oh hey Jake, thanks for snagging us this table,” she says as the lanky server swings his tray around to drop their food off at the table. Jake turns slightly red and nods, placing their plates in front of them and lets his gaze linger on Leigh. Leigh blushes and shoos him away.

“So that’s something, huh?” Mia observes.

"I seriously never thought I'd fall for one of these undergrads, but seriously Mia, he is so not like most of the uppity kids that go here. He works really hard and he's the first to go to college in his family, and he's working this job to pay for as much as he can –" Leigh rushes.

Mia waves a hand, interrupting Leigh, "Hey, I'm just teasing, if you're happy and he treats you right, who am I to judge?" Leigh visibly relaxes and then notices the table is conspicuously missing her hot sauce.

"Ugh, let me know if you see a waitress, this burrito is the best when my mouth is on fire."

Mia nods and begins to dig into her waffles, eggs, and bacon. Leigh waves down a waitress and requests her bottle of hot sauce which is promptly sent to the table.

"Remind me again what you're taking in the spring? Do we have any overlap?" Leigh asks between spicy bites.

"Mostly clinical stuff and social psych with uh, Dawson? I think." Mia says.

"Yes, that's right, so we'll actually have a class together! Is this his first grad course he's teaching?"

"Yeah, so no idea what he's like or how much work it is." Mia sips her water.

"Nice to get an assistant professorship straight out of school." Leigh snarks and briefly chokes on her bite of food. Mia holds out her glass of water, which Leigh quickly takes a gulp of.

Mia laughs, "Yeah, he's gotta be some kind of boy genius. Who skips post-doc?"

"Maybe he's connected?" Leigh coughs once before clearing her throat.

"Maybe he has a reaaaally nice former TA?"

"Mia!" Leigh shrieks with admonishment. Her shout is barely heard over the din of the other diners' conversations.

Mia laughs, "Sorry sorry, I couldn't help it."

"Whatever, it's fine. I've got some industrial/organization specific courses, and obvi the social course. So at least we've got something together." Leigh rolls her eyes.

"Yeah, we can sit in the back and throw spit balls."

"And I'm the one dating the undergrad."

"Ooooh, we're dating now, are we?" Mia teases.

"You know what I mean," Leigh grumbles before rolling her eyes.

"Well I know what a two am text is for sure."

Leigh giggles, "Dude, Mia, the sex is so good. I would not allow just anyone to mess with a good night's sleep. But like, it is a guarantee come every time he uh, comes over."

Mia smiles, "The only way I get that kind of guarantee is with my vibrator." Leigh chuckles and nods. "Oh, I also forgot to tell you about the new asshole my advisor tore for me."

Leigh raises an eyebrow, "That's a strange way to transition this conversation."

Mia waves her off, "She sent back edits of my thesis and I tried to look over it last night and just ended up crying. Thankfully, I had already had two drinks earlier, so I was just a little more numb to it than the usual."

Leigh's face is sympathetic, "I'm sorry, she's the worst." Mia nods in agreement and notices as several men at the table behind Leigh get up and made their way past her table to leave. They are all dressed as if they'd been playing basketball outside, layered with shirts and long sleeve shirts. One man with close cropped brown hair with an athletic build catches her eye. She thinks he glances at her, but she goes back to her meal.

"What are you up to the rest of the weekend?" Mia asks Leigh.

Leigh shrugs, "The usual, reading, writing, and going on campus to run some subjects. Oh, and people are going over to Danny's later, you gonna come?"

Mia wriggles uncomfortably, she had mostly managed to

avoid Danny Meyers since the end of the spring semester. Getting dumped for her classmate sucked, and Leigh knew that, but they had made friends with Danny and his fellow chemistry classmates back during their first year at grad school and Mia knew she'd have to see him again.

"Am I even invited?" Mia mumbles.

"The only one making it weird anymore is you. Danny told me to invite you. Sasha is out of town too, not that she would mind," Leigh quickly adds to the end, referring to Danny's current girlfriend, and Mia's classmate in the clinical psych program.

"Okay, fine," Mia says, but rushes, "but I am not going in without you, so I will show up at least thirty minutes after people are invited and you better be there."

Leigh waves her hand and nods in acceptance. Their server delivers their check while Mia and Leigh finish their food. As they get up and push their way through the still existing crowd to the cashier Mia asks, "What time are people invited over at?"

"Eight. So for you, eight-thirty."

Mia nods, "You better be there." Leigh mimes crossing her heart and slashing her neck and Mia smiles back at her as they each pay their part of the bill.

CHAPTER 3

Mia peeks anxiously at the time on her laptop. She knows exactly how long it takes to get to Danny's place from her apartment and she is not showing up a minute before eight thirty. The laptop clock clicks to eight ten. She figures three more minutes allows for one last makeup touch up, locking up her place, getting into her car, and driving there. Then Mia straightens her back and realizes, *shit, I should bring beer.* Mia figures a peace offering of beer would make the fact that she has been actively avoiding Danny a little less awkward when she shows up at his shared house. Mia runs a hand through her hair, which is now brushed out and soft across her shoulders. She closes the laptop shut and pushes away from her desk. Strolling back to her room she quickly changes into a clean pair of black leggings, briefly devoid of cat hair, a dark red tunic and knee-high camel colored boots. She pops over into the bathroom and quickly touches up her concealer and eyeliner. Compared to brunch this morning, now she looks like she's trying.

Mia walks out of the bathroom, gives Renly a brief scratch under his chin as he rubs against the doorframe, and does a visual check that he has plenty of hard food to tide him over until she gets back home. She grabs her bag and coat and locks the door behind her as she swings her jacket on. Walking out to her car Mia digs her phone out of her bag and checks the time again, figuring that now with the beer stop, she'll get to Danny's after the agreed upon eight thirty. *Whatever*, she thinks, *Leigh will wait,* as she gets in the car and makes her way to the store near Danny's house.

Mia pulls into to the lot of the store and parks under a street lamp, close to the entrance, a habit borne out of fear mongering from her parents. She slams her car door shut and heads into the fluorescent lighting and towards the beer and wine aisle. Clearly on a mission, Mia strolls directly to the American brews, where she flings open the refrigerated door and pulls out a six pack of Fat Tire. She goes to shut the door and spins around to walk back to the registers when her first step lands her into someone else.

"Oh, sorry!" She sputters as she takes a step back to take in the human obstacle. Briefly, Mia notices a scent of oranges and has to remind herself she's in the beer aisle and nowhere near the produce.

He smiles down at her and waves his hand, "Not a problem." Mia gives a tight, closed mouth smile and briefly squints at him, realizing this was the tall cute guy she saw earlier at Eastern's. Except now instead of gym clothes, he is dressed in dark jeans and a light blue sweater that helps her appreciate the clear blue of his eyes. Mia starts wishing she was more aware of who she was bumping into so that she could have held one hand out to accidentally brace herself on what appeared to be well defined pecs.

"Hm, maybe you should be apologizing for being so close?" Mia says lightheartedly as she cocks her head to the side

He laughs, "You're probably right, I didn't realize I was in your way." He reaches past her to open up the refrigerator door and grabs a six pack of his own beer. When he leans over to grab his pack, Mia takes another step back as he comes even closer into her personal space. He smells nice, and Mia realizes the light orange scent came from him.

Mia forgets about the time, hoping to lengthen this encounter and begins to shift her weight from one foot to the other, trying to think of something to say.

"You look familiar, do you work around here?" He asks as he moves back into his own space and shuts the refrigerator door.

Mia nods, "Kind of, I'm a grad student at Earl, so I guess I work and study here…or I'm an indentured servant or whatever." She smiles at him, "I'm Mia."

He holds his hand out to her and she grasps it. They shake hands as he says, "Brett." He peers down at her beer. "Off to something fun?"

Mia is immediately wishing that the something fun would turn out to be an invitation from Brett and then mentally shakes herself, *I don't even know this guy.* "Uh yeah, just hanging out with some friends before the end of the semester craziness really begins." She glances down at his own beer, "Yourself?"

Brett holds up his case briefly and shrugs as he said, "Needing to deal with a bad date."

Mia pouts and gives Brett an "aw poor you" face. "The night's young and the date is already over and that bad?"

Brett grimaces and gives a sheepish smile, "Actually the date was my friend's, and I'm just trying to get him through a tough re-entry into the dating world. She went to the bathroom and didn't come back, so I'm swinging by his place to hang out, drink, and play some cards."

"Well yikes for him, and how nice of you." Mia feels her phone buzz in her person, *shit it's probably Leigh, am I running late?* she wonders.

Brett seems to notice Mia's sudden change of focus and shoves his hand into his pocket. "Well, it was nice to meet you Mia, maybe I'll see you around campus." He turns and walks to a different aisle, leaving Mia by herself.

"Nice to meet you too!" she calls after him as she fishes for her phone with her free hand.

I'm here, I'm going in. Are you coming? Leigh's text reads.

Shit shit shit, Mia thinks, as she begins typing her response back while she rushes to the register. Mia pays while she types back, **I'll be there in 2, wait plz.**

Leigh's response is immediate, **already in, i'll see you soon.**

Mia sighs, and casts one quick glance around as she is leaving the store. She sees Brett at the self-checkout with his beer and a bag of chips, and catches his eye. She smiles at him and does a quick wave as he returns the gesture. As she heads out to her car, under the safety of the streetlamp she realizes she never asked how he'd see her around campus.

CHAPTER 4

Mia is clenching and unclenching her fists, trying to work up the nerve to go into Danny's. He lives in the historic district in an older house shared with three other guys, all graduate students. Mia's been here plenty of times, but not since Danny dumped her in spring. She grabs the beer and hustles up the familiar sidewalk and to the front door. She could kill Leigh for already being inside, knowing that all eyes will turn to the opening front door. Mia catches herself from holding her breath and makes her way inside.

As the door opens, and as Mia predicted, several faces turn to observe the newcomer. Mia is practically certain that a hushed silence fell over the room when she entered, but she reminds herself it's all in her head as several conversations continue on around her. Leigh immediately bounds towards the door and catches Mia in a hug.

"Finally!" Leighs calls out.

"I'm only a little late," Mia mumbles slightly embarrassed.

"It's cool, we can start the movie now," Danny says as he strolls towards the front door from the living room. He pulls Mia in for a one-armed hug. "Glad you could make it."

Mia looks up at Danny, with his close-cut blonde hair and brown eyes and feels herself melt a little. "Yeah, thanks for having me, and," Mia scans around and sees only a few curious faces as she lowers her voice, "sorry for holding things up and being weird or whatever, but uh, beer!" She holds it up and hands it to Danny who smiles and nods. He grabs the six pack, pulls one out and offers it to Mia, who shakes her head. Danny goes and places the rest of the beer in the refrigerator while Mia shrugs off her coat and purse onto a nearby chair. Most everyone else, including several of her psychology classmates and Danny's roommates, begin taking seats on the mismatched couches or around the floor. Mia drops into a free spot on a couch, next Leigh, who saved a spot for her.

"Definitely not awkward." Leigh mutters. Mia gently hits Leigh's arm right as Danny walks to the front of the TV.

"Alright, settle down. This evening, for your bad movie viewing pleasure, we present Don't Tell Mom the Babysitter's Dead. All commentary, jokes, and observations are welcome." Danny mockingly bows to the crowd and takes a seat across from Mia on a different couch. Mia settles into the couch and listens as her friends around her try to one up another with witty quips about the movie, while occasionally glancing at Danny throughout the movie.

About halfway through the movie Danny catches one of her less than stealthier glances and smiles at her. He attempts to scoot over a little on his couch and tilts his head as if to ask Mia if she'd like to sit with him. Mia gives an almost imperceptible shake of her head and turns back to the movie. After the movie ends, Danny announces a brief bathroom and food break and for everyone to come back in the next few minutes for the second movie of the night. While others are slowly trickling back in and returning to their seats with more food or a new drink, Danny announces Glitter as the second movie of the night, praising the voice but not the acting of Mariah Carey, and then plops himself next to Mia before everyone else has sat. Mia slightly stiffens and glances over at Leigh. Leigh's eyes widen but she turns away to pull her phone out of her pocket and respond to a text that Mia heard ring in.

Everyone settles back down as the opening credits roll and Mia feels Danny's fingers begin to gently stroke her hand. *What the fuck*, Mia thinks, feeling both excited and confused. Danny's girlfriend and Mia's classmate Sasha is out of town for the weekend, and as Mia realizes this she immediately feels hot and snatches her hand away. Danny shifts his weight to not be so close to Mia but remains next to her throughout the movie. Mia finds herself hardly able to pay attention to the movie or the jokes. She can barely make out any of her own coherent thoughts, only noticing confusion and a slow burn of excitement.

As the movie ends, Mia shoots up and quickly makes her way to the bathroom in hopes to slow her breathing. She stares at herself in the mirror and whispers, "This is so fucked up. Just say goodbye and go home. Don't get caught up in his game." Mia pulls open the door to the bathroom to find a startled looking Danny.

"Oh, ah, excuse me," Mia says as she turns her body to try and slide her way past Danny. Danny hesitates, then steps aside to let Mia pass as he runs a hand over his hair. He goes to step into the bathroom and just as Mia begins to pass him, she feels his hand on hers.

"Mia," he whispers, and she finds herself stopping and turning herself back to him. She feels her blood rush to her head and somewhere lower, and begin to throb as her heart starts to pound. Danny pulls her close into him, still holding her hand and Mia leans her head against his chest. She feels Danny rest his chin on her head and take a deep breath in, appreciating the smell of her hair. With his free hand Danny tilts Mia's head up, and as her breath catches in her chest he gently presses his lips against hers. He pulls back briefly to murmur, "I've missed you," and leans back in for a second kiss.

Mia jolts herself back at those words. *What the fuck am I doing? How the fuck dare he?* Mia's anger flashes in her eyes and she yanks her hand away from Danny and pushes him away from her. "What the fuck?" she's finally able to hiss at Danny. "Not cool, just….not cool."

Danny looks at her defensively, raising his hands up as if to feign innocence, "I'm sorry, I just haven't seen you in forever, and I don't know what came over me, you just, seeing you, I don't-"

"Yeah, you don't. And you won't again." Mia turns on her heels and storms back out in the living area, only stopping long enough to quickly grab her things and rush out the door. With the blood pounding in her ears she doesn't even hear Leigh call after her. She's almost into her car when she feels hands on her shoulders.

"Get off!" Mia yells and goes to shake off the hands.

"Hey! Hey! It's me! What the fuck just happened?" Leigh says, startled by Mia's violent response. Mia's tense shoulders relax and she turns to face Leigh, her eyes brimming with tears. Leigh's eyes are concerned and her lips are pursed, "What did he do?"

"He kissed me. I kissed him back. Whatever, I don't know why. I shouldn't have come here. I can't believe I did that. He's a prick and I'm an idiot." Mia gasps out.

Leigh pulls Mia in for a hug as her tears begin to fall. "Oh Mia, I'm sorry." Mia's body quietly shakes as she cries into Leigh's shoulder.

"And fuck, I feel awful. I'm not that girl that hooks up with a guy that I know has a girlfriend!" Mia pulls out of the hug and begins to wipe the tears away from her face.

"Of course you aren't. You said he made the first move, and you had a natural response to it. But I'm guessing you also chose to end it." Leigh says to Mia, looking imploringly at her face. Mia sniffs and nods as she wipes another fallen tear. "Yeah, so you are human and made a mistake and then chose to do better." Mia nods, appreciating Leigh's perspective. "Do you want me to go back with you? Hang for a little bit? Make a voodoo doll?"

Mia lets out a chuckle and shakes her head. "No. I'm just gonna go home and get some sleep so I can actually get work done tomorrow."

Leigh pulls Mia in for one more hug, "Fine, but seriously, text me if you need me." Mia nods.

"And you? You're gonna go back and hang out?"

Leigh shakes her head, "Nah, I need to get my stuff, but I'm gonna go home and wait for my two am text." She smiles and does a shimmy, earning the laugh from Mia she was aiming for.

"Alright," Mia turns to get into her car, "I'll talk to you later."

"Kay, drive safe," Leigh calls to Mia as she heads back into the house.

CHAPTER 5

Back at her apartment Mia has changes into pajamas, flannel pants and an oversized t-shirt emblazoned with her undergraduate school's logo. She throws back the covers on her bed and climbs in, but doesn't pull her covers back up just yet. She wanted to get out of there earlier for a number of reasons. Shame, embarrassment, anger, and something else. Mia still feels a dull throb at her core. Something that hadn't stirred since the spring. Since Danny dumped her. She moves restlessly on her bed, heaves an exasperated sigh and leans over to open up the top drawer to her nightstand. Mia grabs the black silky bag that contains her guarantee come, her trusty, if not pricey, vibrator. She loosens the drawstrings on the bag and lets the hot pink vibrator fall out into her open palm. Mia quickly shimmies off her pajama pants and her plain cotton underwear and flicks her vibrator on. The familiar low buzz begins and Mia leans back and settles the vibrator between her legs as she closes her eyes.

Behind her lids she briefly thinks about Danny and that kiss from earlier, but finds herself hot with anger rather than desire. Mia squeezes her eyes tightly and shakes her head as if to throw Danny out of her mental imagery.

Refocusing and taking a deep breath, Mia starts picturing someone else kissing her. Blue eyes, brown hair, hard chest pushing against her. She begins to imagine what Brett's mouth would feel like moving on hers. She imagines his mouth gently opening hers and his tongue slowly, and deliberately beginning to explore her mouth. She visualizes his hand creep up her thigh and begin to tease her opening. As she holds the vibrator to her clit with one hand, she begins to massage her crevice with her other, starting to ease two fingers in. She pictures Brett moving his hands with care, running a thumb over her clit with increasing intensity before he inserts his strong long fingers into her and begins pumping slowly. Mia feels her own moisture on her fingers as the pressure in her center continues to build, sending tingling out to her extremities. She pictures Brett moving his free hand over her breast as she takes one hand and begins to pinch and pull on one of her nipples, enjoying the dual sensations. Mia pulls her legs up higher as the heat in her body continues to burn and a moan escapes from her throat. Her grip on her vibrator leads to her knuckles whitening, and she clenches at her breast as she begins to rhythmically pant. She envisions Brett slipping an additional finger into her, gasping at the tightness but also enjoying the tension. Mia feels the pressure explode as she comes and lets out a loud, grateful moan. She flicks her vibrator off and sighs out as she stretches out her arms and legs.

Mia gets up and cleans off her vibrator before carefully placing it back in its bag and drawer. She pulld her panties and flannels back on and crawls back into bed before flicking off the lights. As she snuggles under the covers, she calls out, "Renly?" and the fat tuxedo cat announces his presence by jumping on the bed and curling up in the nook behind her knees. Mia smiles to herself as she begins to think back over her fantasy. Her happiness over it is short lived, as she thinks, *it's all in your head, remember that, you don't even know this guy and will probably never see him again.* She pulls the covers tighter around herself and closes her eyes, releasing herself to sleep.

Mia's dreams were of no help. They clashed between arousing memories of Danny, disgusted feelings with their encounter that night, and flashes of what she had envisioned with Brett. She wakes the next morning feeling poorly rested and unenthusiastic to tackle the day. She drags herself out of bed and Renly weaves himself around her ankles, mewing for breakfast. She nods and rubs the sleep from her eyes as she makes her way to the kitchen. She doles out some fresh cat food for Renly and grabs her phone from her purse, which she had left on the counter the night before. Two unread texts.

U ok? Leigh.

I'm so sorry, that was super dumb of me. I fucked up. Danny.

Mia sighs and types out a quick response to Leigh, saying she's fine and just going to hunker down and do school work for the day. She pauses over responding to Danny, not sure of what to say. She starts to type a response, only to delete it. *Whatever, he can wait on a response.* She grabs a soda from the refrigerator, pops the tab with the satisfying *whoosh* from the can, and walks into her office to tackle her work.

By the time lunch creeps around Mia's stomach is growling and she's made a big dent in her readings. She glances at the time as she feels her stomach protest over her soda for breakfast plan. She drags herself back into her kitchen to see what she has in there to eat and after feeling disheartened by everything she has thoughtfully purchased just a few days ago, decides she deserves a good bagel. Quickly getting dressed, brushing her teeth and washing her face, she heads out of her apartment to walk to the bagel shop down the street.

As Mia's paying for her bagel and orange juice she scans the bagel shop and sees undergrads in various states of dress. Some still in pajamas, some in their bar clothes from the previous night, and some perfectly coiffed and put together for the day. She also notices a familiar face smiling and waving her over. Jake's goofy grin pulls Mia over to him.

"Hey Jake, how's it going?" Mia observes Jake's stubble and rumpled clothes to suggest that he was in the attire from last night category.

"Good. How are you doing?" He asks with what appeared to be genuine concern in his eyes.

Mia's eyes narrowed, "I'm fine…" she says cautiously.

"Oh okay cool, Leigh said you had a rough night and she was worried about you."

"Yeah, it wasn't the best, but I'll survive."

Jake nods to her to go bag, "Want to sit?"

Mia shakes her head, "Naw, I'm gonna go back and catch up on work."

Jake awkwardly nods again, "Yeah yeah, cool. Um…I get that this is weird, but um…" he pauses as he tries to find the words, "but like, do you have a problem with me dating Leigh?"

Mia is taken aback but composes herself enough to respond, "No. I mean, I tease her a bit, but she's only had good things to say about you, so as long as that's the case, I'm cool with you."

Jake nods appreciatively. "Okay, cool, cause like, I think she's scared to like, be seen with me and stuff and if maybe she knew that you were cool with this, we could actually go out like a real couple."

Mia smiles, feeling reassured by Jake's earnestness. "I'll let her know."

"Thanks. Seriously, thanks."

Mia nods, holds up her bag as if to reiterate her reason to leave, "Alright, well, see you later." Jake waves to her and Mia heads back to her apartment to finish her reading goals for the day.

CHAPTER 6

The next day Mia gets to campus early. She stops into her office in her advisor's research lab and signs onto her computer. The lab is located in the basement in one of the older buildings on campus, and Mia has come to find the musty smell almost comforting. She downloads her most recent thesis draft with her advisor's notes from her emails and glances at the clock. It's the week before finals and she initially intended to have her master's thesis defended by the end of this semester. *Best laid plans,* Mia sighs to herself and sets a new goal in her calendar to defend by the end of the spring semester. She starts to pore over each page, eyes flickering to notes mixed with genuine questions and biting commentary. Mia is dreading her meeting with her advisor today as she already has a day full of lab work, seminars, and final papers to write.

Mia takes sips of her soda between revising sentences,

pulling up reference articles, and searching for additional work to target her advisor's comments. She only breaks her concentration briefly to wave hello to the undergraduate entering the lab whose work study program has them helping with research in the lab. Mia's been instructing Amy on various tasks for the lab, and today she has a mound of data entry that should keep her occupied for the day. Mia's phone buzzes, her calendar reminder alerting her that her class begins in ten minutes. She saves her work, grabs her bag, and heads up a floor to the second level of the old Psychology building where her Cognitive Development class is.

Already seated in her usual spot is Sasha, sipping on her coffee with her notebook and pen already out on the table. Sasha silences her phone and raises her face to see Mia enter the room, her long black hair heavy on her shoulders and her bangs hanging into her eyes. She smiles at Mia as Mia moves to sit in the chair next to her.

"Hey!"

"Hi," Mia replies, still feeling twinges of guilt. She barely notices that she's holding her breath, wondering what Sasha knows.

"Good weekend?" Sasha chirps.

"It was okay, tried to get stuff done…" Mia trails off, "um, what about you? Weren't you visiting family?"

"Yep! Met my new baby niece. It was nice, but you know,

back to the grind." Sasha shrugs with a genuine smile. "Did you go to bad movie night?" she asks without any suspicion.

"Um, yeah. It'd been awhile since I've been to one." Mia says carefully while she watches Sasha's nonverbal cues.

"Nice. Wish I didn't miss it. I hope it wasn't too weird…I know it's been awhile since you've hung out with the whole crew." Sasha drops her voice a bit as other students walk in.

"Um, a little, but it was fine," Mia feels herself squirming internally, practically dying for the conversation to end or for the teacher to start class early or for a bomb to drop on the Psychology building.

Sasha gently touches Mia's arm, "I'm glad though, I know we haven't hung out much, but maybe it'll get less awkward each time." Mia nods, feeling as though the shame is radiating off of her. She feels immense relief as Dr. Samuels scurries into the room like a tornado and Sasha leans back in her chair, with her pen poised and ready.

As the class ends, Mia shoves her notebook and papers into her bag, waves a quick goodbye to a slightly bewildered looking Sasha, and dashes up one more flight of stairs to end up in front of her advisor's office door. Mia takes a deep breath to steady herself and knocks.

"Come in," calls the voice behind the door, and Mia turns

the knob and pushes open the door. Dr. Thompson, her advisor, sits behind an impressive desk in front of a window that affords a beautiful view to one of the campus's quads. The walls on either side of her desk are lined with bookshelves overflowing with journals and scholarly books. Despite all major journals having switched to digital formats, Mia has observed an almost one-up-manship of which professor can maintain the largest and oldest journal collection. Dr. Thompson was definitely in contention for a top third position in that fight.

Dr. Thompson sizes up at Mia from her desktop, her steely gray eyes that matched her short gray hair, and presented Mia with a gentle, if not misleading, smile. "Mia, wonderful. How have you been?"

"Great!" Mia says as she pulls out a notepad to keep track of the discussion and a hard copy of her recently edited thesis.

Dr. Thompson looks pointedly at the large stack of papers, "You've had a chance to review my notes? I hadn't heard from you, so I didn't even know if we'd be meeting to discuss them."

Mia mentally kicks herself for not replying to her advisor's email, "Yes, sorry, I totally forgot. I've been working on your edits since I got them."

Dr. Thompson nods, her eyes softening slightly. "Good,

then let's go through my comments, page by page." Mia, ready and familiar with this process, brings the sheets up to the desk and lays the stack down for her advisor to begin paging through them.

Mia feels the time weigh on her, as they go through each page and comment. Since the suggestions and comments are no longer fresh, she doesn't feel the urge to cry over the more condescending remarks, and practices her doubling numbers routine when they circle around one particularly mean statement her advisor has written. When the hour and a half has passed, Mia's copy of her thesis with her advisor's comments has even more hand written notes in the margins, from both her and Dr. Thompson. Mia's head feels a bit as if it's swimming as Dr. Thompson waves her hand to usher Mia out of the office.

"Close the door behind you," Dr. Thompson calls after her as Mia is still shoving papers back into her bag and grabs the knob with her free hand. With the door closed Mia allows herself a deep, calming breath. She's grateful for blocking off the rest of the afternoon from seeing patients before her seminar so she has time to reset and work more on her thesis. Mia heads back down one floor and strides into the research lab where Leigh works, and knocks on the open door to Leigh's shared office.

"Any interest in lunch?" Mia asks, breaking Leigh's attention from her computer screen, which is covered in statistical code.

"Swamped with this right now, and Greg wants this before he leaves for the day." Leigh says referring to her advisor.

Mia nods, "Okay, maybe later this week." She stalls a bit before turning out of Leigh's office.

"Everything alright?" Leigh asks.

"Yeah…I saw Sasha earlier and she seemed…normal." Mia answers.

"Were you expecting something else?" Leigh asks distractedly as she's gone back to typing more code.

"I, uh, I don't know. Maybe Danny would have said something to her?" Mia switches her weight from one foot to the other, recalling her discomfort from earlier. She had left Danny on read and had no idea what he may have done or said since his girlfriend came back to town.

Leigh stops typing and looks at Mia. "I doubt that. Unless he thinks you'll fill the void she'll leave if she dumps him, which she probably would dump him, he probably won't tell her." Leigh leans back in her chair, thinking it over.

"Ugh, yeah okay. I have no interest in that." Mia runs a hand through her hair and crosses her arms in front of her chest. "Alright, I'll let you to it, I'm gonna go eat. I'll see you later?"

"Yup," Leigh says as she pulls herself back to her work.

Mia briskly walks back down to her office space where she drops off her class notepad and thesis paperwork. She peeks into where Amy is still chugging away at entering data, grabs her jacket, and heads out to the student union where a dining hall and several restaurant options are housed. Mia chooses a chain sandwich stop and gets in line. She pulls out her phone and does a quick scroll through Instagram and Twitter. She sees a story recently posted by Sasha, of her kissing Danny on the cheek with the words *Missed my boo* flashing across the bottom. Following Sasha on social media after Danny broke up with Mia felt awful, but unfollowing her would have led to a mix of emotions and potential awkwardness that Mia also did not want to deal with.

Mia looks up from her phone as she reaches the front of the line and places her order. She follows the queue to grab her completed sandwich and pay. She orders a fountain drink at the register and gathers up her items to wait at the soda dispenser. Just as she is approaching the soda machine she recognizes a familiar profile.

"Brett!" She says cheerily, trying to free a hand from her cup and sandwich to wave. Brett turns, momentarily startled, then breaks into a gorgeous smile. He sees Mia trying to juggle her items and holds a hand out.

"Can I get you something?" he asks as he takes her empty cup.

"Thanks, yeah, Coke?" Mia finds her voice raising at the

end, despite knowing her order.

"You sure about that?" Brett teases her.

"Ha, yes, definitely." Mia feels the heat in her cheeks, chiding herself for suddenly acting insecure. Brett sets his empty cup to the side of the machine and fills up Mia's with ice and soda. He carefully places it to the side and places a cover on it, grabs a straw and hands the cup and straw back to Mia and then returns to filling up his own cup. "Thanks," Mia says. Mia feels a sense of nervousness than says to herself, *fuck it, why not*, as she manages to say to him, "Want to join me for lunch?"

Brett has finished placing a cover and straw in his drink and faces Mia. "I'd really like to, but I actually have a lunch meeting. Rain check?"

Mia nods, feeling disappointed, but trying to hide the emotion from her face. "Yeah sure." *Yeah definitely not gonna happen*, she thinks to herself.

"Do you have your phone?" He asks, gesturing with his free hand. Mia, with both hands occupied, swings her body to the side to showcase her bag hanging from her shoulder.

"It's in the front pocket." Mia says. Brett raises his eyebrows as if to ask permission and Mia nods, so he reaches into the pocket, grabs her phone, and turns the screen on.

"Oh, password protected?" He says as the lock screen lights up.

"Ah yeah, it's uh," Mia pauses, calculating how to get her phone back and punch in the code, all while holding her lunch in either hand and not continue to block people from moving around in the crowded shop. *Whatever* she decides. "It's my birthday, oh-seven-oh-seven."

Brett punches the numbers in and gets to the home screen, where he pulls up the messaging app. "That doesn't seem like a very secure passcode. I'm texting myself from your number so that I've got it. I'll text you later about doing something." Mia nods and smiles, also hoping he didn't see the message from Danny. Brett clicks the screen off and drops the phone back into her bag. "I'll see you later!" He says as he smiles at her one last time, before heading out of the student union with his drink in hand.

Mia mentally shakes herself and moves to the seating area and lays down her drink and food at a two top. She drops her bag onto the bench she's sitting on and pulls her phone out of the bag, punches in her code and pulls up the app. She finds the top message sent to an unstored contact:

You're super sexy, I can't wait to meet up.

CHAPTER 7

Mia keeps finding herself thinking back to the text and smiling stupidly while sitting in her late afternoon seminar. She practically floats through the rest of her afternoon and this lecture as she tries to imagine what hanging out with Brett would actually be like. She also wonders about texting him with an actual message from herself. She isn't sure about what to write. She worries about when to send it because she doesn't want to seem overeager, but she also doesn't want to seem uninterested. That leaves her with being indecisive and having done nothing. As the seminar wraps up, she decides she will text Brett when she gets home and settles in for the evening.

After finishing up dinner and taking a quick shower, Mia curls up on her couch and clicks on the TV. Renly jumps up from the floor, circles the same spot three times before plopping himself on the far end of the couch. Mia turns the channel to The Office reruns and grabs her phone, ready to finally send a message of her own.

Does this mean I think you're sexy or you think I'm sexy?

Mia lets out the breath that she was holding and hits send. She quickly puts her phone back down and tries to focus on Michael Scott. Her phone buzzes.

Yeah, I realized the potential confusion after I sent it. But I wanted to seem charming and cool and not admit the mistake.

Mia laughs, her fingers hovering over her phone, trying to think of what to say next.

Brett's next message arrives before she can respond, **Anyway…i think YOU'RE sexy.**

Mia smiles widely and she feels giddy. **The feeling is mutual**, she sends back.

You also think you're sexy? Brett responds. Mia slaps herself on the forehead, *oh my god I am dumb*, she thinks.

Omg no, I think you're sexy, she sends back to him.

Brett sends back, 😂 **I'm teasing you.**

Mia breathes a sigh of relief and her phone buzzes again. **What are you up to tomorrow night?** Mia stops and thinks, she has a class and several patients tomorrow, but could probably make time to see Brett. No, she decides, she can definitely make time to see Brett.

Nothing tomorrow night. What are you thinking?

Drink at Callahan's? Brett suggests a bar popular with graduate students right near Main Street. **8?**

Mia thinks through her day and calculates that she'll have just enough time after her last patient to scarf down dinner, change, and meet Brett on time.

It's a date! She sends back. She sees the three little dots pop up on her phone as Brett seems to take forever with his reply.

Great, looking forward to it.

Mia squeals, scaring Renly out of his light sleep. "Sorry my little prince," she whispers to Renly and gives him a quick pet. Renly slowly blinks his eyes to suggest he is offended, but not mad and rests his head back on his paws. Mia pauses for a moment and then sends one last text, **Me too, see you tomorrow!**

Mia settles back into the couch to watch one more episode before heading off to bed. She hears her phone buzz again and wonders what Brett might be saying this time, but when her eyes land on the message's sender, her heart sinks. *Fucking Danny*, she thinks, swiping open to read the new text from him.

Still haven't heard from you. We cool?

We cool? Mia thinks, *WE COOL? No I am not cool with you, you fucking prick.* She feels her anger rising as she tries to decide what she would say back to him, if anything at all. As she deliberates she sees the three dots pop up, suggesting that Danny is typing something else to her.

Can I come over to talk?

Absolutely not. Mia is able to text back her response immediately, as the last thing she wants is Danny over in her apartment, late at night, with nobody around to interrupt a terrible mistake.

Then can we talk somehow? Mia imagines she can feel Danny's earnestness in the text.

There's nothing to talk about. Mia huffs and feels ready to throw her phone across the room.

I feel bad. Mia rolls her eyes at Danny's text.

You should, she sends back. Mia sees the three dots pop up again, then disappear, then pop up again. She pictures Danny typing and then deleting responses. *What good is going to come of this? What does he want?* Mia thinks.

So we're just gonna act like nothing happened?

Mia clenches her fists and lets out a strangled cry. *Why can't he just leave me alone? Is it that hard?* she asks herself. Mia carefully types out her response, **We are not cool. We are not friends. There is nothing to talk about. I am going to do my best to avoid you going forward.**

Please respect that.

Mia sees the three dots pop up again and quickly sends one last text, **There is nothing else for you to say. I'm done with this conversation.** Mia turns off her phone and goes to plug in it for the night. She knows nothing good can come from any response he sends her. Whether it's a cry to communicate with him or a cruel, lashing out reply, she knows that either will make her feel miserable. In fact, she observes she already feels crummy. Mia's irritated that the jittery, excited feeling she had earlier from setting a date with Brett has been overshadowed by the contact with Danny.

Mia turns off the TV and lights in the living area and strolls into her bedroom. She's determined to regain her positive mood, to excitedly anticipate tomorrow. She grabs her vibrator from the drawer and flops onto her bed. Mia sets the vibrator next to herself and closes her eyes. She tries taking a few deep breaths in, as an effort to slow her pounding heart. She feels adrenaline rushing from both being asked out and being mad. She reaches under her pajama pants waistband and feels the top of her underwear, which is trimmed in lace. She pushes past the lace and starts to gently swirl a finger on her clitoris.

Behind her closed eyes Mia pictures kissing Brett. She sees herself sitting on her kitchen table, legs spread wide, with Brett pressed against her. She's wearing only underwear, and Brett is kissing her neck, while holding her with one arm, and groping one of her breasts with the other. Mia feels his erection, hard against her, pushing through his pants and against her panties. Mia moans, and pulls Brett in closer and begins to move her hips up against his hard cock. She pulls a hand from around Brett's neck and begins to tug at his waistband in an effort to free him from his pants. Brett steps back, panting, eyes glinting and undoes his pants, stepping out of them. Mia gazes at him, her panting matching his, her panties damp with desire, as Brett pulls his boxer briefs off, revealing his large erection. Brett steps forward and gently pushes Mia to lay down on the table. He grabs her waist and yanks her closer to him. He leans down and gives a quick flick of his tongue on her clit before standing and plunging into her, with Mia exclaiming in pleasure. He thrusts in and out of her, increasingly faster, harder, as Mia feels the oncoming explosion simmering within. She gasps with each thrust, begging for more, for Brett to fuck her harder, to make her come.

The Mia in her bed cries out with the release of her orgasm and slowly pulls her hand out. As the tremors dissipate, and her body fully relaxes, Mia wipes her hand on her pants and feels sudden shame. Her imagination was not entirely responsible for that fantasy, she acknowledges. She replaced Danny with Brett, as it was only a few months ago that Danny fucked her in the kitchen, with his plentiful dick stiff against his pants, his mouth on her clit, and his actions making her come hard. Mia lets out a shaky sigh, places her unused vibrator back in the drawer, and settles in for an uneasy night of sleep.

CHAPTER 8

Mia has already made it through most of the next day, pushing past the previous evening's mixed emotions. There was no reply from Danny to her last text, and she decides to try and shrug off the guilt she felt from using one of their moments together to inspire a different fantasy with a new person. Mia manages to have a fairly productive day, choosing to focus on school instead of her romantic life. She's had a morning seminar, worked on her thesis draft, and already seen two therapy patients in her practicum. She has one last person to see before she would dash home to change. Mia is deciding when and where to grab dinner when she got a text from Leigh, almost as if Leigh could read her mind.

Dinner? Stats finally giving me a break ;)

Mia smiles, thinking she could probably squeeze in a quick dinner with Leigh before meeting Brett for drinks.

Yes! Needs to be fast though, have a date at 8, she sends back.

Oh la la. Noodles? Leigh texts back.

Perfect, 7?

Done.

Mia sets her phone to the side, deciding that she'll dash home after her last patient, freshen up and change, and then head out to her dinner and drinks. She checks the time and quickly reviews her notes from the last time she saw this patient, a forty-year old man struggling with depression. She gathers up her notepad and heads to the clinic's waiting room to meet with her last patient of the day.

At home Mia reapplies deodorant and some make-up. Her date night look is notably different than psychologist in training. She's changed from her black slacks and loose long sleeve blouse to form-fitting dark jeans and a black short sleeve sweater that lays invitingly on her breasts. She's put on knee high brown boots and checks herself over in the mirror. She's chosen to wear eyeliner to accentuate her eyes and lip gloss with a slight pink shade to it. Her hair is brushed out, full and soft. Mia runs a hand through it, feeling confident. For her final touch, she applies a small spritz of perfume on each wrist, before gently dabbing each one behind her ears. She heads out of the bathroom, unplugging her phone from the charger and goes to pack up her purse in the kitchen, moving key items like her wallet, car keys, and eye drops from her school bag to her smaller shoulder bag. Her phone buzzes as a text flies in.

Still on for 8? Brett asks.

Yes! See you soon! Mia shoots back. She glances back at the kitchen table, the scene of both real and imagined sex and feels her heart flutter. She's not sure if it's over excitement for her date, or recalling how well Danny fucked her there. Mia's purse is all ready to go, so she pulls her jacket on and heads back out to her car to meet Leigh before she gets to spend some actual time with Brett.

Leigh had picked one of their favorite dinner spots, a place they frequented many times over the last two and a half years. Mia gets in line to order as Leigh also arrives and joins her.

"Perfect timing!" Leigh says to Mia, and looks her over. "All this for me?" She jokes.

Mia snorts, "Yes, surprise, you're my hot date at eight."

Leigh grins. "As yes, who is this mystery man that you've met and haven't told me about?" Leigh is forced to wait for an answer as each take their turns ordering, filling their drinks, and finding a table for the two of them. Once they're both settled in, waiting for their food, Leigh raises an inquiring eyebrow at Mia.

"Uh, well, I met him when I picked up beers right before Danny's thing on Saturday. But I could swear I've seen him around, and anyway, I saw him again yesterday when I was getting lunch solo," Mia teases Leigh at the end. Leigh says "You're welcome" as if to take responsibility for Mia having a date, as Mia finishes her story, "and we exchanged numbers then. He's hot, tall, seems to be funny."

Leigh nods, "Cool. Well that should be exciting."

"I'm looking forward to it. I definitely need to shake this Danny shit." Mia says, lowering her voice as she scans around the restaurant for anyone that she would not want hearing the conversation. Leigh's eyes lighten as she looks on with sympathy.

"Have you heard from Danny since Saturday?" She asks.

"Yeah, he was trying to talk, but," Mia stops as the server places their dishes in front of them and wishes them to enjoy their meals, "I told him to basically drop it. I mean, there's no point to it."

Leigh has already placed a forkful of food in her mouth and is chewing, holding a finger up to Mia, as she clearly has something she wants to share. Leigh swallows her bit of food, takes a sip of her drink and says, "I wanted to tell you earlier, but couldn't, you know, shared office and all, but I overheard one of Danny's roommates say that he was hoping you were gonna be at the movie night." Mia rolls her eyes as Leigh continues, "I don't think he wants to be with Sasha."

Mia shrugs, "Oh well for him. He made his choice, I'm trying to move forward, and so should he." Mia notices that even though those are the words coming from her mouth, she can't help but to feel some curiosity. Would she consider taking Danny back? Mia internally shakes her head, *no, the sex was good, but definitely not worth being strung along again only to get dumped for someone else.*

Leigh nods, "So what else do you know about this new guy? Where's the date?"

Mia appreciates the change in subject, "His name is Brett, we're meeting for drinks at Callahan's. He's a grad student too."

"Oh, in what?" Leigh asks in between bites.

"Um, I don't know," Mia crinkles her forward in thought and then answers, "I guess that's something I'll ask tonight."

"Well text me when you get home from the date. You know, safety." Leigh says nonchalantly. Mia appreciates it, since they became friends two and a half years ago Leigh and Mia have looked out for each other, especially when it came to going out on dates with someone new. They always sent a "home safe" text after a new date to reassure the other.

Mia and Leigh move on to discuss their work and classes as they eat. Mia shares about her tough meeting with her advisor and Leigh talks about the coding work she had done and then had to redo. Mia keeps a watch on time, as she hopes to be just a few minutes past eight for her arrival to her date. She finds herself shaking one leg, nervous to head out. As Leigh catches her for the third time checking the clock on her phone she finally says, "Is it time? Can you leave yet? You seem ready to rocket out of your seat."

Mia laughs at her, "Sorry, yes, it's time. Thanks for waiting it out with me, I'll text you later." Both women get up from their chairs, hug, and head out of the restaurant to go their separate ways for the night.

CHAPTER 9

Mia walks into a dimly lit Callahan's just a few minutes past eight. It is not wildly busy on a Tuesday night, but a fair amount of people are around, with a smattering of couples and a two small groups of people huddled at their tables or relaxing and laughing. Just as Mia prepares to accept that she's there first and needs to pick a table, she sees movement out of the corner of her eye. She turns to face her date, who has also just arrived. She notices that Brett is wearing dark slacks and a light gray sweater that suggests ripples of muscles underneath.

"Hey, perfect timing!" Mia says with a smile.

"Thank you, it's one of my many great qualities," Brett jokes. He holds an arm out and points out a free table, closer to the entrance but also further from the occupied tables. Mia nods and makes her way over. She takes off her jacket and drapes it on the back of her chair and sits down. Brett takes the seat across from her, giving him a better view of the bar and people as they enter it. Not long after they've seated a server comes up.

"What can I get you?" She asks cheerily. Mia notices the waitress's eyes linger on Brett and feels a flash of jealousy.

"I'll have a whiskey Coke," Mia answers promptly and turns her attention to Brett, cuing him to place his order.

"Heineken." He says, smiling politely at the server, as she nods and turns on her heels to get their drinks. "That's a strong drink for a Tuesday," Brett observes teasingly.

"Honestly, it should have been my drink yesterday, today was far more manageable than yesterday," Mia shrugs.

Brett raises his eyebrows, "What was so hard about yesterday?"

Mia sighs, "Just another really tough meeting with my advisor. It's rare to walk out of those without crying," she pauses and thinks, "or even to not cry in them."

"Jeez, why?"

"She's just really hard on me. And not just me, her older students have also said that she's tough. Like, her comments and questions are usually cutting. She's well-meaning, but also not usually kind." Mia thinks to her last meeting with Dr. Thompson, and starts to worry she's sounding like a crybaby. "Don't get me wrong, she's smart and definitely trying to make me a better researcher. Just interpersonally…it's difficult."

Brett nods knowingly, "Fair enough. You're trying to do right by her and it's hard to get it all right."

Mia nods emphatically, "Exactly." Mia pauses as their drinks are dropped off at their table and their waitress hesitates to leave.

"Thanks, looks like we have everything we need." Brett says kindly, dismissing the waitress.

Eager to change the subject she says, "But really, I don't only want to talk about school, I feel like I do that all the time. Tell me about you!"

Brett laughs, "Okay. This is starting feel like an interview."

Mia grimaces, "Oh my god, no no, I just want to learn about you."

"Well, let's see. I'm actually from Pennsylvania, so definitely appreciating what is considered winter around here, I'm big into sports, whether it's watching or playing, I enjoy comedy shows and going to the movies. Hanging out with friends, playing Halo. I like to eat and read, though not the same things," he jokes at the end and drinks his beer. Mia smiles back. "I feel like I'm still really just getting settled here, though I've obviously been here for a few months." Mia nods knowingly, remembering how she also needed some time to get comfortable to a new city.

"Who are your teams?" She asks.

"Eagles and 76ers," he replies.

"Ah, a Philly boy," Mia says, as if knowing Brett is from Philadelphia provides her more insight into who he is.

"Guilty," Brett grins. "What about you?"

"My teams? I guess whoever is playing against the Patriots and obviously Earl basketball." Mia shrugs, indicating her overall laissez faire take on sports as she takes a sip. It tastes fairly strong, one of the reasons why grad students prefer this location, it doesn't skimp on their ratio.

Brett smiles appreciatively, "Any enemy of the Patriots is a friend of mine." Mia giggles and tosses her hair. "But I actually meant, tell me about yourself."

"Oh," Mia blushes, and while it can't be seen well in the dim lights, she feels it anyway. "Well, mostly I do school stuff, I know I know, I tried to pivot from that, but I read, work out, spend time with my friends, watch reruns of my favorite shows and snuggle up with my cat." Mia smiles, hoping for a positive reaction to her last note. Reactions to being a single girl with a cat have helped her decide whether or not a second date would happen.

"You have a cat?" Brett asks. Mia nods and takes another sip. "Nice, I have, um, had one as well. It's complicated, but I don't have him with me now, but I definitely miss the furry guy." Mia feels relieved, appreciating that Brett hasn't already signed her off as a crazy cat lady. "And tell me what shows you like to rewatch?"

Mia starts ticking the various shows on her fingers, "The Office, Parks and Rec, The Good Place, Superstore, This is Us, Scandal," she then gives a guilty smile, "and of course mindless trash like The Bachelor and Real Housewives."

Brett rolls his eyes, but they twinkle and he laughs, letting Mia know he's not judging her too harshly, "Hey, we all have our vices, right?"

"I guess so…what are yours?" she asks, raising an eyebrow flirtatiously.

"Failing to pick up girls in grocery stores?" Brett says. He finishes his beer and runs a hand through his hair. "Really, I thought I was smoother, but thankfully you spotted me getting lunch."

Mia glances down and feels her face warm up, "Just glad we're able to do this. And speaking of our first actual meeting, how's your friend?"

Brett looks at her blankly for a moment and suddenly recalls her reference, "Friend? Oh yeah, he's fine. He split from his girlfriend, they'd been together awhile and his first actual date with someone new was a mess."

Mia rests her chin on her hand and leans closer to Brett, "Well that was very kind of you to go spend time with him."

Brett folds his arms onto the table and leans into Mia as well, "What are friends for?"

At just that moment the server comes back to the table and motions to their drinks, "Can I get y'all another?"

Brett pulls back and gently waves his empty bottle, "Sure, I'll take another." He motions to Mia and her half empty glass. Mia looks down and shakes her head.

"Just a water for me, thanks."

Brett's face appears disappointed, "Boring you already?"

"Not at all, it's just that Callahan's makes these strong, and it is a school night," she winks at Brett.

"Fair enough," Brett says, indicating he is not going to push her. Mia mentally checks off another box: he's hot, likes cats, and isn't pushing her to drink. She also reminds herself that he reads and looks out for his friends.

"What about family?" She asks, trying to go through her mental list.

Brett takes a sip of his newly delivered beer, "What about family?"

"I mean, tell me about yours." Mia requests more clearly.

"Well, my family is all just outside of Philly. My dad's retired army and my mom still volunteers at an elementary school. My sister, her husband, and her two kids live near them. They're both teachers." Brett ticks off each family member on his fingers as he describes them to Mia.

Mia nods, "So it's tough to be far from them?"

Brett gives a half nod, "Yeah, kind of. I mean, I'm used to being away, but also sometimes I miss out on stuff. You probably know how it is."

Mia nods and traces the rim of her drink, "Yeah, I mostly miss my brother though. He's younger than me and finishing up college this year. I'm really hoping to go visit him this summer. He's in Miami and is constantly telling me how awesome it is."

"And your parents?" Brett questions.

"Ah, they're divorced, but they're both still in Texas, where I'm from. My mom stayed in Austin and my dad moved to Dallas. That was…" Mia tries to think through the dates, "Six years ago?" Brett nods and becomes distracted as someone has approached the table. Mia begins to wonder if she needs to worry about the waitress. She turns her head, ready to make it clear to the waitress to back off, but her eyes darken as she realizes who has come up.

Brett has turned to face the intruder and Mia sees him

smile as encouragement.

"Hey, I'm Danny," Danny says nicely as he stretches out a hand to Brett, who takes it and shakes it, "I'm a friend of Mia's."

"I'm Brett, date of Mia's," Brett says, oblivious to the anger raging in Mia. "Nice to meet you."

"You too," Danny says as he turns his attention to Mia, "Hey, I'm surprised to see you here."

Mia imagines herself throwing her water at Danny's face, she's so irritated he's here and has interrupted her date. She composes herself before saying icily, "Yep, sometimes I leave the office and my apartment." She gives Danny a frozen smile and turns her attention back to Brett, who looks at Mia and then Danny, becoming more aware of the tension.

"Well it was nice to meet you again," Brett says as he turns back to face Mia, sending a signal to Danny that the conversation was over. To Mia he says, "Would you like to get going?" Mia nods immediately in response. Brett stands and gets Mia's coat and holds it out for her, allowing her to pull it on as she gets out of her seat.

Danny nods and awkwardly bounces from foot to foot. "Uh yeah, see you around Mia," he says as he walks back to his table.

Brett stares at Mia's face, unable to read the emotions

behind it, "Let me close out, give me one minute." He walks up to the bar and talks with the bartender while the tab is run. He quickly signs the receipt and cups Mia's elbow as he leads her out of the bar and into the cool night.

CHAPTER 10

Mia takes a deep breath, the cooler air beginning to soothe her. She mindfully relaxes her shoulders, letting them drop, as they had tensed up higher and higher during the brief moment in Danny's presence. *Well I really fucked up this date*, Mia thinks with regret.

Still guiding her gently by her elbow, Brett walks Mia a block down from Callahan's stopping in front of a nearby restaurant under a streetlight. He stares carefully at her face again, though Mia has trouble masking her mix of emotions. Anger, irritation, disappointment, and confusion all swirl within Mia's head. Just as she opens her mouth to apologize for her reaction, Brett stops her.

"What's wrong? Are you alright?" he queries gently, searching her eyes for some hint.

Mia turns her face downward, shamed, and shrugs. "I

don't know, I guess." She lifts her head back to face Brett and lets out a soft sigh. "I'm sorry about that, that was weird."

Brett shakes his head, "I feel like it was weirder for you than me. I'm fine, you just seemed…uncomfortable."

Mia purses her lips anxiously. "Yeah, it's complicated," she says hesitantly.

Brett nods, "I figured by the look you gave him."

Mia's heart sinks. This is not how she was hoping this date would go, or even end, as it appeared to be heading into that direction. *Fucking Danny, fucking up another fucking thing in my life.* Mia feels the tears starting to prickle in her eyes and tries to take a few deep breaths to calm herself. She can feel herself starting to have a negative thought spiral and she does not want that right here right now.

Brett gently rubs Mia's shoulder and arm, "Hey, life's messy sometimes, right?" He pauses, seeming to think over his next words. "I, uh, get it if this is bad timing or something-"

Mia, touched by his tenderness but wary of a misunderstanding, holds a hand up to stop him and shakes her head. "This," she says waving her hand between her and Brett, "is not bad timing. *That* was bad timing." Brett nods his head slowly, still seeming uncertain, as Mia continues, "It's complicated, but it's also not as it's over *and* it's been over."

"Gotcha," Brett says quietly.

"I'm sorry, this clearly has thrown the night off, and I've totally ruined tonight." Mia tries to tamp down the rising urge to cry, insistent that she won't end this date even worse than it was right now.

"Hey, not at all," Brett smiles at her and brushes his hand against her waist. "I've been having a great time. That was," he pauses, "a hiccup. We don't have to end the night on that." He smiles almost mischievously at Mia.

Mia feels her stomach flip. "What do you have in mind?" She asks.

Brett smiles more widely, "Well, I'd ask you back to my place, but honestly I don't want to assume anything. So what if we just sit for a bit somewhere else and talk more?"

Mia nods, feeling calmer. She looks around, "Ah, but um, where?" The last thing she wants is to go somewhere and be disturbed again, or have Danny show up. She thinks through the options nearby and decides to make her suggestion quickly before she loses the nerve. "How about we just sit in my car for a bit? I know it's weird but-"

Brett is already nodding, "That sounds good. No one to bother us, and you can kick me out when you get tired of me." Mia laughs. She grabs Brett's hand and walks him back to her car, passing Callahan's and into a small parking lot on a side street, half full of other cars. She unlocks her car and slides into the driver's seat as Brett climbs into the passenger side. She pushes her keys into the ignition and turns the car on to have the heat and radio going.

Brett mocks warming his hands by the vent, "Oh thank god, it's freezing out there." Mia tilts her head back and laughs. She turns down the volume of the radio so that the music sounds like a steady murmur.

"So where were we?" Brett asks, facing her. Mia bobs her head, thinking. "Family, right? You're from Texas and your parents are divorced?"

"Yeah. That happened before I went to graduate school, while my brother was still in high school. It was definitely harder on Luke. I was at least at college, but he was home while their fighting got worse and when my dad finally moved out."

"Do you see them much?"

"Um, I sometimes go home for Christmas and stuff, but I don't really head back too often. I have to split time between Austin and Dallas, which is a pain in the ass. And," Mia smiles sadly, "it's just not really the same since they split. Home isn't home." She shrugs. "Don't get me wrong, I think we're all better off with them divorced, but there isn't a home base anymore." Brett's forehead wrinkles as he looks at Mia with sympathy.

"I guess I have probably taken that for granted myself," he says quietly.

"Oh, I didn't mean for it to be taken that way," Mia says quickly, worried that she said something off-putting. She shifts in the seat, drawing a little closer to Brett, her heart beats a little harder and the air in the car begins to feel warm. He moves similarly, adjusting his position such that Mia finds him almost in her space, leaning in and inches from her face.

"Not at all," Brett murmurs, gazing at Mia's mouth. Mia leans in and closes her eyes as Brett's mouth lightly touch hers. The kiss begins gently, with Mia and Brett delicately and slowly moving their lips against each other, both physically trying to adjust in their seats to get closer. Their kiss becomes more frantic, as Brett slips his tongue into Mia's mouth. She kisses him back, flicking her tongue against his before pushing her tongue into his mouth. Mia is itching to get closer, the car's small console between them suddenly feeling like the Grand Canyon holding them apart. Brett's hands are in Mia's hair as she grasps the back of his neck, their kissing becoming more passionate.

Breathless, Mia pulls back and her eyes shining she whispers, "Push your seat back." Brett, also on the verge of panting, reaches down to the side of his seat and pulls the lever while pushing back with his legs, forcing the seat to slide as far back as it goes. Gingerly, Mia climbs over the console and straddles Brett. He holds her waist to steady her. She leans back in to kiss him again, but Brett takes one hand and runs his thumb along her bottom lip, staring with hunger at her. Mia tucks her chin, allowing her to take Brett's thumb into her mouth, and she sucks on it, gently bobbing back and forth. Mia feels a stirring beneath her and begins to move her hips, encouraging Brett's penis to continue to stiffen. Brett moans and pulls his thumb out of her mouth. He wraps his arms around her and pulls Mia in and kisses her hard and long. Mia and Brett begin to move in synchrony against one another.

Brett pulls away and takes a breath and Mia feels his heart pounding through his shirt. He runs his hands up and down her denim legs. She feels herself throbbing, her body starting to ache for something more. "Shoulda worn a skirt," she whispers as she moves against Brett, leaning down and kissing his neck.

Brett laughs appreciatively and moves his hands under Mia's sweater. His hands graze over her chest and yanks down the cups of her bra to release her large breasts into his hands. Mia moves back to kissing Brett on the lips and while he encircles her nipples with his fingers.

"I want to taste you," Brett whispers hoarsely. Mia moans in response, her body beginning to move more urgently against Brett, her need for him to be inside her growing. Mia moves to attempt to unbuckle Brett's slacks.

Tap tap tap.

Mia and Brett shoot apart as much as they can in the confined space as the sound of something heavy knocks on the now-fogged up windows of her car. Mia throws herself back into her seat, adjusting her bra through her sweater. She doesn't pay attention to Brett as he moves to try and conceal his erection and she rolls down her window. A short muscled cop is standing outside her window, his flashlight in hand. He shines it into the car, and both Mia and Brett squint into the light, making it difficult for them to see the police officer.

"Ma'am, sir, I'm going to have to ask you to move along." The authoritative voice booms at them both.

"Um, yes, officer." Mia says shakily.

"Don't let me catch you out here doing this again. You've got dorm rooms for this." The officer says chidingly as he turns away and strolls back to his squad car. "College kids," he mutters as he walks away.

Mia rolls her window back up and turns back at Brett. They both burst into laughter. Tears comes to Mia's eyes and her peals of laughter slow into hiccups.

"This has been an eventful evening," Brett observes with another laugh.

"Yep," Mia says with a giggle. She glances at the clock and is surprised by how late it got. Brett catches her checking the time.

"Need to call it a night?" He asks.

"Unfortunately, I think so. I have a good bit to do tomorrow." Mia smiles ruefully.

"Shall we do this again sometime?" Brett asks without a trace of irony. Mia raises an eyebrow and smirks. Brett laughs, "I meant like hang out again, but maybe more of this specifically but less so in a public parking lot."

Mia grins, "Yeah, I'd like that. Hang out or maybe more of that specifically in a more private place." Brett smiles back and leans over the console to kiss Mia again. His tongue quickly caresses hers and he pulls back.

"Can't get started again. I'll get arrested. I'll text you about getting together again. When are you free?" Brett says as he moves his seat back into its previous position.

Mia casually runs her tongue over her lips and thinks before saying, "Well, the rest of this week is kind of crazy as classes wrap up. But how about this weekend?

Brett nods, "That'd be great. I'll text you later." He gives Mia one last quick kiss and gets out of the car. He waves as he says, "Have a good night," and closes the car door and heads in the direction of his own car.

Mia lets out a contented sigh. *That was not bad. That was…good,* she thinks happily. She pulls out her cellphone and types out a hasty message to Leigh.

Good date. He's so hot. Gonna see him again.

Headed home now.

Leigh quickly sends back a thumbs up emoji. Mia goes to lay her phone back down when another text comes in.

It's later. I had fun tonight. Can I see you Saturday? I'll make you dinner? Brett's message reads.

Mia giggles, and sends her message back. **I had fun too. Dinner Saturday. Just send me time and location.** Brett's message with his address and note to arrive by seven comes in. Mia texts her own thumbs up emoji, places her phone down and drives herself home, all while enjoying the slight scent of oranges lingering in her car.

CHAPTER 11

Mia finds herself swamped during the rest of the week. The last few days before finals week is filled with seeing patients before they leave for the holidays, attending the last of her seminars, working on her thesis, and starting her final papers. Mia's annoyed with herself for waiting to start on her three final papers at the last minute. Her courses all require a paper instead of a final exam, and while she had made rough outlines for all three of them, she had not begun writing the bulk of any of them. Instead of leaving her office to head back home during what she would consider normal hours, Mia ends up staying late each day so not to be distracted from her deadlines. That's why on Friday, when Leigh stops by Mia's office, Mia's desk is scattered with papers and several sodas with varying levels of the beverage left. A blanket hangs over Mia's chair, as her office becomes unusually cold during the evening hours.

"I'm sorry, do you live here now?" Leigh asks sarcastically as Mia looks up from the final paper she's working on.

"I mean, basically." Mia's face is paler than usual, her eyes dark with exhaustion.

"Yikes, Mia, you need to take a break," Leigh says with concern. "Let's go get some fresh air."

Mia sighs and rubs the back of her neck, "I don't know, I really need to finish this paper."

"It's a walk. You'll be back to keep working. C'mon," Leigh smiles encouragingly. Mia stretches out her arms and yawns.

"Okay, but just a short walk." Mia pulls her jacket out from under the blanket and pulls it on. She follows Leigh out of her office and out of the building. The cool air hits her face, feeling both refreshing and shocking. She and Leigh stroll down the path that takes them to the school's chapel, a walk they've done many times before.

"I haven't heard about your date since you texted me," Leigh says as she shoves her hands into the pockets of her jacket.

"Oh man, Leigh, it was good," Mia sucks in some cold air, "well, most of it was good. We had a couple of drinks at Callahan's and then Danny showed up and *came to our table to introduce himself*," Mia says with an incredulous tone at the end, "and somehow the date ended with us trying to fuck in my car and a cop interrupting."

Leigh throws back her head and laughs, "Seriously?"

Mia nods and smiles, feeling lighter, "Seriously. It was so hot. I don't know the last time I wanted to jump a guy like that."

Leigh raises an eyebrow questioningly at Mia. Mia rolls her eyes, "Okay, fine, I know the last guy I wanted to jump like that, but it has been awhile and honestly, after Danny dumped me, I just wanted a break."

Leigh gives a half-smile and nods, "What did Danny even say when he came up?"

Mia shrugs. "Just hi and introduced himself to Brett, and then I turned into an ice queen and we got out of there and into my car," she sings the final words. "He's got some balls to do shit like that."

Leigh nods slowly, thinking it over. "Well, you know he and Sasha have been fighting," she glances at Mia, trying to gauge her reaction. Mia rolls her eyes and shakes her head. "Yeah, Sasha told me he's been kind of a dick to her lately, ever since she got back."

"Ever since he kissed me," Mia spits out the correction. She quickly looks around, checking to make sure none of their classmates were in earshot. "Danny seems to only want what he doesn't have. I'm done with it."

"Alright," Leigh says skeptically.

"What's that supposed to mean?" Mia asks sharply.

"No, it's just, I agree with you. He's a grass is always greener guy. You were so into him though, and so hurt by what happened, I didn't know if you'd take him back, given the chance." Leigh responds gently, her eyes sympathetic on Mia's face.

Mia shakes her head vigorously, "No, I'm done with him because of how he hurt me. And because he thinks it's acceptable to come after me *when he has a girlfriend. The girlfriend he dumped me for.*" Mia emphasizes her last words.

"Well good, I'd hate to see him do that again to you."

Mia calms down and nods. They walk in silence for a bit, taking in the now bare trees and numerous students hustling quickly to their own classes. Mia worries she's hurt Leigh's feelings by snapping at her and changes the conversation with hopes to move past the awkward moment.

"Um, how are things with Jake?"

Leigh brightens and smiles. "Good, like insanely good. We've decided to date for real, like meet friends and families and go out in public on an actual date, once the new semester starts."

Mia nods at her friend and smiles back at her. "Why next semester?"

Leigh casually shrugs, "Just to make it feel like there was a whole semester between us getting together instead of a couple of weeks."

"Ah," Mia says gently. "Well, I can't wait to see the both of you out. Together."

"Thanks," Leigh smiles with gratitude. "So what's next for you and Mr. Car Sex?"

"That's Mr. Almost Car Sex, thank you," Mia and Leigh both laugh, "and I'm going over to his place for dinner tomorrow night."

"Dinner?" Leigh grins mischievously. "You bringing dessert?"

"Dahhling," Mia drawls, "I *am* dessert." Mia tosses her hair flamboyantly with each hand as both women laugh. Mia and Leigh reach the chapel and stop for a moment to appreciate the Gothic architecture before they turn back to their offices. Upon reflecting more seriously on Leigh's question, Mia utters, "I guess I should probably bring something else to eat? Or wine?" Leigh nods. "Mmmkay, I'll figure something out." Mia feels a bubble of excitement, thinking about being in a room with Brett again. This time without any exes, car consoles, or cops to get in the way.

Mia and Leigh reach the entrance of their building. They stop and each gaze up. Mia feels less appreciation than she did for the chapel, and begins to notice a surge of stress. She inhales deeply, hoping for the cool air to soothe her one more time.

Leigh turns to face Mia, "Don't wear yourself out." Mia nods. "Really, get some work done and go home at a normal time and just rest." Mia nods again. "I mean it, get a good night's sleep. You'd tell that to your clients!"

Mia lets out a laugh, "Okay, okay. Thank you, Dr. Black."

"Still a dissertation away from that title, but I still like the sound of it." Leigh jokes back.

"Uh huh, back to the grind, I'll talk to you later," Mia says as they enter and go their separate ways to their offices. Back in her office, Mia logs back into her computer and does a quick assessment of the goals she wants to achieve by the end of the day. She figures she can finish a first draft for her Cognitive Development class and then focus on a draft for her Principles of Third Wave Therapies class. Mia tests out the volume left in each can of soda, throwing the empty ones into the small bin for recycling under her desk, and taking a big swig from one that is still mostly full.

"Let's get shit done," she whispers to herself as she settles in for an afternoon of writing.

CHAPTER 12

Leigh's **go home** text arrived thirty minutes before Mia packed up her things. Feeling mentally spent, Mia already made the determination to pick up Chinese food for dinner and crash at home. She walks into the door of her apartment, with a to-go bag hanging from one arm and a bag laden with her laptop and stray research articles from the other. She flicks the lights on and sees Renly make his way out of her bedroom and down the hallway. He goes to weave in between her ankles, purring and rubbing himself against her.

Mia places her bags on the counter and leans down to scratch behind Renly's ears. "Missed me, buddy? Let's get you some dinner first." Mia grabs a can of cat food from the small pantry and pulls back the top. She pours out the food into his food bowl and watches as the cat eagerly devours his meal. "My turn," she says turning to her things on the counter. Mia removes her jacket and hangs it on the back of a kitchen chair. She grabs the bag with her food and lays the containers out on her coffee table. She makes one more trip back into the kitchen to get a glass and pours an already open bottle of cabernet sauvignon into her glass. She settles back onto the floor by her coffee table and begins to eat chicken and broccoli and rice. Mia turns the TV on and chooses a marathon of old *Law and Order: SVU* episodes as Renly jumps up onto the couch, eyeing her meal.

Halfway through her dinner, Mia hears her phone buzz, but chooses to ignore it. Then it buzzes several times in row. Sighing, she pushes herself up and points a finger at Renly, who is looking at the coffee table with renewed interest.

"Don't you dare," she says and quickly grabs her phone from her bag and sits back down, putting herself between her food and the cat who had managed to creep a little closer to the chicken. Mia presses the screen on to her phone and finds a missed call and three text messages, all from Luke.

Mia.

Pick up.

Pick up.

Where are you?

Mia's heart starts to pump harder, and quickly presses the

button to call her brother back. It rings twice and then he answers.

"Meeeeee-ahhhhhh," Luke shouts into the phone. Mia hears the din in the background, finding herself less worried and more annoyed that Luke is calling her from somewhere noisy and is already drunk at nine.

"Hey Luke, is everything okay?" Mia asks.

"Yessss! I just wanted to call and say I miss yoooou!" Luke slurs into the phone.

Mia's annoyance disappears as she listens to her brother. "Thanks," she laughs.

"I was just telling Matt, your name's Matt, right? Yeah, I was just telling Matt how cool you are and how you're studying to be a psychologist. He wants to be a psychiatrist, and I said he had to talk to you. Can I put him on?" Luke is already not listening as Mia tries to protest.

"Hey?" a voice says hesitantly.

"Hey Matt, could you put my brother back on?" Mia asks gently.

"Yeah sure, here he is." Mia hears the phone being fumbled between hands.

"He sounds cute, right?" Luke says once he's back on the phone.

"I can't tell. But you sound pretty drunk, are you going to be safe to get home?" Mia finds herself beginning to worry.

"Oh yeah, I'm at a party with Erica and her boyfriend, he's DDing tonight." Luke says referring to his best friend and roommate, Erica.

"Okay, good. How are you this drunk this early?" Mia asks, still feeling worried.

"Classes ended and finals don't start till Monday. So. It's. Time. To. Get. Drunk." Luke enunciates each word. Mia laughs, feeling a little more reassured that her brother is with friends and cutting loose for a reason. She knows he'll likely regret it in the morning however.

"Well it's good to hear you're having fun. How about we talk some other time? Like maybe when you're sober?"

"Yesssss. I will call you tomorrow! But you should come down here, we can go dancing!"

Mia laughs, "Yes, I'll make a plan to come down for your graduation, and we can do that. Why don't you go dance now? I'll talk to you tomorrow."

"Alrighty, byyyyyye Mia, love you!" Luke shouts into the phone.

"Love you too! Be safe!" She says as Luke hangs up, hoping he caught her last words. Mia turns back to her dinner and show. She's grateful for having a brother that wants to call her, even when he's drunk. She and Luke had never been particularly close, but when he started college and came out to their family, Mia made a concerted effort to be a better sister. Their father struggled to accept Luke and so she felt responsible for filling that gap. She made sure to call him weekly during that first year he was in Miami, and after that they spoke fairly regularly.

Mia finishes up her dinner and takes the empty containers to the kitchen where she rinses them out and places them in the recycling bin. She determines she can either try to get some more work done now, or head to bed early for an early start tomorrow. Mia stretches her neck, pours the rest of the wine into her glass and chooses to relax for a little longer before heading off to sleep.

Feeling a little buzzed now from her two glasses of wine, she picks up her phone again and punches out a message to Brett.

Can't wait to see you tomorrow. Hope you're a good cock.

Mia's eyes blink at the message and widen with mortification. "Oh fuck," she says and quickly tries to correct her typo.

Good cook. Omg I meant good cook.

Why not both? Reads the message Mia gets back. Mia laughs and breathes out a sigh of relief.

I guess we'll see. Mia ends her text with a winking emoji. She shuts off the TV and places her glass by the sink to wash later. As she flicks off the lights she calls out, "Renly, come!" and the cat bounces off the couch and trails Mia to her room as she gets ready for bed.

CHAPTER 13

Mia feels good about the progress she's made on her papers. She's revised her final paper for Cognitive Development and it's at the point where it's good enough for her to turn in. She knows it's not her best work, but there isn't enough time for her best work anyway. She's also managed a completed first draft for her Principles class, meaning she can probably revise it tomorrow and then focus on her last paper. Mia's only stopped long enough to eat a quick breakfast and lunch. As the time creeps into the later afternoon she starts to feel anxious for the evening to arrive.

As the sky darkens Mia takes her cue to start getting ready. She takes a hot shower, scrubbing herself with her favorite vanilla body wash. She carefully shaves her legs and her bikini line, then washes and rinses her hair out. As she leans her head back into the stream of water she briefly imagines Brett's hands running through her hair again. Her lips part and she drops one hand down her body to briefly and gently swirl her finger over her clit. Mia's body tingles and she stops, wanting to save this energy for tonight. She turns off the shower and wraps her hair in one towel and her body in another. After she dries herself off she applies lotion and small dabs of perfume at her wrists and one spot above her cleavage. She quickly blow dries her hair and applies a light amount of make-up, again choosing to focus on accentuating her eyes. Mia walks to her room, still in her towel, trying to determine what to wear. Thinking back to the moment in the car, Mia picks a dark green, form-fitting sweater dress and black boots. She slips into a lacy thong and matching bra before donning the rest of her outfit, tossing her towel into the hamper. Mia goes back to the bathroom to check herself over. She feels good, as just the sensation of the thong itself seems to alert her body that something exciting is on its way.

Mia goes to make her way out of her place when she stops dead in her tracks. *Crap, a wine*, she thinks. She quickly gazes over her sad little wine rack in her kitchen, and grabs the only bottle left, a Merlot that had been sitting there longer than she'd like to admit.

"Renly!" She calls and the cat trots into the kitchen to get his dinner. "Be good," Mia whispers as she gives him a pet once he's begun eating. Mia heads out the door with wine and purse in hand, and makes her way to Brett's home.

Brett lives in townhome about halfway between Earl and the local airport. His place further from campus than Mia's place, but in a neighborhood commonly occupied by graduate students and faculty. As Mia pulls up, she observes the pleasant suburban vibe, appreciating the trimmed shrubs and wreaths on the doors. She parks in the second open spot for Brett's home, as the first is occupied by what she assumes is his car. She takes a deep breath and makes her way to his front door and rings the bell.

The door swings open, with Brett filling the opening. He smiles at Mia, taking her in, and gestures for her to come in as he says it.

"No problems finding my place?" Brett asks, holding out a hand to free up Mia's hands. She gives him the bottle of wine.

"Yes, super easy. Um, also, hopefully that wine is good. I'm sorry, I didn't have time to stop earlier." She says embarrassed.

Brett waves off her comment, "Thanks for bringing it! I've got others if you end up not liking it." Mia relaxes and peers around. The main floor of Brett's townhome opens to a kitchen that looks onto a small dining/living room combination space. She can see that directly to the opposite side of the kitchen is a door that leads into a bathroom, and after that is a staircase that leads upstairs. Brett's home is sparsely decorated. He has the furniture for the dining room and living room, and plain curtains over his windows. A bookshelf on one wall holds various books and photographs. A single panoramic framed photograph of Philadelphia hangs on the wall. Brett observes Mia trying to satisfy her curiosity.

"I'll give you the grand tour later. I know my aesthetic leaves a little to be desired. But who am I kidding, decorating this place hasn't been a priority." Brett shrugs with a smile.

Mia nods, "Well it's very nice from what I've seen. No Sport Illustrated swimsuit posters," she teases.

"Oh, those are in my bedroom upstairs," Brett jokes back. "But why don't you take a seat, dinner is ready."

Mia pulls her jacket off and lays it on the arm of a couch. She sits down at the table, where it has been set for two. Brett slides a plate in front of her and heads back into the kitchen to uncork the wine she's brought.

"I hope you like chicken parmesan. It's the only good thing I can make." He says as he pours the wine into two glasses.

"What would you do if I was a vegetarian?" Mia asks, draping her napkin on her lap, waiting for Brett to join her. He looks up, startled and concerned.

"Are you?" he asks.

"No, this is perfect," Mia says gently, letting him know

she was teasing him again.

"Phew, cause I have no back up to this," Brett replies, bringing the glasses of wine over and settling into the chair across from Mia. He raises his glasses to Mia, and she clinks hers to his. "Bon appetite."

They each take a sip of the wine. Mia chokes it down and Brett tries earnestly to not make a face.

"Oh my god, this is terrible. I'm so sorry." Mia laughs as Brett tries to keep his composure. Brett laughs as Mia pretends to gag.

"Let me see what I have instead." Brett heads back into the kitchen and peers into his refrigerator. "I've got some Pinot Grigio and beer," he calls to Mia.

"I'll take the Pinot Grigio," she calls back.

"Perfect, there's enough for you and I'll have a beer." Brett returns to the table with their new drinks and sits back down. "Let's try this again," he says.

Mia clinks her glass to his bottle and says, "Take two. Thanks for dinner *and* the drink." She takes a bite and nods appreciatively. "Well if this is the one thing you can cook, you cook it well."

"Thanks, my mom insisted I learn how to make at least one good meal." He chuckles. As Mia and Brett eat and continue to take sips of their drinks they settle into an easy conversation.

"How has your week been?" She asks.

"Pretty light, mostly doing prep work for next semester. I'm teaching a new course and just want everything in order before the break. I doubt I'll get much done over Christmas. How about you?"

Mia feels mildly envious that his workload is light, making a mental note that some of Brett's funding clearly comes from a TAship. "Pretty exhausting, actually. I have a paper to finish up and another to basically write, so I've been busy." Brett nods sympathetically. Mia's eyes land on a photograph of an orange tabby. "Is that your cat?" she asks.

Brett nods, "Yeah, that's Tyrion."

Mia laughs, "My cat's Renly. I guess you're also a Thrones fan." Brett chuckles and nods. "So where is he?"

Brett wipes his mouth with his napkin as he finishes his meal and takes another swig from his bottle. "Staying with a friend, we kind of share ownership."

Mia pouts, "Aw, poor kitty." Brett gives a sad smile. "Or should I say poor Brett?"

"I'll survive, but I look forward to getting him back in a few months."

Mia nods at his answer. She finishes her glass and places her napkin on the table. "Let me clear these." Brett goes to stop her and she shakes her head. "No way, you cooked, I can clean this up." Mia grabs the plates and rinses them off in the sink and loads them into the half-full dishwasher. She comes back for their glasses, dumps the mostly untouched Merlot and washes out the wine glasses, leaving them to dry on the counter. Brett comes into the kitchen to toss his empty bottle.

"Thanks for that," he says, placing a hand on the small of Mia's back. She turns to face him.

"Happy to. Dinner was great." She smiles, feeling more nervous excitement begin to build.

"Well, should I give you the tour?" Brett's offer seems innocent, though a flash in his eyes suggests something more.

"Yes, please!" Mia says and feels a thrum of excitement shoot through her, as Brett takes her hand and guides her out of the kitchen.

"Kitchen," he says and points with his free hand.

Mia nods, "Mmhmm, yes, seems right."

Brett walks her to the living/dining room and points as he says, "Dining room. Living room."

"Yes, looks familiar." She giggles.

He points across the way, "Bathroom?" Mia shakes her head in response and so Brett continues to guide her up the stairs. Mia's heart begins to beat harder as they move up the steps. At the top of the stairs Brett points to one open door, and as Mia glances in she sees a space set up with a desk and bookshelves. "Office." Mia nods, anxious. They pass another open door and as Mia peeks in she sees a simple room with a bed and dresser. "Guest room." Mia's heart begins to race as they stop at the last door at the end of the hallway. "Master suite." Brett stops in the doorway and faces Mia, gazing down at her as he holds her at her waist.

CHAPTER 14

Mia, feeling as though her heart is about to burst through her chest in anticipation, exhales and looks back up at Brett. She runs a hand over his chest and notices him catch his breath. Brett closes the gap between them by pulling Mia in closer and kisses her. Mia wraps her arms around Brett's neck and moves her mouth more urgently against his. Mia kept her desire at bay all week, and finally relents to her urges. *I want him in me,* she thinks. Her sweater dress is already feeling stifling hot and she's itching to feel his skin against hers. Brett runs his hands down her backside, cupping her butt as they continue to kiss and stumble towards his bed.

Once the back of Mia's legs bump up against the bed, Brett gently pushes her down to the bed and she scoots back on to it, making room for him. Brett climbs on top, carefully placing himself between Mia's legs. He props himself up slightly so not to place all his weight on her, and Mia kisses him deeply. She spreads her legs, wrapping them around Brett. The action pushes her dress up a little, starting to expose her thong. Brett trails his mouth from hers and begins kissing her neck, running his tongue against Mia's earlobe. Mia's body jerks with delight and Brett's free hand caresses her breast. Mia lets out a soft moan and wraps her legs tighter around him. She feels herself longing for more and begins to rhythmically move against Brett. Brett smoothly runs a hand down from Mia's clothed breast to her thigh and runs it up her leg to the junction between her thighs. He strokes a thumb over the crease and Mia jerks against him, moaning again. She pulls his face back to hers and kisses him deeply, flicking her tongue against his as he continues to encircle her clit through her panties. His thumb moves faster, and both Mia and Brett breath heavily.

"God, more, I want more," she says breathlessly. Brett pushes himself off of her and pulls Mia's boots off and her dress up over her head in quick succession. His eyes roam over her, gazing at her breasts as she breathes. Mia reaches behind herself and unclasps her bra, letting her breasts fall loose. Brett leans back down, continuing to rub Mia with one hand as he gently holds a breast with another and kisses her along her neck. Mia whimpers and arches her back, aching for more of a connection. Brett's lips moves to her ear.

"I want to taste you," he whispers seductively.

"Yes," Mia murmurs back, her heart pounding, racing for

this moment. Brett peels himself off of Mia and stands up. He grabs the sides of her thong and slowly pulls it off her as she raises her hips slightly to let it go. Brett tosses the thong to the floor and leans back down to kiss Mia's breasts. Mia grasps at him, tugging at his shirt and belt loops. "Off," she demands. Brett makes quick work of his shirt and pants, throwing them to the same pile of Mia's discarded clothes. He leans back down and Mia runs her hands along Brett's chiseled chest. She moves as if to kiss his pec, but instead he bends down to catch her nipple in his mouth. He sucks hard.

Mia moans, "God I need you to fuck me."

"Not yet," he replies with a mischievous grin and kneels at the edge of the bed. He grabs Mia's legs and yanks her closer to him. Brett places his face between her thighs and flicks his tongue against her clit. Mia cries out, as the tension in her continues to tingle. Brett inserts one long finger in her and begins to slowly slide it in and out as he continues to tongue Mia's clitoris.

Mia breathes hard, "More. God, more." Mia briefly tenses when she feels the pressure of an additional finger and then relaxes into the sensation. Brett begins to pump his fingers more vigorously and Mia finds her body moving with him. Brett's tongue continues to lash her clitoris and Mia feels the sensation throbbing, the oncoming orgasm ready to rip through her. Her hands pull lightly at his hair and Brett pulls off, his eyes bright and his face flushed.

"Stop?" he asks huskily.

"No, fuck me. Please fuck me," Mia begs. Brett pulls himself to stand and Mia sees his erection bulging against his briefs. She sits up and grabs Brett's hand, feeling her slickness on his fingers. She guides them into her mouth, gliding them in and out. She reaches to stroke his cock with her free hand and Brett lets out a quiet grunt. He takes his hand from her mouth and pulls his briefs off, stepping out of them. Mia hungrily grabs at his thick penis with one hand and wraps her mouth around the top. She gently eases the length of Brett's cock into her mouth, sliding her tongue against it and pumping back in forth. Brett rans a hand through her hair and moans appreciatively. Mia feels his cock tense and she pulls off, observing a slight beading of semen at the tip. Brett almost seems to wince when Mia breaks away.

"Condom?" Mia asks, aching for the moment of Brett entering her. He nods and grabs one from his nightstand drawer. Brett rips the wrapper off while Mia lays back onto the bed and he rolls it onto his generous erection. Brett stands between Mia's legs and poises himself at her entrance.

"I need you in me," Mia licks her lips, still tasting the mixture of her and him in her mouth. Brett nods, leans down and kisses her passionately once more. He pushes himself forward, spreading Mia as her body graciously accommodates his girth. Mia moans as he fills her and begins to steadily pump against her body. His hands roam over her breasts and Mia clutches the comforter beneath her.

"Harder," Mia begs and Brett moves his hips faster, pushing into her, her breasts jiggling under his hands. Mia reaches down with one hand and rubs a finger against her clit, increasingly quicker. The fire inside grows as they both move more desperately against each other. Mia's back arches, "Yes, yes, yes, fuck me, fuck me," she cries and Brett begins to pound against her. Mia's orgasm tears through her, and she cries out as she comes. Brett continues to pump against her as she comes when he ejaculates and falls onto her, breathing heavy and exclaiming as he finishes.

He rolls off of her and both Mia and Brett pant as they stare up at his ceiling. Mia smiles lazily and gives herself a shake. She runs a hand through her hair and turns her head to face Brett. His eyes are closed and he's resting one hand on his chest as his breathing begins to steady.

"Good cook and good cock," Mia whispers in his ear. Brett laughs and turns to face her, he pulls her in for a long kiss, followed by a short peck. Mia snuggles into Brett, breathing in the smell of his sweat mixed with oranges, curving her body against his as he wraps his arms around her.

CHAPTER 15

As Mia begins to feel the sex haze lift from her brain she starts to worry. *Am I staying the night here? I did not plan on that. Does he want me to go now? I did not think this through enough.* Mia begins to squirm, and Brett lets her go as she pushes herself up. Mia rummages around the room to find her discarded clothes. She begins pulling on her underwear and bra, and pulls her dress over her head. She pulls her hair out from the neckline and grabs her boots. Brett has turned to his side and has been watching her process.

"Watching you get dressed is way less fun than undressing you," Brett murmurs as Mia sits on the bed to pull her boots on.

Mia grins at him, "Well I don't want to overstay my welcome."

Brett shakes his head and starts to say something, but

stops himself. He watches as Mia zips up her boots and turns to face him. "I'd offer a drink or dessert…but all I have is stale Oreos."

Mia smiles, still feeling uncertain about what he's thinking or wants, "I didn't even know those could go bad. And while it's a tempting offer, I think I'll pass."

Brett pushes himself up and grabs his briefs and pants from the side of the bed and pulls them on. He turns to Mia and cups her chin with his hand. He looks searchingly into her eyes and kisses her again. His lips are gentler this time and Mia returns the kiss, beginning to feel herself flush and eager for more. Brett pulls back and smiles at her, "I want to do this again sometime."

Great, Mia thinks sarcastically, *I jumped right into bed with him and now this is going to be all that he expects. I'm such an idiot sometimes.* Mia gives him a strained smile as she mentally berates herself.

"Maybe something in public. So that I'm less likely to rip your clothes off right away," Brett continues. He pushes back a hair that has fallen into Mia's face. "Don't get me wrong, I'd really like to rip your clothes off again, and I'd like to hang out with you with your clothes on."

Mia feels some of her anxiety breaking and lets out a breath she did not realize she was holding. "I would like to do something again too." She traces a hand along Brett's bare chest and watches at him from under her eyelashes.

"Then it's a date. Another date." Brett brushes his lips against hers. "A clothing date."

Mia laughs, "Sounds like a plan. Perhaps after finals? I've got to wrap up some papers and I'm going to be useless until then."

Brett nods, "Sure. Unless you need some kind of relief from all that work?" He raises an eyebrow suggestively.

Mia giggles, "That's not a clothing date."

Brett makes a dramatic pouty face before winking at Mia, "Fine. How about next Friday night? Celebration for the end of the semester? Drinks and then dinner out somewhere?"

Mia nods her head as she says, "That would give me something good to look forward to."

Brett stands and holds out a hand for Mia. As she takes it, he helps pull her up from the bed. "Then that's what we'll do. Let me think about where. Any preferences?" Mia shakes her head as they make their way back downstairs. She gathers up her purse and jacket and walks to the door, with Brett's hand on the small of her back.

"Brett, thank you again for dinner," she turns to face Brett and smiles up at him.

"If that's how I get thanked every time I make dinner I

will definitely cook more," Brett replies. Mia laughs and lifts her head up for one last kiss. Brett leans down and kisses her one last time. Mia steps back to enjoy the visual of Brett and his bare chest.

"Have a good night, I'll talk to you later," Mia pulls open the door and waves as she makes her way to the car.

"You too!" Brett calls and he remains at the door, letting the cool air in, as he watches her drive off.

Back at home, Mia changes back into her pajamas and completes her routine for bed. She settles into her bed and picks up her current library book. Mia's barely had time to read for pleasure during graduate school and she has easily renewed her copy of *Eleanor Oliphant Is Completely Fine* four times. Mia settles into reading her current chapter and Renly curls up next to her. She lazily scratches under his chin while she turns to the next page. As Mia finishes the chapter and yawns, she closes the book and sets it back on her night stand. She grabs her phone to shoot off a few last texts.

Hope you got home safe! To Luke.

I have to tell you about my date. Brunch tomorrow? To Leigh.

After a brief hesitation of second guessing herself, Mia sends one more message. **I had fun tonight** to Brett.

Brett's response quickly rolls back in, **Me too, will be**

thinking of you tonight.

Mia sends back a winking emoji and shuts her phone off, double checks her alarm for eight am, and switches off the light. She hooks an arm around Renly and lets herself drift to sleep, with a slight smile on her face.

CHAPTER 16

Mia's already seated with her bagel when Leigh comes through the door. Earlier in the morning they had already texted over when and where to meet. Given the likelihood that Eastern's would be jammed from hungover students celebrating the end of classes, they decided on The Bagel Shoppe, further from campus and less likely to attract the same crowd. Leigh quickly makes her way through the line, gets her order, and sits down across from Mia.

"Sorry for running late. Jake was slow to move this morning," Leigh sips on her coffee.

"You just got up?" Mia asks surprised as it was past eleven.

"Oh, we've been up," Leigh starts into her bagel.

"Ah," Mia nods, taking the hint. "So he's a morning person."

"I don't know if I'd say he's a morning person so much as he's a person with morning wood," Leigh shrugs and continues to devour her bagel. "Anyway, how was the date?"

Mia grins, excited to tell someone about it. "It was good. He was funny, he's from Philly, he likes cats, and his cock was perfect."

Leigh chokes on the bite she was working on and takes a swig of her coffee. "So he was dessert?"

Mia laughs and shrugs. "At first I was kicking myself for having sex with him so quickly, but I'm just so drawn to him, it felt magnetic. I couldn't help it. I thought for sure I fucked this up again, cause the last time that happened, Danny happened." Leighs nods knowingly and Mia continues, "But he wants to have another date. He even joked that it needed to be in public cause he'll just want to have sex again otherwise."

"Well that's good. When's that gonna be?"

"After my papers are in, I just need to focus on those and this draft." Mia wipes her hands off with a napkin.

"What's he study anyway?" Leigh finishes off her bagel and takes another drink.

Mia starts to say and then realizes she's never asked. She stares off beyond Leigh and gives a slight frown before laughing with embarrassment. "Um, I can't believe this, but I don't know. We haven't even talked about school that much. He's a TA?" She offers at the end as some kind of apology.

"Sex so good you forgot you're in grad school." Leigh wipes her hands off and pushes her tray away from herself.

Mia shrugs, feeling uncomfortable. "I guess we'll talk about that at our date."

Leigh smiles back at her gently, "Hey, just teasing. It's nice to spend time with someone and not have to think or talk about something stressful."

Mia nods slowly, "Yeah."

Leigh, sensing Mia's discomfort, changes the subject. "Anyway, speaking of stressful, what's left of your work?"

Mia and Leigh launch into the papers they have left to write and their plans for wrapping up the semester. As the conversation slows and begins to stall Leigh checks her watch.

"Well, it's probably time to get back to it anyway. Let's grab lunch or something during the week." Leigh gets up and grabs her tray, waiting for Mia.

"Yeah, sounds like a plan." Mia follows Leigh to dump their trash and return their trays. They share a quick hug outside and walk back to their respective cars.

Once Mia is back home, she settles back into her writing. She's revising her second paper and thesis, alternating between the two each time she gets frustrated with one. Renly sits in the box in the office as Mia hunches over her laptop. Even with these important distractions Mia has a nagging thought she can't shake.

How have we not talked about school? How do I not know what he studies? She wonders. Mia's sense of self-deprecation grows as she thinks she's been short sighted or coming off as uninterested. She tries to shake off the worry as she reminds herself that it didn't naturally come up in conversation and that it'll give them something to talk about on Friday.

After finding herself making no progress on her revisions after an hour because of her distracted thinking, Mia leaves her office and grabs her phone from the kitchen. Her fingers pause over Brett's number, as she contemplates texting him and asking. *It'll look stupid if I suddenly ask him this out of nowhere*, Mia thinks. *I can wait, it's not that big of a deal.* Mia sighs and puts her phone back down. *I'm overthinking this. I'm acting insecure because of the Danny stuff.* Mia practices these thoughts to reassure herself.

Mia goes and grabs a fresh can of soda from the refrigerator. Back in her office she sets her soda down and pulls up her music on her laptop. *Let's dance it out*, she thinks. As her playlist blasts from her laptop speakers, Mia bounces around her small office, pumping her arms in the air. Renly pokes his head out of the top of his box, seemingly alarmed.

"C'mon Renly! Let's dance!" Mia goes to scoop Renly out of his box, but he darts through her arms and runs out of the room. Mia laughs, shakes out her arms, and settles back into her chair as a song winds down. *Okay, back to work*, Mia says to herself as she recommits to writing.

The next day Mia had originally planned to finish up her *Principles* paper at home, so she stayed up late the prior night writing, and allowed herself to sleep in more than usual the next day. Mia checks her email from her at-home office when she finally pulls up her calendar to confirm for herself that she does not have any patients scheduled for the day. Mia scans her calendar and her eyes widen. An appointment with Dr. Thompson is in the calendar and it's in thirty minutes. Mia rushes out of her office and quickly changes into jeans and a sweatshirt, and gathers up her bag. She's barely brushed her teeth and run a brush through a hair before she decides against putting make up on. Mia grabs her things and runs out of her apartment to drive as quickly as possible without earning a ticket. Her heart races at the thought of being overly late to this meeting as she thinks *shit shit shit* over and over again.

Mia rushes into school and throws her coat and bag into the office. Mia can't remember why she has this meeting scheduled when she has not even sent back the latest of her revisions to Dr. Thompson. Mia quickly sifts through the paperwork in her bag and pulls out drafts and statistics print outs. Once she has everything she thinks she could possibly need, Mia dashes back out and makes her way to the stairs. She takes steps two at time and quickly finds herself panting at the end of the three flights. She's already late by ten minutes and steeling herself for the well-earned look of disapproval. Walking down the hallway to Dr. Thompson's office, Mia takes a few deep breaths to slow her breathing and stops at the door.

Mia listens closely and hears the muffled laughter of Dr. Thompson and a man. Mia breathes out a sigh of relief. *Her previous meeting has run over, she won't know I'm late,* Mia thinks. She debates knocking or waiting longer, uncertain if her advisor would be more upset at the tardiness or the interruption. Mia makes her decision and holds up her hand to knock, and barely gets one in before it swings open.

Standing in front of her at the door is Brett, mouthwateringly handsome in dress slacks and a pressed button-down shirt. Mia gawks at Brett with shock and Brett's eyes also widen in surprise.

"Mia, come in, come in," calls Dr. Thompson from behind Brett. "I'd like you to meet Dr. Dawson, he's the newest faculty hire in social psychology."

CHAPTER 17

Mia's heart is pounding in her ears and feels as if all the blood has drained from her face. Brett stares at her helplessly and Mia feels as if hours have passed. She shakes herself, plasters a smile on her face, and quickly holds out a hand.

"Dr. Dawson, nice to meet you, I'm Mia James." Brett slowly takes Mia's hand and shakes it, still seeming to unable to find something to say.

Dr. Thompson, unable to see either of their faces clearly, jumps in, "Brett, Mia is my third year student. She was the one I was mentioning may have some overlapping interests with your research. Mia, I know you have already formed your committee, but perhaps you may want to rethink things given Dr. Dawson's expertise."

Mia dryly smiles at Dr. Thompson and then Brett, trying to find what to say next. Her heart is still racing and she's certain a faint sheen of sweat is visible on her face.

"Let's set a time to meet, Mia," Brett says cordially and then turns to face Dr. Thompson, "Jean, thank you for taking the time to meet with me. I don't want to intrude anymore into your next meeting." He turns back to lock eyes with Mia once more as he heads out the door. "It was nice to meet you, Mia," he says, with a smile on his face that does not reach his eyes. Brett walks out of the office and Mia shuffles the rest of the way in, shutting the door behind her.

Dr. Thompson, still seemingly oblivious to Mia's reaction, sits at her desk and sorts through various papers as she waits for Mia to come sit. Mia practically collapses into the chair, startling her advisor into glancing up.

"Is everything alright?" Dr. Thompson asks.

Mia wipes her fingers across her forehead. "Yes, sorry, I, uh," Mia tries to focus and find her words, but can only seem to think about seeing a very surprised Brett opening the door. "Just tired, working hard on my final papers," Mia finally manages to say.

Dr. Thompson nods knowingly, "How have classes gone this semester?"

I can't believe this, Mia thinks. *He's the new fucking professor. I fucked the new fucking professor.* Her heart begins to pound again. *Oh my god and I look like shit right now,* she realizes. Mia finds herself beginning to panic and doesn't realize she hasn't responded to her advisor.

"Your classes?" Dr. Thompson repeats herself.

"Uh, good, they went well. I found Principles of Third Wave Therapies really useful. Um, particularly for some of the patients I see," Mia says. She takes a deep breath and tries to slow the racing of her heart.

Dr. Thompson nods again, mildly bored. "Mhmm, and what about your statistics course?"

Mia's brow furrows and she snaps back to the moment. "Oh, that's not until next semester. It's the structural equation modeling class and um, the new social psychology course." Mia bites down on her bottom lip, thinking about sitting in a seminar room while Brett teaches that course. Her heart thuds.

"Ah, the new one with Dr. Dawson? That'll be good. I do think you should reconsider your committee. He would be an excellent addition. Though it might ruffle some feathers to remove someone. Let's think about that maybe for your dissertation committee." Dr. Thompson says with a smile.

Mia nods and tries to smile back, feeling a mix of emotions. Anxiety over having Brett as her teacher, excitement at the thought of seeing him regularly, annoyance at the idea of changing her committee to suit her advisor's whims, and a resumed panic as another thought forms in her head.

Oh my god, is this even allowed? She wonders about her and Brett. *I'm gonna get kicked out,* she starts to worry.

"Anyway, remind me why we are meeting today, because I don't have your revisions back," Dr. Thompson interrupts Mia's thoughts.

Well double shit, Mia thinks to herself.

"I, uh, I'm not sure either," Mia says quickly and smiles apologetically. "Perhaps we set this one up some time ago? Not realizing we'd have discussed my draft last week?"

A brief flash of annoyance flies across Dr. Thompson's face, but she composes herself and finally takes in Mia's slightly disheveled appearance. "Well perhaps let's just end early today, and you can take the time to finish your final papers. Email me when your next draft is ready for me to review."

Mia nods gratefully, "Thanks, I will do that." She gathers her things and makes her way to the door. "I will email you soon," she says to Dr. Thompson while heading out the door.

Dr. Thompson nods and gives a small wave of her hand to indicate to Mia to leave, "Sounds good, bye Mia."

"Bye," Mia says as she pulls the door shut and finds herself alone in an empty hallway.

What do I do now? Mia wonders as she feels another rush

of emotions, feeling ready to crumble under the sudden weight of them. She peers up and down the hallway, wondering if Brett is behind one of the many closed doors. She moves as if to check her phone, realizing she left it in her bag downstairs. Mia makes her way back down to her office, anxious to find a way to talk to Brett.

CHAPTER 18

Back in her office in the basement, Mia sits at her chair and stares at her bag, where her phone waits within. *Has he already messaged me? Is he waiting for me to text him? Did he know? How did I not know?* Mia's thoughts swirl. *Is this prohibited? Are we going to get in trouble? Does it matter that it happened before he was my teacher? Before we knew?*

Mia logs into her computer and opens an incognito tab in her web browser. Mia quickly types in "faculty student relationship earl university policy" and hits enter and quickly begins to scan the links that appear.

The first link she sees and clicks on is a memo from almost twenty years ago. She quickly scrolls down to the paragraphs outlining faculty-student consensual relationships and reads closely.

No current faculty member shall be permitted to enter into a consensual relationship with a current student falling under that faculty member's authority. The situations of authority include teaching, mentoring, research supervision, and any employment of a student as a research or teaching assistant. Other situations of authority include exercising responsibility for grading, establishing honors, administering disciplinary action, or awarding degrees.

In addition, no current faculty member may take authority over a student with whom he or she has or has had any consensual relationship without agreement with the appropriate dean. No faculty member may allow the student to enroll in a course which the faculty member is teaching or supervising; direct the student's independent study, thesis, or dissertation; employ the student as an assistant of any kind; participate in decisions related to a student's grades, honors, degrees; or consider disciplinary action involving the student.

If a consensual relationship exists or develops between a faculty member and a student involving a situation of authority, that situation of authority is required to be terminated. Termination includes the student withdrawing from the course taught by the faculty member; transferring to another course or section, selecting or being assigned to an alternate advisor, and changing the supervision of the student's assistantship. For these changes to be ratified appropriately, the faculty must disclose the consensual relationship to his or her superior (i.e. the chair, division head, or dean) and reach an agreement for remediation. In case of failure to reach agreement, the supervisor shall terminate the situation of authority.

Mia breathes deeply and rereads the memo. *He can't be on my committee. He can't be my teacher.* She wonders about the gray area, *do we need to report this? This happened before either of us knew. Maybe he can be my teacher if we stop? We can stop. This only just started, we're not in too deep, we can stop. We can stop.*

Mia reassures herself, slowing her breathing and feeling

calmer. She closes her eyes and pictures Brett, feeling a sudden ravenous urge for him. She opens her eyes and slouches, crestfallen. While her academic career does not seem to be thrown away just yet, her love life has taken yet another significant hit. *Just when I get excited about someone, this shit has to happen. So unfair.*

Mia reaches down for her bag, bracing herself to finally check her phone. She pulls her phone out and drops her bag back to the floor. Mia takes one more deep breath to brace her and pushes her screen on and taps in her passcode. Her home screen indicates a text is waiting for her. She clicks it open and already knows it's from Brett.

we need to talk asap

No flirtation, no emoji revealing his own emotions. Mia feels shaky again, beginning to mourn the loss of something she's barely had. She checks the time of his message and sees that he clearly sent it immediately after leaving Dr. Thompson's office. She quickly sends one back

yes, when?

Brett's response is almost instantaneous. **I'm in my office, 213, free now.**

Mia frowns and sighs. She gets to get prematurely dumped while also looking like a complete mess during finals week. *Couldn't have asked for this to go any better*, she thinks sarcastically. Mia responds *on my way* to Brett and grabs her things to go to his office. She figures she'll head right back home after this, knowing she'll want to cry in the safety of her home rather than in her campus office. Mia locks up her office and returns the stairs she only just took two at a time. She climbs them more slowly, landing at the floor beneath her advisor's office. *How have I not seen him all semester? I have classes on this fucking floor*, Mia berates herself. She arrives at room 213, the plaque displaying the number, yet the slot with the occupant's name still empty. She knocks once.

"Come in."

CHAPTER 19

Mia pushes open the door and gently closes it behind her. Brett sits behind his desk, with his head down in his hands. His face pops up at her as she closes the door. Mia takes a deep breath and moves to take a seat on the opposite side of his desk. She looks around his office, which is more decorated than his home. An undergraduate diploma from the University of Pennsylvania hangs on the wall next to his graduate degree from Harvard University. Two book shelves are lined with various textbooks with a scattering of Funko Pop figurines from Game of Thrones and the Marvel Universe. Picture frames sit at his desk, their images hidden to Mia. As Mia sits across from him, they both stare helplessly at each other.

"I had no idea-" Brett starts.

"I didn't realize-" Mia begins at the same time. They both stop and open their mouths again to talk. Mia lets out a nervous laugh.

"Fuck," she snorts. Brett gives her a sad smile, sighs, and runs a hand through his hair. Mia can't help but admire how attractive he is even when he seems stressed.

"I'm not going to tattle on you, Brett, if that's what you're worried about," she says hurriedly.

Brett gives her a more genuine smile, though his eyes are sad, "Honestly, that's not the first thing I was worried about." Mia furrows her forehead and tilts her head at him, urging him to continue. Brett sighs. "I like you. I had fun with you. I did not expect this." He pauses, seeming ashamed, "and then I was worried you would think I was coercing you and would report it."

Mia shakes her head almost violently. "There was no coercion and you know that. This," she says waving a hand between the two of them, "was mutually consensual. If either of us had known, I think we would have behaved otherwise."

Brett nods, "I agree. I guess now we have to figure out what's next."

Mia's eyes drop down, disappointed and waiting for the other shoe to drop. She looks back up to see Brett's imploring expression. "I wish I could keep seeing you," he says as he reaches a hand out across his desk to her, his palm up inviting hers. Mia places her hand in his and rubs her face with other hand.

"I….I don't think we can." Mia pulls her hand back, "I was Googling," Mia starts and pauses to appreciate Brett's chuckle, "and Earl has a policy about consensual relationships. I'm in your class next semester. I'd have to drop it, and obviously I couldn't have you on my committee." Brett nods slowly. "And honestly, even if we made those two things work, we'd still have to report it to the Dean." Mia's breath catches in her throat, but she continues, "And in a small community like this, everyone would find out and there'd be a big question mark looming over me. Or people thinking I've slept my way to my Ph.D. And I, I can't do that." Mia's voice falters. Tears start to brim in her eyes. It hurts to face this and she's angry thinking about how appearance-wise it is bad for them both, but mostly for her. That she would be judged and scorned and that he would likely get attaboys and slaps on the back in approval.

Brett gets out of his chair and walks around his desk to sit in the chair next to Mia's. He wipes a tear that has fallen off her cheek and Mia's breath catches at his gentle touch. He gazes at her face and moves as if he is going to respond, but Mia continues herself.

"And to be honest, I don't want to drop your class for next semester. For a number of reasons, some more logical and some probably more sadistic. I want to finish this program sooner rather than later, so I just can't put off my social psych course." Mia continues to silently cry, feeling sad and frustrated.

Brett leans back in his chair and runs a hand through his hair and then across his forehead. "I think this is the quickest I've been dumped," he says with a half-smile. Mia chuckles lightly through her tears. "Obviously, I am going to respect your decision with this. I guess this will mean goodbye until next semester?"

Brett stands and pulls Mia up to him. Mia gazes up at him and nods, first with certainty, but as she looks into Brett's eyes her nod slows and she begins to question herself.

It's not fair, she thinks. *I find someone fun and hot and the sex was good and then this is how it turns out. Why does it matter anyway? Why should I care what other people may think? Why can't I do want I want? Why can't I be with him?* Mia's sadness and frustration begin to melt into defiance.

Mia rests her head against Brett's chest and her folds her into his arms. She breathes in deeply, trying to appreciate his scent, forcing herself to remember it as she knows she won't have this chance again. Her tears slow and she begins matching her breaths to Brett's steady heartbeat.

Feeling calmer, Mia pulls herself out of Brett's embrace. Staring into his eyes, she feels a pull towards him, desire beginning to bubble, and her resolve quickly melting. Her breathing begins to speed up again and she strokes a hand down his chest. Brett stares at her, his lips parted and his breathing also picking up. Mia feels a heat between them grow and the air around them thicken with tension. Mia tilts her head up at him, wanting him and knowing she shouldn't.

"This is a bad idea," Brett whispers, his eyes still focused on Mia, drawn to her lips.

"I don't think I care," Mia says whispers back.

Brett pulls her back in and kisses her passionately. He runs his hand over her back and down her butt, while Mia has thrown her arms around his neck and shoulders. Mia's heart pounds as Brett pushes his tongue into her mouth and caresses hers. Mia pulls a hand free and strokes Brett's chiseled chest. Brett moves to kiss Mia's throat and gently nibbles her earlobe. A quiet moan escapes from Mia and Brett rubs one hand between her legs. Mia moans louder and Brett pulls back.

"This is not the best place," He whispers again, his eyes roaming over Mia, his face flushed. Mia's heart is thudding and nods in agreement. She stares steadily at Brett, then turns back to the office door and resolutely pushes in the lock.

"I'll be quiet, can you?" She murmurs as she pulls Brett's dress shirt out of his pants. She begins unbuttoning it in between kissing his neck.

Brett closes his eyes and tilts his head back. "Yes," he whispers, barely audible.

Mia pulls off Brett's shirt and begins kissing down towards his chest. She gently bites on his nipple and Brett gasps with a glance back down at her. Mia runs a hand across the front of Brett's pants to find that he is hard. She goes to unbuckle his pants when he grabs her wrist gently and stops her.

"Are you sure?" He asks. Mia nods. Brett reaches down and pulls off Mia's sweatshirt. "Positive?" Mia nods again and Brett unbuckles and unzips her pants as she hurriedly steps out of them. She goes to kiss Brett, but he stops her again. "This ends the moment you want it to," he says.

Mia unhooks and throws off her bra, she grabs Brett's hand and places it on one of her large freed breasts. She pulls him back down to her and kisses him, hungrily searching for his tongue in his mouth. Pulling back from him and panting, Mia says "I don't want this to end. I need this."

Brett leans back in and gently squeezes her breast, his thumb running over her nipple, encouraging them to stiffen and harden. His mouth roam back down her neck and up to her earlobe where he sucks harder. Mia lets out a heavy sigh, trying to stay quiet. Brett begins to rub her clitoris over her panties and returns to kissing her on the lips.

"How do you want me?" he whispers. Mia pulls back and her eyes glint. She licks her lips and begins unbuckling and unzipping Brett's pants. She yanks them to the ground, revealing Brett's large hard cock rigid in his boxer briefs. Mia places her hands on both sides of the waistband of the black briefs and pulls them down. She licks the pad of her thumb and rubs of head of Brett's penis slowly. Brett closes his eyes and moans. As he opens them and moves to pull Mia in for another kiss, she drops to her knees in front of him.

With one hand on the base of his penis, Mia slowly licks the length of his shaft before reaching the top. As her tongue reach the head of his penis, she opens her mouth and takes in his generous erection. Mia slowly guides her mouth up and down Brett's cock, her tongue a steady stroke against his shaft. Brett moans and his hands tangle into her hair, resting one on the back of her head, only being moved by Mia's motions. Mia begins to pick up her pace, feeling Brett's cock stiffen and twitch, and pumping her hand along with her mouth. She squeezes Brett's ass with her other hand, holding him close to her as she continues to bob up and down on his penis, working hard to fit as much of the shaft as she can into her mouth.

Brett's breathing quickens and he's panting with Mia's effort. "Fuck," he grunts, "I'm gonna come." Mia continues at her steady pace and Brett's hands tighten in her hair. He moans again and Mia persists in her sucking. Brett lets out in indecipherable grunt as he orgasms, spilling semen into Mia's mouth. She continues to pump as she tastes the overly sweet semen and quickly swallows. Mia pulls back and wipes her mouth with the back of her hand and then gazes up at Brett. His eyes are closed and his face rests in a state of relaxation. He gives himself a shake, opens his eyes, and grins at Mia.

Brett pulls Mia back up to her feet and holds her body close to his as he kisses her again. Mia reaches up and runs her hand through Brett's hair as his hand roams around her body, grasping her ass and stroking her breasts. Brett pushes one hand under the band of Mia's panties, running the tips of his fingers over the light dusting of her pubic hair. He runs a finger between Mia's legs, making his way to her clit, where he begins to slowly swirl his finger.

Brett drops to whisper in Mia's ear, "You're so wet," before he nibbles on her earlobe again. Mia's knees buckle slightly and Brett kisses her down her neck. He sinks one finger into her and Mia leans her head back. "Do you want more?" he asks between kisses.

"Yes," Mia moans softly. Brett slides a second finger into her and continues to slowly move them in and out. Mia clutches at Brett, wanting more contact. "I want you to fuck me," she hoarsely whispers.

Brett pulls back, his eyes dark with desire, "I don't have a condom. Tell me what else I can do for you," he whispers back.

Mia steps back, pulling his fingers out of her. She pulls her panties off as Brett watches and backs up to his desk. Mia gently sits herself onto his desk, then gently places her feet on each chair, spreading her legs. "I want you to fuck me," she repeats. Mia leans back on one hand while she begins playing with herself with the other. She guides her own finger into herself, feeling her saturated need, aching for Brett to enter her. She glimpses at Brett, who watches all of this intently, his hand now stroking his own cock, which has stiffened again. "I want you to fuck me," Mia presses once more.

Brett, feeling both desire and pain, shakes his head, "I want to, I do." He takes a step towards her, seeming to fight an internal battle. Brett walks closer to her again and Mia spreads her legs wider. Brett pushes her hand out of the way, allowing Mia to support herself with both hands. She closes her eyes and braces herself for Brett to enter her when she feels his mouth at her crevice. She only opens her eyes briefly to see him kneeled before her.

He looks up at her briefly, his eyes pleading, and Mia nods and closes her eyes again, leaning her head back and letting herself fall into the sensation. Brett presses on, alternating between licking and rubbing her clit. He slips two fingers back into her and pumps them with increasing pace. Mia begins to quietly moan, her blood and heart throbbing in her ears. Spurred on, Brett's pace quickens and he continues to draw and flick his tongue over Mia's clitoris. Mia's chest rises and falls quickly with her breathing, as she strains to stay quiet. "More," she moans raggedly. Brett pushes a third finger into her and Mia jerks to the sensation. As the tingling sensation within her grows, louder and louder moans begin to escape from her lips. Mia reaches down and grabs Brett's free hand and places two of his fingers in her mouth. As the tension within her explodes, Mia wraps her lips around Brett's fingers tightly and moans against them, struggling to stay as quiet as she can.

Brett pulls himself back up Mia's body by kissing his way from her thigh, up her stomach, across her breasts, up her neck, and back to her mouth. Mia grabs the back of his neck and pulls him in for a long kiss as the tremors in her body slowly dissipate. She sits up straight and Brett stands back. They stare at each other wordlessly, both flushed, and finally allowing themselves to process what they have done and where they did it.

"Now what?" Mia asks quietly, feeling stunned for a new reason. She begins to gather her scattered clothes and dress. Brett is already doing the same, trying to smooth out the wrinkles in his clothes. Once dressed he sits back down in one of the chairs Mia had rested a foot in just moments ago. He puts his head back into his hands.

"God we're fucked. We're right back to where we started." He says pained.

"No," Mia says shaking her head, feeling more resolute. "This was it. I just, needed to get it out of my system." Brett's expression is wounded and he quickly tries to hide the emotion. Mia catches the moment and feels herself weaken. *Not the time, do what you need to do* she thinks as she braces herself. "I don't mean for this to be cruel, I really like you," her voice falters and she takes a deep breath, "but we both know this won't end well. So let's stop it here, on a good note." Mia forces her eyes to the window, purposely controlling her breathing, wringing her hands to keep them to herself.

Brett blinks and lets out an unsteady sigh. "Sure," he says and then more firmly, "you're right. Just…collegial from here on out." He stands and holds out at hand to Mia. She looks at it for a beat, knowing that only seconds ago that hand caressed her and made her come, and takes it and shakes it.

"It was nice to meet you Mia, I look forward to having you in my class next semester," Brett says stoically.

"I look forward to it too, Dr. Dawson," Mia smiles sadly and lets go of his hand and makes her way to the door. She unlocks the door and quickly walks out. Mia practically slams the door behind her, and before she can change her mind, runs down the nearest staircase and speedwalks to her car, feeling the cold air freeze the tears against her face.

CHAPTER 20

Mia spends the next two and half days in a haze. Her waking hours are either in front of her laptop trying to knock out her last two papers, or sipping wine in front of a parade of chick flicks in the evening. She's letting herself sleep in, or rather sleep off the wine two mornings in a row. Sensing her despair, Renly even snuggles up on her lap while she works in the office, eschewing his preferred cardboard box. While Mia reads and types during the day, she hardly acknowledges the painful interaction just days earlier. As the third night of wallowing in her self-pity rolls in, Mia chooses to drown herself again in a movie where at least someone is happy in the end.

I am such a cliché, she can't help but think to herself. Rather than choosing to do something about it, Mia pours herself more wine and pulls an afghan up to her chin, settling into an evening with a romantic comedy marathon. When her phone buzzes, Mia chooses to ignore it. She wants it to be Brett, but knows better. She doesn't want it to be Leigh because she's afraid of Leigh asking about Brett, and wants it to be Leigh so that she can have a shoulder to cry on. Mia's sure it's not either of her parents because they rarely text her, and worries that if the message is from Danny she'll do something she'll regret even more. Mia figures she can hole up at her apartment for a few more days, emailing in her final papers to her professors, and dedicate herself to her thesis during the winter break.

Mia finishes off her glass of wine, and gingerly makes her way to the kitchen to place her glass in the sink. Feeling dizzy, Mia rests a hand on the kitchen counter, steadying herself and walks back to the couch, where she flops herself down. Renly, rudely awoken by the significant shift on the couch, jumps and leaves with a haughty glare back to Mia. She pulls the afghan back around her and sighs deeply.

This is embarrassing, Mia chides herself. *I barely knew him.* But even as Mia tries to talk some sense into herself, her thoughts swirl around her other perceived romantic failures. Danny chose someone else over her, the string of really bad dates before hooking up with Danny, the on again and off again roller coaster with her college boyfriend that went on for two years, the random hook-ups in college that on occasion she had hoped would turn into something more, and her high school boyfriend that she never seemed good enough for. Mia recognizes that this break up particularly hurts because they both seemed equally eager for one another and she will not be able to escape him. Mia lets herself wallow some more, wiping away the tears that arrived and sniffling.

Her phone buzzes again. And again.

"Fuck, what is it?" Mia grumbles and grabs her phone from the coffee table. Mia feels a mixture of relief, worry, and sadness when she sees one text from Luke and two from Leigh. She almost giggles to herself, suddenly seeing the juxtaposition of their names and appreciating that the two people she is closest with are *almost* named for the Star Wars twins. *Yep, drunk*, Mia thinks to herself. She unlocks her phone and reads the messages.

Talk soon? From Luke. Mia punches back a reply and sends it. **Sure, tomorrow. I'll call.**

What are you up to? Leigh's first text, and then the second one that came later, after Luke's: **Alive?**

Mia sighs and contemplates what to text Leigh. Realizing she will have to eventually rip the band aid off and see her friend, Mia texts her back. **Been writing these last few days. Just relaxing now.** Mia adds an emoji of a wine glass and sends it to Leigh.

Leigh's response is immediate, **Hang out tomorrow?**

Mia sighs loudly again, as if her friend's kindness is

suddenly a burden. She shakes herself at that thought. *Why am I scared of seeing Leigh?* Mia knows her friend would support her. Nodding to herself, Mia texts back a *sure*, and Leigh texts her to come over tomorrow night to hang out. Mia confirms and puts her phone back down. She snuggles back into the couch once more, and Renly rejoins her, snuggling up against her chest, kneading and purring into the afghan.

Mia wakes up the next morning, partially because of Renly's insistent meowing in her face and partially because her body ached for her to move and stretch. She fell asleep on the couch, yet did manage to turn off the TV at some point, though she couldn't recall when. Mia rubs her eyes and checks the clock. It's not yet lunch time, giving her enough time to quickly read over her last two final papers one last time and then send them off to their respective professors.

Mia stretches and walks into her kitchen, choosing to drop two slices of bread into the toaster and pulls out the tub of butter from the refrigerator. As the bread warms she fills a glass of water from the sink and drinks half of it quickly. She then grabs the Advil bottle from a nearby cabinet, pops off the top and tips out two pills. She tosses the two pills into her mouth and swallows them with another swig from her glass. The toaster dings and sends up her slices, and Mia gingerly grabs one, quickly butters it, and leans over the sink to eat it, allowing the crumbs to fall. After devouring the first slice, she quickly repeats it with the second slice. Mia wipes off her hands and finishes her glass of water. Mia briefly wishes for something greasy to manage her slight hangover, but chooses to go into her office and begin working.

After two hours of staring at her laptop screen, making slight revisions, and feeling proud of one paper and bitter acceptance of the other being good enough, Mia sends each final paper off to her professors. Feeling accomplished, and wanting to take a break before working on her thesis, Mia decides to treat herself to lunch. Heading back into her bedroom she quickly pulls on fitted exercise pants, a sport bra, a t-shirt with her undergraduate college emblazoned on the front, and a thick sweatshirt with *Earl* displayed on the front. She pulls on her cross-trainers and shoves her phone and a small wallet into the kangaroo pouch of her sweatshirt. Mia heads out of her apartment and starts a brisk walk.

Mia takes several long, deep breathes of the cool winter air, feeling it slightly burn her lungs. She pulls the hood up over her head and shoves her hands into the sweatshirt's pockets, regretting that she didn't layer more. Somehow, she observes, it got a lot colder over the last few days when she decided to be a hermit. Mia picks up her pace to her favorite Thai restaurant, which is a mile walk from her apartment. She keeps her eyes on the sidewalk in front of her, ignoring the cars soaring by. She passes by a nearby park, hearing the sounds of some younger kids squealing and the noise of a basketball hitting a backboard. She turns and scans her surroundings, and her breath catches momentarily. She stops and sees a group of men playing basketball, squinting to get a better view. One tall guy with brown hair has his back to her and Mia inches closer to the entrance of the park. The tides turn in the pickup game and the men race down to the opposite end of the court. Mia catches a glimpse of the brunette's face, realizes it's not Brett, and quickly turns back to her steady walk along the path.

What would you have done anyway if it was him? Mia scolds herself. *Stop being obsessive.* She hunches her shoulders, picks up her speed, and focuses on getting to her lunch.

One hot Thai dish and a brisk walk back to her apartment later, practically running past the park, Mia settles in. She's decided to give herself the afternoon off from work. She lazily picks up her phone and calls Luke. He quickly answers with the video chat on, turning her camera on too.

"Hellooooo!" Luke practically shouts into the phone. He's tan and smiling, sitting outside.

"Hey," Mia says, finally cracking a smile for the first time in several days.

"Either the lighting in your place sucks or you look terrible," Luke kindly quips.

"Both?" Mia shrugs, but rubs at her eyes and tries to fluff

up her hair.

"Finals?" Luke asks assured.

"Kind of, yeah," Mia replies, not wanting to get into details of her failed romance over the phone with her brother. "Anyway, are yours done? How have you been?"

Luke shakes his head, "Nah, I have two more, but you caught me taking a break from studying. Have you decided if you're going to be at mom's for Christmas?"

Mia cringes, "Ah no, I haven't decided." Mia's graduate student stipend didn't afford her many plane tickets back home and she had previously determined to never ask her parents to help her visit.

Luke rolls his eyes and sighs, "That's just Mia code for 'no.'"

"I didn't say no!" Mia furrows her brow.

"Yeah, whatever. It'd be nice if you did come down for Christmas." Luke says.

"Okay, *mom*, thanks for that." Mia replies sarcastically.

Luke pouts at her, "I'm sure mom would like you there too."

Mia waves her free hand, eager to change the subject again, "So who was that guy you put me on the phone with the other night?"

Luke grins into the camera, "That would be Matt. I've walked past him in the quad almost every Tuesday and Thursday going to my advanced political theory class. I finally uh, ran into him, a few weeks before classes ended," Luke says giving a conspiratorial wink. "We started talking and have hung out a few times. He's nice, Erica likes him. He's pre-med and a junior. He's pretty active too, so we've gone on a few runs." Luke, a former cross-country athlete, smiles again. "He's super shy though, and we haven't had a *date* date, but we've hooked up."

Mia nods, carefully asking her words, "Is he out?"

Luke nods vigorously, "Yes. He's just quiet with new people, but he's hung out with me and Erica and Alex and has warmed up. Maybe if you come down to Miami this winter you could meet him?"

"If I don't have money for a ticket to Texas, I don't have money for a ticket to Miami," Mia sighs.

"So you're not coming home!"

Mia narrows her eyes, "Probably not. But are you saying you're not either?"

Luke shrugs. "I don't know, it'd suck if you weren't back too."

Mia frowns, feeling bad that her decisions are influencing her brother's. There's no reason why he can't visit without her. "Mom would be so sad if neither of us went home. You should go. I will try to figure it out for myself," she promises. Luke shrugs half-heartedly, not seeming to trust her words.

"How about you? Anything exciting on your end?" Luke asks.

Mia takes a deep breath and sighs, "Um, no. Just buckled down and focused on my work."

Luke nods, seeming distracted by something Mia can't see off camera. "Mmhmm, all work and no play makes Mia a dull conversationalist."

Mia laughs, "Sorry, you're right. But really, the last few days have all been work." She pauses, then adds, "And honestly some less than stellar social stuff, but it'll work itself out."

Luke looks sharply back at the camera, "What happened?"

Mia shakes her head and waves her hand as if to indicate it's nothing, but still says, "It's nothing. It'll all blow over in time."

"Does it have to do with Danny?" Luke asks protectively.

Mia, deciding it's easier to talk about Danny than Brett, nods, "Um, yeah. But like I said, it'll not be a thing. I asked him to leave me alone and I haven't heard from him since."

Luke nods, clearly comfortable with her answer and not wanting to get more details than necessary, replies, "Fine," he pauses and sighs, "but if you want to talk about it, we can."

Mia shakes her head and lets out a light hearted laugh, "I think we're both good *not* talking about certain things." Luke cringes and laughs, recalling their failed attempt to discuss their individual sex lives. While they both dated men, they each still found a significant gross factor in talking about their sex lives with one another.

"Agreed. Well, I'm gonna get back to studying. Love you!" Luke waves.

"Love you too," Mia says before ending the video call. Mia sets her phone down, and decides with the time left to kill before heading over to Leigh's place she'll veg out and finally take a shower.

CHAPTER 21

By the time Mia gets to Leigh's place that evening she recognizes a couple of cars in the parking lot of the apartment complex. Mia notes that both Jake and Sasha are likely here too and feels her heart beginning to sink. She had been hoping for a low key night with just Leigh and now has to put more effort into the night. She sighs and knocks on Leigh's door.

"Come on in," Leigh calls from inside. Mia lets herself and closes the door behind her. Leigh is on the couch in front of the TV, draped across Jake. Sasha is curled on the second, smaller couch that is adjacent to the larger one. Leigh turns around from her seat, and upon seeing Mia sits up and smiles.

"It's been a while, I thought you fell off the face of the planet," Leigh says jokingly.

"Nah, just busy with final papers, you know," Mia shrugs

nonchalantly, glancing at Sasha. "Did you get yours in today too, Sasha?"

Sasha nods, "Yeah, it's nice to have them done."

Leigh gets up from the couch and walks over to Mia. "I saw Sasha at the library this morning and invited her over too, just a way to relax after getting everything done." She searches Mia's face, knowing Mia was probably surprised by the additional guests, but Mia doesn't let her disappointment show. "And Jake was actually just leaving, right?" Leigh says as she turns to see Jake already pulling on his jacket.

"Yep," he says. He pulls Leigh in for a quick kiss and then turns to Mia. "It was good to see you, maybe I'll stick around to hang out another time," he says, directing the second half more to Leigh instead of Mia. Leigh rolls her eyes and motions for him to go.

"You too, see you later," Mia responds, as Leigh and Sasha both wave to Jake and he leaves the apartment. Mia examines Leigh with a questioning eyebrow, "I thought bringing him around friends was happening next semester?" Sasha giggles from the couch and Leigh rolls her eyes at Mia. "I guess there's no timeline for love," Mia continues lightly.

Leigh rolls her eyes again at Mia, "Whatever." Both Mia and Leigh head back to the couches and flop down on opposite ends of the big couch.

"How you been, Sasha?" Mia asks.

"Fine, I guess. I hated that principles paper, but that's over with. Just happy to be out of the library and around normal people." Sasha grumbles.

"Who isn't normal?" Mia asks. Leigh shoots a quick admonishing look at Mia, and Mia instantly regrets asking.

Sasha takes hesitant breath and slowly answers, "Danny's just been, difficult. The last few days he's been picking fights for no reason."

Mia purses her lips anxiously and nods, "Sorry, that sucks."

Sasha nods and gives a forced smile, "Yeah. But uh, we don't have to talk about that."

Mia waves her hand nonchalantly, "Really, it's fine, if you want to trash Danny, I'm very good at that." She gives a genuine smile.

Sasha laughs, "I'll keep the offer in mind." The air feeling lighter around them, all three women visibly relax. Mia had mostly avoided conversations about Danny around Sasha, or excused herself when Sasha would talk about him. This would be the most words the two had shared about Danny since Sasha approached her months ago and apologized for hurting Mia's feelings. Mia didn't feel that Sasha needed to apologize, it was Danny who was being dishonest and it was Danny who dumped her. However,

Mia knew Sasha wanted to make sure things were smooth between the two of them since they'd continue to see each other almost daily, even if Mia and Danny didn't.

Leigh gives Mia's leg a nudge with her toes, "Well what about you? Have you seen Hottie McPerfect Cock?"

Sasha's eyebrows raise and she smiles at Mia. Mia's mouth flatten into a line and she shakes her head. She's still uncertain about telling Leigh who Brett actually is, but she definitely does not want to share it with Sasha. Whether or not Sasha and Danny are on the outs, she doesn't want this failed romance getting back to Danny.

"Have you heard from him?" Leigh pushes.

Mia feels ready to smack Leigh, wanting her to shut up. She shakes her head again, momentarily catching Leigh's eyes and trying to signal with her own to stop asking. Leigh's face finally registers Mia's reluctance.

"Um, what do you guys want to watch?" She asks, picking up the remote. Sasha sits back on her couch, her face showing disappointment. Leigh clicks through the channels until she lands on a show they all can agree on. After a couple of hours of mindlessly watching TV Sasha stands and stretches.

"Alright, I'm out. I'll see you guys around," she says as she leaves. Mia and Leigh both wish her a good night and after the door is shut, Leigh turns and faces Mia.

"What was that about?"

Mia sighs loudly. "I just don't want to talk about this stuff in front of Sasha is all."

"Okay, noted. But now that she's gone, can you talk about it?" Leigh asks gingerly.

Mia shrugs again, trying to be nonchalant. While watching TV she decided there was no good reason to share everything about Brett. Since they agreed to quit and try to move forward as a student and teacher, there was no need for Leigh to know details. Rather, as Mia reasoned, it would be worse if anyone else knew anything, as it could put both Mia and Brett at risk.

"We did talk again," Mia starts, "and I kind of realized we weren't a good fit," she finishes with a statement that only feels like half a lie. "And I don't want another Danny situation, hooking up with someone that I know isn't good for me and having it go nowhere, and get hurt again."

Leigh nods, her face understanding. "Fair enough. That sucks though."

Mia nods, "Yeah, but whatever. Anyway, I'm getting tired too, I think I'll head back home."

"Well let's do something else sometime. Maybe hit the gym? A good sweat might help you feel better?" Leigh says encouragingly.

Mia agrees with Leigh and nods her head. She grabs her things and heads out of Leigh's apartment, thanking her for having her over and wishing her a good night.

Back in her car, Mia pulls out her phone and checks to see if she has any messages. She finds herself disappointed when she sees none, and realizes how much she wants to see Brett again. She pulls up her text exchange with him, the one that last happened when they realized their dilemma. She starts to tap out a message, writing that she wants to see him again, and then deletes it. She types out a **how are you** and then deletes that too. *Don't be stupid*, Mia says to herself and shoves her phone back into her bag and drives herself home.

At home, laying in her bed, Mia scrolls through Facebook and Instagram. She looks over old photos on her phone, swiping past pictures of her and Danny. She feels some regret over not having a single photo of Brett. She pulls Facebook back up and does a quick search for Brett Dawson. Thousands of profiles populate and Mia does a brief scroll, quickly giving up. She briefly weighs searching for him on Instagram, but decides against it, figuring he'd be harder to find on there. Mia sighs, frustrated, and pulls up her text exchange with Brett again. She weighs the idea of texting him now.

It's late, she thinks, *and any text I send now will be deemed a booty call. Is that I want? I mean, I definitely want to sleep with him again, and I want more than just the head we gave each other in his office. And does he even want to see me again? Would anything good come out of me texting him?* Mia's thoughts swirl, as she goes back and forth between wanting Brett and chastising herself for not being smarter.

It's gotten late while Mia vacillated between berating and encouraging herself. She plugs her phone in after realizing how her text would be perceived at the current hour and tosses it to the floor to charge. She shuts off her lamp light and curls up under her covers. She turns away from her phone, not realizing the notification light is blinking to signal a message has been received.

CHAPTER 22

Mia wakes up from what finally feels like a good night's rest, acknowledging that not drinking the night before probably played a role in that, and pads off to the kitchen to feed Renly and herself. She scrambles some eggs and pours out some orange juice, sitting herself on the floor by her coffee table, slowly enjoying her eggs while watching reruns on HGTV. After finishing her breakfast she cleans up the dishes and places them to dry, heading back into her room to make her bed and grab her phone.

Despite her mood last night, Mia's finally feeling herself come out of her fog. She prides herself on not sending that text, on not sharing anything with Leigh or Sasha that isn't going to amount to anything, and for not drinking last night. Mia sweeps back the covers of her bed and runs her hands over the comforter to straighten it out. She grabs her phone and swipes it on to see the home screen.

There, glaring up at her, as if to taunt her for making her own decision to remain silent last night, is a message from Brett. Mia's heart begins to pound and she pulls up the text she missed.

I've been thinking about you.

Mia lets out the breath she didn't realize she was holding. The uncertainty she felt in herself last night rises again as she thinks through how she wants to respond. It's the opening she wanted last night, the one that would bring them back together, the one that would let her be with him again. And it's also a doorway to a potentially reputation-shattering, or even education-ending, path. Mia hesitates before tapping out her response, then takes a deep breath and sends it.

I know the feeling. Want to talk?

Feeling jittery from sending the invitation, Mia works to focus on brushing her teeth and finding something comfortable to wear. She keeps glancing back at her phone as she moves about her apartment, anxiously waiting for a response.

He probably sent that last night and totally regrets it. He's not going to text me back. It was obviously a text meant for a late night visit. I shouldn't have responded. I am so dumb. Mia's thoughts create an avalanche of doubt and self-criticism. Deciding to distract herself, or at least tire herself out, Mia changes out of the sweats she had just settled into and into running tights. She pulls on her sports bra and layers a t-shirt and sweatshirt. She arranges her hair into a high ponytail, ties on her running shoes, and grabs her iPod. Mia switches on her music and chooses the playlist Luke put together for her to encourage her to run. Mia briefly hesitates, wondering whether to bring her phone with her, at minimum for safety reasons. Knowing she would only be distracted, Mia leaves her phone on the counter and heads out for a run.

Mia makes her way around a small loop in her apartment complex. Since she opted not to bring her phone, she chooses to run laps around the perimeter, maintaining a steady pace. She breathes deeply and feels the cold air burn her lungs. Mia passes by the same buildings over and over, letting herself go into autopilot, focusing only on her music and the slap of her feet against the pavement. Finally feeling exhausted, Mia slows to a walk, and walks one last lap, slowing her breathing. She returns to her building to kill time and stretches out her legs, extending her break away from her phone.

Back inside her apartment Mia pulls off her sweatshirt. Despite her irritation for having no self-control with her phone, she quickly grabs it off the counter. Her frustration soon melts into relief as she pulls up the missed text from Brett.

Yes, are you free today?

Mia's heart pounds, suddenly feeling stressed again after

cooling off from her run.

This afternoon? She sends.

Brett's response is immediate this time, **Yes where?**

Mia pauses before responding. Meeting in public would definitely stop them from clawing each other's clothes off, but would also mean having a very private conversation in public. Preferring discretion, particularly in their small college town, would likely mean meeting at one of their homes.

Mia texts Brett her address, adding to come over at one. Brett sends back an **I'll be there** and Mia clicks her screen back off. She scans her apartment, noticing various things that need to be cleaned up. She starts rushing around, moving stacks of papers back into her office, rearranging throw pillows and the afghan on the couch. She pulls out the secondhand vacuum she bought after adopting Renly and does a once-over in the common space. Thinking twice, Mia also rolls the vacuum into her bedroom, trying not to convince herself that they'll end up back there.

After wiping down the kitchen, almost haphazardly, Mia jumps into the shower. Since she just washed her hair the day before, she focuses on scrubbing herself clean. She carefully shaves her legs and trims up her pubic hair, paring it down to a small tuft. Once out of the shower, Mia dries herself and applies lotion. She eyes her counter top and makes the snap decision to lightly apply perfume, gently dabbing it to her wrists and behind her earlobes. Feeling her excitement continue to grow she applies a light amount of makeup and moves onto her closet back in her bedroom. Sifting through her clothes, Mia's stumped.

This isn't a date. It may be a hook up? It may be an actual conversation. Fuck, what do I wear for this? Mia shifts her weight from one foot to the other, and paws through the clothes in her closet. Her eyes land on the sweater dress she wore on their second date and her stomach flips, remembering the evening. She pushes it to the side. Finally, Mia decides on an oversized camel colored sweater and black leggings, assuring herself it is casual and a safe option for anything that occurs. Mia allows herself one decision to satiate the mounting desire as she pulls on a lacy thong and matching bra to wear underneath.

I'll be happy for these if that happens, and if it doesn't I can still feel confident and sexy. Mia checks herself out in the mirror, feeling good about the entire ensemble. In attempt to kill time before Brett arrives, she makes herself a sandwich for lunch and watches TV, only half-focused on the episode. Mia brushes her teeth once again, choosing to be prepared *just in case*, she thinks for the millionth time, and clears up the kitchen once more. She curls back up on the couch, finding herself watching the clock more than the show.

Perfectly on time, there's a knock at Mia's door at one

pm. Her heart racing, she jumps from the couch and races to the door. Taking one last deep breath and trying to steel herself for whatever is happening next, she pulls it open.

CHAPTER 23

Standing at the door, slightly hunched and with a hoodie pulled over his head, Brett stands with his face trained down at his feet and then quickly up into Mia's eyes. Mia notices his face seems tired, with light bags under his eyes, yet still ravishingly handsome.

"Um, come in," Mia says, holding the door open and standing to the side. Brett steps inside and quickly glances around. Renly throws a glance behind him as he saunters into the office.

"No roommates?" Brett asks. Mia shakes her head, realizing they've been too intimately distracted to discuss basic personal facts.

"Nope," Mia says, "Just me and Lord Renly." She closes the door behind Brett and wrings her hands nervously. Brett pushes his hoodie back and stands silently, his eyes darker and his lips parted. Mia stands across from him, unsure of what to do or say next. She gives a small smile and gestures towards the kitchen, "Um, can I get you anything to drink?"

Brett starts to shake his head but appears to change his mind, "Actually yeah, water."

Mia nods, grateful for something to do amidst the tension and grabs a glass from a cabinet and fills it with water. She hands it to Brett, who takes several big gulps and places it back down on the counter. "Thanks," he says. He glances over at the couch, and Mia breaks herself from staring at him.

"Have a seat! Sorry, I just-" she stops herself, not even sure of what she wants to say. Brett sits on the couch and Mia folds herself onto the opposite end. "So, how have you been?" She asks slowly.

Brett pulls off his sweatshirt, appearing less rigid. He gives Mia a sad smile. "Honestly, I've been better."

Mia begins to relax and lets the tension out of her shoulders. "Me too," she replies quietly.

"I really hate how things ended the other day," Brett says, his eyes cast down.

Mia nodded, her own eyes now back down at her hands.

"And I can't stop thinking about you. How you've been doing, how you've been feeling," Brett continues and then pauses, "and how I want to touch you again."

Mia's startled into facing Brett, who is gazing at Mia intently.

"And I know that it's a bad idea, and I probably shouldn't have texted you. I just figured…I don't know what I thought. I guess I thought if you responded maybe you felt the same way, and if you didn't then I'd let it go." Brett looks at her questioningly. Mia tries to steady her breathing, which has been steadily picking up pace.

"And look, you can tell me to go away, and I will, but I need you to tell me that." Brett runs a hand through his hair. Mia lets out the breath she was holding. She pushes herself off the couch and takes the few steps to stand in front of Brett. She places her hands on his shoulders as he lays his at her waist. Mia gently lowers herself onto Brett's lap, straddling him. She looks at him carefully, both of them breathing heavily. She runs a hand down his chest, feeling his heart pounding. She takes one of his hands and lays it on her heart. She traces his lips with her other hand. They stare into each other's eyes, silent and searching. Mia leans in slightly and Brett stretches forward to kiss her. Mia feels a thrill of excitement shoot through her as the gentle kiss turns into something more needy. Brett runs his hands down Mia's back and then up under her sweater, stroking her back and squeezing her butt, pulling her into closer to him.

Mia feels a mounting pressure swirling inside her, as she continues to kiss Brett with her arms wrapped around his shoulders. She starts to grind against him, the thin layer of panties and leggings becoming moist with her desire. Brett unclasps her bra and fondles her breasts underneath her sweater. Mia pulls back for a moment and yanks off her sweater and bra. Brett cups one of her breasts in his hand and begins to suck on the other. Chills run through Mia's body and she moans, her head rolling back. Brett lets go of her nipple and Mia begins tugging at his shirt, so he swiftly pulls it over his head. Mia leans back into kissing Brett, her fingers roaming over his back, and his arms around her, pulling her in tightly. Mia continues to rock against Brett's body, and notices a stiffening beneath her. She scrambles up, and with Brett watching, yanks off her leggings. He moves forward on the couch, sitting on the edge, and kisses her right above her thong on her stomach. His fingers trail to her waist, as his lips move downward, teasing her slowly. Brett sneaks one finger underneath the fabric and runs it along Mia's opening.

He pulls back, his eyes glistening as he looks up at her, "You're so ready for me."

Mia, panting at the anticipation of where his tongue may go, nods and whispers, "Yes, you do this to me."

Brett reaches down and undoes his jeans. He lifts his hips and in one swift motion yanks off his pants and underwear as one. His large cock stands at attention, and he rubs it with one hand, his eyes trained on Mia.

"I want to fuck you raw," he says huskily. Mia's heart pounds and she nods. She wants to feel him without the thin layer of latex. She wants to feel his skin and she wants him inside of her. Brett peels off Mia's thong, stroking one finger between her lower lips. "I'll come outside of you, okay?" Mia nods and licks her lips.

"Sit back," she says, gently pushing Brett back into the couch. He leans back and Mia climbs onto him, aiming herself above his penis. She steadies herself with one hand and lines him up with her with the other hand and slowly lowers herself onto him.

"Fuuuuuck," Brett whispers as Mia's body envelopes his erection. He cups her breasts and Mia begins to slowly ride him, their bodies moving in unison. Mia moans delightfully when Brett takes her breast into his mouth again, steadily kissing and sucking on her with increasing force. Mia's pace picks up with the intensity of Brett's actions. She feels his throbbing cock slide in and out of her and she places one hand at her clit. She flinches with pleasure as she gently rubs, feeling herself tighten within.

Brett grabs her neck gently and pulls her down for a kiss. His tongue reaches for hers and Mia moans between between kisses. Brett smacks Mia's ass and Mia cries out appreciatively. Her breasts shake in his face as she continues to fiercely ride him, her cries becoming steadier. Mia feels the beginning of her sweet release vibrating, coursing through her body, ready to explode. She kisses Brett and whispers into his ear, "I'm gonna come" as her orgasm hits her, causing her to cry out once more. Brett quickly maneuvers Mia onto her back on the couch and continues to thrust through her convulsions. His pumping steadily increases until he suddenly pulls out, and while rubbing his engorged cock, ejaculates onto her stomach. Mia watches as Brett appears to let go of the breath he was holding as he comes. He leans back down to her and kisses her gently.

"Let me clean you up," he whispers, and struts into the kitchen. Mia watches his toned ass until it disappears from her view and smiles at Brett as he returns with a paper towel. He kneels down next to her and gently wipes away the evidence of his passion. He crumples up the paper towel in one hand before turning his attention back to Mia. He runs a hand along her jaw and up to her lips, where he drags a finger across them. Mia gives a playful nip at his finger and they both laugh.

"I think we're back to square one of our dilemma," Brett says quietly. Mia nods, and pushes herself up. She grabs her sweater, suddenly feeling self-conscious and pulls it on, she spies her thong on the ground and quickly pulls that back on too. Following her lead, Brett gathers up his pants and t-shirt and gets dressed. They stand taking each other in, Mia's breath quickening out of anxiety this time.

"Well, I can't storm out of my apartment, so now what?" she hesitantly jokes.

"Now we talk," Brett replies seriously.

CHAPTER 24

Mia hands a refilled water glass to Brett, who is sitting back down on the couch and waiting for Mia to join him. She sits on the opposite end, her legs curled up beneath her, still without her leggings. She pushes a stray hair back behind her ear. Renly slinks out of the office to cuddle up against Brett, and Brett lazily scratches around the cat's ears after Renly settles in. The apartment feels thick with tension again, as each one waits for the other to start.

Mia rubs her face with her hand. "Well, we can't keep our hands off each other, but we can't be together. At least not for next semester," She quickly adds at the end.

"You can't take a different course?" Brett asks hopefully, with a tinge of demand in his voice.

Mia shakes her head, "It just wouldn't work." She gives Brett a sly look, "What if you just beg out of teaching it?" knowing that is not an option either.

Brett's lips push together into a thin line, "Fair enough. We each have obligations we can't avoid."

Rubbing her neck and resting her hand in her chin, Mia cautiously offers, "What if we just put this on pause? For the semester?" Mia's brow is furrowed and her eyebrows are pulling towards each other. Brett seems to flinch at the word "pause," and quickly composes himself.

"I'm not really crazy about that."

Frustrated, Mia throws up her hands, "Well then what's your suggestion?"

Brett shrugs and takes another sip of his water.

"If we don't figure out a plan we're going to end up doing something stupid. And stupid will probably translate into something bad for me. A pause will allow us to, I don't know, maybe get to know each other more, but not sleep together?" Mia says.

Brett shifts on the couch, disturbing Renly, his discomfort obvious. "I don't like this idea of a pause. What does that even mean?"

"We just, I don't know, try not to fuck each other's brains out while you're my teacher?" Mia supplies.

"I can appreciate that. I just-" Brett stops himself and sighs. Mia looks at him imploringly. "I got burned that way once before. My ex…" Brett turns his face away from Mia, "My ex wanted a break and I just got hurt in the end. Honestly, I haven't dated since her cause it's been so hard to build trust with someone else again. So to start something with what is essentially a break under a different name, feels doomed and shitty from the get go."

Mia reaches out and lays her hand gently on Brett's knee. He looks back at her, his face pained. "I'm not trying to hurt you," she says gently, "and I worry about this hurting me in the end." Brett takes her hand and their fingers entwine.

"Yeah, I worry about this being bad for you too," he shares. "I definitely don't want to mess up your graduate education."

Mia nods, "Yeah, that, and you're not the only one who's had trust issues. I'm not eager to jump into another doomed hook up and get slut-shamed out of school." Brett nods and pulls his hands back to himself, leaving Mia to draw back to her corner of the couch. Mia tries to think through other options, but finds herself hitting a mental block.

Brett gives her a sad smile, "So, is this it? Again?" His eyes show defeat and he rubs his hands down his face.

Mia frowns, feeling frustrated with the situation. "Does it have to be?"

"Well, what other options are there? We stop, and I mean we really stop or you drop the class and we keep this up, or I don't know, we sneak around and try not to get caught through this next semester." Brett sounds exasperated as he throws his hands up at the last option.

Mia wrinkles her forehead and shifts her weight, as she measures the last choice. "What would sneaking around mean?" She asks cautiously.

Brett shakes his head, "That's a terrible idea, I shouldn't have even said it."

"Well out of the options of quit spending time together in a uh, social manner, " Mia shoots a sheepish grin at Brett and then returns to being serious, "and delaying my graduate career, both suck, so what would sneaking around look like?"

Brett shakes his head again, though seeming less certain the second time. "It's a bad idea, it sets us both up for trouble."

Mia nods, "It sets us up for trouble if we don't have a plan. So let's just spitball here and think of what a plan could be." Mia felt uncertain when she first grabbed onto Brett's spontaneous suggestion, but is now beginning to feel some hope as she clings to the idea.

Brett sighs, "I don't know if I'm comfortable with this."

Mia rubs her neck, "I'm just saying let's think about what it could be, and if that seems impossible, then we quit. We just stop, okay?"

Brett gives an almost indiscernible nod, "Yeah, so just

brainstorming…what would keeping this secret mean?" He thinks and adds, "For the semester, I don't want to be sneaking around forever."

Mia sits up straighter, feeling more confident. "We could designate zones, boundaries. Certain places and situations are professional only. Rules that help keep us professional."

Brett nods, "So, for instance, my office is a professional only space?" Mia lets out a breath with a smile and nods.

"Yes, all of campus. You'd be Dr. Dawson and we would be strictly student-teacher interactions only."

"Alright," Brett pauses, still sounding skeptical. "But even if we stick with being polite and cordial in class, there's also Jean wanting me to be on your committee," he says, referring to Mia's advisor.

Mia scrunches her nose in thought, "I could probably try to hold that off until my dissertation proposal, and by that time, the semester would be over and we could inform the dean, and then there's no way you could be on my committee. I can hold her off until next fall. Or we could come up with some excuse as to why you can't be on my committee."

Brett's eyes narrow at her last suggestion, "It'd be hard to find an excuse, you'd have to hold her off. What's your timeline for your dissertation?"

Mia sits back and sighs, thinking through her failed plan to defend her master's earlier in the semester that just ended. "Well, I'll be defending my master's this spring, and then will need to form my committee for my proposal, and maybe present my proposal in the fall?"

Brett makes a face, suggesting his disbelief in that plan. Mia nods, feeling more sure, "I can work on a proposal before the committee is together, have a full draft for my advisor as soon as the summer ends, so in the fall it'll be getting committee members and editing the proposal. I'll just get a head start on writing."

Brett nods again, his action seemingly bolstered by Mia's confidence. "Okay, and where is it appropriate for us to be together?"

Mia's confidence starts to slip. It's a small town, so dinners and movies and dates around the college city suddenly feel impossible. She stares at Brett helplessly and shakes her head slightly. "I think, I think just at our homes," she whispers.

Brett frowns at the suggestion. "And would I even mention to anyone that I'm dating? I mean, I brought it up in passing to my new faculty mentor and he might ask about it."

Mia's taken back and asks sharply, "New faculty mentor?"

Brett nods, "Yeah, new assistant professors get paired with tenured faculty members to sort of, guide us in our first year or two, help us get some footing and support beyond our departments. The friend I went to hang out with that night I ran into you? That's him. He got divorced and he's dating again, and whatever, it's all beside the point, of what do I say?"

"I'm not sure," Mia shrugs, "whatever feels best for you to say. No? Yes? Yes but nothing serious? Yes and it's a student and shh don't tell?" Brett looks at her serious face and laughs.

"I can figure that out myself. So campus is professional, homes are dating, you hold out on your committee formation, and we hold off on details with others." Mia nods as Brett ticks off the rules. "Anything I'm forgetting?"

"All communication needs to be professional during general working hours, like nine to five on weekdays," Mia adds, thinking of one of Brett's first texts to her, calling her sexy. Brett nods in agreement.

"Alright," Brett says, extending a hand out to Mia, "let's try this."

Mia smiles, and grabs Brett's hand to shake it, "And either of us can pull the plug on this whenever. If either of us are going to have some serious consequences, no questions asked, it's done." Brett nods again and smiles, letting go of Mia's hand. He scoots over on the couch and tilts Mia's face up to his by her chin. He leans down and kisses her gently, and then more passionately. Mia wraps her arms around him and he pulls her on to his lap. She flicks her tongue into his mouth and nibbles on his bottom lip. Brett pulls out of the kiss and rests his hands on Mia's bottom and gazes at her intensely.

"Well that's settled, what now?" Brett asks with a sly smile. Mia throws her head back and laughs.

"Now we order in and have our first secret date," Mia says smiling. She pries herself away from Brett and grabs her phone from the kitchen. "Pick your poison: Chinese, Thai, or pizza?"

CHAPTER 25

Brett scoops more rice onto his plate and helps himself to another serving of beef and broccoli. Both he and Mia had kept the conversation light after striking their deal, focusing on how Brett's settled into the area and what Mia's discovered about the city in the last few years, suggesting her favorite restaurants and bars. Once the food arrives, they both dig in, suddenly realizing the appetites they had each developed from earlier. Mia has finished the servings of lo mein and szechuan chicken she craved and packs up the containers to save the rest for later. Brett makes quick work of the last of his dish, wiping his mouth with a paper napkin and sighing, now satiated.

"Too bad this place isn't closer to me," Brett says referring to the restaurant they ordered from.

Mia waves her hand dismissively, "My favorite Thai place is even better, I'll take you there next." Both she and

Brett stop, her words hanging in the air between them, as she remembers she won't be taking Brett out anywhere any time soon. "Or we'll just order that in too." Brett nods and the corners of his mouth lift in a slight smile.

"So ah, what's next for you, after grad school?" Brett asks as he gathers up the empty containers and drops them into the large paper bag they came in. Mia grabs her leftovers and puts them in the fridge, and places the trash by her front door to take out later.

"I'm not sure entirely. I mean, I think I want to do research and conduct therapy, but I guess a lot really depends on where I get matched for internship and if I could land a good post-doc after that," Mia answers. She shrugs, trying to communicate her relaxed attitude about the future, "it's basically impossible to get a tenure track job these days, so I figure I need to be flexible."

Brett nods and moves to sit back on the couch, where Mia joins him. She sits on the opposite end, with her legs stretched out, allowing her to still be in contact with him. "I mean, not everyone seems to have your luck," she adds.

Brett grins, "It was hard work, not luck."

Mia's eyebrows raise as her face shows her hemming and hawing. "No advantages? Not even just having good connections?"

Brett ducks his head, "Fair enough, it was hard work and

my graduate school advisor is well connected. But I also was going to be coming in with grant money."

Mia nods slowly and gestures as she makes her next point, "That your advisor is maybe co-investigator on, making it more likely you would have been awarded those grants?" Brett frowns at Mia, seeming to become frustrated with her reasoning. Mia holds up her hands in defense, "I'm not saying you're not smart or capable, you're clearly both. And, it probably didn't hurt to have the connections you had." Brett nods, his irritation seeming to lessen. "Anyway, maybe an academic medical center, but also, maybe private practice or industry, or I don't know. I get burned out by something different each year and reassess my future constantly," Mia returns to the original topic, hoping to avoid any further conflict with Brett. "And you? Was it always becoming a hot shot professor at a big time university?" She teases Brett and pokes at his leg with a toe.

Brett smiles at her and grabs her foot, his earlier annoyance seemingly gone. "I guess so? I kind of figured that research and teaching would be my future once I applied to graduate schools. I definitely didn't think I'd be at some place like Earl so quickly, so the pressure is on, I guess."

Mia nods, feeling more empathy for the stress that she figures he must be feeling over proving himself. "I'd imagine there are a lot of expectations for you."

"Yeah, I feel like I've had a good couple of months to set up my lab and work on manuscripts, and next semester I'm interviewing for my first grad student and teaching my first graduate level course. It's kind of crazy. Cause I was just a grad student myself. And now…" Brett trails off and lifts his hands up helplessly. "It's that imposter syndrome all over again."

Mia nods emphatically, "So feeling like you're the odd man out and they made a mistake picking you doesn't ever go away?"

Brett laughs, "I hope it does! I mean, it got easier in grad school. It's just this transition, kind of makes you question your abilities again. And it didn't help that-" Brett stops suddenly and glances down finishing, "it didn't help that my relationship kind of imploded towards the end of grad school." Mia looks at Brett with gentle concern as he shrugs.

"Was this the 'break' ex?" Mia asks kindly. Brett nods and gives another shrug, appearing to be nonchalant, though shifting his weight as if he is uncomfortable. Sensing he isn't eager to divulge more, Mia takes over, "It's tough to make a big move, big changes, and not have the support you thought you had." Brett seems relieved that she spoke first and nods with a small smile. "Sometimes the personal impacts the professional and vice versa. I fell behind on getting my master's done when the guy I was seeing dumped me out of nowhere and started seeing my friend." Mia shrugs, feeling self-conscious. "I've since pulled it together and will get it done, but it definitely sucked and threw me for a loop."

"Did that happen to be the guy I met at our first date?" Brett asks cautiously, mindlessly rubbing Mia's foot.

"Ah, yeah," Mia says, her mind taking her back to her anger at him showing up and then further back to him kissing her, and her kissing him back. She feels herself flush with embarrassment. "I've mostly avoided him since the summer, but obviously, with shared friends and this city…" Mia trails off.

"Life's a lot easier when you can move several states away from your ex," Brett pats Mia's foot comfortingly.

Mia snorts, "Any suggestions on getting rid of him?"

Brett grins, "Murder?"

Mia laughs, "I meant on how to get him to move, but sure, let's add murder to our secret relationship." Brett laughs in return.

Glancing at the time displayed by Mia's TV, Brett turns back to her and jerks his head at the clock. "I should probably head out, let you get back to your things."

Mia smiles, but feels disappointed, hoping to have him stay longer. "Are you sure?"

"I don't want to overstay my welcome. Let's make a plan

to get together again soon," Brett stands and reaches out a hand to Mia. She takes it and he helps to pull her up from the couch. She looks up at him, her stomach jumping, and he leans down and kisses her. "I'm glad we talked."

"Me too," Mia murmurs against his lips. She kisses him again, lingering on his bottom lip, her hands reaching around to play with his hair.

Brett gives her one quick peck and pulls himself away from her. He squeezes her arm gently, "I'll text you." Mia nods and walks him to the door. Brett scoops up the paper bag that held their trash from earlier and turns to walk out the door that Mia has opened. She grabs his arm and Brett turns around and kisses her quickly once more. "We'll give this a try." Mia nods once more and watches Brett make his way back to his car. She closes the door and suddenly feels her apartment is now weirdly empty. She pads back into her bedroom and changes into her sweatpants from earlier, and eventually crashes back down on her couch, feeling calmer and ready to binge watch some more TV.

CHAPTER 26

Mia wakes with a start, realizing she's dozed off in front of the TV. Her stomach growls and she rubs the sleep from her eyes. Renly is staring up at her, as if he'd been sitting and watching her for some time.

"I guess we both need some dinner," she says out loud. Mia grabs her own leftovers from the kitchen and sets them to reheat in the microwave. While her food warms, she scoops some cat food out for Renly and gives him a quick scratch as he goes to eat his own meal. The microwave beeps and Mia grabs the plate and settles it down on the coffee table in front of the TV, along with a fresh glass of water. She turns on her phone's screen as she begins to twirl lo mein noodles onto her fork and sees two messages waiting for her.

The first one is from Brett: **free this weekend?** Before responding, Mia checks her second text, from Luke. With only the word **surprise** and a picture of plane tickets with her name on one and Luke's on the other, Mia sees that someone has purchased a flight home to Austin for her for the next week, leaving on the weekend. Mia immediately pushes the call option next to Luke's name.

"Hey!" Luke says cheerily as he picks up.

"Did you buy those?" Mia asks, skipping any formalities.

"Ah no, dad did…" Luke replies hesitantly. "We were just chatting about Christmas, and he surprised me with the tickets. He asked me to share it with you…since he knew you'd fight him about it."

Mia's worry subsided, she hated the idea of Luke spending his meager savings on a flight for her. She wryly observes that her father made a sneaky, but wise, move of having Luke presenting the ticket, as she wouldn't argue with him about it.

"Are you mad?" Luke asks quietly.

"No no!" Mia exclaims. "I just didn't want you to spend that kind of money on me. I don't love it that dad did, but it looks like I can't do much about that now. Plus, this means we get to hang out, so no not mad."

"Okay good. I wasn't sure of what exact dates would be good for you, but I looked at your school's calendar online and you're definitely off starting this weekend, which is why I had dad get the ticket for then. And then we both get to return for New Year's, since I figured you'd rather spend it with friends."

"I'd be happy to spend it with you as well, but I appreciate the thought." Mia looks over the online ticket again, "So this flight is for Saturday?" She starts making a mental checklist, as she thinks through what she'll have to take care of in order to be gone for a week.

"Yep, I hope it's not too short notice?"

"No, I just need to make sure I get a pet sitter," Mia says, also thinking of trying to squeeze a date with Brett in before she leaves. "Um, email me the link to the ticket so that I've got it."

"Already done," Luke replies. "It'll be good to see you."

Mia smiles, feeling genuinely happy, despite her consternation over her dad buying the flight, "Me too. Maybe mom can hold off putting up a tree for a couple more days and we can help."

"Dad also mentioned he's gonna come in from Dallas for a few days too, so we'll probably end up splitting our time."

Mia rolled her eyes, frustrated with the inability of her parents to be in a room together. "Yeah, okay. Well, I've got to go start pulling stuff together to make this happen. I'll see you soon!"

"Can't wait! Bye!" Luke replies.

"Bye!" Mia repeats back into her cell and hangs up. After finishing her dinner and cleaning up after herself, she grabs a piece of paper from her printer and begins writing a list of things to do and arrange in order to visit home. The top of her list is finding care for Renly, so she quickly leaves a message for a local pet sitting service she has used before. Mia also starts pulling out clothing to pack and does a quick inventory of the laundry she needs to do as well. In her office she sifts through the various piles of paper and grabs the most recent edits from Dr. Thompson and begins putting together a bag of her work to bring with her. Mia continues to hustle about her apartment, trying to complete all the last minute travel tasks on her list.

The end of Mia's list includes letting a few key people know that she's headed out of town. She sends a quick email to Dr. Thompson, informing her that she will be working on the latest revisions during her time home and will send them back ASAP. She shoots a text to Leigh saying she'll be back for New Year's Eve and to keep her posted, which Leigh automatically responds with a thumbs up emoji and a wish to have fun.

The last message she needs to send is to Brett. She types out her text and sends it to him.

Last minute trip home for me. Leaving Saturday, back after Christmas. Free tomorrow instead?

Mia returns to her clothes, sorting through what she

needs to wash tonight to pack tomorrow. Her phone buzzes with Brett's response.

Can't, faculty semester close out thing.

Mia feels disappointed, thinking over what other options she could offer. She sighs and tosses her phone back on her bed, returning to the pile of mixed up warm and cold weather clothes. Her phone buzzes again.

I could come over after. It'll be late. stay and drive you in the am?

Mia feels conflicted over the offer. She absolutely wants time with Brett before she leaves for the week, but hates what sounds mostly like a booty call and friendly lift to the airport. The late night aspect of it feels reminiscent of Danny and Mia feels wary about agreeing to it. However, if she says no, it would mean over a week before seeing Brett again. *At least he's trying to find a way to see me*, she rationalizes. *Just because it's a late night thing doesn't mean this is going to turn into another disaster*, Mia tells herself.

Sure, let's do that. Just let me know when you're headed over, she texts to Brett.

Will do, he sends back.

Mia starts her laundry and puts away the clothes she doesn't plan on taking with her to Texas. She picks up her phone when the pet sitter calls and arranges visits for Renly. After the phone call ends, she checks in the pantry to make sure there's enough food for the pet sitter to give him and is reassured that there's a stockpile in the event of a nuclear catastrophe.

Mia picks up her phone to make one more text and phone call. She sends a short message to her mom, letting her know that she's excited to see her soon, and then dials her father.

"Hello?" Gregory James picks up the phone, with a friendly timber in his voice.

"Hey dad," Mia replies, "Luke just sent me a ticket home and said it was from you. I wanted to call and thank you for doing that. You know you didn't have to."

"I'm happy to do it, you haven't been down here in months and it'll be nice to see you. I assume you'll be staying with your mother?" he asks, knowing full well that with a destination of Austin on her ticket Mia is not likely to drive to Dallas.

"That's the plan. But Luke says you'll come into town for a few days?" Mia tries to steer the conversation away from her mom.

"Yes, I'll AirBnB some place nearby and stay for a few days. You two could come stay there if you'd like," Greg offers.

"Maybe, we'll see. But we'll definitely see you and hang out," Mia answers, hoping to avoid such a plan. "Anyway, thank you again, I gotta keep pulling myself together for this trip. Can't wait to see you!"

"It'll be nice to see you too, love you Mia," Greg says.

"Love you too, Dad, bye!" Mia waits for her dad's farewell and hits the end button to the call. Her initial excitement about going back to Texas and seeing her brother starts to dwindle as she thinks about navigating time between her parents. *You'll just have to make it work and deal,* Mia scolds herself. Rather than focus on the anxious pit in her stomach, Mia busies herself with packing and putting out a set of instructions for the pet sitter.

CHAPTER 27

By eleven in the evening the next day, Mia's packed and ready for Texas. Renly's needs are completely accounted for and Mia's been waiting for the text from Brett to indicate he's on his way. She is not familiar with the faculty event he mentioned in his text, but doesn't think much of it, as she assumes there are likely several things that occur with faculty members she is not aware of. Mia flips through the channels aimlessly while also occasionally picking up her phone to scroll through Facebook or Instagram.

Mia does a fresh search on Brett Dawson on Facebook and tries to scroll through the many faces. She narrows the search to Philadelphia and doesn't find him, before changing the city to hers and still not having any luck. Mia sighs with annoyance and sets her phone back down. Time feels like it's crawling slowly. She thinks about texting him to check and see if he's on his way. *Does it break a rule if it's not during normal working hours but it is during a work function?* Mia wonders and then shakes her head deciding it's not worth the risk. She gets up from the couch and goes back into her bedroom, where she changes into her pajamas, a worn pair of sweatpants and clean t-shirt. As she grabs her phone to check once more, she sees a message has come from Brett.

On my way, be there in 15.

Mia checks the time, noting that it's after midnight. Brett's late night arrival feels increasingly like a booty call and she can't shake the feeling of being annoyed. *Why did I agree to this in the first place if it was going to rub me the wrong way?* She asks herself. However, Mia knows exactly why she agreed to it. She was hoping to see him again, to feel him again, to have whatever this was continue at whatever the cost. Mia chides herself for getting so wrapped up in someone she barely knows. She's so busy berating herself that she hardly notices the knock on her door, until it occurs a second time, more loudly.

Mia swings it open to see Brett standing in the dark. He's dressed in slacks and sport jacket, his pressed shirt matching his eyes. He gives Mia a sloppy smile and steps inside, pulling her to him in a kiss without saying hello.

Mia kisses him back, tasting the faint whispers of alcohol on his breath and pushes herself away from him. "Hey, are you drunk?"

Brett shakes his head, closes the door, and drapes his jacket on one of her kitchen tables. "Nah, just had a couple of drinks with my mentor after the semester review. That's why I'm late. I'm sorry about that, I probably should have texted you," he smiles lightly and strokes Mia's hair. "I thought about it, but I didn't know the rules and if that was breaking one."

Mia relaxes a little bit, feeling mildly less irritated than earlier. "Yeah, a text would have been nice. Maybe in the future, there's leeway for texting important information." Brett nods and begins undoing the buttons on his shirt. He pulls it off and hangs it on another kitchen chair, exposing his sleeveless undershirt and toned arms. He kicks off his shoes before removing his slacks, folding them carefully and setting them on one of the seats. Mia crosses her arms, watching him undress, feeling her annoyance rise up. *It's going straight to a booty call. Goddammit,* she thinks.

Brett motions to Mia, "Ready for bed? You look comfortable."

Mia glances down at her ratty sweatpants, suddenly realizing that Brett's strip show was not for sex, but so that they could go to sleep. "Um yeah, come on, do you need any sweats? I may have a large pair somewhere?" Mia leads him back to her bedroom. Brett shakes his head at Mia's question.

"Nah, I'm good in this," he says as he pulls back the

covers and crawls into the bed. He pats the open spot next to him, "C'mon."

Mia chuckles and turns off the lights. She curls up in the bed, allowing Brett to spoon her as she pulls the covers up under her chin. He wraps his arm around her and pulls her closer to him. He gives her a light kiss behind her ear, "Goodnight," he whispers.

"Goodnight," Mia murmurs back, allowing herself to close her eyes and let go of some of her worries.

Mia's awoken several hours later as the weight on the bed shifts and Brett leaves the room silently. She glances at the clock to see it's only been a few hours. She listens as she hears him flush the toilet and run the sink. He quietly makes his way back into the room and into the bed. Mia turns to face him and touches his cheek.

"Sorry, didn't mean to wake you," Brett whispers, "go back to sleep."

Barely able to see him, Mia cranes her neck forward and kisses the outline of Brett's jaw. She moves one hand to stroke his side and sneak it up under his undershirt. She throws one leg over his hip, pulling herself closer to him. Brett responds to her touch, catching her lips with his own and holding her hips close to him. His kiss becomes more insistent and his hand moves under her shirt, circling her nipples and cupping her breasts. Mia feels the urge to grind against Brett and gives in, trying to rub against him.

Brett takes his hand from her breasts and pushes it under the waistband of Mia's sweatpants, quickly finding she's not wearing underwear. He traces a finger between her legs and gently slides it into her. Mia moans and tightens her leg around Brett, kissing him in response. Brett slips a second finger into Mia and steadily moves in and out. Brett pulls his fingers out and Mia quickly removes her sweatpants. Brett fumbles under the sheets and tosses his underwear to the side before pulling Mia to sit on top on him. He pulls her shirt over her head and throws it before pulling her back down for a kiss. Mia gently rocks on Brett, sliding herself on him, feeling his cock stiffen beneath her.

"Does this feel good?" Mia whispers into Brett's ear, between kissing his jawline and nibbling on his earlobe. She catches the scent of oranges once more, gently wafting from his skin.

"Yes," he breathes out.

"Do you want more?" Mia practically purrs.

By reply, Brett holds Mia by the waist and tosses her onto her back. Crouching over her, he kisses his way down her torso until he reaches her pussy, alternating with his fingers and his tongue as Mia writhes and jerks in reaction to the insistent pleasure. He stops suddenly and leans back down into Mia's ear.

"Do you want more?" he croons. Mia grabs him by the neck and pulls him down for a forceful kiss, her tongue demanding. Brett pulls back, Mia gasping for more. "Do you want more?" Brett asks again. Mia nods into the dark, her heart racing and her clitoris throbbing. Brett, unable to see Mia's reply, lets his hands roam across her chest, circling and pulling at her nipples as he kisses her neck. Mia's body arches into his as she yearns for more contact. "Tell me you want me," Brett murmurs into her ear as he passes back to suck on her earlobe.

"I want you, god please, I want you," Mia cries quietly. She slaps the nightstand beside her and barely gasps out, "Condoms." Brett grabs one from the drawer and rolls it on in the dark. With her permission, Brett quickly buries himself into Mia, as she gasps with his entrance. He pumps steadily against her, her breasts jostling with each push. She pulls Brett back down to her, kissing and biting his shoulder, suddenly intent on marking him as hers. Brett withdraws suddenly, leaving Mia to feel empty.

"Sit on your knees and face the headboard," Brett says, and Mia scrambles to get into the position, kneeling and facing the wall. Brett places himself behind her, urging her to lift her bottom as he wraps his arms around her, kissing her back and shoulders. He runs his hands over her breasts and Mia feels his cock, slick from her, hard against her back. "Are you ready?" Brett whispers into her ear.

"Yes," Mia whispers to the wall. She grabs onto the

headboard to steady herself as Brett enters her from behind. He bites and sucks on her shoulder, while caressing her clit with one hand and holding her close to him with the other. Mia leans her head back onto Brett as he thrusts into her. She takes one hand from the headboard to rest it on his hand, the one moving her closer to orgasm. Brett takes his hand away, to pull and tease her nipples, as Mia continues to rub her clit.

"Come for me," Brett whispers between sucks and nibbles on Mia's shoulder. Mia's hand moves faster on her clitoris, allowing the budding sensation to finally bloom throughout her body, feeling her orgasm unfurl. She cries out as Brett holds her close to him, steadying her as the tremors slow. Brett holds her tightly as he orgasms, quietly cursing, before pulling out. He wordlessly hops out of the bed and disappears momentarily out of the room. Mia snuggles back down into the bed, choosing to forgo her clothes. When he returns, Brett gets back in with her, pulling her close and kissing her. Without another word, Mia falls asleep against him.

CHAPTER 28

Mia's alarm goes off early, rudely waking her for her eight am flight. She rolls over and peeks at Brett, who is sleepily rubbing his eyes and groans. She gives him a quick peck on the jaw and hops out of bed, dashing around her room to get dressed before heading into the bathroom to brush her teeth. She's practically completed her morning routine and pops back into her room to see Brett has rolled over and may have gone back to sleep.

"Hey, you want any kind of breakfast? Or something to drink?" Mia calls out kindly to Brett. He groans in response. "I'm sorry, I didn't catch that," she says, and goes to sit by him on the edge of the bed.

"Coffee?" He mumbles.

Mia grimaces as he lazily opens his eyes, "Sorry, I don't have any. I can offer you a soda?"

"What self-respecting grad student doesn't have coffee?"

Brett grumbles as he pushes himself to sit up.

Mia shrugs, "The kind that doesn't drink it?"

Brett rubs his eyes again and yawns, stretching out his arms above his head. "Alright, then never mind. I'll just get something on my way home."

"Are you sure?" Mia asked.

Brett nods, "Yeah, it's fine. I do think I might have had a little more to drink than I realized."

Mia pushes herself off the bed as she murmurs, "Mmhmm." She goes to grab the last of her toiletries to pack and throws everything into her bag before zipping it up. Brett is still sitting in her bed, watching her move around the apartment with lightening efficiency.

"You're some kind of morning person," he observes.

Mia shakes her head, and runs out to the kitchen to feed Renly before returning to her room. "Nah, just have a schedule to keep in order to leave on time," she answers, her eyes narrowing as Brett does not seem to take the hint. He rubs at his face and yawns again, before pushing himself out of bed and padding into the bathroom. Mia notices her quiet annoyance at his leisurely pace, as well as his belated admission about how much he drank the night before. Mia sighs and goes to sit on her couch, as Brett eventually leaves the bathroom and comes out into the living area and begins to get dressed. Mia tries to push down her irritation, reminding herself that Brett means well and that she won't be seeing him for a week. *Don't let this little stupid stuff sour shit before you go*, she tells herself. She takes a deep breath and lets a genuine smile creep onto her face.

"Sleep okay?" She asks.

Brett grins at her, "I slept great. Particularly after I got attacked." Mia giggles. Brett buttons up his shirt and tucks it back into his slacks before throwing on his coat and running a hand through his rumpled hair. Renly, having finished his breakfast, weaves his way between Brett's legs, and Brett bends down to give the cat a quick pet. Renly marches over to the couch where Mia sits and jumps up to sit next to her.

"Sorry to do this to you bud," Mia says to her cat as she gives him some scratches behind his ears, "but I'm gonna be gone for a week. Eva is gonna come take care of you. Be good and don't puke in my bed." Brett smiles at Mia when she she's done petting Renly.

"Ready?" he asks. Mia nods and goes to grab her suitcase from her room. As she heads to the front door, with Brett in tow, he grabs the bag from her. She starts to protest, but he waves her off and heads out the front door. After locking up, Mia follows Brett to his car, an old Toyota Corolla with a faded paint job. "Your chariot," Brett says with a smile as he places her bag in the backseat. Brett casts a quick look around before getting into the car, and quickly slapping his sunglasses on, though the dawn has barely approached.

Mia climbs into the passenger seat and buckles in as Brett pulls out of his parking spot and begins to make their way to the airport.

"So what are your plans for Christmas and New Year's?" Mia asks casually, while she confirms her flight is on time on her phone.

Brett glances over at her, "Probably home for both. Philadelphia, I mean. We usually do holidays there."

Mia nods absently. "Any big plans?"

Brett shakes his head, "No, just uh, family time. Probably see some friends from college, that sort of thing." He smiles at Mia, "What about you?"

Mia rocks her head and shoulders back and forth slightly, "Splitting time between my parents and awkwardly avoiding talking about the other one with each. Hanging out with my brother, doing Christmas with my mom, seeing friends from high school. That sort of stuff. I'll be back for New Year's though, we usually do a party at someone's place for it." Mia stops and thinks of how, even if Brett was around for New Year's Eve, he wouldn't be able to come and be her kiss. She frowns at the thought and works quickly to push it away.

"Sounds like fun," Brett says, quickly adding, "Except for

maybe the awkward family stuff?"

Mia snorts and nods, "Yeah. It's been convenient to be away for the most part, but," she says with a shrug, "what can you do?"

Brett nods more solemnly, stealing another glance at her, "Divorce is hard on everyone." Mia's face is solmen and she nods, glancing at Brett, whose attention has returned to the road. College and graduate school have allowed her to escape, and while she's grateful for the opportunities, she tries to push down the guilt for feeling like she abandoned her brother. Brett pats her leg gently, "Sorry, didn't mean to bring you down."

"No, it's fine," Mia says quietly. "Just you know, it hasn't been too terrible for me cause I haven't had to be there for most of it. I just feel like I could have probably been more there for my brother. Not that he'd say anything or blame me for anything, but I definitely just sort of, peaced."

Brett nods, seeming sympathetic, "I get that. Escape is way easier." Mia nods and shrugs again, wanting to move past the conversation.

"Anyway, when do you think you'll be back?"

Brett grins at her briefly, "Already gearing up to ask for a ride back?"

Mia laughs and shakes her head, "No, just want to figure

out when I can see you again."

Brett barely shrugs his shoulders, "Not entirely sure, it kind of depends on how things are in Philly."

"Huh?" Mia asks.

"Just like, I don't know, if I'm getting antsy or having fun. It'll be nice to see everyone, but um, you know, home isn't what is used to be, I guess," Brett takes the exit for the airport and Mia nods in agreement.

"Home isn't what it used to be."

Brett gives her a knowing smile back and pulls up to the single terminal of their small airport. "Don't forget me while you're away."

Mia laughs and playfully hits his shoulder, "Obviously. Don't have too much fun in Philly."

Brett grimaces, "I'll try not to."

Mia feels nervous but tentatively asks, "Will you be in the office at all? What are our communication rules?"

Brett rubs his chin, pretending to be deep in thought, "Well, since the semester is over, and any work in the office is technically on my own time, let's say we're in the clear unless either of us have a uh, interfering event?"

Mia nods and smiles, "Sounds good. She does a quick glance around at the people getting their luggage out of cars and gives Brett a peck on his cheek. "Don't worry about getting out, I'll grab my stuff."

Brett nods and gives her thigh a quick rub. Mia hops out of the car and grabs her suitcase from the backseat. Brett has rolled down the window of the passenger side, so Mia leans down and blows a kiss at him. "Have a safe flight, text me later," he calls through the window.

"Yes sir," Mia says with laughter in her voice and she waves goodbye as she heads into the airport.

CHAPTER 29

The next few days in Texas pass quickly for Mia, as she crams her waking hours spending time with various configurations of friends and family. Time with just Luke, time with just mom, time with Luke and Mom, time with Luke and Dad, and when she's able to break away, visiting some friends from high school that she's kept up with mainly through Snapchat and Instagram. Mia keeps fairly busy to the point where she doesn't think twice about the limited exchanges between her and Brett, as the texts between them are mostly check ins about their days or what they're each up to in their respective hometowns. Luke catches her smiling at her phone a few times, and while he's raised a curious eyebrow at her, Mia simply shakes her head and clicks off the screen, deftly changing the subject to avoid the Luke's curiosity.

Christmas morning breaks and Mia finds herself in the kitchen with Luke, as they work together to make pancakes, hoping to surprise their mother with a tradition she had originally begun. Mia's phone buzzes in her pocket, but she chooses to focus on scrambling eggs and searching for the pancake mix. Mia's phone buzzes again, and Luke is distracted from the bacon he's frying on the stove.

"You gonna answer that?" He asks.

Mia presses her mouth into a thin line and pulls her phone out of the pocket of her sweatshirt, to see two texts from Brett, but only able to read the first one on the screen, wishing her a merry Christmas. Mia smiles and drops her phone back into the pocket.

"So you're not going to answer that?" Luke says, watching her. Mia shrugs and digs back into the pantry, triumphantly pulling out the pancake mix.

"Dude, every time you look at your phone you are smiling. Who's the guy?" Luke cuts straight to the point. He waves a fork at Mia, "And don't lie and say it's no one."

Mia blushes, trying to think of what to say.

"Ugh, please don't tell me it's Danny," Luke grumbles.

"Oh god no, absolutely not," Mia exclaims, and begins to mix the ingredients for the pancakes in a bowl. "It's someone else from school, but it's new, and I don't know, no need to talk about it yet."

"Uh huh," Luke replies skeptically.

"Seriously, it's not Danny," Mia responds more assertively.

Luke holds his hands up in mock defense, "Okay okay, I believe you."

Mia relaxes and begins pouring dollops of the batter into the heated pan, watching carefully for the edges to bubble and inform her to flip the pancake.

"But you're not going to tell me anything?" Luke asks more gently.

Mia hesitates, uncertain what to share with Luke. She knows she'll have to satisfy some of his curiosity, but worries about giving too much information. She's known Luke to use Google to act as a private investigator for every guy he's ever liked and she's not eager for him to turn his internet sleuthing on her.

"His name is Brett, we met at a grocery store. He's smart and hot and funny. And seriously, it's just begun and nothing may come of it," Mia answers, trying to act casual.

"Uh huh, and does Brett have a last name?" Luke asks sweetly.

"Yes," Mia responds curtly and gives Luke a wide smile, indicating that's the only answer he'll get.

"Touché," Luke replies, carefully removing the cooked slices of bacon and laying them on a paper towel to soak up the excess grease. Mia stirs up the eggs some more, deftly switching between the two pans and taking out pancakes as they finish.

"Anyway, have you been hearing from Matt?" Mia asks, hoping Luke will take the bait.

Luke nods, "Yeah, he's home with in parents in Florida. He's doing well. I'm gonna fly back to Miami in time for New Year's, and we're gonna go out with Erica and Alex. Alex was able to hook us up with tickets to some party downtown, I'm sure they cost a bunch but he said it's for letting him live rent free with us."

Mia nods, "Alex is over that much?"

Luke shrugs, "I mean, he basically lives with us, but it's cool. I'm sure after graduation Erica will move in with him somewhere. They only reason they're not at his place more often is cause he's got a car and it'd be a pain for him to drive Erica back to campus every day." Mia nods, while turning off the burners and starting to plate three breakfasts. She feels her phone buzz against her once more. "Oh my god," Luke says with exasperation, "please go answer that already."

Mia laughs, quickly places the plates on the table and hurries off to her old bedroom, shutting the door and pulling out her phone. Three texts from Brett.

Merry Christmas!

Do you have a present for me ;)

Sorry, was that not ok to ask?

Mia giggles at her phone, observing Brett's anxiety between the second and third message. She quickly types back and sends it.

Merry xmas to you too. What kind of gift are you looking for?

While she waits for his response, Mia opens up the photo gallery on her phone and scrolls through the various pictures. She has one in mind that she's trying to locate. While her current make-up free face and bed ruffled hair isn't camera ready, she has a picture from last spring that she could send. Mia squirms a bit as she scrolls through the gallery. Danny took the photo, and texted it to himself. In the photo Mia sits on her bed at her apartment, her legs curled under her and the curve of her ass slightly visible. The strap of her thong lacy against her hip. Mia's laughing in the photo, and she recalls the moment, her trying to emulate a pin up girl and feeling ridiculous. She's holding her arms up behind her head, pushing her hair out and up. Her raised arms force the cropped shirt she's wearing in the photo to rise just above the lower swell of her breasts, revealing the bottom curves of her chest and hinting at the hard nipples just covered by the top.

Deciding to not wait on his response, Mia quickly sends the photo to Brett, burying the slightly gross feeling of sending a photo to him that was originally meant for someone else. She chews on her lip, waiting for a response, hoping for something soon as she keeps an ear out for noises to suggest anyone approaching the door. Mia's breath catches as she watches the three blinking dots appear on her screen, letting her know Brett is responding.

Wow.

Wow.

Damn.

Brett sends three quick texts in succession and Mia blushes. A picture suddenly also comes through from him, showing his lower torso and upper thighs, the latter clothed in tight boxers, and a large erection straining against the cloth.

This is what you do to me.

Mia licks her lips at Brett's latest reply. She feels an urge budding inside of her, a desire to play with that feeling and herself until she comes, but she knows it's only a matter of time before her mom comes down for breakfast or Luke interrupts this conversation.

Wish I could help you with that ;) Let's chat later.
Mia sends her reply, trying to push down her growing

want for release, and mentally dousing cold water on herself with the thought of her family intruding.

Call me when you can, Brett replies and Mia texts back a thumbs up emoji before heading back out to the kitchen.

Luke is placing the final touches on the breakfast smorgasbord and assesses Mia's face when she returns. She casts her eyes down, slightly abashed, reminding herself that no one knows about the texts she sent and received.

"I'm not gonna ask," Luke mutters, and then waves towards the food, "Ta-da! Now where's mom?"

Mia takes in the impressive display, catching a slight sense of sadness over the three settings, instead of the four she grew up with. "Looks great," she says with a smile and gives Luke's arm a squeeze.

As if reading her mind, Luke nods and gives Mia a gentle smile.

"It does look good," Mia's mother, Valerie, says from behind her. "You two did all this?"

Mia turns and smiles at her mother. "Merry Christmas!" she says as she hugs her mother. Valerie, a thin woman with a short gray bob and light brown eyes, hugs Mia back and gives her a quick kiss on the cheek.

"Merry Christmas to you too, sweetie," Valerie lets go of

Mia and wraps Luke in another hug and repeats the sentiments to him. "I love what you two have done, shall we sit and enjoy this?" Luke nods and pulls a chair out for Valerie to sit in, which she quickly sits in. "Thanks hun," she says as she scoots herself in, "I don't even know where to start with all this."

Mia and Luke join her at the table and begin passing around the plates holding the pancakes, bacon, and eggs for each of them to heap helpings onto their plates. Mia makes sure to slather her pancakes in excessive amounts of butter before drizzling syrup on them. Luke is already digging into his meal as Valerie pushes eggs around on her plate.

"It's so nice to have you both here," Valerie says softly, "I wish I had you here more often." Mia and Luke glance at each other, and Mia feels the guilt rising. "I know it's not easy for either of you to come visit, it's just…nice to have you back," Valerie smiles at her children. "I miss you two."

Mia sets down her fork and pats her mom's hand, "We miss you too, Mom, and I'm glad we could do this."

"Yeah Mom, we totally miss you too! Maybe you and Mia can come out to Miami sometime soon? It'll definitely be warmer out there then up north where Mia is," Luke crinkles his nose at the thought of cold weather.

Mia laughs, "I'd hardly call North Carolina northern."

"It's in the name!"

"It's below the Mason-Dixon line."

"Whatever, it still gets more winter than Florida."

Mia shrugs, admitting defeat. Valerie smiles at her children, appreciating the meaningless bickering that has been gone from her house for several years.

"Perhaps after graduation, we'll all come for a visit?" Valerie suggests. Luke's face suggests he's mildly disappointed and Valerie waves her hand dismissively. "Don't act like you want me there during spring break and I'm not flying for just one short weekend."

Luke nods, "Fine, graduation. Mia?" He peers at Mia with hope.

Mia hesitates, thinking of the cost of a ticket, then reminds herself that Luke will only graduate from college once. "Yes, of course I'll be there for graduation, and I'll see if I can stay for a little bit after too. But you're totally going to want to hang out and celebrate with your friends."

Luke forks more food in his mouth and rolls his eyes, "I have the whole summer before law school for that."

"You haven't heard back from anywhere yet, right?" Mia checks.

Luke shakes his head, "Should know from most places by

end of January. I'll probably be leaving Miami, and I'll want a few weeks in the new city before classes start, which definitely gives me at least a month in Miami after graduation. So this will be your last chance to party in Miami with me, you'll have to take it."

Mia smiles at Luke as Valerie tries to hide her eye roll at Luke's final statement, "Okay, will do."

As the three of them wrap up their meal Mia feels her phone buzz and chooses to ignore it, while Luke immediately pulls out his phone, reads the message on the screen and promptly shoves his phone back into his pocket. His obvious attempt to hide what just happened tells both Mia and her mother that the message was likely from Gregory, and Mia's able to assume that buzz on her phone was also from him.

"You can answer him, I won't be offended," Valerie says kindly, beginning to clear the table.

Mia gently swats her mom's hand off the dish and grabs plates from the table, "We'll take care of this." Luke nods and begins to help Mia clean up. As Valerie leaves to relax in front of the never ending stream of Christmas movies on TV, Mia and Luke efficiently tackle the dishes and pans that need washing and drying. Once Valerie is clearly out of earshot, Mia turns to Luke. "What's dad saying?"

"Just wants to see us at some point today. Think you can do it?"

Mia nods, "Yeah, how about a late lunch? Maybe we can borrow mom's car and head out there?" Their father had already left the nearby AirBnB he had been renting and was back in Dallas, meaning a long drive for Mia and Luke.

Luke looks at her skeptically, "You up for that drive back and then your early flight tomorrow?"

Mia nods, she doesn't relish driving that much in a day, but would feel guilty not seeing her dad, especially after he bought her flights. "Maybe see if he's willing to meet in Waco, tell him I fly tomorrow morning." Luke types back to their father and Mia feels the phone buzz in her pocket as the group text is sent. She continues to wash the dishes and hand them to Luke to dry as what can only be their father's response buzzes in her pocket.

Luke puts the dishes he's stacked away in the cupboard and checks his phone. "Um, Waco it is…let's see, he's sent an address of a restaurant, I hope he's made sure it's open." Luke clicks on the address link and grins, "Yep, Chinese food."

"Great, tell him we'll be there, um, around one-thirty? I've got to shower and get ready." Mia turns off the sink and dries her hands on the dish towels hanging from the oven. Luke quickly sends back their reply and Mia begins walking back toward the bathroom. "Also not it, you have to tell mom," she calls over her shoulder, teasing her brother. She hears him shouting her name as she closes the bathroom door.

CHAPTER 30

A shower, one slightly awkward conversation with her mother, and a two hour drive later, Mia and Luke are sitting across the table from their dad, with various steaming bowls of rice and plates of spiced chicken and veggies in front of them. The already halting conversation quickly died once the food arrived and Mia and Luke began doling out the second family meal of their day. The low rumble of other diners around them help to fill the silence.

After taking several mouthfuls of his kung pao chicken, Gregory breaks the silence. "So, back early tomorrow, right, Mia?"

Mia nods with a mouthful of lo mein. She covers her mouth as she tries to eat and reply, "Yep, I really need to buckle down and finish a draft for my master's thesis."

Gregory lifts a questioning eyebrow at her, "I thought

you were already supposed to be done with it?"

Mia shifts uncomfortably in her chair, her dad's innocent question reminding her of how derailed her thesis got after Danny dumped her. "Yeah, it just got, pushed back, but my advisor and I determined I can defend it this coming spring." Mia kicks at Luke's foot, hoping he catches her desperate silent plea to change the subject.

"Pushed back? What happened?" Gregory asks with concern. Mia nudges at Luke's foot again and he glares at her, annoyed at her at first, and then recognizing the plea in her eyes.

"Probably Mia went overboard and her advisor is making her scale back now," Luke lightheartedly jokes. "Anyway, when are you gonna come visit me?" he directs to Gregory.

"I thought we were all coming out for your graduation?" Gregory asks carefully. "Or are we splitting graduation too?"

Luke and Mia glance at each other, trying to figure out who is going to save the conversation now. Mia breathes in and gives an easy smile, "I'm pretty sure Miami doesn't do double ceremonies to satisfy divorced families."

Gregory doesn't respond and returns to his food.

"Obviously I am expecting you there for graduation, Dad. As long as you want to be there, I want you there," Luke says more emphatically.

"Why wouldn't I want to be there? Cause your mother is going? You're my son too and I am also proud of you and helped pay for your college education. So of course I want to be there," Gregory's reply is tinged with annoyance and sadness.

"Great, so everyone is going to graduation and it's going to be a ton of fun and now we can change the topic! Watching anything good?" Mia exclaims. Gregory is briefly irritated and then sighs, moving along with the subject change as the three of them debate which dramatized documentary they think is best on Netflix.

After finishing their meal, and managing to have a smoother conversation during the second half, Mia makes sure to thank her dad once more for the plane tickets before she and Luke hug him goodbye. Luke promptly falls asleep in the car on the way home, so Mia scrolls through various radio stations to find songs to sing along to on her drive back.

The brief questions about her master's thesis are still rolling in her mind, as Mia's disappointment and embarrassment roll together. She hates that she fell behind on her academic and career goals all because her relationship at the time went up in flames and she had a hard time coping with it. Mia's thoughts turn into more self-flagellation as she also picks apart the irony of her poor coping skills while in the context of learning to become a therapist. *Nobody is expecting you to be perfect,* she tries to remind herself, while also observing an underlying chant. *No boy is going to get in the way again* the chant goes. Mia takes a deep breath and calms herself. *I know better now, I take better care of myself now, I make better choices now,* she reassures herself. She nods to herself with each assertion, despite the niggling feeling that some of those statements could still be called into question.

By the time they get back to Austin, Mia's a mix of emotions. Luke breezes into the house, only to turn back around to head out and see some friends. Mia is ready to hide out in her room and kill time before she goes to bed, ready to be on a flight back home. However, Valerie has called to her from the family room, and Mia joins her to see a bottle of wine and two glasses out.

"Care to join?" Valerie smiles and gestures for Mia to sit on the couch. Mia smiles and plops down, curling her legs under her and pulling an afghan over her.

"Are you cold?" Valerie fusses over Mia and Mia shakes her head. Valerie pours wine into each glass and hands one to Mia before settling with her own onto the couch. "You seemed a bit tightly wound," Valerie observes after taking a sip.

Mia drinks from her own glass, appreciating the smooth taste of the wine as it begins to warm her belly. "Guess I'm just stressed about things I need to tackle when I get back." Valerie nods, her eyes still trained on Mia while she takes another sip. "I really need to be focused and get my writing done." Valerie continues her silent stare, as Mia swirls her wine and takes another small sip. "And…" Mia trails off, contemplating how much she wants to share with her mom.

"And?" Valerie questions.

Mia shakes her head, still weighing what she wants to share with her mom. "And I just don't want to get thrown off again, like over the summer."

"Well, honey, I don't see that happening again. That whole thing with that boy, it's not like you'll be dating him again." Valerie says compassionately.

"No of course not," Mia replies.

Valerie pauses, looking intently at Mia's face, as if searching for an answer. Mia's eyes drop back down to her wine, feeling uncertain under her mother's gaze. "Is there something else?" Valerie asks. Mia shakes her head. "Hm, is that a no or a no I don't want to talk about it?" Valerie muses.

Mia looks up and wryly smiles at her mother, "Are you sure you the one training to be a therapist?"

Valerie smiles and quickly retorts, "Is this where we discuss your use of humor as a defense mechanism?" Mia rolls her eyes while letting out a snort. "But really, sweetie, if there's something going on and you'd like to talk about it…" Valerie trails off.

"There's nothing to talk about, I'm good. I'm doing my best to avoid," Mia imitates her mother's earlier intonation, "that boy." Mia sighs and continues, "It's not always the easiest, he's dating my classmate and we share a bunch of friends. I can't go avoiding all my friends too." Valerie nods sympathetically and gently pats Mia's arm. Mia purses her lips, again deliberating on what she wants to share with her mom, deciding to leave out anything involving Brett, but feeling safe that she can talk about Danny. *Mom already doesn't like Danny, but there's no need to tell her about Brett now, plus she'll want details I just can't give her.* "And the other night we were all hanging out watching some movies and Danny cornered me and kissed me. I pushed him away and told him to leave me alone, and he texted me a few times after that. But that's really it." Mia takes a big swig of her wine, avoiding eye contact with her mother.

Glancing back at her mother, Mia sees Valerie's brow is furrowed with concern, and Valerie carefully asks, "Is he harassing you?

"Oh my god no, Mom. Our last conversation was over text, I said to leave me alone, and he has. Seriously. This is not a thing for you to get up in arms about." Mia suddenly regrets sharing that bit of information with her mom.

"Yes, but if he - " Valerie starts, but Mia cuts her off.

"If he does anything that is harassing, believe me, I'd report him. But he hasn't." Mia finishes off her glass of wine. "Don't worry about it, ok?" Valerie nods slowly and Mia rolls her eyes knowing that her mom's silent acknowledgement was not an indication that it would be let go. Mia peeks at the clock over the TV, "I'm gonna go read for a bit and then head to bed, okay?"

Valerie starts as if to say something, but stops herself. She nods her head while saying, "Okay, I'll see you in the morning."

Mia gets up and kisses her mom on the head, before placing her wine glass next to the kitchen sink and going back into her childhood bedroom.

CHAPTER 31

Back in her room, Mia's flopped onto her bed and pulls out her phone. Her jumble of emotions from earlier only seems to be raging harder after the glass of wine and conversation with her mom. She clicks the screen on to her phone and punches in her passcode. Mia scrolls in her contacts and quickly lands on Brett. *He said to call later,* Mia reminds herself, while also feeling nervous about calling. *Who talks on the phone anymore?* She asks her herself. Mia's mental back and forth is finally settled by the light buzz from the alcohol and she presses the call button. The phone rings a few times and just as she is about the hang up she hears Brett's voice.

"Hey, didn't think I was going to hear from you!" He sounds cheerful. Mia lets out an internal sigh, pushing aside the anxiety about calling.

"Yeah, it's been a busy day. Merry Christmas! How's yours been?" she asks.

"Busy too, mostly stuff with my parents and sister's family. We did this polar express train ride thing last night, to see Santa off, and I swear I am still frozen from it," Brett laughs. Mia smiles into the phone. "And today was presents and breakfast and more presents and then watching some traditional and not so traditional movies, so you know, Christmas-y. How about you?" Brett sounds lighthearted and Mia doesn't want to bum him out.

"Um, breakfast with my mom, and then my brother and I went out to meet my dad for a late lunch that went long, and then back home and had some wine with my mom, and now just hanging out in my old bedroom." Mia suddenly feels like her Christmas day was lacking, a sense she pushes aside and does not feel like acknowledging.

"That sounds nice," Brett says genuinely. "And what's left for your time home?"

"That's actually it, I head back tomorrow. What about you?" Mia hopes that Brett ends his trip early, giving her a chance to spend time with him before the town picks up again with students returning and classes resuming.

Mia catches a brief pause on Brett's end before he says, "Ah, well, actually taking a guys trip with some friends to Vegas, and then coming back to Philly for New Year's."

Mia's optimism dissipates, but she quickly pushes it down and tries to refocus. "Vegas, huh?" She asks lightly.

Brett chuckles on his end of the connection. "Yeah, we'd been kicking around the idea and with no bachelor parties on the horizon, we all decided to just go. It's a bunch of my friends from high school. It should be fun." He pauses again and teases Mia, "Obviously I'll be well-behaved."

Mia lightly snorts, "I mean I wasn't worried about that until you said it." She hears silence from Brett's end and quickly tacks on, "I'm kidding, I'm not worried. I hope you have fun. Really." Mia pauses and then adds brightly, "What happens in Vegas stays in Vegas, except for communicable STDs."

Brett laughs, finally stopping and saying, "Noted." A silence slowly settles over the phone conversation.

"It's too bad I won't get to see you at New Year's," she says carefully. As soon as it left her mouth, Mia immediately regrets it, thinking she sounds needy. "I mean, it would be nice to hang out before the semester starts," she rushes to add.

"I'm sure we can find a time when I get back and before classes start. I know it'll be harder once, uh, we get back into the swing of things" Brett replies.

Mia's mood dampens again at the thought of how careful they'll need to be once they both get back. With the wine buzz starting to wear off, she decides to change the subject while she still has the courage for it. "Anyway, how'd you like the photo I sent?"

"I really liked it. Made me wish you were here with me."

Mia smiles mischievously and presses forward, "What would you have done if I was there?"

Brett pauses and Mia hears him take a breath in. "I would have had my way with you."

"Mmhmm, tell me how," she lowers her voice, her eyes darting towards the door and confirming she locked it earlier.

"I would have laid you down on your bed and begun kissing you from your heel to your hip," Brett says huskily. Mia reaches her free hand down her pants and begins to swirl a finger against her clitoris.

"And then?"

"I'd make my way to your pussy, and write out a second dissertation with my tongue."

Mia bursts out laughing and stops touching herself, as Brett also laughs on his end. "Sorry," he says, "I've literally never done this before."

Mia's laugh slows into giggles, "Me neither, but I don't think dissertations are normally included in phone sex."

"Well since you seem to be better versed in the rules, why don't you take the lead, hot shot?" Brett teases.

Mia takes a deep breath before beginning. "I would push *you* down onto the bed and straddle your hips. I would rub my pussy back and forth along your hard cock, making you beg me for entry. You'd reach your hands up under my shirt and gently play with my nipples." Mia pauses, licking her lips and returning to her manual stimulation. Mia pushes forward and changes tenses, "I'm moaning now, slick against you, also wanting you inside of me. Instead, I sit back and hold your cock with one hand as I slowly lick you from root to tip, and gently place the tip of you in my mouth." Mia hears Brett breathing more heavily into the phone, as her breath begins to quicken too. "I'm sucking your cock, hungry, going faster and faster, and you are moaning and begging for me to let you fuck me." Mia's thrumming with excitement and she slips two fingers inside of herself, and begins to pump. "So I stop sucking you, and I climb on top and very slowly, very carefully, lower myself onto you, and it feels so good to have you in me. With your hands on my hips, I start to move, sliding up and down on your thick, firm, cock. And you move me faster and faster," Mia's breath begins to catch and Brett's breathing sounds heavier. "And it feels so good to have you fuck me, I want this all the time. You fuck me so good," Mia whispers hoarsely, feeling the momentum within her starting to crest, "and you're gonna make me come, cause you're so good at making me come, and you're squeezing my ass and fucking me and oh my god you're making me come fuck me fuck fuck me oh my god," Mia's last words run into each other as her orgasm electrifies her body.

She barely hears Brett's grunted "fuck" as he presumably finishes himself off.

Mia lays panting for a moment in her bed, feeling like an eternity has passed. She's trying to find the next words to say, feeling both satisfied and slightly embarrassed.

"You are…way better at that than me," Brett says quietly, breaking the silence. Mia laughs, feeling her tension break.

"I could probably flesh it out better next time," Mia demurs, feeling more relaxed.

"Well it worked for me, and it sounds like it did for you too," Brett sighs. "And now I just want to get my hands on you more."

Mia smiles to herself, feeling a mixture of content and sadness. "I guess you'll just have to wait until after the new year."

"I can't wait," he says quietly. "It'll be nice to just, relax with you."

Mia giggles, "Is that what we'd call what just happened?"

"No, I just mean to do both *that* and relax you. Just get back into the swing of things. You know, holidays are crazy and I have this trip, so I'm just, ready to be back and be with you." Brett awkwardly explains.

"Gotcha, well, me too. I guess I'm gonna head off to bed now, can't really end my day on a higher note." Mia hears

Brett respond with a laugh. “Good night,” she says.

“Good night, thanks again for my gifts,” he replies. Mia grins and ends the call.

CHAPTER 32

Mia's back at her apartment following a smooth flight and uneventful Uber ride the next day. She breathes a sigh of relief once she's inside, and is pleased to see Renly marching out of her room, meowing at her return.

She crouches down to scratch Renly's ears and he purrs appreciatively. "Glad to have me back, huh?" She croons to him. After a few more scratches, Mia begins to busy herself with settling back in. She cleans up Renly's food bowls and litter box, as well as unpacks and starts a load of laundry. She sets her laptop back up, and sits her stack of draft notes next to it. Mia regards the work setup sadly, regretting that she didn't touch her thesis while in Texas. Finally, she does a quick scan in her refrigerator and pantry and jots down a grocery list. Before heading out to refill her kitchen she sends out two short texts.

Back, you around? She sends to Leigh.

Made it back, what are you up to? She sends to Brett.

"Sorry, Renly, I'll be back!" Mia calls over her shoulder to the scowling cat as she leaves for the grocery store.

Mia's on full auto-pilot mode while food shopping, making her way up and down each aisle, grabbing what she needs while also trying to cross items off her list. She almost walks right past Sasha in the pasta section, who is waving at her with a big smile.

"Hey Mia!" Sasha says brightly. "I figured I was the only one back!"

Mia, initially startled, quickly recovers and replies, "Hey, sorry, was totally caught up in my list. How are you? How has your break been?"

Sasha shrugs and pushes aside a stray hair and straightens her glasses. "It's been alright, I guess. Went home for a bit and then," she pauses briefly, "went to Danny's for Christmas with his family." She pauses again. "It was nice. How about you?"

Mia has kept the same light smile on her face, nodding along and observing Sasha's slight hesitancy to mention Danny. *She doesn't want to hurt me,* Mia reminds herself. "Just Texas for a few days. It was good."

An awkward beat follows Mia's response and both women go to speak before they both laugh and insist for the other to go ahead.

"Do you know what you're doing for New Year's?" Sasha asks, taking the lead.

"Ah," Mia thinks. Her friends usually have a party together, and a party with her friends means Sasha, and Sasha going would inevitably mean Danny going, which has the potential to make ringing in New Year's miserable for Mia. Mia's suddenly realizes she's taking a long time to respond to Sasha and begins to blush.

Sasha rushes in to fill the silence, "I was just wondering, cause someone usually takes the mantle to throw the New Year's party, but no one has yet, so I thought maybe I would?"

"That'd be great!" Mia says honestly. "I didn't even realize no one offered yet?"

"Yeah," Sasha shrugs, "I don't think anyone from the last couple of years wanted to do it again."

"Well, if you're gonna throw it, let me know what I can do to help." Mia offers.

"I will totally take you up on that!" Sasha grins.

Mia nods, and peers into her cart, "Well just let me know what you need, I'm gonna finish out this shopping trip though."

Sasha nods back, "Sounds good, I'll see you later!" Sasha and Mia wave at each other as they head out of different ends of the aisle. Mia carefully navigates the rest of her grocery shopping to not run into Sasha again, anxious about having any other potential awkward moments. Mia is also feeling uncertain about what was a truly genuine offer. She does want to be helpful to Sasha, and also does not want to spend any extra time alone with her too. Mia still feels gross from kissing Danny back, and feels terrible about Sasha not knowing. Mia sighs internally, wishing Leigh was back so that she could hash out these thoughts and feelings with someone she trusted. Mia quickly glances at her phone while the cashier checks her out, hoping for a response from either text she sent earlier. Relieved, Mia sees responses from both Leigh and Brett, and decides to get back to them once her errands are done.

After getting back home and unpacking her groceries, Mia settles down on her couch with a bagel, Renly, and her phone. She pulls up Leigh's response.

Still at home, coming back on 30th. Wanna be my ride from the airport? ;) Mia smiles and texts back, **Sure thing, send me arrival info.** This means just a few more days of wrestling with her thoughts alone. She resolves to take the time to be productive, rather than hemming and hawing over dealing with Sasha. Mia quickly clicks on Brett's response, **Layover on my way to Vegas. Still thinking of our phone call ;).** She smiles, relishing the idea that their phone sex was still on his mind. She types out and sends **Round 2?**

Figuring that a response from either would be awhile, Mia finishes her bagel and pulls out the draft of her thesis, along with her paper agenda. She counts the days before classes resume and starts developing a plan for what to focus on for each day, with the goal of a final draft to her advisor on the first day back. Segmenting her thesis and identifying morning times for researching articles to include and afternoons to write, Mia also allows herself breaks around New Year's and a buffer day to move around according to when Brett gets back. She sits back, mulling over her calendar and plan, feeling satisfied. *I can do this*, she tells herself confidently. It feels possible with little to no distractions between now and the semester resuming, Mia observes with a rare bout of optimism.

Her work ethic renewed, Mia goes over Dr. Thompson's notes from her last draft, marking where she needs to make significant changes and do more research. Having left her phone on the couch, Mia becomes absorbed in her work, and only breaks to have dinner, and finally checks her phone again.

Landed in Vegas! Don't know about a round 2…won't have much privacy. Mia's disappointed in Brett's response, though she admits to herself that she should have expected as much. *He's going with friends and wants to have fun with them*, she tells herself, *he's not your boyfriend, so don't be a buzzkill.*

No problem ☺ Have fun! She texts back.

But not too much, right? Brett's reply immediately flies in.

Mia giggles and texts back, **Just enough fun. No more no less.**

Good, that's my plan. First up to is lose money gambling. Brett's my name, craps my game, and I suck at it.

You just need someone to blow on your dice for good luck, Mia texts back with a grin.

Brett texts her back with three eggplant emojis followed by **Are you volunteering?**

Celebratory BJs if you hit it big in Vegas, she sends back.

And if I lose? Brett responds.

Condolence BJs, Mia replies.

I guess I am lucky.

Have fun! Text me the results ;) Mia sends. With that last text, Mia sets to making some dinner and watching random reruns on TV, determined to continue her focus on work for the next few days.

CHAPTER 33

Mia spends the next several days devoted to her plan and faithfully tackling her thesis. She adds in one more task as well, restarting her birth control pill and making an appointment with her doctor to ensure she has refills as well. She takes breaks to flirt with Brett over text and to check in with her brother. She crashes in the evening, watching movies sometimes with a glass of wine in hand. Each night feels like an accomplishment, having stuck to her plan and seeing her work progress. It may not be the most exciting, but it's getting shit done, Mia acknowledges. When December 30th rolls around, she's seeing significant improvement with her thesis and it's finally time for Leigh to be back. Mia's allowed herself to become a hermit over the last few days, rarely leaving her apartment except to go to the gym, along with running some errands per Sasha's request for the New Year's Eve party.

As Mia pulls up to the arrivals lane to pick up Leigh she's

surprised to not just see Leigh, but Jake along with her.

"Hey!" Mia puts the car in park and gets out to hug Leigh and open the trunk. Jake grabs Leigh's bag and hoists it into the trunk, and throws his duffel bag on top. Mia gives Jake a brief hug and shuts the trunk.

"Surprise!" Leigh says with a grin. Everyone piles into the car and Mia glances at Leigh, with an eyebrow raised. "Jake surprised me the last two days and uh, came out to meet my family."

"Aw," Mia says, glancing back at Jake through the rearview mirror, "that's sweet." Jake blushed slightly and shrugged. Mia genuinely feels happy for Leigh, though she was hoping for some time to chat without Jake present.

"It was," Leigh says, turning back to smile at Jake before she turns to look at Mia, "don't worry about driving him to his place. You can take us to my apartment and I'll get him back." Mia nods. "How was your Christmas?"

Mia shrugs, "Good, and awkward. The usual for my family I guess."

"Sorry," Leigh says with concern.

Mia waves her off with one hand, "Nothing to be sorry about it, it is what it is. I've been back for a few days and been really productive, so I'm good. I'm also ah, trying to help Sasha some with the party."

"Oh?" Leigh asks gently.

"Yeah, ran into her and offered, so I've gotten some food and liquor for it."

"That's nice of you," Leigh muses. Mia glances at her briefly and sees Leigh's concerned face.

"Yep," eager to not discuss further in front of Jake, Mia tries to shift the conversation, "You're going right?"

"Of course!" Leigh exclaims.

"What about you, Jake?" Mia asks, peering into the mirror to see him again.

Jake squirms in his seat, trying to make eye contact with Leigh, who seems to be refusing to look back at him, "Ahhh, probably not? I don't know? Leigh?"

"Probably not," Leigh says quietly. Her eyes dart over to Mia, "It's just another week or so till the new semester, and I'd rather that, you know, we look like this started then, rather than…earlier."

"Gotcha," Mia says cheerily, trying to cover over the awkward beat, "Well what are your plans, Jake?"

Jake, now glum in the back seat, shrugs. "Not entirely sure, most of my friends won't be back, but I'll figure something out." He gives another shrug, attempting nonchalance. Mia tries to gauge Leigh's mood through her peripheral vision, but can't catch the expression on her face.

"Well I'm sure something will be going on," Mia says reassuringly. Jake nods from the backseat, with less certainty than her. "Anyway, it's still really sweet you surprised Leigh. How'd you like your trip?"

As Mia continues to drive them back to Leigh's, Jake and Leigh share how their break went. Mia's half-listening, with nods and affirmative sounds to show that she's listening, while she quietly thinks through how her friend is doing. Leigh seems more nervous about her dating Jake coming into the open soon, it's not like the week before a new semester will make a difference, Mia observes. As Mia weighs Leigh's hesitation, she also begins to wonder if Leigh could be supportive with her own predicament. Mia wishes she could share what is happening with Brett, starting with who Brett actually is. It'd be nice to have someone to confide in, Mia tells herself. *But you both agreed not to*, she sternly reminds herself. Mia's still lost in her thoughts as she pulls up to Leigh's place.

"How about I take us both to Sasha's tomorrow? I can help you both set up?" Leigh offers, as she's getting out of the car. Jake is already pulling their luggage from the trunk.

Mia snaps out of swirling thoughts to put a smile back on

her face and nod, "Yeah, sure, that's a great idea. Eight work?"

"Perfect, I'll see you then! Thanks again for picking us up!" Leigh calls as she shuts the door. Mia nods and waves as they both head up to Leigh's apartment. She sighs, regretting she didn't have a chance to share her worries about Sasha and Danny, and knowing she'll only have a few minutes to do that just before the party.

After getting back home, and still feeling disappointed, she shoots a text to Brett, **When's the party over?**

Today. Headed back tomorrow, Brett replies.

Mia sighs with frustration, unsure if back means Pennsylvania or North Carolina. **Does that mean I get a New Year's kiss?** She types out her text, and hits send before she can second guess herself.

It'll be late when I get in, but I'll head to your place from the airport, if you want.

Mia feels lighter as she reads the text, **Yes, just text me when you get in.**

Sounds good. By the way, I broke even, what does that mean for me?

Celebratory and condolence BJs canceled out each other. You'll have to settle for a New Year's booty call. Mia texts back.

It's not settling, Brett replies and Mia smiles to herself.

CHAPTER 34

Leigh picks Mia up promptly at eight and drives them both to Sasha's, where they spend an hour helping Sasha decorate, lay out drinks, and prepare some food. Mia listened and dropped "mmhmms" at the appropriate times as Leigh and Sasha updated each other on their winter breaks. Mia only briefly snapped out of her overly focused task completion when Leigh nudged her after Sasha asked her about her trip back to Texas. As the hour closed in on nine, the women surveyed the apartment and felt fairly satisfied with their work. Sasha poured each one of them a drink and handed out the plastic cups.

Raising her cup, with Leigh and Mia following suit, the women clink their solo cups together, as Sasha says, "Good teamwork, ladies. Here's to ringing in a good new year!" Both Leigh and Mia smile back at Sasha and they all take a sip to Sasha's toast. "And now we get to see who is punctual and who is fashionably late," Sasha says as she sits down on a couch.

"Well," Leigh laughs as she perches on the armrest of the couch, "Mia is already here, so that checks one off of fashionably late."

Mia flashes a smile at her friend, "Hardy hardy har. I'm always running late, very funny." Mia leans against a countertop, swirling her drink and occasionally taking sips. Her short black dress with a v-neck inches up slightly and Mia gently tugs the hem back down. "Anyway, are we expecting the usual suspects? Cause if that's so, everyone will be here in thirty minutes."

"Basically," Sasha nods and ticks off various members of their year in the psychology program, along with a few older and younger classmates, as well as Danny and his friends from the chemistry department. "Oh, you two are both taking the social course with Dawson, right?" Sasha asks. Mia feels her throat clench and nods, trying to keep her face neutral, while Leigh simply nods at Sasha. "I totally forgot to tell you two, I saw him during finals week, he actually had his office door open, and damn. I mean, damn." Sasha draws out the last damn and pretends to fan herself.

Leigh grins at both of the women, "Oh really, that hot?"

Sasha nods, "Yeah, it might actually be distracting during class." Mia clenches the countertop while smiling, knowing just how distracting it will truly be for her, as she is far more familiar with all of Brett's attractive parts.

"We've never had a hot young professor before. The department is all…" Leigh trails off to find the right word.

"Mature?" Mia gently provides. All three women look at each other and burst out laughing.

"Yes, quite mature. They were gonna need some fresh blood anyway. It's just a nice bonus for us that he's hot," Sasha grins.

"Well it's not like any of us will be taking advantage of it beyond oogling," Leigh comments, "Between Jake and Danny, and um," she glances quickly at Mia realizing she's highlighting her presumed singledom, " I'm sure departmental rules, um, yeah, you know. You know what, I'll stop talking?" Leigh finishes awkwardly.

Mia felt her stomach twist during Leigh's comment, unsure of where she was going, but felt sudden relief as her friend tried to save face. Mia laughs kindly, "It's cool, Leigh, I'm very single," while crossing her fingers behind her back. *It's not a lie*, Mia tells herself over a very clear lie to her best friend, *it's the pretend truth for the time being.* Another part of Mia's brain is shouting LIAR LIAR at her while she spins around and grabs the wine bottle nearest her. "Aaaaaanyway, who needs more?"

Both women raise their cups as Mia replenishes their drinks and the knocks on the door begin. Slowly, but steadily, Sasha's apartment begins to fill up with their classmates and friends, everyone bringing some kind of dish or drink. Mia helps to arrange the food and beverages as they come in, trying to clear out anything that has been finished and squeeze new arrivals onto the small kitchen counter.

Between catching up with other classmates about their breaks, attending to the spread, and trying to keep her own drink refilled, Mia initially doesn't even notice that Danny sidles up next to her as she pours her next drink.

"Hey," Danny leans against the counter, blocking Mia's exit from the kitchen. Mia looks up, slightly glassy-eyed, and definitely annoyed, the alcohol wearing down her politeness.

"Hey yourself," Mia says and puts the bottle back down and picks up her drink, to indicate her intended departure from the kitchen. Despite this, Danny does not move.

"Did you have a good break?" Danny persists.

Mia sighs. "Yes. I heard Sasha went to meet your family," she says pointedly.

Danny blinks, "Um, yeah. But tell me about your break?" He reaches out to gently stroke Mia's arm.

"Nope," Mia says bluntly and pushes her way past Danny and out of the kitchen. She quickly finds Leigh and starts to listen intently to the conversation Leigh is having with a classmate a year below them, complaining about a class Leigh previously took. Leigh is briefly startled at Mia suddenly showing up at her side, so Mia tries to nonchalantly tilt her head back to the kitchen. Leigh eyes Danny making his way from the kitchen back to Sasha in the living room and rolls her eyes at Mia before returning to her conversation. "Yep, he's a really tough grader," Leigh empathizes.

As the clock ticks closer to midnight, the time at which Mia has promised herself she is allowed to leave one way or another, Mia finds herself jumping in and out of conversations, trying to avoid Danny, who consistently seems to appear wherever she is. Mia accepts a shot from Sasha as she hands them out, and then another, as she continues to try to elude Danny. Without intending it to happen, Mia realizes she is drunker than she wants to be.

I wonder if Brett's still on a plane or if he could get a text right now. Mia escapes to the bathroom, grabbing her purse along the way. Once inside, she pulls out her phone, which she hasn't checked since she got to Sasha's. Her phone's blinking indicates she has a missed text.

Last plane trip for the day. Will see you soon. Brett's text was from a couple hours earlier. Mia checks herself over in the bathroom mirror, feeling and looking a little flushed. She fluffs her hair out a bit and rearranges her top to have more cleavage show. Trying her best to make a come hither face, she bites her lip and raises an eyebrow before taking a picture in the bathroom mirror. Attaching the photo to her text (**I can't wait**), she sends it off and leaves the bathroom. She scans the room for Leigh, hoping she can convince her to take her home soon. Mia moves around the crowded apartment, trying to find her friend when she runs into Sasha back in the kitchen.

"Hey, have you seen Leigh?" Mia asks Sasha.

"Oh, she told me to tell you she went to Jake's. I think she wanted to officially ring in the new year with him," Sasha says as she clears some trash off the counter.

Damnit, Mia thinks. Mia's frustration and disappointment with her friend feels heightened with all the alcohol she's had.

Sasha notices Mia's change in demeanor, "Hey, it's alright. I told her I'd get you home, don't worry."

Mia gives a tight smile to Sasha, "Thanks, but I was hoping to go kind of soon, and obviously you'd want to stay around till people have left..." Mia trails off, "Whatever I'll just get an Uber or something."

Sasha shakes her head, "And get gouged on surge pricing right now? No way. Just wait a little till after midnight, I promise."

Mia sighs internally and nods, leaving the kitchen and finding the safest conversation she can join while the final minutes to midnight tick down. As the couples around the room seem to magnetically come together, Mia sees Danny brush aside a stray hair from Sasha's face and whisper in her ear. Mia turns away and tries to focus, though poorly, on her classmate's face as they all start to chant the countdown.

"Three, two, one, HAPPY NEW YEAR!" is chorused throughout the apartment while the TV blares Auld Lang Syne and the ball in Times Square is flashing as it hits its base. All around her, the couples kiss, and Mia gets and gives various hugs from friends as they all wish each other a happy new year. As the bodies hustle around her, with everyone eager to share with one another, Mia finds Danny in front of herself again.

"Happy New Year, maybe new year, new friendship?" Danny asks Mia, holding his arms out slightly for a hug. Mia stares at him, and Danny drops his arms. "Hey look, Sasha said you need a ride home, but she needs to stay here, so she volunteered me."

Feeling exhausted and drunk, as well as ready to just be home, Mia feels her resolve falter. "Yeah, whatever." She searches around the crowd and gets Sasha's eye contact long enough for both women to wave goodbye to each other. Mia barely notices Danny's hand on her lower back as he leads her out of his apartment and into his car.

CHAPTER 35

Once ensconced in the passenger seat of Danny's car, Mia tries to focus on her phone, checking to see if Brett has responded. Nothing yet, so she clicks the screen back off and shoves her phone back into her purse. Danny keeps glancing over at her as he drives, all while Mia keeps her eyes trained firmly out the window. Mia, suddenly aware that she never pulled her neckline back up from the selfie she sent Brett, self-consciously tries to fix it. As she squirms her hemline creeps back up and she tries to yank it back down. Danny glances back over and reaches to place a hand just above Mia's knee.

"You look really pretty tonight," Danny says quietly, resting his hand on her leg.

This fucker, Mia thinks. She scoots herself closer to the door, forcing Danny's hand to drop off her leg.

"I'm sorry about all this weirdness between us. I just keep

thinking about you…about us lately. I really messed up." Danny glances again at Mia, which she catches in the window's reflection. "I wish I knew what to do to make this right. Between us."

Mia continues to watch out the window, her mouth pursed, with rage and fear boiling within. *I just need to get home, please let me just get home safely,* she thinks.

"Are you going to say anything?" Danny asks.

Mia's eyes widen as she stays turned toward the window, seeing the car turn into her apartment complex. Danny slows the car down considerably as he drives to her building.

"Are you just going to ignore what I'm saying? I'm apologizing," Danny persists.

Mia takes in a big breath, "Thank you for apologizing." Mia's phone buzzes in her purse, and she pulls out it to see the **on my way over** text from Brett. She breathes out a sigh of relief, still feeling some tension from the current moment but eager for later.

"Who's that?" Danny asks, craning his neck to see. Mia clicks her screen off and shoves her phone back in her purse.

"Leigh," she lies. Danny pulls into an open spot in front of Mia's building and she immediately goes to unbuckle her seatbelt. She feels Danny's hand on hers as she clicks down on the release button.

"I want to try to be friends." Danny says, holding onto Mia's wrist.

Mia opens the car door with her free hand and wrenches her wrist from Danny's grasp. "Be less creepy, stop touching me, stop hitting on me when you're dating my friend, and stop eyefucking me and maybe when hell freezes over we'll be friends." Mia stumbles out of the car, slams the door, and hurriedly makes her way up to her apartment, listening carefully for any steps behind her. Hands shaking, she digs her keyring out of her purse and jams her key into the lock, throwing herself into her apartment and quickly slamming it behind her before locking it again.

Mia crumples down to the floor, finally letting out the ragged breaths she held on to at the end of the ride. Mia rests a hand on her abdomen and tries to slowly and steadily return her breathing to normal, closing her eyes and envisioning her lungs expanding and contracting, as she often talks her clients through. After a couple minutes of mindfully breathing, Mia finds herself feeling calmer. Renly wanders out from her office and crawls into her lap. Mia smiles and gives Renly a scratch under his chin.

A loud rap at the door sends Renly flying off Mia, and she pushes herself up and looks through the peephole. The overhead light by her front door cast some shadows, but the dark hair on the man reassures Mia enough to open the door.

"Hey," Brett says with a smile as Mia swings the door open. His smile quickly fades as he sees the tear streaks down Mia's face, "Whoa, is everything alright?" Brett steps inside, shutting the door, scanning Mia's face.

Mia feels the panic from earlier swell in her as she spits out, "I'm fine, it's just this guy, that not complicated guy, I needed a ride home, he's my friend's boyfriend, she asked him to give me a ride, he's just a fucking creep, but I'm here you're here I'm fine."

"Did he do something?" Brett asks, alarm creeping into his voice.

Mia shakes her head, "No, no. He's just a fucking creep." She gazes up at Brett and takes another deep breath. "I'm fine, really."

"Is there something I can do?" Brett asks.

Mia smiled up at him, "Yes, make me feel better." A big smile spreads over Brett's face.

"You look gorgeous by the way," Brett says as he leans down and brushes his lips over Mia's. Mia grabs his neck, pulling him close to her and she hungrily kisses him. Brett's mouth parts and their tongues dart between each other's mouths. Brett runs his hands down Mia's back to cup her butt.

Mia disentangles herself from Brett, both of them slightly out of breath, and both of them flush now. Mia reaches up under her dress and pulls her panties off, letting them drop down her legs, as she kicks them off, one foot at a time. She backs herself against the front door, as Brett advances and removes his jacket and shirt, and he leans down, nibbling on her earlobe, and kissing down her neck and across her cleavage. Mia moans, leading Brett to whisper in her ear, "I love the noises you make." He presses his mouth to hers once again before taking a step back. Mia grabs him by the belt loops of his pants and pulls him forward, moving her hands swiftly to unbuckle and unzip his jeans. She yanks them open to reveal Brett's erection, bulging against his underwear. She reaches in with one hand, grasping his firm cock, slowly pumping it, while pulling Brett's head back down to her lips.

Mia moves her kisses from Brett's lips up along his jawline to his earlobe. She gently sucks on his earlobe before a she gives it a quick nip. "I love how you fuck me," she whispers back to him. She hears Brett's breath catch, and he pushes her dress up above her waist, as she pulls his erection out from his boxer briefs.

"Are you ready?" Brett asks huskily, his mouth roaming Mia's neck, cleavage, and mouth.

"Yes, fuck yes," She moans between kisses. Brett quickly grabs a condom from his pants pocket, tears it open and rolls it on. He then lifts her up and Mia wraps her legs around Brett as he penetrates her, pushing her up against the front door. Mia's head gently thuds against the door with each pump, as Brett pushes into her, burying his face in her cleavage. Mia moans and whimpers with pleasure with each gentle bite Brett lays across her chest. Brett raises his face back to hers and kisses her deeply as he fucks her against the door. Mia feels the oncoming orgasm, and her breathing accelerates. "I'm gonna come," she moans between kisses, just as the warmth and pleasurable explosion spreads through her body. Mia goes limp in Brett's arms and as she drops her legs from around his waist, he lowers her feet back to floor.

Brett steps back, still fully erect, his eyes still lustful. Mia pulls her dress off over her head and unclasps her bra. Her nipples fully hard, Brett reaches down and rolls one between his fingers, pulling Mia in closer with his free hand, and dropping his face down to kiss her again. Mia kisses him back then gently pushes on his chest and Brett backs away. "Lay down," Mia commands. Brett lays out on the cold tiles by the front door and Mia straddles herself over his erection. She lowers herself onto his thick cock slowly, enjoying the steady expansion and fulfillment in her own body. Mia closes her eyes, lips parted, and rhythmically moves up and down Brett's cock. He keeps one hand on her waist, with the other reaching to stroke her breasts. As Brett moves both hands to her waist, urging her faster, Mia fondles her own breasts and pulls on her nipples. Both she and Brett move more frantically as she feels a second orgasm ready to echo the first. "Oh god," Mia moans, her head rolling back, her back arching, and her orgasm tearing through. Brett's fingers dig into her waist as he stiffens and lets out a long groan, with a final convulsion that shakes through his body. Mia extricates herself and flops down next to Brett on the tile. She turns towards him and he sleepily grins at her.

"Best homecoming I've ever had," he says. Mia barks out a laugh as he pulls her close and holds her tight.

CHAPTER 36

Brett and Mia eventually peel themselves off the tile floor and gather up their tossed clothing. Brett grabs the luggage that Mia didn't even see him bring in and they both head back to her bedroom to take turns getting ready for bed. They each sink down under the sheets, and Renly hops up and curls himself between the two as they lay facing each other.

In the dark, barely able to see him, Brett reaches out and gently strokes Mia's cheek with his thumb. "I missed you."

Mia yawns and mumbles out "I missed you too."

Brett laughs, "Very convincing."

Mia smiles into the dark, "No really, I did. It's just been a long night."

Brett's voice is hushed and concerned, "Do you want to talk about it? What happened? With this guy?"

Mia scowls at the thought of Danny. "Not particularly. But in an effort of full disclosure," she takes a deep breath, "his name is Danny. He's a grad student in the chemistry department. He's the guy who messed me over last spring. We were, um, hooking up, and clearly I felt more strongly about him than he did about me. He dumped me out of the blue and started dating a friend of mine, she's in my cohort, Sasha. She didn't know much about us. No one really did, except for my best friend. We kind of snuck around. Or really, he had us sneak around, which was probably a red flag, but I chose to ignore it." Mia takes another deep breath, "Anyway, I was really hurt, and it felt like a slap in the face with how *public* he was with her. And we shared a lot of the same friends, so I kind of just retreated from everyone." Mia pauses. "It sucked. It was really lonely." She feels Brett rubbing her arm, soothing her. "And as of late, he's either hitting on me or pretending to want to be friends? I don't know." Mia stops and waits for Brett's response. She tries to make out the expression on his face but struggles with doing so in the dark.

"And tonight?" Brett presses carefully.

"Ah, tonight. Well, a few weeks ago, actually the night we first ran into each other at the grocery store, he kissed me," Mia stops and rushes out, "I didn't want him to, he basically cornered me when a bunch of us were hanging out and after it happened I ran out."

"Okay."

"And then he reached out and I told him to leave me alone. And honestly we've had no contact until tonight." Mia finishes.

"Except for when he showed up at Callahan's," Brett says.

"Yes, sorry, except for when he managed to crash our first date," Mia nods.

"And tonight?"

"Well Leigh, my best friend, was supposed to be my ride tonight, but she ditched me for her secret boyfriend, and Sasha, who was having the party insisted on giving me a ride home, but then she asked Danny to do it. And at this point, I don't know, I was drunk and tired, and clearly against my better judgment went along with it."

"And?"

"And he hit on me in the car, like, feeling up my leg, and was apologizing for his behavior and when we got to my apartment he, like, grabbed my wrist," Mia feels Brett's hand stiffen on her arm, "but I basically threw myself out of the car and ran inside. And that's it."

"You were scared." Brett's says, clearly not questioning her.

"Yes," Mia whispers, holding back a tear.

"Has he hurt you before? Done anything before?" he prods.

"No, not like physically, no. And I don't know if he would, but the vibe I was getting…" Mia trails off.

Brett leans over and kisses Mia gently on the forehead, and goes back to stroking her arm. "Yeah, it was creepy. I don't blame you for being freaked out. Is there anything I can do?"

Mia smiles, "What, like go beat up my ex-boyfriend? Ex-hook-up, whatever?"

Brett chuckles, "I don't know about that." His voice turns more serious, "But yeah, if he hurt you."

Mia shakes her head against her pillow. "No, having you listen and know helps."

"Well, if he does anything again, whatever it is, let me know," Brett says reassuringly.

Mia nods into the dark, "Okay." She stares in the direction of Brett, wishing she could see his face. "Sorry if it's weird to listen to me talk about an ex."

"It's not. This is something else. And besides, you're a grown woman, I'd be dumb to assume you had no past."

"Ouch," Mia teases, "No past, huh?"

Brett laughs nervously, "I don't mean it like *that*. You know what I mean…I mean…I keep trying to think of how to say this without it sounding terrible and I'm failing." He pauses and then continues, "It makes sense you have exes. I do too. We're not middle schoolers experiencing our first relationship."

Mia pats Brett's arm to reassure him, "I know what you're trying to say, just teasing you. Since you got to hear all about my last horrible ex, does this mean I get to hear about yours?"

Brett pulls Mia in closer, disturbing Renly who jumps off the bed, and hugs her to himself. He kisses the top of her head before resting his chin there. "Enough of exes for tonight, let's get some rest." Mia nods into Brett's chest and yawns, closing her eyes and settling in to sleep.

CHAPTER 37

"I forgot to wish you a Happy New Year," Brett whispers in Mia's ear as she blinks into the morning sun. She groans and rubs her temples. "Ah, a little hung over?" He teases. Mia groans again and pulls the cover over her head.

"Happy New Year. It's too bright out." Mia's voice is muffled from under the blanket. Brett laughs, and Mia feels the bed shift as he climbs out.

"I don't think the sun is the problem. I would offer to make you some coffee, but I know how you feel about that." Brett's footsteps seem to take him out of the room and Mia pushes the covers back down and squints as she looks around the room.

"Yuck to coffee. But um, do you want some? I could run out and get something for you?" Mia calls out to Brett, wincing at the volume of her own voice.

"Naw, I'm good. I'll get some on my way home," Brett's voice floats from the bathroom. Mia drags herself out of bed and starts rustling around her room, changing out of her pajamas and into running leggings and an oversized sweatshirt. After running her hands through her hair a few times she pulls it into a messy bun on top of her head. Brett strolls out of the bathroom and sees Mia as she moves to switch rooms with him. "Going for a run? Seems a little ambitious right now."

Mia snorts, "No, just finding something comfortable. Though now that I am thinking a little more clearly, I should run over to Leigh's and yell at her." Mia gets to busying herself in the bathroom, washing her face and brushing her teeth before applying some light makeup.

"Yeah, what exactly happened there, again?" Brett calls from Mia's bedroom. "She left for a secret boyfriend?"

"Yeah. I guess he's not so secret, or he won't be soon," Mia comes back into the bedroom and leans on the doorframe as she watches Brett get dressed. "He was an undergrad in a class she TAed," Brett's eyebrows raise at the description and Mia shakes her head, "and they started hooking up *after* the class ended. But they've been sneaking around cause Leigh's freaked out that people will assume otherwise and that it would cause all sorts of problems."

Brett nods solemnly, "Yeah, can't imagine what that's like," before breaking into a silly grin. Mia leans over to grab a pillow from her bed and launches it at him. He bats the pillow down and picks it back up from the floor before placing it back on Mia's bed. "So uh, if you know about Leigh's secret boyfriend…?" Brett cocks his head and raises an eyebrow.

Mia sighs, "She doesn't know. Or rather, she knows I had this great date, and ah, great sex, and then I kind of told her when we talked more I discovered it wasn't a good match so I ended it. I obviously never gave any detail to exactly who you are, so yeah, she basically doesn't know. I assume you want to keep it that way for now?"

Brett nods. "Yeah, I mean, the fewer people that know, the less likely we are to get into trouble." Mia nods and glances away. "And I don't want you to freak out about that. I know you said last night that your ex also had you sneak around, and maybe this is starting to look the same way, but I swear, I am not intending on this to stay that way. Sneaky. Seriously. I think we just both agree to be, um, discreet, for the time being." Brett's word nervously rush out.

Mia nods, as the worry of a Danny situation 2.0 begins to crystalize in her mind. *How could I be so dumb to not see this parallel? Or is it different because we're both choosing to hide this relationship? Or am I just in some kind of sex haze again and refusing to see red flags?* Mia goes to run her hands through her hair, forgetting she tied it up, resulting in her playing with the top knot.

"And I've made you worry now. Hey, like we said before, if at any point you're not cool with this, we can stop," Brett comes around the bed and gently clasps Mia's arms. "I'm not trying to hide you, or us, for some kind of shame or something. It's because we both don't want to jeopardize our careers. But I also understand if you don't want to do that. Of course, for us, the only alternative right now would be-"

"Nothing. The alternative would be cutting ties as much as possible and not having any kind of relationship. I know." Mia finishes his sentence. "No, I am choosing this with you," she says to reassure Brett and assuage her worries. "We just need to make sure we continue to communicate is all." Mia smiles nervously up at Brett and he leans down and kisses her.

"I promise to communicate," he says and draws his mouth up her jaw, "though I'll admit it's hard to talk when you jump me constantly."

Mia throws back her head and laughs, "Noted, I will stop jumping you. Gosh, you're making me out to be some kind of sex fiend with a sordid past."

"Don't stop jumping me," Brett murmurs, running his hands down Mia's back to hold her ass. He brushes his lips over hers again. "Just let me get some words in every now and then."

Mia feels her heart beginning to thud, and her body

starting to thrum in anticipation. "You can get some words in. You can get some other things in." She feels Brett's smile on her mouth.

"That would be very tempting right now," he says, giving her one last kiss before straightening back up. "But I definitely need to unpack and make sure my place didn't burn down while I was gone."

Mia steps back and nods. "Sure, um, I guess..." she goes to lead Brett back out.

"I'll text you," he says earnestly. "We'll do something before the semester starts," he says as he wheels his luggage out to the front door.

"Maybe we'll talk." Mia smiles.

Brett laughs, "Yes, maybe we'll talk." He plants on last kiss on Mia's mouth and lets himself out. Mia waves him off and closes the door.

As she spins around to face her emptier apartment, she sees Renly staring accusingly at her from the living room. "Yikes, okay, let's get you some breakfast." Mia picks up her purse, which she left by her front door last night, and drops it onto the counter as she moves into the kitchen and prepares some food for her cat. Renly scarfs down his food, as though he's been starving for days, while Mia digs into her purse and takes out her phone. The telltale blinking green dot tells her she has a text message.

Bracing herself, and hoping it is not another missive from Danny, Mia clicks on the screen and taps in her code.

I believe I owe you a huge apology. Leigh's first text. **Sasha told me she had Danny take you home**. Leigh's second text. **I am such an asshole for ditching you like that.** Leigh's third text. **Please tell me you got home ok.** Leigh's fourth text. **Again, I am so incredibly sorry.** Leigh's fifth text.

Mia scrolls through to check the time on the texts and sees that Leigh sent them early this morning. Mia leans against the counter and tries to think through a response. With the alcohol from last night faded, the mix of emotions of dealing with Danny dull, and her earlier sex haze gone, she realizes she's pretty pissed at Leigh. *It was a dick move*, Mia thinks, *to leave was selfish and to not tell me directly was not okay either.* As Mia tries to think through how to respond, another text from Leigh rolls in.

I wish I had a good excuse for my behavior. Like, Jake was in some kind of danger and only I could have rescued him but that's not the case. He texted me about seeing me at midnight and I just wanted to be with him as soon as I could. I should have handled it differently. I should have given you a heads up, at minimum, and really should have taken you home. I'm really sorry.

Mia sighs with frustration, annoyed with Leigh, but also empathizing with some of Leigh's actions. She shoots back her text to her friend, **Let's get lunch and talk.** Mia sends a second text indicating a nearby sandwich shop and time, and then settles in for some mindless TV watching until it's time to confront Leigh.

CHAPTER 38

Mia's already sitting with her soda, sandwich, and chips as Leigh hustles in and quickly orders at the counter. She gives Mia a quick smile and brief wave, and after paying and getting her order, slides into the seat across from Mia.

"I am an asshole." Leigh says directly. Mia raises an eyebrow. "And I am really sorry. I made a choice and it actively hurt you. I texted Sasha this morning asking if she needed any help cleaning up and I ended up finding out you left right after midnight, *and that she had Danny take you home*, and as soon as I found out I freaked out and have been worried about you. I figure you probably hate me right now, but I just want to make sure you're alright." Leigh's expression is pained and she pushes the food around on her tray.

"You are an asshole," Mia agrees, but then shakes her head, "You acted like an asshole. I'm really shocked you didn't even tell me."

"Which I totally should have! I got caught up in the text and couldn't find you and waiting a few more minutes wasn't going to kill me." Leigh reaches a hand out to touch Mia's hand. "I am sorry. I will never behave like that again."

Mia nods, "Good."

Leigh lets out a nervous breath she had been holding, "And you're here, but how was it getting home?"

Mia pulls her hand back and rests her hands in her lap. "Not great. Danny hit on me," Leigh makes an annoyed face at the reveal of information, "and then grabbed me and tried to get me to, I don't know, but he had my wrist and I yanked myself away and out of the car."

Leigh's mouth drops in shock, "Are you fucking kidding me?" Mia shakes her head. "What the fuck?"

Mia shrugs. "Yeah, I don't know. He was talking about how he mistreated me and how he wanted to be friends, but he also was putting his hands on me and complimenting me, and it obviously freaked me out when he was gripping my wrist."

"Yeah, of course," Leigh says, her surprise now mixing with shame. "Fuck, Mia, if I had any idea that your night would have played out like that, never, and I really, I mean *never*, would I have done what I did. I'm so sorry." Leigh rubs her face and sighs, "I'm really fucking sorry,

Mia. I put you in that position."

Mia shakes her head, "No you didn't. I should have taken an Uber home. Or waited till Sasha would have taken me. And Danny chose to behave that way. Clearly I cannot be around him at all at this point."

Leigh nods effusively, "Of course." She starts to eat some of her meal, as does Mia. After a few quiet moments of chewing she asks, "Are you going to tell Sasha?"

Mia squirms in her seat. "I don't know, I hadn't thought about that."

Leigh nods, "Right. I mean, part of me feels like Sasha should know her boyfriend is a fucking creep."

Mia tries to rub the stress out of her jaw and forehead. "Yeah, but I'm not trying to be involved in Danny's life at all at this point. I just want nothing to do with him."

"It's going to be impossible to avoid Sasha, though," Leigh says reasonably.

Mia sighs, "True." She throws her hands up in exasperation, "I don't know. I don't know what I'd say. Like 'hey Sasha, I used to fuck your boyfriend but no one really knows about it and then he dumped me to date you but he's also trying weird shit with me behind your back.'"

Leigh's eyebrows are raised as she nods her head, "Uh,

yeah. You'd say that."

Mia shakes her head at Leigh, "No. It'll just start some kind of drama and make things weird and I'll go back to being some loner without friends."

"I'd still be your friend."

"Well you fucking have to be after last night." Mia grimaces, "Sorry, that was harsh."

Leigh waves it off, "Nope, valid, you have a few more of those left before I think we're even."

Mia laughs, "Okay. But seriously, that kind of conversation will probably find a way to make things worse for me. And I could really do without that right now."

Leigh puts her hands up, as though to admit defeat and nods, "It's your choice. But," she says and Mia tilts her head questioning, "if he continues to be creepy, I would suggest reconsidering it."

"I'll think about that. Hopefully he won't have another opportunity. And anyway, classes are going to start up again soon and we're all gonna be busy, so avoiding Sasha and Danny in social groups won't be that hard." Mia returns to her lunch, noticing Leigh's concerned gaze lingering on her.

"Right. Well I'm sorry your new year didn't really get off

to the greatest start," Leigh says as she finishes up her lunch.

Mia feels a slight flush crawl up the back of her neck, as she remembers the rest of the evening going much more pleasantly. Mia's lie comes out, even as she regrets it, "It's fine, I went right to bed, too much to drink, you know." As she says it, Mia realizes that this may be one of many lies she may end up saying to Leigh, and hopes she can minimize that from happening as much as possible. Eager to redirect Leigh, Mia asks, "But how about you? How was the rest of your night?"

Leigh wiggles her eyebrows at Mia and both women laugh at the insinuation. Mia relaxes, feeling grateful things are smoothed over between the two of them, with only a twinge of regret about her dishonesty.

CHAPTER 39

After returning home from lunch with Leigh, Mia lays around her apartment for some time, finding it hard to muster the motivation to do any sort of work. She scrolls through Instagram and Facebook, liking various photos of others' celebrations. Just as she scrolls past Luke's latest post she suddenly realizes she never heard from him. Mia taps her contacts icon and quickly selects Luke from her favorites for her phone to dial. After four rings she hears a click.

"Hey," Luke's voice is groggy.

Mia glances at the time on her phone, "It's two in the afternoon, am I waking you?"

"It's two in the afternoon after New Year's during my senior year, so yes," Luke grumbles into the phone.

"Well, happy New Year little brother," Mia says sweetly

into the phone.

"Happy New Year," Luke says, the final word interrupted by a yawn. "How was your night?"

"Eh, not great, really bad, and good," Mia rattles off mindlessly. "And you?"

"Uh, very descriptive. Mine was awesome. The party Alex got us into was insane. I legit saw JLo. From really far away. At least, I think it was JLo, it wasn't super well-lit and I was kind of drunk, but I felt like I was in the presence of JLo." Luke's voice perks up and Mia laughs. "We all ended up crashing at Alex's place downtown." Luke's voice grows quieter for a moment, "I didn't tell you, but Matt actually picked me up from the airport when I got back, we even had dinner with his parents."

"Wow, dinner with his parents? I don't even remember the two of you having a date yet?" Mia asks.

"Well," Luke sighs, "he kind of introduced me as a friend. They came to town and we all got dinner together."

"Yikes, Luke, a friend? I thought you said he's out?" Mia's protective concern rises.

"He is, he is. I think it's just that we hadn't really made our thing uh, official, or anything at that point. After that we kind of talked about it and I guess it's official now? Exclusive? Yeah." Luke responds.

"Okay," Mia responds hesitantly. "So his parents know about you? Officially?"

"Um, I don't know?" Luke hedges.

"Luke," Mia says admonishingly.

"It hasn't come up again!" Luke sounds defensive, "I'll circle back to it with him some time. Just chill, Mia."

"Sorry," Mia says warmly, "I love you and worry about you and just want to make sure you're being treated well."

Luke sighs into the phone, "I love you too, and I am. Don't get all crazy just yet. Anyway, what sucked about your night? Did you see that Brett guy?"

Mia breathes in, practically holding her breath as she weighs what she wants to share with her brother. "Well, the good part was seeing Brett. I saw him after my friend's party. The bad part was some stuff with Danny, but it's totally fine."

"Mia," Luke's voice is now the one filled with concern.

"Really, it's fine. He was a creep, but nothing happened, and I am handling it," Mia says trying to reassure both her brother and herself.

"Was Brett at the party?"

"Oh, no, he was flying in from out of town," Mia says

honestly. It also begins to dawn on her that the chance she could ever have Brett over to a party with her friends, even after they're out in the open could be awkward.

"So a New Year's booty call?" Luke coughs uncomfortably into the phone.

"No," Mia says sharply, though Luke's words seem to ring slightly true. "It's not like that, it's, I don't know, I can't get into it."

Luke imitates Mia's tone from earlier, "I love you and worry about you and just want to make sure you're being treated well." Mia doesn't respond and a silence spills across the connection. After a beat she hears Luke sincerely say, "I'm sorry. I *do* care."

"I know," Mia responds tiredly. "This thing with Brett, is kind of complicated, and I don't know how much of it I can really get into it with you."

"Complicated how?" Luke asks.

Mia's brow furrows as she weighs what to share with Luke. On the one hand, he's not here and obviously wouldn't tattle on her, on the other hand, which is what is holding her back, he'll likely reflect back to her all the facts that make her relationship with Brett completely inappropriate.

"Mia?" Luke asks again.

Mia's resolve breaks. She's determined Luke is the *only* person she can safely confide in and not being able to talk with anyone about what's going on will eventually drive her nuts. "Ugh, fine, I'm going to tell you this, but you cannot, and I really mean it, *you cannot* tell anyone."

"Okay," Luke responds slowly, drawing out the initial vowel.

Mia takes a deep breath, "I met Brett a few weeks ago and we'd been on a few dates, and um, really connected. And then kind of um, discovered, that ah, well that he's actually a new professor in my department and I'm taking a class with him this semester." The last words of Mia's explanation rushes out and she winces as she hears it out loud.

"Well, shit," Luke breathes into the phone. "So you're still seeing him? Is that allowed?"

Mia sighs loudly, "Yes and kind of yes and no."

"Mia!" Luke exclaims into the phone, "What does that mean?"

"We are still seeing each other. Kind of, secretly right now? *Which is why I require your discretion,*" she adds firmly. "And it's allowed so long as we alert the dean and um, he's not in any position of power over me." Again, Mia flinches at her admission.

"So, like, being your teacher for a class? That would make it not okay?" Luke presses.

"Correct," Mia says quietly. "Hence the secret part."

"Mia!" Luke exclaims again. Mia rubs her forehead, working out the tension that has built as she shared with her brother. "Look, I'm not going to tell you that you are being dumb-"

"Thanks," Mia interrupts.

"-But don't be dumb. This just feels, I don't know, kind of like a Danny situation all over again. You're dickmatized."

Mia bursts out laughing, "Dickmatized?"

"Ugh yes, you're, ugh, I can't believe I am saying this to you, you get hypnotized by dick." Luke sounds exasperated and grossed out.

Mia giggles, "Come on, Luke."

"You do! You got wrapped up in this Danny stuff, and you two were also just hooking up, and now this guy wants you to sneak around too? So basically sex and no relationship?" Luke takes another breath, "Which if you were just wanting to hook up with someone, fine, that's fine, but you didn't seem to do so well when that happened with Danny, so I worry that this will be the same."

Mia's smile fades from her face as she faces the facts she knew Luke would lay out for her. "I think this is different," she says quietly. "I don't think Danny and I were on the same page. I know we weren't. Cause I wanted more and he never did. But Brett and I have discussed this. We both do want more. It's just that any public aspect of a relationship will have to wait until the semester is over." Luke is quiet on the other end of the line. "It's hard to keep this from everyone I care about. I told you, Luke, because I trust you. I know it doesn't all sound good, but I guess I was hoping you'd support me."

Luke sighs once more into the phone, "I do. Just…just like I said, don't be dumb, Mia."

"Yeah, alright," Mia replies, feeling dejected.

"Just keep me posted?" Luke says, sounding kinder.

"Yeah," Mia says, sounding defeated. "Well, go tell everyone I wish them a happy New Year,"

"Will do, I guess we'll talk later, bye Mia," Luke responds.

"Bye." Mia hangs up and stares at her phone. Luke pointed out her exact concerns that this scenario is going to repeat of last spring. *But that's not the case*, she reminds herself, *Brett and I have actually discussed this. We don't want to sneak around. This is temporary.* Mia absently scratches Renly's head. Her emotions swirling and the tension she feels preventing her from focusing on much. Instead, she sinks deeper into the couch and turns on the TV to avoid having to think or feel much more.

CHAPTER 40

The next day Mia awakens with more resolve to focus and get work done. With classwork completely out of the way for the brief time being, she gets back to reading in the morning for her thesis and writing in the afternoon. Her work is only interrupted a few times by a couple of text messages. One from Brett, asking her over for dinner later that week, and another from Luke, reminding her that he loves her and to be careful.

See, Mia reassures herself with Brett's text, *we're doing date-like stuff, even if it is in private. He could only be texting me at ten pm to come over and then we'd be in booty call territory. This is not like Danny.* Mia shakes herself a bit. Luke's text message also felt like an olive branch after yesterday's conversation. While it didn't go the way Mia hoped, at least her brother reached back out. Mia texts both men back, thanking her brother for his concern and promising to make smart decisions, and confirming a date with Brett the next night.

By late afternoon, Mia's eyes begin to burn from staring at her laptop for so long. She saves her work and pushes away from her desk, ready for a break. She heads into her kitchen, rummaging around cabinets and the refrigerator, trying to determine what to have for dinner. She reluctantly settles on a frozen pizza, and scrolls through the news on her phone as she waits for the oven to preheat.

Mia's attention is broken by a knock at her door. Feeling confused, as she is not expecting anyone, she walks over and peers through the peephole. To her dismay she sees Danny standing out there.

"Go away," she shouts through the door.

"I just came to apologize," Danny calls back.

"Don't. Just go." Mia insists.

"I'm really sorry. I just came to say that."

"For what? Being an asshole last spring? Being an asshole the night you kissed me? Being an asshole the other night when you grabbed me? Go away." Mia's heart starts to pound.

"All of it. I'm really sorry. You know me. You know I'm not that guy. Really, Mia. I'm sorry. I'm not trying to hurt you."

"Noted. You can go away now."

"Mia, I do want to be friends. Could we try?" Danny's voice sounds more desperate behind the door. "Can I come in and we can talk?"

"No, Danny. Seriously, I want you to go. I don't want to be friends. We were never really friends." Mia holds her phone close to her, starting to feel anxious and wondering if she needs to do something more to get him to leave. Calling the police seems almost excessive, he's not trying to barge in. She can't call Brett right now, as that would potentially complicate this more. Mia's not even sure if calling Leigh would help. She hears Danny rest his head against the door.

"Mia, I'm sorry, I just want everything to be cool between us," Danny says. "And um, I was hoping you wouldn't say anything to Sasha about the other night. I mean, we both had had a few drinks-"

Mia feels her temper surge. "We? *WE? I* did nothing, *you* grabbed me in your car. *Twice.*" Mia takes a deep breath and tries to steady her voice. "You need to leave now, or I will tell Sasha."

"Oh, so now you're going to hold this over me?" Danny's voice sounds darker. "She wouldn't believe you over me. Why would she? You'll just come off as some jealous, lonely, slut." His last words spit out at her.

"Fuck off, Danny," Mia says through her teeth.

"Whatever," Danny laughs at the door, "fuck you too. And the guy who came to fuck you after I dropped you off? He'll fucking figure you out too. Just an easy fuck."

Mia's heart drops to her stomach. *He was watching my place after I went in*, she realizes with alarm. Mia tries to hold her voice steady, "For the last time, Danny, leave."

"Already gone, bitch," Danny shouts. Mia peers through the peephole again to see Danny walking away and towards the steps to lead him out to the parking lot. After he disappears from that view she runs over to her office window, where she can see the parking lot. She watches to makes sure he climbs into his car and drives off.

Mia lets go of the breath she hadn't realized she was holding. She notices she is shaking and slowly lowers herself to the floor. She feels like she should call someone, but is unsure who. Danny's comment about Brett terrified her that Danny was *watching* her place the other night. And having Brett over could potentially expose their relationship. Calling Luke, or her parents, would just freak them out. Finally deciding, Mia clicks on her phone and sends a quick text to Leigh.

Can you come over? Kind of an emergency.

Leigh's response arrives in seconds. **On my way.**

CHAPTER 41

Leigh's mouth hangs open, her eyes wide in shock, as Mia finishes recalling her encounter with Danny. She did leave out the small detail about Brett, but kept the rest of the events intact.

"Holy shit, Mia," Leigh breathes out, finally leaning back on the couch.

"Yeah," Mia looks down at her hands, which have finally stopped trembling.

"That's not cool, you know that right?" Leigh gently reaches out and touches Mia's arm.

"Yeah, I know," she replies.

"Do you feel safe here? Did you need to call the police? You can if you need to, you know that?" Leigh shakes her head in disbelief.

"I think I'm okay. I didn't think I needed to escalate at the time by calling the police. But maybe…" Mia trails off, unsure of what to say.

"Maybe if he ever comes here again you just go ahead and call." Leigh insists.

"For what? It's not like he was trying to break down my door." Mia asks, feeling exasperated.

"I don't know, for stalking or harassment or something? But like make the fucking call," Leigh stares at Mia intently. "Seriously, that's fucking scary and needs to be stopped."

Mia nods, "Yeah, yeah, I know." She pauses and nods again with more certainty, "You're right, I'll call if it happens again. I don't think it will. I think maybe I scared him off with the idea I'd tell Sasha."

Leigh shrugs, "Maybe, but it definitely made him mad. Just, avoid him if you can, you know?"

Mia laughs uncomfortably, "Obviously."

"Are you sure you feel safe here tonight?" Leigh asks again.

Mia nods, "Yeah, I don't think…I just can't see Danny doing something like that. He got mad, he said some shitty stuff, but again, he wasn't trying to knock down my door and come after me. I'll be fine."

Leigh appears mildly placated. "Well, how about I stay for a while? We order in some food?"

Mia nods, glancing at the kitchen, where her frozen pizza managed to sit out and melt during all of this.

"Good, Thai sound good?" Leigh asks, then catches Mia's glance at the pathetic melted pizza, "Or pizza?"

"Thai's fine," Mia says with a smile, and writes down her order for Leigh as Leigh calls in their dinner.

A few glasses of wine, a full stomach, and two light hearted movies later with Leigh, Mia feels much more at ease than she had earlier.

As Mia gets up to stretch, and then collect Leigh's empty glass, she says, "Thank you again for coming tonight."

Leigh waves her off, "I would do it again in a heartbeat. Seriously, maybe if he ever shows up again, call me sooner and I'll bring Jake with me and a baseball bat."

Mia laughs at her friend's brashness. "Hopefully it never comes to that and you being arrested for assault." Leigh shrugs and gets up, helping herself to a glass of water in Mia's kitchen.

"It is getting kind of late now," Leigh says as she glances at the clock on the stove, "if it's okay with you, I'm gonna head home."

Mia nods, "Of course. I will be fine." Leigh tilts her head as if to double check. Mia smiles at her, "Seriously. I feel a lot better, I just got really shook up, but I am good. Thank you for coming over. Go home." Leigh nods and gathers up her things, giving Mia a quick hug goodbye before darting out door and heading to her car. Mia locks up after Leigh leaves and flops on her couch.

Double checking the time herself, Mia realizes it is late. *It's probably pretty inappropriate to text Brett now*, she thinks, knowing that her asking him over at this point would lead to sex and only sex. Her thoughts swirl around each other as she tries to fight off lingering the accusation from Danny and the words of concern from Luke. What she really wants in this very moment, to be having sex with Brett right now, seems to almost make those earlier comments truer than she'd like them to be.

Instead, Mia washes her face, brushes her teeth, changes into her pajamas and crawls into her bed. Renly hops up and snuggles in beside her, kneading the blanket and purring. Mia wraps an arm around the cat and closes her eyes, reminding herself that the next day can only be better than today.

CHAPTER 42

Just as she'd hoped, Mia's next day was calmer and less eventful. She focused on her thesis writing and otherwise took various breaks when she felt drained from the work. Mia felt like this day was also easier knowing that she'll be with Brett later, *and not just for sex*, she reminds herself. Remembering that, she sends him a quick text to see if she can bring anything over for dinner.

Nope, just you. Can't wait to see you. Brett replies. Mia smiles and sends back a thumbs up emoji. Plugging her phone in to charge, Mia heads back to her bathroom to shower and get ready. As she bathes, working the shampoo into and then out of her hair, Mia lets her mind wander to Brett's body. Her nipples harden as she pictures him, chiseled and naked, his cock thick and ready. She feels a slow burn humming in her body and lets her fingers slip down to her clitoris. She begins to rub herself, gently at first, and more vigorously as she imagines having Brett's mouth on her neck, his erection pressing against her body.

A sudden crash from outside the shower curtain leads to Mia shrieking and her pulling back the curtain to see Renly sheepishly righting himself amongst a pile of fallen makeup supplies. Renly glares back at Mia and walks out of the bathroom, no longer ashamed. Mia pulls the curtain closed again and with renewed focus, finishes washing her hair.

After getting out of the shower and blow drying her hair, Mia heads back to her bedroom and closet and begins rifling through her clothes. Feeling self-conscious of her lack of willpower around him, Mia turns away from the dresses in her closet and quickly selects clothing that will take more effort to remove. A simple green sweater and form fitting jeans, along with a pair of black ankle boots. While she purposefully picked an outfit to keep her clothes on, Mia allows herself to select underwear that's meant to be seen. A lacy black thong and a matching bra that barely contains her breasts, Mia adjusts herself carefully once her sweater is on, reminding herself that too much movement will jostle her breasts free of the balconette. Lastly, Mia stops back into the bathroom to apply some coverup, blush, and eyeliner. She dabs some perfume on her wrists and neck and views herself once more in the mirror.

Feeling confident and sexy, Mia leaves the bathroom and grabs her coat, phone, and purse and heads out of the apartment. She carefully locks the front door and does a quick scan around. While she doesn't feel unsafe per se, she reassures herself that there's no car in the parking lot that looks like Danny's before she makes her way down to her own car. The drive to Brett's is easy and Mia feels herself growing more eager to see him. Once there, she parks in the front and rings his doorbell.

Brett swings the door open after a beat and grins at her, "Come in!" He steps back to make way for Mia and she follows him in. "Let me take your jacket," he says, reaching for it as Mia tugs it off. He goes to hang it up in the closet by the front door as Mia makes her way to the kitchen.

"Smells good. What is it this time?" She calls out as Brett approaches.

"Well, I kind of cheated, I didn't cook." Brett smiles slyly, "I ordered chicken picatta from a local place, it's just staying warm in the oven."

"It's still dinner, so it works for me," Mia turns to face him and smiles. "Thanks so much for this."

"Well I already have some salad and bread out on the table, do you want to start with that?" Brett asks, gesturing to the table.

"Absolutely!" Mia makes her way to table and grabs a seat, as Brett sits across from her. He already had wine and water poured for each of them.

"You look gorgeous by the way," Brett says as he lifts his wine glass to toast.

Mia grins at him, "You're not bad looking yourself," as she clinks her glass to his. Brett grins back at her.

As they break into the salad and bread, Brett asks, "So what have you been up to?"

"Ah, mostly trying to get some work done. Leigh came over and hung out a bit last night," Mia replied, uncertain of how much she wanted to share with Brett about Danny. Given Danny's comment indicating he was watching her apartment the night he dropped her off, she worries about scaring off Brett.

"How's the thesis coming along?" asks Brett, breaking into Mia's thoughts.

"Good, good. I think I'll get another draft to my advisor before classes start. At least, that's my goal. What about you? What have you been up to?"

Brett winks at her, "Mostly prepping for my class. And also revising a few papers for resubmits. And writing a new draft to make my dissertation publishable."

Mia nods, "So you've been plenty busy." Brett nods back as he eats his food. "So how are you feeling about the class?" she asks carefully.

"Well I feel great about teaching it," Brett says, "but definitely nervous about having you in there. I'm worried I'm going to be overthinking how to behave in there with you."

Mia laughs, "Yeah, tell me about it." Brett smiles sheepishly. "I mean, I've never really been one to fantasize about my teachers, but knowing exactly what I know about you, definitely will be hard to not daydream." Mia winks at him.

Brett coughs and takes a swig of his water. "Yep. I'm worried this will be a There's Something About Mary situation and I'll have to make sure not to go in with a loaded gun every time."

Mia throws back her head to laugh, "Well, you know how that went. Just uh, make sure you have a tissue?" Brett laughs with her. "I'd offer my services, but that would be strictly against the rules."

Brett licks his lips and smiles at her, "Yeah, it would be." Mia's thoughts briefly flash to the last time they were in his office and her cheeks begin to flush with the memory.

"Um, anyway-" she starts.

"So tell me-" Brett also begins at the same time. Mia closes her mouth and motions for him to continue. "So tell me how Texas was with your family." Brett clears off their salad bowls and comes back from the kitchen with plates heaping with pasta and chicken.

"Wow, this looks delicious. You should cheat more often. I mean, like, pretend to make dinner and bring something in." Mia giggles. Brett smiles at her as he sits back down. "Texas was alright. It's still a little weird sometimes with each of my parents." Mia shrugs, "It is what it is. Luckily Luke was there, so it helped to smooth over any awkwardness. I do feel kind of guilty at times, being so far, and I guess unavailable to all of them."

Brett nods as he eats. "Makes sense. It sounds like it's been a tough adjustment for everyone since your parents divorced."

Mia looks down at her plate, "Yeah, I guess so."

Brett clears his throat, "Sorry, didn't mean to be a downer."

"No, you're not. How about you? How was your Christmas? And Las Vegas?"

"Home was pretty good. Nice to see my parents, my niece and nephew. It was great to be out in Vegas. Last time I was there was, um, a bachelor party, and this time felt much more laid back." Brett shifts around in his chair.

"Sounds like it was a good break for you," Mia says.

"For the most part, yeah, it was," Brett smiles.

“Some of it wasn’t?” Mia asks.

“Ah no, it was fine,” Brett says.

Mia eats more of her dinner and starts to push her food around her plate, wondering if she needs to tell Brett about the latest with Danny. She takes a sip of her wine, watching Brett as he eats. He stops and watches her. “Do you not like it?”

“No, no, I do, it’s delicious. Um, I figure you should know that Danny came around my place.” Mia says hesitantly.

Brett puts his fork down, his attention now focused fully on Mia. “What happened?”

“Nothing really, he just yelled some mean shit from the other side of the door when I said I wanted him to go away and didn’t want to be friends.” Mia takes another sip of her wine.

“Did he threaten you?” Brett’s voice deepens.

“Not really, not like, physically, if that’s what you’re asking. Just like, I shouldn’t tell his girlfriend, which I wasn’t planning on doing anyway, there’s too much there and I’m not trying to have any drama.” Brett’s brow furrows as Mia speaks. “I guess the most important thing you really need to know is that he apparently saw you come into my apartment on New Year’s.” Mia quickly adds, "He doesn't know who you are or anything, he just mentioned having seen a guy come into my place."

"So he was watching your apartment?" Brett asks alarmed. Mia shrugs and nods at the same time.

"I'm really sorry, I don't think he knows who you are, but I figured you should know," Mia says quietly.

"I'm not worried about him seeing me, I'm worried that this guy is threatening you and watching your apartment. Does that not concern you?" Brett's face is scrunched up and he reaches a hand out to touch Mia's.

"To a point, sure, but I don't think he'd do anything," Mia tries to say reassuringly.

"Why didn't you call me?" Brett asks. "I would have come over and helped."

Mia shakes her head, "I guess I thought having you suddenly show up would make it worse, or I don't know, it would be too much exposure for us, and it just didn't feel like a smart idea at the time, I don't know, it was hard to think in the moment."

Brett sighs, "Next time call me."

"Okay," Mia responds. "I mean, next time I might call the cops if he shows up at my place again like that."

Brett nods, "Fine, call the police and then call me."

Mia nods again, "Okay, I will."

"Good." Brett wipes his mouth with his napkin, "I think I'm done, how about you?" Brett grabs his plate and Mia's as she agrees with him. After dropping the plates off in the kitchen he comes back to the table and holds a hand out for Mia, which she takes and he helps her up. Brett pulls Mia in for a hug and strokes her back. Mia wraps her arms around him and he kisses the top of her head.

Mia lifts her head up and Brett kisses her as she intended. Mia runs her hands up Brett's back and into his hair. Brett drops one hand to cup Mia's butt, bringing her hips closer to his. Mia's kisses become hungrier and Brett's hands begin to roam to the side of her body, moving up from her hips to the side of her breasts. Brett reaches one hand under her green sweater and strokes across one breast, immediately popping a breast out of the tiny cup of her bra. He gently nibbles on Mia's lower lip as he strokes a finger across her freed nipple, feeling it harden under his touch. Mia catches her breath and takes a step back, breaking their embrace.

"Sorry, I…I purposely dressed to make it harder to have sex, and I totally regret that right now." Mia blushes.

Brett raises an eyebrow and smiles devilishly. "You wanted to make me work for it tonight?"

Mia giggles, "No, I wanted to have a date that maybe

ended in sex, rather than a strictly hook up only night."

"If you have dinner and spend the night, does that count as more than a hook up?" Brett murmurs as he steps in towards Mia, gently brushing one hand over her still hard nipple.

Mia bites her lower lip and feels butterflies in her stomach, "Probably need some conversation in there too," she whispers.

Brett lowers his mouth to her ear, saying, "We did talk. And we can talk some more after," before he kisses along her neck. Mia drops her head back, letting Brett kiss down her neck and across her throat. His hands are back on her waist, this time guiding her to his couch. Brett breaks his kiss to sit down on the couch and pull Mia towards him. Mia straddles his lap and leans down to kiss Brett, her tongue slowly playing with his. Brett places one hand on her waist again, and the other back under her sweater, groping her free breast and squeezing her nipple. Mia rocks on Brett's lap, feeling the lace of her thong gently rub against her clit. Brett pulls his hand back out and pulls Mia's sweater off over her head. His eyes widen as he takes in her bra.

"This was supposed to make it harder to have sex?" He asks incredulously.

"The jeans were the deterrent, the bra was…" Mia trails off as Brett runs his hand over her cupped breast, gently squeezing it out of the bra. He takes the newly freed breast into his mouth and starts to gently suck on her nipple, while fondling the other breast. Mia moans and rocks again against Brett.

"Can we do something about the jeans?" Brett asks, his eyes bright.

Mia nods, clambering off Brett, and slowly peels her tight jeans off. At the same time, Brett pulls his shirt over his head and swiftly removes his own pants, revealing his large erection barely encased in his boxer briefs. Mia pushes Brett's legs apart and kneels down between them. She has a glint in her eyes and licks her lips. "Take off your briefs." Brett quickly complies, kicking them to the side, and exposing his throbbing cock. Mia grasps his manhood with one hand, and slowly licks him from the base to the tip, maintaining eye contact with Brett the whole time. With her mouth hovering at the tip of his penis, Mia flicks her tongue at the tip a few times, before opening wide and placing his cock in her mouth. Mia sucks and pumps with her hand, slowly, gripping Brett's leg with her other hand. She feels Brett's hands in her hair, resting in there, occasionally clenching as he moans. A few more pumps and Mia feels Brett pull her up. She lets him drop out of her mouth and she stands up. Brett grabs her by the ass and pulls her close. Mia goes to remove her thong.

Brett shakes his head, "Leave it on." He pulls her closer

and Mia climbs back on him, with only a thing piece of lace separating the two of them. Brett buries his face in her chest and Mia shifts her hips back and forth over Brett. Excitement builds in Mia and she doesn't want to wait much longer.

"Condom?" She breaths out.

Brett is dazed and takes a beat, "Um, shit, upstairs."

Mia shakes her head and leans down and whispers, "Just pull out."

Brett nods and he slips a hand between the two of them, moving the lace of her thong to the side. Mia, feeling the new skin to skin sensation moans. "Fuck, you are wet," Brett whispers. He rubs his fingers along Mia and brings them out to his lips, licking them. He grabs Mia's hips and urge them forward, lifting her slightly. Mia hovers briefly over his thick erection, before lower herself down slowly. "This feels so fucking good," Brett says huskily, his mouth kissing and sucking along Mia's neck. Mia moans in agreement, slowly riding Brett. His hands move across her ass, her hips, and her breasts. His lips find their way to her nipples and mouth. Brett urges Mia faster with his hands on her hips. She tries to move quicker, her breasts rocking outside of their cups.

Brett lifts Mia off of him, and taking her hand, guides her to the armrest of the couch. He turns her to face away from him, as he kisses her neck and ear, strokes her breasts and gently rubs her clit. "Bend over," he whispers. Mia complies, her hands resting on the armrest, her legs slightly spread. She feels Brett stroke her ass, and trace the sides of her thong. He reaches around and rubs her clit and Mia moans. She feels Brett's erection rub against her opening and then plunge inside her. Mia cries out in pleasure, enjoying the sensation. Brett grasps Mia's hips, pumping steadily. Mia frees a hand from the couch and rubs her clitoris, more vigorously as Brett's pace increases.

Brett moans from behind her, "You feel so good."

Mia gasps and moans, "Harder." Brett's pumping quickens more, his pumping turning more into pounding, and Mia moans, "Fuck yes, fuck yes. Fuck me harder." Brett grunts and continues, and Mia feels a sharp sting on her ass as he slaps it and then rubs the cheek. Mia moans again, and feels the rising pressure of an orgasm. "Don't stop," she gasps out. Brett continues to fuck her, occasionally moaning, and whispering how good she feels. "Fuck me," she cries again as tension mounts. Brett slaps her ass again, and Mia's orgasm erupts. She cries out and feels Brett pull out and a hot splash hit her ass.

"Fuck," she hears hoarsely behind her. More calmly, "Wait a second." Brett pads away and when he comes back, she feels a tissue wiping his semen off of her. He gently slaps her butt. "All clear."

Mia turns around and admires Brett, and eyeing his still

hard cock. She grabs him and kisses him.

"I uh, hope that was okay?" Brett asks sheepishly.

"Yeah, that was great," Mia assures him. Brett grins and pulls Mia close to him, kissing her on the mouth roughly.

He pulls away and whispers in her ear, "You feel like fucking heaven."

Mia giggles as her heart skips, and kisses Brett's neck, breathing in his familiar orange scent, "Thank you."

CHAPTER 43

A little while later, Mia finds herself lounging in one of Brett's shirts while they're curled up on the couch, watching the latest movie edited for TV on TBS. She's comfortably settled against him, her legs under her and his arm around her. Brett occasionally strokes her hair, twirling a strand between his fingers as they both laugh at the perfectly timed punch lines. As the credits begin to roll, Mia pushes herself up and shakes her hair back from her face.

"So how about that promised conversation?" She asks with a smile and a wink.

Brett laughs, "Alright, what do you want to talk about?"

"Well, you know about my most recent ex and the obvious mess it has become. What about you?" She asks innocently.

"What do you mean? Are you asking for a full accounting?" Brett responds hesitantly.

Mia shakes her head, "No, not that. You just previously mentioned an ex, and I don't know…I guess I was curious as to what happened." Mia pauses and watches Brett's face as he keeps it neutral. "But if you're not comfortable talking about it..." Mia trails off.

Brett shrugs. "I'm not sure there's much to say about it. Emily and I, that's my most recent ex, were together for a while. We grew apart during grad school, and she ended up cheating on me, so we broke up." Brett shrugs again.

"I'm sorry," Mia says comfortingly. "Grad school can definitely strain relationships."

"I guess," Brett says as he leans back and runs a hand through his hair, "though I don't think that excuses her behavior."

Mia moves her hand to her chest defensively, "Oh, of course not. I never meant that. I just meant that grad school requires a lot of time and energy and sometimes not everyone gets that."

Brett nods, "Yeah, we uh, had been together since college," he glances at Mia who has filed away that information to agonize over later, "and she went to work and I kept going to school. And I think our paths just kind of diverged from there. Her work day would end, and mine wouldn't. She'd go socialize with friends and colleagues and I…I guess where I failed is that I was determined to be on a certain path professionally, and that meant sacrificing time with her." Mia nods sympathetically. Brett sighs and shrugs again, "Anyway, she hooked up with a coworker and we tried to make it work after that, but I don't think either of us were really trying at that point."

Mia's forehead furrows, "That's a really long time to be with someone and then let them go. That's got to be tough."

Brett shifts around uncomfortably, "Yeah, well, it is what it is. And then I moved down here, so it allowed more of a clean break." He pauses and gestures to a photo on the shelf, "That's actually who Tyrion is with." Mia is confused for the moment and glances in the direction of Brett's hand, her eyes landing on a picture of his cat. "I guess you could say Emily and I share custody of him? We got him together when we graduated from college. She has him now, but we're going to switch off in a few more months." Brett falls silent, waiting for Mia to say something. Eventually he touches her shoulder, brushing her hair to the side. "Was that too much?"

Mia gives him a slight smile, "No, I appreciate your honesty. I mean, hell, I've told you about my last relationship and it's more scandalous than your college sweetheart breaking your heart." She pauses and rubs the tension out of her neck, then looks back up at Brett. "I guess I'm just feeling very aware that you're coming out of a serious long term relationship."

Brett gently strokes her arm, "It was over before it was officially over. And would it help if I said there may have been a Tindr hookup or two before meeting you?"

Mia laughs at his goofy smile, "I don't know. I don't need to know." Mia shifts again on the couch, grabbing Brett's free hand, "Well, thank you for telling me."

"So you got your conversation?" He asks with a raised eyebrow.

Mia playfully sticks out her tongue, "I got a conversation, yes."

Brett leans in and gives her a kiss, "Good, then let's go to sleep.

While nestled up to Brett, whose steady breathing suggests he is asleep, one arm thrown over his chest and another under the pillow, Mia sighs out. Finally feeling like she has a moment to think, she starts to work through what Brett shared. She tries to estimate just how long his relationship was, with the short end being five years and the long one being nine years. *If he was with someone for all of college and all of graduate school, he could be trying to make up for lost time. Sow wild oats or whatever,* Mia frets. *Or,* her rational side chimes in, *he's serious about monogamy and he's not a wild oat sower.* She feels the pull between the thoughts, trying to find a middle ground. Mia shifts in the bed, extracting herself from Brett, a new line of worry occurring to her. *Oh my god here I've had hookup after hookup and he's just had this really long relationship for most of his adult life, he must think I'm some kind of slut.* Mia curls up, facing away from Brett. She feels him move behind her, scooting up next to her, wrapping an arm around her and holding her close to him. Mia closes her eyes and breaths out to let herself relax into the cuddle, telling herself to worry later and sleep now.

CHAPTER 44

Mia wakes the next morning, blinking into the sunlight escaping between the slats of the window blinds. Brett is propped up against his headboard, scrolling through his phone, which he clicks off as he sees her stir.

"Morning," he says and smiles. Mia throws an arm over her face. "Or not?"

She pulls her arm back down and rubs the sleep out of her eyes, "G'morning."

"Would you like some eggs for breakfast, since you don't like coffee?" Brett says. Mia makes a face at the word 'coffee.'

Mia stretches and yawns, "That'd be awesome."

Brett nods, "I'm going to shower and then start that." He gives Mia a quick kiss on the cheek and makes his way to his bathroom. Mia stretches again and throws the covers off as she hears the water in the bathroom running and the sound of the shower curtain opening and closing. Mia pulls off the shirt and shorts she borrowed from Brett and walks to the bathroom.

She knocks as she enters, hoping to not startle Brett. "Hey?" he calls from behind the curtain.

Mia pokes her head into the shower, enjoying the view of Brett's backside. As she speaks, he turns his neck to peek at her, "Okay if I hop in?" Brett grins and motions for her to come in.

Mia climbs into the shower and Brett moves back, allowing her to come under the hot spray. As she closes her eyes and lets the water run down her hair, she feels Brett take a washcloth and start to rub down her shoulders and back. Mia notices the light aroma of oranges again and opens her eyes, finally spotting the source of Brett's ever-present scent. A bottle of body wash sits on the edge of his bathroom tub, one she recognizes as a more feminine brand. She quickly leans down and picks it up, waving it with a smile as she glances over her shoulder at Brett.

"Now I know why you always smell so good," Mia grins.

Brett chuckles, "I guess you've discovered my secret." Mia turns back to face the shower head again, placing the bottle back in its place. She moves to turn around and start talking to Brett again, but his lips on her neck stop her. He lowers one hand to cup her breast while his other hand finds Mia's small patch of pubic hair. One of his fingers finds her clit and he begins a slow circular motion with his finger. Mia's lost her train of thought and leans against Brett's chest and she moans quietly. He kisses along her shoulder, giving small nips along the way, and slides a finger into her. Mia shudders under the hot water and Brett presses forward, sliding another finger into her, slowly sliding in and out of her. Mia's nipples harden and she braces herself against the shower wall with one hand.

Brett pulls his fingers out, and turns Mia around to face him. His face is determined and Mia throws her arms around him, pulling his face down to hers, kissing him. Brett grabs Mia's waist and pulls her into him, and she feels his slick body against hers, his erection hard against her stomach. Brett's hands roam over Mia's soaked body and he squeezes an ass cheek.

Mia's worries from the night before have disappeared under the steam and the sensation of Brett's body against hers. As they break apart from a kiss, she breathes out quietly, "I need you in me." Brett nods and he guides Mia to turn and face the shower wall. Mia spreads out her legs and places both hands against the tile. Mia drops her head down, as the hot water hits her side, and she feels Brett position himself behind her. He leans down and kisses her neck, before nibbling on her ear. "Ready?" he whispers to her.

Mia nods, adding a whispered "Yes," barely audible over the running water. Brett enters her slowly and then places one hand next to Mia's on the tile. The other hand on her hip, Brett begins to steadily thrust into Mia. Mia's breasts bounce with each plunge of Bret's cock and she moans. Brett goes back to playing with Mia' clitoris and she sucks in the air at the sensation. Brett's thrusting speeds up and his fingers on her clit move apace. Mia moans again, feeling her legs begin to weaken as the heat within her grows. The water splashes off of them from the shower head and from the contact between their bodies. Mia moves to encourage Brett's pace, her cries becoming louder, her 'yeses' becoming less clear. She comes suddenly, crying out, trying to clutch at the smooth tile. Brett continues to pump, sucking and nibbling on her neck as she orgasms. Mia's tremors weaken and subside, as Brett's pace increases more and he suddenly pulls out, and she hears a quiet drawn out, "fuck" from behind her, as he ejaculates into the downward stream of the shower. Mia turns back around to face Brett, who immediately cups her face with his hands and kisses her intensely, both panting as they break apart. Brett glides a finger over a sensitive nipple and Mia shudders again, the feeling sending aftershocks through her.

Mia steps back, allowing herself to land fully under the stream of water and pushes her hair back and smiles. She turns back around, allowing the falling water to rinse off the body wash from earlier. Brett chuckles from behind her, "Who needs coffee right?"

Mia laughs and they each take turns finishing up under the pelting water. Brett shuts the shower off and grabs the closest towel to hand to Mia before grabbing the other for himself. Mia wraps herself up and steps out of the shower, with Brett trailing behind her. He watches as she dries off her body and then wraps the towel around her hair, leaving her naked under his gaze.

"I could go for a round two, but don't know how much you want breakfast right now," he practically growls. Mia smirks and pulls off the towel that Brett has wrapped around his waist. Settling onto her knees in front of him, she begins to stroke his penis, and it quickly hardens under her touch. Wasting no time, Mia takes him into her mouth, doing her best to suck him from tip to base. She pumps her hand that's wrapped around his cock, and moves her head back and forth quickly, and feels the towel fall off and Brett's fingers entangle in her hair. He moans, and moans again more audibly, "I'm going to come." Mia persists and feels Brett's fingers pull a little in her hair. She hears him again, as if a warning, "I'm going to come," he gasps, as her mouth is suddenly filled with his hot seed, quickly swallowing down as he orgasms. Mia lets him drop from her mouth and wipes her mouth. Brett pulls her up to face him and draws his thumb over her mouth before kissing her again.

"Now breakfast," Mia says with a satisfied smile when they break apart.

CHAPTER 45

After finishing off breakfast, and mutual promises of seeing one another before the new semester starts, Mia finds herself back in her apartment. She's alone with the exception of Renly, who only briefly acknowledged her return before resettling in his box in her office. Mia's changed out of her outfit from the night before, everything now tossed into her hamper, and comfortably settled into sweats in front of her laptop.

Determined to work on the most recent revision from Dr. Thompson, Mia sets to work. She works with the hard copy of notes from her advisor next to her computer, as she also sifts through various articles she has printed or saved on her laptop. She keeps an eye on the time, pushing herself to work for two hours before she allows herself a break, her eyes burning from the screen and the small print.

Mia's short break involves more screens, an irony she

notes to herself, as she quickly scrolls through Instagram. She has another thought and pulls up Facebook and goes to type *Emily* in the search bar, before realizing she has no clue what Brett's ex's last name is. Mia shakes her head, admonishing herself. *What were you going to do?* She asks herself, *internet stalk her?* Mia's already answering the question in her mind, a version of her vigorously nodding her head, eager for more information. Her fingers hover over the keyboard, wanting to know more. She types in *Brett Dawson Pennsylvania* and begins to scroll through the profiles. None of the thumbnails seem to show the one she knows, and the list keeps autofilling as she scrolls down. Mia lets out a frustrated sigh. She navigates the webpage to Google and types in *Brett Dawson Emily* and scrolls through, mainly finding LinkedIn profiles and a fan-generated Wiki for a network TV show.

"Whatever," Mia grumbles, frustrated with her inability to learn more about Brett and his ex. She struggles to pinpoint why she's trying to discover something. *It's not discover something, like there's anything to hide, it's just to know more. I feel like I have so much more of a past than him,* Mia reasons with herself. Despite being alone, Mia shifts in her seat self-consciously. Her worries about her history compared to Brett's rise again, now that she's alone without a distraction. She doesn't feel judged by him, but her own judgement starts to weigh heavily.

Mia pushes back from the computer, and rolls her eyes. *Why should I judge myself? I've had some bad taste in guys, but it's perfectly fine for me to have sex with whoever I want to have sex with.* Mia goes into the kitchen, needing a break from her abysmal detective work, and searches in her refrigerator for something to eat. She settles on making a peanut butter sandwich along with an apple, and crashes in front of the TV, allowing herself one sitcom before returning to her actual work.

Mia's next few days continue to follow a similar routine. While she dropped her effort to try and internet stalk Brett or his ex, she focuses on her drafts, with brief breaks to eat, watch a show, or text with Leigh or Brett.

As the start date for the new semester approaches, Mia finishes her latest edits on her thesis draft and sends it to her advisor, reaching her goal of turning it in by the first day back. She texts Leigh and Brett each, excited to share the news. While her phone buzzes to indicate someone has replied back to her, Mia quickly scrolls through her new emails and her stomach drops.

An invitation to her department's back-to-school dinner sits at the top of her unread emails. Mia's stomach turns a little, as she opens and reads through the invitation that she's already familiar with from years past. Each year the chair of the entire psychology department hosts a dinner at the beginning of the fall and spring semesters. The former to welcome new students and encourage them to get to know older students and faculty, the latter a feeble attempt at reconnection over the course of the short winter break. This dinner, Mia realizes, marks the beginning of where her relationship with Brett truly becomes dicey. She feels nervous thinking about them being in the same place, having to act as though they are not intimately familiar with one another, having to pretend like she doesn't want to rip off his clothes, or having to breathe like normal even though her heart races around him.

Mia sighs loudly, and clicks the *yes* button on the invitation to indicate her RSVP. She grabs her phone and sees the text from Leigh first.

Congrats! A celebratory drink? Downtown tonight?

Mia feels some stress lift just at the thought of hanging out with her friend and immediately confirms the plans with Leigh. The second text she scrolls to is from Brett.

Great news! How about one last dinner and sleepover before shit gets real? Brett's text contains a screenshot of the dinner invitation. Mia smiles sadly at her phone.

I can't do dinner tonight, tomorrow? She sends, though that would mean waking up next to Brett in the morning and then seeing him at the department dinner that evening.

Brett's response is quick, **Can't tomorrow, meeting with my own mentor.**

Mia pushes aside the start of a judgmental thought and texts back, **Are you willing to come over late tonight? I'm getting drinks with a friend, but you could come stay after?**

If you're ok with that, than I am too. Brett replies.

K, I'll text when I'm on my way home. I'll try not to be too late. Mia types out and sends.

I'll be up. Brett's text includes an eggplant emoji and a winking face, and Mia laughs out loud.

Perfect, she replies.

Mia lets herself relax the rest of the afternoon, before making a plain dinner out of a frozen meal and getting ready to go out and have a drink with Leigh. After eating, she showers and dries her hair before carefully applying her makeup in the bathroom mirror. Back in her room and searching through her closet, her skin gets goosebumps as her fingers skim past the green sweater, now clean and hanging up, she last wore when she saw Brett. Instead, Mia pulls out a wine red blouse and lays it out on her bed with a pair of black jeans. She catches a glimpse of herself, still in her towel, in the full length mirror that hangs on the door to her closet. Impulsively, she grabs her phone and drops her towel to the floor. Holding one arm over her breasts, she takes a quick picture of herself in the mirror, torso up, and her breasts bulging out around her arm. She looks over it quickly, making sure she's not blinking or blurry, and sends it to Brett before she thinks twice about it. Mia then quickly gets dressed and hangs up her towel in the bathroom.

When she returns from the bathroom, Brett's response is flashing from her phone. **Can't wait to see you later, too**. Mia smiles, grabs her coat and purse and heads out to meet Leigh at Callahan's.

CHAPTER 46

After few watered-down mixed drinks each, Mia and Leigh continue to laugh and reminisce at the time they went speed dating during their first year.

"No, the worst was the guy from the math department who kept trying to play footsie for the full five minutes," Leigh insists.

Mia holds her hands up, admitting defeat, "Fair enough, he was pretty bad."

"Yeah, and even though I *did not match with him,* he found me on Facebook and asked me out!" Leigh exclaims.

Mia smiles and shakes her head, "Yeah, he was…" she trails off trying to find the words.

"Creepy," Leigh finishes for her. Mia nods and both women giggle.

"Well you're doing better now," Mia says with a slightly tipsy smile and an arched eyebrow. Leigh flushes slightly and laughs.

"Yes," Leigh throws her hair back with a hand, and grins, "much better now." Her face grows more serious, "But what about you?" Her voice lowers, despite them being in a fairly noisy bar, "Have you heard from Danny again?"

Mia's back straightens and she quickly scans the crowded bar, recognizing some faces, but no one close enough to listen or care. "No, thankfully. I also haven't really been anywhere either, so I haven't seen him."

Leigh nods. "That's good, I'm sure we can also find ways to avoid him going forward too."

"You mean avoid Sasha?" Mia asks skeptically. "That's not exactly going to be easy or possible. I'll just have to figure something out." Leigh takes another sip of her drink and nods. Eager to change the subject, Mia asks, "So will Jake be joining as the department dinner?"

Leigh chokes on her drink before clearing her throat. "Yeah, that's a no." Mia cocks her head to the side, as if to ask Leigh why, as the dinners always allowed significant others. "Are you for real? We're definitely together, and will be, for lack of a better word, *out*, amongst friends, but I don't think I could bring him to a department party just yet. That feels…bordering on inappropriate still?"

Mia shrugs, "Okay, just didn't know if you'd be taking that next step with him."

Leigh just shakes her head in response. She grabs her phone from the bar and glances at the screen, "Speaking of which…he's headed over to my place now, so I'm gonna head out."

Mia nods, and the women flag down a bartender so they can each close their tabs. While Leigh is momentarily distracted with her own bill, Mia sends a text to Brett to let him know she's leaving the bar shortly. After both Leigh and Mia have taken care of their bills, the two hug outside of the bar and head off in different directions to their cars.

As Mia heads home, she feels her skin beginning to vibrate and her heart starting to beat a little faster in anticipation of seeing Brett again. She's barely arrived back in her apartment, throwing down her jacket and purse on the kitchen counter when she hears a knock at the door. Mia quickly glances through the peephole to confirm it is Brett and swings the door open with a smile.

"Hey, sexy," she says, still feeling warm and loosened up from her few drinks. Brett grins and steps inside, closing and locking the door behind him. He bends down to kiss Mia, and she wraps her arms around his neck, pulling him in for a deep kiss. When they break apart, Brett is slightly panting, and Mia feels his cock beginning to strain against his jeans. She grins and hooks a finger into the top of his pants and walks him into her bedroom.

Once inside, Mia kisses Brett again, her hands busy with his belt, buttons, and zipper. Brett runs his hands through her hair, before pushing them under her blouse. He pulls away from her momentarily to pull her blouse over her head and toss it to the side. Brett leans back down and kisses Mia from her shoulder, up her neck and back to her lips. Brett's fingers fumble at the jeans.

Mia takes a step back and points up and down at Brett's clothes. "Off," she demands, as she undresses from her own jeans. Brett complies, enjoying Mia's take-charge manner. Their clothes now piled on the floor, Mia closes in on Brett and kisses him hungrily again. She pushes him gently toward the bed, and Brett lays down, one hand down his briefs as he watches Mia clamber on top of him. Mia straddles his waist and leans down, letting her cupped breasts brush across Brett's chest before kissing him again. Brett reaches around and unclasps Mia's bra, pulling it off and throwing it to the side. Mia lifts herself up slightly and Brett maneuvers a nipple into his mouth as Mia moans in response. Mia rocks against Brett, feeling his hard cock between her legs, her panties moistening as her body responds. Mia sits back up, as Brett's hands go to her waist and encourage her to continue to move on top of him.

Mia pauses to lean over to her night table and grab a condom from the drawer. She pulls off her panties and

Brett follows suit with his briefs, before rolling on the condom that Mia handed to him. Mia climbs back on Brett, poised over his sheathed erection, with her vibrator now in hand. Brett watches as Mia turns on her vibrator and holds it against her clit, immediately moaning at the sensation. Brett grips Mia's thighs as she lowers and lifts herself on him slightly, only allowing the tip of his penis to penetrate. Brett's breathing quickens with each subtle move, and he tries to urge Mia all the way onto himself. Mia grins at Brett and takes one of his hands to hold the vibrator for her. Mia moans again as Brett holds it steady against her clit and she lets him plunge into her. Brett continues to grip her thigh with one hand, as Mia's own hands roam over her own body, across her breasts, pinching her nipples, up to her mouth, through her hair, as she rocks back on forth on Brett.

"Fuck," Brett whispers as Mia's pace increases, her moans growing louder, and her body tensing. Mia drops a hand behind her and reaches to cup Brett's scrotum, her back arching.

"Do you like how I'm fucking you?" Mia's voice is soft.

"Yes," Brett says hoarsely.

"Do you want to make me come?" she teases.

"Yes," he whispers.

"Good," Mia lets go of Brett and leans down to kiss him.

His hand drops the vibrator away from her and Mia grabs him and puts it back to where it as, the renewed shock of the vibrations almost putting her over the edge. "Make me come, Brett," she gasps. Brett lets go of the vibrator, letting Mia hold it instead and holds her against him with both hands as her back arches and her head leans back. Mia cries out with the orgasm, still moving in unison with Brett. As the aftershocks and ripples of pleasure leave her body, Mia blinks down at Brett and grins sheepishly. "It's your turn. What do you want?"

"To fuck you. Hard," Brett says roughly.

Without batting an eye, Mia climbs off and props herself up on all fours next to Brett. She looks over at him expectantly, "Then come fuck me." Brett positions himself behind her, one hand squeezing a cheek, the other stroking her clit. Mia moans at the sensation, her clit still tender from earlier. "Yes," Mia sighs. Brett pushes himself inside Mia at that word, and begins to increase his pace as he thrusts into her. The force of his pumps jostle Mia's breasts and he reaches to hold on as he fucks her.

"Harder," Mia cries out and Brett complies, their bodies slapping together as he fucks her with increased force. "Yes, fuck yes," Mia pants and feels a sharp sting on her ass where Brett has smacked her. "Fuck me, Brett," she cries out again. Brett grabs the end of Mia's hair and wraps some around his fist, gently pulling her head back a little as he continues to pound into her. Mia feels the urge to beg him to rip off his condom and fuck her raw before coming, but silences herself. She moans again instead, her yeses devolving into cries of pleasure as Brett grunts and reaches his own climax.

Brett's plunges slow and stop, and after he pulls out, he collapses next to Mia on the bed. Mia's limbs feel weak and she also lets herself lay down, resting a hand on Brett's chest. Brett takes the hand to his mouth and kisses it, before placing it back on his chest, his own hand resting on top. After a few minutes, each taking a moment to catch their breath, Brett rolls off the bed and walks to the bathroom. Once he's back Mia sees he's removed the condom and placed his boxer briefs back on before laying back down into the bed.

Mia rolls to face him, and he gently strokes one of her nipples. "That was good," she says with a smile.

"That was incredible," Brett replies. He pulls her close to him and kisses her, Mia wrapping a leg over him. Mia rests her head against his chest and sighs. She closes her eyes and feels herself melt into the bed, forgetting that she wanted to discuss the upcoming dinner.

CHAPTER 47

Mia opens her eyes to what is beginning to feel like a familiar routine. Brett is already awake, out of bed, and seems to moving around in the kitchen. She rubs the sleep from her eyes and drags herself out of bed. She rummages around a nearby drawer for an oversized t-shirt and pulls it on before padding into the kitchen. As she walks through the small apartment the smell of coffee hits her, and she sees Brett sitting at her kitchen counter with a cup of coffee, emblazoned with the local bagelry's logo, and two bagels sitting out.

"How do you function so well this early?" Mia teases as she climbs onto the chair next to Brett.

He grins at her, "I don't think I had quite as many drinks as you last night."

"You didn't seem to mind," Mia grumbles, not actually annoyed.

Brett takes a sip of his coffee, "Oh, I'm not complaining," he grins again, "I just figured you could use some carbs to soak up whatever alcohol may have been left." Brett gestured to the refrigerator. "I also got some cream cheese, and I wasn't sure what kind of bagel you liked, so I just got a plain one."

Mia glances at his everything bagel, somewhat jealous, and smiles back at Brett. "Well thank you, this will definitely work. In the future, make it two everythings." She winks at Brett. He nods in acknowledgment, and goes to grab the cream cheese after fumbling through drawers to find a knife to spread it with. Both of them settled back down to eat as Mia remembers the few things she wanted to address with Brett.

"So, tomorrow night's the department dinner," she starts hesitantly. Brett nods solemnly, unable to respond with a piece of bagel in his mouth.

"So it begins," he says after swallowing his bite.

"So it begins," Mia repeats. She pauses, uncertain of what to say next.

Brett clears this throat, "Well we know the ground rules, and we have already technically met." Mia blinks, momentarily trying to recall beyond their first encounter at the grocery store. "Your advisor introduced us in her office," he gently adds.

"Right, of course, duh, that day," Mia shakes her head at herself.

"Plus, how much interaction is there really between the students and the faculty at these things? You'll probably be catching up with your classmates and do the courteous thing to acknowledge your professors. But overall, this may be the easiest part." Brett shrugs. Mia nods, reassured. She realizes he has a point, as a large department gathering often means the faculty and students end up self-segregating quickly.

"Right, so we probably won't even interact much, and even if we did," Mia glances at him, "I imagine we're both capable of not tearing the other's clothes off in front of everyone."

Brett winks at her, "I mean, I am, but based on last night, I don't know about you." Mia rips of a piece of her bagel and throws it at Brett, who laughs, and pops the bread into his mouth.

Mia shifts in her chair, deciding whether to voice her other thought, the one that she worries may make her sound like a stalker, but would also satisfy her curiosity. After finishing her bagel she wipes her hands and decides to give in to her desire for knowledge. "So I can't seem to find you on Facebook."

Brett raises an eyebrow, though unfazed by the abrupt change in subject. "That would make sense, cause I'm not on it."

"Oh," Mia replies. "I guess that would make sense then."

"Been searching for me?" Brett's voice suggests he's teasing her.

"Well, yeah, I mean, doesn't everyone Google the other people they're seeing?" Mia replies, slightly defensive.

Brett nods, "Yeah. I just…well I deleted it after my ex cheated. I kept wanting to look up the guy and then I kept wanting to look her up and see if anything had been posted with the both of them." Brett shrugged and wiped his own hands after finishing his bagel. "It wasn't doing me any good, so I deleted it."

Feeling sympathetic and slightly chastised, Mia nods, "Yeah, that also makes sense."

Brett touched Mia's arm gently, "If there's something you want to know about me, you could just ask."

Mia rolls her eyes and replies sarcastically, "But where's the fun in that?"

Brett nods seriously, "Right, I mean it's much better to Google someone and come up with all sorts of information that might not even be true."

"Exactly! You get it!" Mia exclaims and laughs as Brett smiles.

"So, is there a question you have for me?" He asks her.

Mia shakes her head, "No, just general internet stalking curiosity."

"Ah, great. Well next time, ask if there's something you want to know. There's a lot of Brett Dawsons out there, and I'd hate for you to find my murderous doppelganger in name-only." Mia raises her own eyebrow now as Brett grins at her. "Anyway, what are your plans these last few days before the semester starts?"

Mia sighs and shrugs. "Veg? Maybe work out? Just relax before another semester takes over my life?"

Brett nods, "And other than the department party, and uh," he coughs slightly, "my class you're starting this week, when do you want to get together again?"

Mia feels life drain out of herself, as she had been willfully ignoring the fact that Brett's Monday/Wednesday seminar will start the day after the department dinner. "Ugh," Mia groans.

"The class isn't going to be that bad," Brett says, startled.

"It's not that," Mia quickly says, stroking Brett's arm, "it's that I've purposely pushed that from my mind. Shit's gonna get real really fast."

"That is true," Brett says, before leaning over and kissing Mia on the neck, "but that doesn't mean I don't want to see you again soon." Mia leans her head back and feels her nerve endings beginning to tingle. Brett moves his lips slowly up her neck to her earlobe and whispers a questioning "Hmmm?"

Mia rolls her head back to face Brett again and pushes her hair to the side. Brett sits back to look at her. "How about we get through the dinner and first seminar and plan for next weekend?" Mia says. "It'll be celebratory. Like hey, we were in the same room together twice and didn't fuck one another?"

"So the third time's the charm?" Brett grins.

"Well," Mia bats her lashes at Brett and smiles, "every time has been charming, but yes."

CHAPTER 48

After agreeing on their next date and quickly helping Mia clean up, Brett kisses Mia goodbye and heads out. He's gone before she even remembers to ask about his dinner the previous evening and she makes a mental note to ask him next time it's just the two of them. Mia hops into the shower and quickly bathes before toweling off and crashing on her couch. Content that she's earned the chance to veg out before classes start, she turns on the TV, calls over Renly and settles down to binge watch whatever she can find.

The rest of Mia's day passes uneventfully, as she occasionally makes moves to eat meals or check various social media apps. She considers texting Leigh to make plans to carpool to the dinner, but changes her mind given that their last carpooling plan ended terribly. She thinks about calling Luke, but realizes it's mostly out of boredom and doesn't want to end up in a conversation about Brett. Instead, she lets herself sink deeper into the couch and lets the day go by her.

Mia almost treats the next day similarly, waking up late and uncertain of how she plans to pass the time until the dinner. After checking her emails and eating a bowl of cereal, she decides to feel less useless compared to yesterday. Mia changes out of her pajamas and into her gym clothes and makes her way to her apartment complex's gym. Of the three treadmills, one on the far end is occupied by another twenty-something man, most likely another graduate student, so Mia elects to hop on the treadmill at the opposite end of the row. She glances over at the other runner, who does a brisk nod of acknowledgement and returns to face forward, away from Mia. Mia had smiled back, but quickly turns her focus onto her work out, placing her earbuds in and selecting her speed. Mia skips through songs as needed to try and have the beat keep pace with the pounding of her feet against the rolling tread. She lets her eyes unfocus slightly as she runs, allowing her mind to change gears to autopilot and block the anxious thoughts waiting for her.

By the time Mia's out of breath and sore, the other gym goer has already left. She slows the pace of the treadmill to a walk and allows herself to cool down and her breathing to even out. After stopping the treadmill and hoping off, she does a few stretches on the mat and walks back to her apartment, through the parking lots of the complex. The cold air feels refreshing as she breathes in, even though it chills the rest of her body, as she opted out of a jacket or sweatshirt for the brief walk.

Once back in her apartment Mia grabs a protein shake from her refrigerator and begins to sip it as she leans against the kitchen counter and scrolls through her phone. She has a text from Brett that she didn't notice come in while she was at the gym.

Ready for tonight? It says.

Not really, but as you said, tonight should be the easiest, Mia sends back.

It'll be the easiest. And just imagine everyone in their underwear. Or is that only the advice for speaking in public?

Mia smiles at the message. **I definitely do not want to imagine most of that group in their underwear.**

She gets a laughing emoji back from Brett, followed by **Fair enough**. Mia sees the three dots suggesting Brett is typing, followed by them disappearing, and coming back again.

Spill it, she texts.

I was going to say I will be imagining you in your underwear, but then panicked that it broke a rule, Brett responds.

Mia feels her stomach do a flip and smiles, **It's not rule**

breaking just yet, we're still "off hours" so you can say whatever you want.

Well in that case, I will be imagining you naked. Brett replies.

Naked with your cock in my mouth? Mia teases over text.

Fuck. How long are we forcing ourselves to wait?

Third time's a charm, remember? Just hold yourself together till the weekend. Mia ended her text with a wink, and placed her phone down, choosing to cool herself off again, this time with a shower. After she's showered, dried, and done her hair, she sees Brett only replied with his own winking emoji.

Given that she forced herself to work out, Mia allows more time on her couch in front of the TV. These are the last moments before school gets hectic again, and she won't have these opportunities often. Keeping an eye on the time, she eventually peels herself off the couch to start getting ready for the dinner. After a few years Mia's learned she doesn't have to dress particularly fancy for these events, with the exception of no jeans for the graduate student candidates' interview dinner, but she does have to appear reasonably polished.

Mia grabs a pair of dark wash jeans and a simple black sweater, along with leopard print flats for the evening.

She doesn't place much thought into her underwear choices for the evening, knowing that they'll go unseen, and settling on a plain pair of cotton panties and a basic black bra. After getting dressed Mia applies some makeup in the bathroom, opting again for a more subtle style than her usual date night choices. Once she's already ready, she sends one last text to Brett.

Ready or not, here we go.

CHAPTER 49

The department head is a tenured professor who got into academia during its glory days. Between him and his pharmacist wife, he's managed to settle into one of the nicest neighborhoods outside of the school's campus. The long private driveway winds up to a massive well-lit home, with murmurs wafting from the opening doors. Mia parks on the street, along with what appears to be at least half of the psychology department. She locks her car before making the trek inside. Normally she would plan ahead with Leigh to make sure at least one friendly face was there, but as she already recognized several cars of her classmates she chooses to head right in. Mia also did a quick glance up and down the street to determine if she can see Brett's car, but with the darkening sky is not sure.

Mia catches up to several classmates a year behind her as she makes her way to the house, and they all take the time to say hello and briefly catch up on what they've been up to, before falling into speculation about which professors will actually show up tonight and what kind of food will be served. They're all greeted at the door by Mrs. Sherman, the department head's wife, who is perfectly polished and almost Stepford-like with the exception that she's allowed herself to age gracefully with gray hair and laugh lines.

"Welcome! Come in, come in! You know the drill, serve yourself, find a place to sit, make yourselves comfortable!" Mrs. Sherman ushers them in, smiling and gesturing as she talks. Mia and the other students all let out a chorus of "hi" and "thank you for having us," before they all split apart, searching for various friends or avoiding specific professors.

Mia gazes around the room and is surprised to see Dr. Thompson there, so quickly decides to greet her before finding her own friend. She heads over to her advisor, who is talking with Dr. Fox, an associate professor in cognitive neuroscience, and waves as Dr. Thompson sees her.

"Mia! So good to see you. Did you have a pleasant break?" Dr. Thompson turns her attention to her student.

"Yes, and fairly productive, I sent you my latest drafts and revisions for my master's." Mia smiles and says after nodding at Dr. Fox.

"Yes, yes, I saw that. Hopefully I can get to it by the end of next week. Just send me a reminder next week and I'll try to get to it soon." Dr. Thompson replied.

Mia, feeling slightly deflated, nods and maintains her smile, "Of course, I will do that." Mia shifts from one foot to the other, now uncertain how to disengage from the two professors, when Dr. Thompson appears to look past her and wave someone over.

"James," she says to Dr. Fox, "I believe you've met Brett, the new hire in social." Dr. Fox turns and nods and holds a hand out to Brett as he approaches Mia and the two professors.

"Yes, of course," Dr. Fox says as the two men shake hands. "Ready to teach this semester?"

Brett smiles at the group and nods, "Yep, it's time I finally contribute to the department." Both Dr. Thompson and Dr. Fox laugh and Mia trains her eyes down to her feet. She didn't expect to see Brett so quickly into the night and her heart feels like it is racing as she tries to figure out what to say next.

Before she can say anything, Brett has turned to her and says, "Mia, so good to see you again. I hope you had a good break and are ready for class tomorrow."

Mia makes eye contact with Brett, whose face is a perfect mask, and gives a slight smile back, "Yeah, yes, looking forward to it."

Dr. Fox commands Brett's attention again, "So has Hank prepared you for teaching graduates versus undergrads?"

Mia, clearly recognizing she's no longer part of the conversation, gives a slight nod to indicate her goodbyes, particularly to Dr. Thompson, and makes her way out of the trio and towards the buffet set up.

That was manageable, she tells herself. *He was cool and collected and I was a fucking weirdo, but all of us are fucking weirdos at these things because it's so fucking awkward, so it's okay that I was all around awkward.* Mia attempts to reassure herself while stoking her anxiety. Mia glances again around the rooms visible to her, searching for Leigh, when her eyes land on Sasha. She feels her stomach drop when she notices that Sasha is not alone. Danny is here with her, his hand resting on Sasha's lower back as she balances a plate of food and a drink, while she talks with another classmate.

Of course he's here, Mia mentally kicks herself, *why wouldn't Sasha bring him? Fuck fuck fuck.* Mia looks around and jumps when she feels a hand on her shoulder.

"Hey," Leigh says as Mia turns around. She follows Mia's eye line to see Danny. "Ew, gross," she grabs Mia's arm and pulls her to the other end of the buffet, away from Sasha and Danny.

"I should have realized she'd bring him," Mia whispers to Leigh.

Leigh shrugs, "We'll just do our best to avoid him." Mia stifles a hysterical laugh while Leigh pushes her toward the tables of food.

Leigh and Mia make the proper exclamations over the impressive food display and load up their plates before winding their way through the increasing crowd to find a table with open spots. They find one table occupied at the far end with some first year students, and settle in with their plates on the opposite side.

Leigh takes a bite of her food and turns to Mia, covering her mouth as she speaks, "I saw your advisor is here."

Mia nods, "Yeah," and quietly adds, "hell has apparently frozen over. She never comes to these things."

"Maybe she's putting in the effort cause of the new hire?" Leigh says casually.

"Hmm?" Mia asks, focusing on her food.

"The new assistant professor in psychology? I feel like more of the department is here than usual. Maybe they're trying to be welcoming?"

Mia nods, stuffing more food in her mouth, making it so she can't respond.

"Which, by the way, have you seen him?" Leigh continues, her voice dropping to a whisper, "he is gorgeous."

Mia briefly chokes on her food, her cheeks blushing for various reasons. "Um, yeah, he's cute." She says quickly.

"Ooooh, who's cute?" a voice says from behind Mia and Leigh. Mia turns to see Sasha pulling out a chair next to her and settling down, as Danny, a few steps behind her, moves to sit on the other side of Sasha.

CHAPTER 50

"No one," Mia says as Leigh replies, "The new professor." Sasha looks back and forth between the two women and shrugs, digging into her own plate.

After swallowing some food, Sasha leans past Mia to ask Leigh, "Where is he?"

Leigh tilts her head to indicate where Brett is standing, and Sasha's head whips around, lacking all subtleties as she attempts to spy out Brett. Mia tries to shrink into her chair and keeps wishing the moment away. Everything about this feels uncomfortable, the conversation, the proximity to Danny, this conversation in the proximity to Danny. Sasha seems to find Brett and turns back to Leigh and Mia to make a face as if to say "he's hot," while simultaneously fanning herself off.

"What's going on?" Danny asks, suddenly pulled to the conversation. Mia freezes, panicking at the thought that

Danny's attention will also be turned to Brett.

"Nothing, I was just asking Leigh where Jake was tonight," Sasha says nonchalantly.

Leigh quickly goes along with the lie, "Yeah, he wasn't feeling up to a dinner with all of his former teachers, so he opted out."

"Does that include you?" Danny says not entirely kindly.

"Hardy hardy har, Danny, you're very witty," Leigh rolls her eyes, her sarcasm not entirely reflecting her distaste.

"Mia," Sasha says, clearly trying to redirect the conversation, "I haven't seen you since New Year's! What have you been up to?"

Mia, at this point, feels her skin tingling and her nerves raw with every conversation feeling like a time bomb. She forces a smile at Sasha, "Just writing and laying around before classes and clients start up again." Sasha nods with understanding, and Danny next to her seems to tense and then relax as he hears her response.

"Well we should all do something again soon, it doesn't have to be crazy like New Year's," Sasha says wholeheartedly.

"Yeah, definitely," Leigh chimes in, "maybe a girls' night?" Mia feels grateful to her friend for preemptively excluding Danny in their next social activity.

"Yesssss," Sasha declares.

"Aren't most of your hang outs a girls' night? Isn't your department like ninety-five percent girls?" Danny asks. Sasha rolls her eyes and waves dismissively at him. "Whatever," he grumbles and goes back to his own plate.

"Maybe after our soc psy class tomorrow we'll need a girls' night to decompress," Sasha says quietly with a conspiratorial wink to Mia and Leigh. Leigh barks out a laugh and Mia shakes her head and smiles. As Mia looks back up she sees Brett passing by their table, which he glances over, and briefly makes eye contact with her, though he maintains a poker face. Mia's stomach twists and she reminds herself to calm down before she starts to blush again.

"How long are you all staying tonight?" Leigh asks, already anxious for an excuse to leave.

"Not long honestly, my advisor saw me, I talked shop for thirty seconds, I ate, I am basically ready to go," Mia admits.

"Same, though I still need to talk to my advisor before I go," Sasha nods. She tilts her head to Danny, "Plus if I keep him out past midnight he turns into a gremlin."

"A pumpkin," Danny corrects her, his tone condescending, "it's a pumpkin after I stay out past midnight, a gremlin if you feed me after midnight."

Sasha seems to smile, but it's more strained after the latest comment from Danny, "Well you all get the idea."

Mia takes a deep breath and wipes her hands on her jeans, suddenly realizing her palms have been sweaty. She grabs her plate and stands, "Well, I'm going to call it, I'll see you all tomorrow." Leigh and Sasha wave at her, while Danny barely acknowledges her departure. Mia quickly finds a trashcan, dumping her trash, and glances around the house once more to see if she can find Brett, even if she doesn't plan to say goodbye to him. Having no luck, Mia quickly heads out and walks back to her car, down the long dark driveway, with her keys between her fingers as was ingrained in her from adolescence.

Once in her car, with the heat running, she quickly grabs her phone from her purse and sends a brief text to Brett before focusing on the drive home.

Didn't know how to say goodbye, hope you enjoyed the dinner.

CHAPTER 51

By the time Mia's arrived back in her apartment, her nerves finally feel like they've settled. She's changed into her pajamas and she's nursing a single glass of wine before heading to bed. After she's settled onto her couch, and Renly has curled up beside her, she checks her phone to see Brett has replied.

It was enjoyable, and we both behaved!

I feel like my night may have been harder than yours, Mia texts back. Brett replied with only a question mark. Mia replies to his inquiry, **My classmates kept talking about the hot new professor and I felt so transparent.**

What did you say? Brett sends back.

Nothing incriminating, really, nothing if I could manage it.

Ouch

Well would it have been better if I say yes he's super hot and is amazing in bed?

For my ego, absolutely. Brett's text ends in a winking emoji. Mia snorts to herself and pauses for a moment, weighing whether to share the other nerve-wracking part of the night. She starts to type and then delete, only to have Brett call her out as she did earlier.

Spill it, he texts.

Mia sighs and taps in the text, **The ex was also there and that was uncomfortable**. Mia feels like a century passes as she sees the three dots appear, disappear, and reappear on Brett's end.

Finally, a text from Brett comes in, **That guy at the table with you?**

Yes. He's dating my classmate, she brought him.

I thought he looked familiar.

Mia remembered that Brett had briefly met Danny a few weeks back at the bar.

Did he say anything to you?

No, Mia replies. **He mostly spent his time being an ass to my friend.**

This guy sounds great, can't imagine why you're all drawn to him.

Mia stares at the text from Brett, feeling surprisingly hurt and uncertain how to respond. She takes a sip of her wine and pets Renly, trying to work out something to say back, but Brett sends another text before she can.

Sorry, that probably came out wrong. The guy sounds terrible, I'm glad he didn't give you any trouble tonight.

Me too.

Ready for class tomorrow?

Yes, very eager to be learning from the esteemed Dr. Dawson.

It sounds like I do have some eager students.

I should not have told you they called you hot. Clearly it's inflated your ego.

Brett texts her a laughing emoji followed by, **I promise I won't start thinking too highly of myself.** A brief pause, and then Mia receives another text, **Any chance I could get a goodnight photo?**

Mia feels herself roll her eyes at no one, and then, holds her phone out and takes a selfie of herself as she is, lifting her wine glass as if to toast to the camera. She sends the picture to Brett.

That's perfect, you're gorgeous. Goodnight beautiful.

Goodnight, see you tomorrow. Mia sends the final text, before finishing off her wine and rinsing her glass in the sink. She finishes getting ready for bed by washing off her face and brushing her teeth.

Climbing under her sheets she calls for Renly, who lazily makes his way into her room and onto her bed, before curling up at her feet. Mia shuts off her bedroom lamp and scoots under the covers in the darkness. *Tonight was easy,* she tells herself, *now to do it again in a small classroom with several classmates for ninety minutes with an inevitably of having to interact with Brett appropriately.*

CHAPTER 52

By the time Mia arrives for her afternoon seminar that Brett teaches she's already attended a didactic for her current CBT rotation and supervision for her eating disorders clinic. She also quickly skimmed the articles from the syllabus for today's class while she ate lunch. Up until this point, Mia's tried to treat the day like every other day in graduate school, choosing an outfit according to whether she was seeing clients that day. As she was not seeing clients today, she stuck with jeans, a plain gray shirt, and a black duster cardigan.

Mia's office is in the basement but her Social Behavior and Personality seminar is on the third floor, so she is also slightly out of breath as she arrives in the classroom. Sasha is already there, as are other graduate students from the clinical section, social group, business school, cognitive section, and the developmental specialty. As Mia drops into the seat next to Sasha, Leigh breezes in next, taking the other seat next to Mia. Mia and Leigh had both planned to take a social psychology course together long before they knew what class or who was teaching as it was a rare opportunity for them to have an overlap in their schedules.

Mia greets the various students she knows before sliding her laptop out of her bag and setting up. She pulls up the articles she attempted to read earlier along with a blank Word document to take notes.

Mia feels her heart thumping as she waits for Brett to enter the room and start the class. She jiggles her leg under the table and feels Leigh's foot gently stomp down on hers.

"You're shaking the whole table," Leigh says quietly, referring to the slightly vibrating conference table they're all gathered around.

"Sorry," Mia mumbles. Leigh gives Mia a side-eye and before she can say anything, the door to the room opens again and Brett strides in, carrying his laptop and a stack of what Mia assumes are research articles. He places everything down at the head of the conference table, pulls the chair out, and sits down. Brett glances down the two sides of the conference table and smiles warmly at everyone.

"Welcome to my first ever graduate course. As much as I hope to be teaching something new to all of you, I am also aiming for this class to be an opportunity for me to learn from you so that this course can continue to evolve and I can also grow as a teacher. I was in your position not very long ago, so I hope I am also able to set some pretty reasonable expectations. Before we start discussing the assigned readings for today, I'd like to get to know each of you. I know many of you already know each other, but most of you are new to me, so if we could go around the table, and you could say your name and what you study, that'd be great." Brett finished his spiel and turned immediately to his left to urge the first student, a social psychology third year, to start the process.

Mia sat through the usual introductions, counting down to her turn and her well-rehearsed bit that is asked to be performed at the beginning of every new class. After Sasha finishes, Mia looks directly at Brett and smiles.

"I'm Mia James, I'm a third year clinical psych student and work with Dr. Jean Thompson. I'm currently working on my master's thesis, exploring the role of self-concept in the effectiveness of various third wave therapies." Mia finishes by her mini-speech and then glances towards Leigh, as a silent passing of the introduction torch. Mia observes that Brett is taking notes on a notepad as each student introduced themselves, and thought she saw a raised eyebrow or smile at her mention of self-concept.

Eventually, the first class introduction ritual ended, Brett clapped his hands together once, with a "Great!" and launched into quick review of the syllabus. Mia, who had just reviewed it this morning, was nodding along with the other students, though not entirely focused on what Brett was saying until closer to the end.

"And with the final paper, which is in lieu of a final exam, I am going to ask each of you to turn in a draft two weeks before the final due date. We'll schedule one-on-one meetings to discuss any potential revisions or changes before the final version is due. The ultimate goal with this paper is to have a review that is publishable, so I think it can really help to meet and discuss additional directions."

Mia feels a tap on her shoulder and sees that Leigh has typed out something on her screen. Mia glances quickly to read it.

A great opportunity to get his name on fifteen publishable reviews and fatten up that CV for tenure.

Mia quietly snorted, in agreement with Leigh, and turned her attention back to Brett, who had by now moved on to discussing the first of the several research articles he had assigned for the first day. Mia and her friends mostly listened as the social psychology students dominated the conversation. The social psychology students clearly felt more comfortable with the material and were eager to make an impression on the new professor.

Mia was trying to find herself at ease in the seminar, making sure to add an occasional comment so that she was visibly participating. She felt mildly unnerved each time she spoke up and made eye contact with Brett, but keeping herself focused on the discussion helped stopped the nervous energy from pouring out. Mia reminded herself to breathe when he seemed to smile at her. She keeps catching herself from shaking her leg after a quick shake or two. By the time the seminar began to wrap up, Mia felt like her breathing was normal, and as she made the observation she realized she felt like she'd been holding her breath for the last ninety minutes. The seminar ended with Brett reminding them to email him if they have any further questions from today, and he packed up his items, leaving the classroom without looking back.

Mia and her classmates were also packing up their things, as Sasha turned to her and Leigh.

"What are you two up to now?"

Mia shrugged, "Nothing now, maybe head back to my office and get a head start on some other reading. I start back with patients tomorrow, so just taking it easy today."

Leigh's pulling her bag over her shoulder and pushing away from the table. "Running participants, all day every day." She grins at both Mia and Sasha and waves as she makes her way out, "See ya!" Mia and Sasha say their goodbyes to Leigh as she leaves.

Once Mia's things are gathered up and she starts heading

to the door, she hears Sasha ask, "Mind if I come chat for a bit?"

"No not at all, come on down to my dungeon," Mia replies warmly, despite the sudden growing worry. *What does Sasha want to talk about?*

Back in the lab space that belongs to her advisor, Mia and Sasha settle into the office that Mia shares with a fifth year student in her lab, who is conveniently never in the lab. Sasha plops herself into the empty office chair across from Mia and Mia settles in, doing a quick check of her email, before turning around in her chair to face Sasha.

"What's up?" Mia asks.

Sasha pushes her swivel chair back and forth, not quite making a full turn and sighs. "You were there last night, and heard Danny. I feel like he's being such a jerk to me."

Mia presses her lips together, uncertain how to respond, even though she completely agrees with Sasha.

"I mean, am I wrong? Was I misunderstanding it? I know sometimes I misread cues, but I feel like 'asshole' is a universal language." Sasha presses.

Mia hesitates, while Sasha stops swinging in the chair and looks intently at Mia.

"Mia, I'm not dumb, I know you two hooked up before Danny and I started dating, and I'm asking you this because you also know him."

Mia glances down, feeling ashamed to think that she figured Sasha was ignorant this whole time. She also notices a flash of frustration, wondering if Sasha knew about her and Danny, then why would she get together with him so quickly.

"Mia?" Sasha asks again.

"I don't know exactly what to say to you, Sasha," Mia starts. "Yes, I think Danny was being a jerk to you last night. But I also think that Danny *is* a jerk, so I don't think I would interpret his behavior any other way." Mia pauses, "And I didn't realize you knew that Danny and I hooked up."

Sasha looks at Mia with surprise, "I mean, it's a small department, it's not like secrets stay secret."

Mia snorts, both at the truth of the statement and at the weight of what that statement means for her currently.

"Well did you know that Danny dumped me for you? Like, I didn't know he was starting something with you while stringing me along?" Mia responds, some of her frustration coming through.

Sasha's mouth drops a bit, "Uh, no. He told me you guys hooked up a couple of times but it was long over by the time we started talking."

"Well, he lied. Again, falls under my interpretation that Danny is a jerk."

This time Sasha closes her mouth into a thin line as she appears to digest this information.

"Look, I'm sorry how all this is coming out - " Mia starts, but Sasha waves her off.

"No, I'm sorry I didn't come and talk to you directly sooner. I just need to figure out what I want when it comes to Danny." Sasha says when she cuts Mia off.

"Well, I definitely don't think I'm the right person to help you sort through that." Mia says gently.

Sasha smiles and nods, "Yeah, fair enough. Can we be more open going forward?"

Mia hesitates, thinking about Danny's recent threats, knowing she does not want any further interactions with him, and makes a decision. "Yeah, going forward, let's be more honest with each other."

Sasha says with relief, "Good. Thanks for tolerating this wildly awkward conversation with me."

Mia laughs, "It could have been worse, glad we've come to some understanding."

Sasha nods and stands while grabbing her things from the floor. "Me too, I guess I'll head out now. Thanks again."

"See ya," Mia says as Sasha leaves her office. Once Mia hears the door to the lab shut she lets a deep breath and cusses quietly.

Mia pulls out her cellphone, weighing whom she can talk to. Texting Brett right now would break the rules, so that option is ruled out. Even though she knows Leigh probably isn't available, she shoots a quick text to her, **I think Sasha and I just had it out? Call me when you can.**

Mia put her phone back down and turns back to the old desktop on the lab desk. She pulls up the syllabi for her current courses and starts downloading the articles for her next classes. After completing the reading and taking notes, Mia decides to pack up and head home, as she only gets a few days now when she isn't seeing patients later into the evening.

CHAPTER 53

Mia knew she had to wait until at least five in the evening before texting Brett, per their agreement, but ends up texting him closer to seven, after she realized time had gotten away from her.

Congrats on your first day teaching graduate students!

Mia still hadn't heard from Leigh yet either, and assumed she was working a late day running subjects for her own advisor's studies. Her phone buzzes at her to alert her to a new text message and Mia sees the reply from Brett.

Thanks ☺ I think it went well. And we made it through another event without ripping off each other's clothes. I'm very proud of you.

Mia laughed as the reference to the other night. **I guess we have evolved beyond our animal instincts**, she sends back.

Maybe not entirely…I thought of you the rest of the afternoon, had to run out of the class before the excitement hit me, Brett responds.

Mia grinned at her phone, **And now?**, she texts back. Brett's response is a picture of him from the waist down, his boxer briefs pulled taut around a long, thick erection. **Looks like you could use some help**, Mia texts.

I could, Brett texts with a winking face. Mia hops off the couch and heads into her bedroom. She paws through her underwear drawer until she finds a matching white lace bra and panty set and quickly changes into them. After quickly checking and fixing her makeup in the bathroom, she heads back into her room and takes a few selfies in front of her full length mirror, trying different faces and poses. She settles on a picture with a come hither look in her eyes as she pulls down one strap of her bra. Mia sends it to Brett.

I didn't think it was possible to get harder.

What would you want to do if I was with you right now? Mia replies.

Spread your legs, lick you until you begged me to fuck you, tease you with the tip of my cock until you're ready to come and then fuck you to put you over the edge.

Mia feels a thrill shoot through her body and automatically reaches a hand down to touch herself. She circles her clit with her finger and texts back Brett with her free hand, **That sounds perfect. You're getting me all wet now.**

Brett doesn't respond right away, and Mia takes the opportunity to lean into the image Brett created, imagining him teasing her with just the tip of his cock into her, as she slips her own fingers inside. Mia closes her eyes and leans her head back, dropping her phone to the floor so that she can use one hand to rub her clit while the other plunges two fingers in and out, steadily quickening her pace. She ignores the buzz of an incoming text, focusing instead on pleasing herself, picturing Brett thrusting his hard cock into her, and letting the imagined orgasm become a real one as the sensation peaks and spreads through her body.

Mia takes a moment to settle her breathing and grabs her phone to check the text. It turns out there are two, one from Brett, (**Fuck I want to touch you now**) and one from Leigh (**Sorry, free now, call?**).

"Shit," Mia mutters. She types out a quick text and sends it to Brett, **I actually just handled myself** with a winking face. She adds to it, **This Saturday?**

Brett replies, **I guess I'll go manage my business until then**. He ends it with a smiling emoji, reassuring Mia of the tone of the text.

Before she can get too wrapped up in more messages with Brett, Mia pulls up Leigh's text and dials her from the text thread. Leigh picks up after the third ring.

"Hey, sorry for not getting back sooner. You know, subjects, dinner, Jake, and so on. So tell me what happened?" Leigh says.

Mia quickly summarized the exchange with Sasha, covering the parts of Danny being rude the night before, Sasha informing her that she thought it was a brief hook up, and the agreement to be more honest with one other. Mia stops at that point and waits for Leigh's reply.

"Soooo, did you tell her about New Year's?" Leigh asks.

"No." Mia says.

"And I'm guessing you also did not tell her about the other time Danny tried to kiss you before New Year's, when she was out of town? Or when he came to your place and threatened you?" Leigh presses.

"Yeah, also a no," Mia says with a sigh.

"So this honesty thing…?" Leigh trails off.

"I am interpreting it as honesty going forward. I don't know what Danny will do if I told her any of that, and I really would rather not find out. So if Danny does something going forward, which I really hope he doesn't, I'll tell her."

"Mia," Leigh says seriously over the phone, "Shouldn't Sasha know that her boyfriend is a creep that threatened you? Like, several times?"

Mia sighs, "I don't know. He didn't threaten her, it was specific to me."

Leigh begins to sound exasperated, "But if he does it to you, what is stopping him from doing that to her?"

"I don't know, Leigh! Okay, I don't know," Mia answers, her voice rising.

"I'm not trying to upset you, and I'm not blaming you for anything. But maybe it's worthwhile and important for Sasha to know what has happened." Leigh sounds calm, though Mia imagines her friend is annoyed.

"And I'm saying that I don't want to start anything that doesn't have to be started if it doesn't need to be," Mia says, becoming upset with her friend. "I hope you can respect that," Mia adds carefully.

"I can," Leigh says defensively, "I won't say anything, you asked that of me. I'm just suggesting you reconsider sharing with Sasha."

Mia shakes her head and rubs her temple with her free hand. "Okay, I hear you."

"Alright," Leigh says quietly.

"I'm gonna go, I'll see you tomorrow maybe," Mia says tiredly.

"Okay, bye," Leighs responds and Mia clicks the end call button.

Mia examines herself in the mirror, her back hunched against her bed, her feelings wildly different than moments earlier. Mia feels the urge to text Brett and ask him to come over and comfort her, but worries that discussing this situation with him will also result in him suggesting the same as Leigh. Instead Mia changes out of the bra and panties, returning the bra back in the drawer and tossing the panties into her laundry. She pulls on her pajamas and makes her way into her tiny office. She grabs her statistics textbook and settles into the assigned chapter, knowing she'll be reading and rereading passages until she gives up and goes to bed.

CHAPTER 54

Much of Mia's Thursday and Friday pass uneventfully. She ends up not seeing Leigh, choosing not to seek her out at any point, and Leigh appears to be doing the same by Mia's observation. Mia goes to her statistics course on Thursday, attends didactics for her therapy practicums, sees patients, and continues to manage lab work for her advisor. If there's one thing she's particularly grateful for this year, it's having a research assistantship instead of a teaching one, allowing her to easily switch back and forth between working on her own research and her advisor's. Her first two years she worked as a TA, having to teach sections to students in large, introductory psych courses. It was time-consuming and tiresome, and depending on the professor she was assigned to it could also be unpleasant. With a new influx of grant money for Dr. Thompson's lab, Mia was granted a research assistantship, freeing more of her time.

Mia's Friday is set to conclude with two evening patients,

individuals she has not seen since prior to winter break. She grabs a quick dinner at a restaurant near the clinic at five pm and breezes through the first patient at six pm. Mia's last patient at seven proves to be more difficult. As Mia listens to him speak and begins to catch the concerning lines of, "I don't know if it's worth it," and "I'm ready to be done," her stomach starts to sink and she begins to probe. As Mia had worried, her patient begins to more openly express suicidal ideation. With his own confirmation of his current state, Mia briefly ducks out of the therapy session to contact her supervisor through a text indicating an emergency. Her current supervisor calls immediately and reviews with Mia the protocol to follow for her patient.

Mia ends up finding herself lucky, as her patient has agreed to contract for safety until their next meeting, and decides to have a friend come get him instead of leaving by himself. She waits with him until he is safely ensconced in his friend's car. By then it's almost nine at night, leaving the campus and the clinic she works at eerily quiet. On the outskirts of campus, it doesn't draw the undergrads, who wouldn't even be out just yet.

Mia bundles herself up into her coat and ducks her face into her scarf. She grabs her cell from her bag and dials Brett, feeling safer having someone on the phone while she makes the trek to her car, inconveniently parked nowhere near the clinic.

"Hey! How are you?" Brett says as he answers.

"Good," Mia says, "leaving my clinic and walking to my car."

"Wow, that's really late. You normally see folks this late?" Brett asks.

"Ah no, I had a patient in crisis, so I ended up staying later to deal with it." Mia responds.

"Wow, that sounds terrible. Is it a long walk? Do you feel safe doing it now?" Brett asks her, his voice warm.

Mia snorts, "I mean, it's a decent walk at night on a deserted campus, it doesn't feel great."

"Let me give you a lift to your car," Brett says.

"Aren't you home by now? That's silly," Mia tries to brush him off.

"No, it's fine, tell me where the clinic is and I'll swing by. I can be there in ten minutes, I'm already heading out to my car," Brett insists.

"You don't need to do this," Mia says, however, she's already stopped walking and turns back to the clinic.

"I want to, where's the office?" Brett says, with sounds of a radio now floating under his voice.

Mia gives him the address and heads back to the clinic, sitting down under a bench by the front door. While the clinic itself is closed and dark, the lights out front illuminate the entryway.

"Alright, see you soon," Brett says and the call ends. To kill the time, Mia scrolls through Instagram. She sees that Luke has posted about returning to classes and makes a mental note to call him soon. Mia eventually sees a car roll into the parking lot and cruise up to the entryway, window down.

Brett leans out the window, "Need a lift?" he asks with a grin.

Mia mockingly swoons, "My knight in shining armor." She gets up from the bench and hurriedly gets into the car, warming herself against the hot air blowing from the vents. "But really," Mia says more sincerely, "thank you, you didn't have to."

Brett smiles, "Happy to, gives me an excuse to see you. So where exactly is your car?"

Mia directs him to the far off parking lot where her permit allows her to park and Brett makes the drive around the campus to get there.

"How late are you usually here?" Brett asks, glancing over at Mia, who has now unbuttoned her coat and removed her scarf against the heat.

"I'm usually out by eight, and normally don't even see folks that late. Plus there's usually another student or two leaving around the same time and we'll walk together." Mia shrugs, "Tonight was just a different circumstance."

"Does that happen often?" Brett asks, "A 'patient in crisis'?"

Mia shrugs, "Not all the time, it's not the first time, and honestly this went a lot smoother than other times it's happened. The first time I had a suicidal patient in the office I think I almost crapped myself." She smiles at Brett, who nods more seriously. "But I've had great supervisors and support and feel like I have a much better handle on what to do. It's never easy, but I feel more confident in my skills."

"That's impressive," Brett replies. "I don't think I'd be very well equipped, ever, to handle someone who is suicidal."

Mia shrugs again, "There are degrees to it, of course it's harder and I'd be more freaked out if the client refused to make a safety plan or go to a hospital. I guess I've been lucky in that that hasn't happened."

"Have you had a client kill themselves?" Brett asks, glancing at her again.

"No, that would be….that would be awful. Really. I've had a supervisor that has gone through that though. It's rattling and awful and you're so limited as a clinician as to what you can do after that happens. You can't go to the funeral or necessarily send condolences. You question everything and every appointment that happened. Or at least, that's how it seems. I mean, even patients I've worked with and we've ended therapy on a good note, where they've made progress and were ready to graduate, I still wonder about them at times too. Like, are they still doing well? Have they achieved the things we worked on? Have they needed to return to therapy for one reason or another? I think no matter what the end to a therapeutic relationship looks like, a lot of us wonder. Cause we've been honored to be a part of a difficult process and sometimes don't always see the end result." Mia muses. She turns back to Brett and realizes the car has stopped and he's parked next to hers.

"It sounds like you put a lot of thought into your therapy work. You sound more, I guess, excited about it than your research?" Brett observes.

"It flip flops, depends on the day," Mia smiles. She sighs and looks at her car out the window. "Well, thank you again." She pauses, still looking at her car, her mind still elsewhere, "We should do something tomorrow."

"I'd like that," Brett says.

Mia turns back to Brett and leans in to kiss him, but stops short. "Is this allowed? It's after hours, no one is here."

To answer her, Brett reaches out to stroke his thumb over her cheek and lips, before closing the space left between them and kisses her. His mouth is light on hers and what begins as gentle quick kiss goodbye intensifies. Mia grabs Brett's shirt to pull him closer to the console between them and opens her lips to tease him with her tongue. Brett's hand goes into her hair, keeping Mia close to him as he returns the kiss. Mia feels her heart racing, as the kiss continues to deepen. She pulls back, slightly out of breath and motions that she is climbing over the console, giving Brett enough time to slide his seat back and make room for her.

As carefully as she can, Mia clambers over, now straddling Brett, her hands roaming over his chest and he pulls her face back down to kiss her again. Brett breaks the kiss to move his lips along her jaw and up to her ear, gently sucking on her earlobe before whispering, "Let me make you come."

His words arouse Mia and she moans quietly, now moving her hips back and forth, enticing a response from Brett's body. Brett grips her waist with both hands, encouraging her to continue, and Mia returns to kissing Brett. She feels his erection grow beneath her, his sweatpants and her dress slacks leaving little to the imagination. Brett pulls Mia's blouse out from her slacks, allowing him to stroke and squeeze her breasts.

Brett breaks apart from her, his eyes staring into hers, "I

want to make you come," he says again, with more desperation in his voice.

"Yes," Mia whispers and writhes against his erection, feeling her own excitement grow.

Brett now takes both hands to gently tug at Mia's legs, she glances down and realizes he's grabbing at her pants, which are not going to easily come off in their current entanglement.

"Fucking pants," Mia swears, causing Brett to lean back and laugh.

"Fucking pants," he agrees.

Mia leans back, letting both her and Brett catch their breath and slow their movements.

"We probably shouldn't be doing this here, anyway," Mia says slowly.

"Next time wear a skirt," Brett says at the same time. They both stop and laugh at each other.

Mia lets out a big sigh, "Ugh, yeah, I guess I need to head home."

Brett raises an eyebrow at her, "And leave me hanging?"

Mia suddenly feels the exhaustion of the evening hit her and slumps a little. "Come over tomorrow and fuck my brains out?" She offers sweetly.

Brett smooths down Mia's hair, which had been rumpled during their encounter. "I'll take whatever you'll offer."

Mia nods, "I'm about ready to crash, come over tomorrow, we'll be unencumbered." She motions to her pants, the car, and the parking lot.

Brett smiles and nods, "Done." He leans in and gives Mia a quick kiss before she opens his car door and half-topples out. Brett fixes his seat as she quickly walks back to the passenger side and grabs her bag.

"Thank you again for the ride," she says to Brett.

He winks at her, while adjusting himself, "Anytime."

CHAPTER 55

Mia chooses to treat the next day as an opportunity to decompress from yesterday's therapy appointments. She decides against texting Leigh or Luke and knowing she'll probably reach out to both the next day. Instead, Mia focuses on managing her own stress and mental health. Before Brett is scheduled to arrive she takes one last look in the bathroom mirror. She's applied a light layer of makeup and brushed her hair out. Mia also decided to go straight for seduction and is only wearing the white lacy bra and panties that she recently wore in the picture for Brett. Feeling a little self-conscious, she also throws on her duster cardigan from the days before, telling herself she shouldn't open her front door only in her underwear. She goes to leave the bathroom and sees Renly throw her a dirty look before making his way into her bedroom.

"Don't judge me," Mia scolds the cat. She goes out to the kitchen, where she pulls out two wine glasses and a bottle of unopened red wine, and a bottle opener. She glances at the clock, and goes to check out the window, and sees Brett has already parked and is making his way to the steps of her building, his shape illuminated by the lights of another car in the lot. Mia runs her fingers through her hair again, feeling excited and uncertain as to why she's sensing some nervousness.

Brett knocks on the door, and Mia pulls it open, a hand on her hip, her cardigan open.

"Hey - " Brett starts before fully seeing Mia. He comes inside quickly and kicks the door shut behind him. He pulls Mia to himself and hungrily kisses her, while also trying to shed his jacket, shirt, shoes, and pants. He breaks away from her to fight with his belt buckle and Mia takes a step back.

She gestures to her legs, "No pants!"

Brett's pants are now a puddle on the floor with rest of his clothes, only his boxer briefs left on him. "No pants," he says with a smile despite his voice being more a growl. He presses himself into Mia and pulls her cardigan off of her, his hands now roaming across her butt, over her breasts, and through her hair as they breathlessly kiss each other.

Brett lifts Mia up and she wraps her legs around him, and he walks her over to her kitchen table. He sits on her on the table and breaks her grip around his neck.

He kisses her again and pulls back to say, "Lay down," and Mia immediately complies, leaning back to rest against the table. Brett drops to his knees and with both hands pulls Mia's panties off and buries his face between her legs. Mia feels Brett's tongue lashing at her clit and her body jerks involuntarily with pleasure. Brett uses one hand to steady her and hold her in place and the other to slip two fingers into her as he continues to flick his tongue at her clit. Mia moans and tries to grab at the table but finds no purchase. Brett begins to alternate between his tongue and his fingers to stimulate Mia's sweet spot and Mia cries out with the sensation.

"Oh god, Brett," Mia whimpers, "I'm going to come."

"Not yet," he says, and pulls back. Mia hears the crinkle of the condom wrapper and then feels Brett start to gently enter her. Her body swells with anticipation of his entire thick cock, but he doesn't fully penetrate her. Instead, Brett continues to tease her with the tip of erection, entering just a little and coming out, Mia continue to clench at the table and gasp.

"Please, Brett," Mia whimpers again, as Brett rubs at her clit and continues to only press the tip of his cock into her. "Please, god, Brett," she starts to beg. Brett leans over her and sucks on her neck. He moves his mouth down to her breasts and pulls them out of the cups. Brett licks and sucks on one nipple and then the other, while Mia wraps her legs around his waist and digs her nails into his shoulders. He continues to rub at her clit with one hand. Brett moves back to Mia's mouth and kisses her hard, pressing his tongue in and then pulling back to nibble on her earlobe.

"Beg me," he whispers into her ear.

Mia writhes between the hard table and Brett's body, she grabs his ass with one hand, trying to pull him in. "God, fuck me Brett," she moans, her other hand digging into his shoulder, "please fuck me. Fuck me. Please. I need you in me. Fuck - " Mia's words are cut off with a gasp as Brett quickly straightens up and plunges into her, his hands on her waist. Mia unwraps her legs and lifts them over Brett's shoulders as he thrusts into her, with Mia crying out at each thrust.

"Yes, Brett," Mia's cries are louder and begin to dissolve into incomprehensible "Oh gods" as before bursting with one final cry of "I'm coming, I'm coming, oh my god I'm coming." Brett continues to fuck Mia through the aftershocks of her orgasm and pulls out after her moans subside. Mia props herself up by her elbows and eyes Brett with a sex-stunned grin. He's still holding his erection in one hand and jerks his head for her to get up.

Mia scrambles off the table and pulls Brett close to her, his erection sticky against her stomach, and kisses him deeply. Brett kisses her back, before breaking apart and turns her around the face the kitchen table. Mia pulls off her bra, tossing it to the floor and Brett kisses her shoulder while reaching around to fondle her breasts. He pulls on her nipples and she drops her head back to rest of Brett's chest. He kisses her neck and fingers her clit before whispering in her ear, "Ready?"

Mia whispers "Yes," before spreading her legs and gripping the kitchen table. Brett slaps her ass and then rubs and squeezes her butt. Mia feels Brett arrange himself at her opening. "Fuck me," she says, bracing herself.

Brett plunges into her again, holding her waist to steady himself as he pumps. Mia takes a hand to rub her own clit as Brett continues to fuck her. She hears him grunt from behind her and she moans in response. "You feel so good," she says breathlessly, "your cock is so hard. And you fuck me so well."

Brett's pace increases in response, and his thrusts become more forceful. He slaps Mia's ass again and she cries out in pleasure.

Mia feels the sensation begin to bloom again, the explosion about to break all through her body. "Fuck," she cries out, "I'm going to come again. Fuck me hard. Fuck me hard with your thick cock."

At those words, Brett's thrusts turn into a pound and Mia lets go of herself to hold onto the table as her orgasm hits. She cries out one final time, "Fuck, I'm coming, oh god." She hears Brett cuss and feels him tense from behind her, before his thrusts stop and he rests his chest and head against her back. She feels him panting and the sudden emptiness as he pulls out of her. Mia lets herself sink to the floor, where she lays down, facing up to the ceiling. Brett gazes down at her, a lopsided smile on his face. He paces away and returns, now with his boxers on and gently lowers himself to the floor to lay next to Mia.

Mia raises an arm limply, "I'm spent." She giggles and Brett laughs as she drops her arm back down with a thud.

"So it was well worth the wait." Brett confirms.

Mia rolls over and throws an arm over Brett's chest, "Oh yeah."

CHAPTER 56

After a few more minutes on the ground, they've each pulled themselves together, with Brett having put his pants back on and Mia lounging in flannel pajama bottoms and a t-shirt. They're on either ends of her couch, but Mia has stretched herself out to rest her feet on Brett's lap as he mindlessly rubs a thumb against her ankle. Their now half-full wine glasses sit on the coffee table and Renly has settled on the floor, whipping his tail at the rudeness of being excluded from the couch.

"So how did you like the seminar?" Brett asks.

"It was good, you seemed to know what you're doing," Mia answers.

"Anything else? Did your friends say anything about it?"

"Ah, no?" Mia says.

"Cause at one point it looked like Leigh said something and you giggled about it," Brett muses.

Mia flushes, "Oh, well, yeah. She just, um, made an observation that the final paper seems like a good way for you to get some co-authorships. Easy co-authorships."

Brett smirks, "She isn't wrong. When I planned the class my mentor kind of suggested it. As a possible way to buff up my CV when I go up for tenure. Even if only a few students take me up on it, it's publications and examples of mentorship and so on." He sees Mia has raised an eyebrow at him, "The tenure clock started ticking the day I was hired, I got to do what I got to do. Maybe you'll want to publish one with me?" He teases her and squeezes her ankle.

"So your mentor?" Mia starts.

"Yeah, Hank. Hank Simmons," Brett fills in his name. Mia's breath catches momentarily, knowing the name and realizing this discussion will soon pivot.

"Ah did your mentor have any other suggestions?" She asks, mentally shaking herself.

"Get on committees, collaborate, publish as much as quickly as possible, land a giant grant, don't sleep with a student," Brett winks at Mia.

She gently kicks his thigh. "He did not."

"No, he didn't. I think we're all already supposed to know that?"

Mia rolls her eyes at Brett and takes a deep breath. As casually as she can, she says, "So, um, I know Dr. Simmons."

Brett now raises his eyebrow at her. "Don't tell me you've dated another professor before? He seems a bit old for you…" Brett's tone is teasing but his face is serious.

"Oh, dear god no. No not like that at all. He's um, a chemistry professor, right?" Mia sees Brett nod his head. "Yeah, he's Danny's advisor. I've met him a couple of times, just from swinging by Danny's lab. But that's it."

Brett nods his head, his shoulders seem to drop down and let go of tension. "Interesting."

"Have you been by his lab?" Mia asks, now curious if Brett has seen Danny again.

Brett shakes his head, "No we meet at his office, not his lab space, or have dinner out somewhere."

Mia lets go of the breath she was holding. "Okay, well good. Cause, I guess that could get awkward…if like…you know…" she trails off.

Brett nods his head seriously. "Yeah, I guess it could."

An awkward silence fills in the apartment and Mia sits up

and grabs her wine glass, taking several sips before setting it back down. Brett appears to be staring off into the distance as Mia scoots over on the couch and gently touches his arm.

"Thoughts?" She asks him.

Brett shakes his head, "Nothing really."

"How about a change of subject?" Mia says, and then winking at Brett, "I'm curious, do you have any fantasies?"

Brett now seems more alert to their conversation and grins. "Fantasies?"

"Yeah, you know, things you want to do, like, sexually?" Mia presses.

"I know what you mean. I guess, yeah, everyone does," Brett fidgets.

"Well…?" Mia asks, giving his arm a gentle pinch.

"You'll laugh, and honestly it's kind of embarrassing," Brett says while shaking his head. "What about you?"

"C'mon, you won't tell me?" Mia teases. "You never know…if you tell..." she hints.

Brett shakes his head again, "Why don't you go first?"

Mia rolls her eyes and sighs. "Fine. I guess it's not really a fantasy per se, but I get excited about the potential for getting, um, caught."

"So you're an exhibitionist?" Brett asks confused.

"No, not quite, I don't think I want someone to watch me, I just get excited by the idea of having sex somewhere where I *could* get caught. I don't want to get caught and get some kind of charge or whatever." Mia clarifies.

"I guess that explains why you keep jumping me in parking lots," Brett says wisely.

She play punches his arm, "I believe we are both at fault for that thank you very much." She squeezes his thigh and bats her eyelashes at him. "Now, your turn." Brett squirms against her. "I won't laugh," Mia swears.

"It's just, uh, like a student-teacher fantasy," Brett mumbles.

Mia raises an eyebrow at him, unable to conceal her smile.

"Not quite like what we're doing, more like," Brett sighs and rubs his face, refusing to make eye contact with Mia. She can see him starting to blush. "More like, 'oh Dr. Dawson what can I do to improve my grade?' sort of thing."

Mia smiles more widely at Brett and he glances down at

her. "You're not allowed to laugh."

Mia holds up a hand, "I'm not laughing. So we're talking plaid skirt school girl begging for an A from Dr. Dawson?"

Brett coughs. "Yes."

"Anything else?"

"I mean, sex is involved."

"Duh," Mia giggles.

"You weren't going to laugh," Brett admonishes, but smiles at Mia.

Mia mimes zipping her lips, but ends up grinning. "Any other fantasies?"

Brett shrugs, "Probably just standard stuff from there, like a threesome or a random hot stranger having awesome sex with me, I don't know."

"Mmmkay," Mia answers.

"So what now? We can't exactly attempt to have sex in public," Brett says.

Mia shakes her head, "No, well at least not right now. I was just curious is all."

"Satisfied?" Brett asks.

"Always," Mia murmurs and kisses Brett. She snuggles up against him and the two settle into finishing their wine and watching movies on TV before going to bed.

CHAPTER 57

Brett leaves after breakfast, ducking under his baseball cap that Mia didn't even see him bring with him. They agreed to another date for next weekend, switching off to his place instead, and allowing themselves to each focus on their own work during the week. Mia has mixed feelings about trying to compartmentalize their relationship to primarily the weekends, as she'd like to see him more but worries about blurring the lines when she needs to maintain a sturdy façade.

After going to her complex's gym, showering, and grocery shopping for the week, she sits down at her laptop to skim over the articles for this week's classes.

Mia figures it's also been long enough to go without talking to Leigh and sends her a text, **Are we ok?**

Mia also glances at the clock and determines it is late enough into the day to call her brother, assuming he's awake by noon. Luke picks up after the third ring.

"Hellooo," Luke practically sings into the phone.

"Hey," Mia says, "how was your first week of classes?"

"Fine, uneventful. I've got a couple of easy ones, cause you know, senior year, so it's whatever." Luke answers while Mia pictures him shrugging his shoulders casually during his response.

"Okay, well that's good. Have you heard from mom or dad at all?"

"Yeah, mom's good. It sounds like she's going to start teaching a class at the community center? Like a meditation thing? I don't know."

Mia nods into the phone, "That should be good for her. And dad?"

"Eh, dad's dad. We spent twenty minutes talking about the weeds in his yard and the weeds in the neighbor's yard."

Mia laughed, "I guess I don't need to call either to get updates then."

Luke sighs, "I mean you should so that I'm not the only one talking to them."

Feeling chastised Mia replies, "Yeah, you're right, I

should." She pauses and then continues, "Anyway, how's everything else? How're things with Matt?"

"Matt's good, we're good."

"And any word from law schools yet?"

"Uh, it's too early for most of my applications, but I should hear back about my early decision from Earl pretty soon."

"It'd be pretty exciting if you ended up here," Mia says warmly.

"Yeah, but I'm sure we'd both be pretty busy."

"I would make time for my little brother," Mia says with a twinge of defensiveness in her voice.

"Yeah yeah, I know. It'd be funny, right? After so many years in different states we'd finally be in the same place?"

"It could be nice," Mia says. "We could have mini family dinners."

"You mean we could go out to eat and I can now legally drink with you," Luke corrects her.

"Well, that too," Mia replies. "Just, keep me posted, okay?"

"Sure, of course," Luke says, "anything else?"

"What do you mean?" Mia asks.

"Well last time we talked you told me all sorts of crazy stuff about your dating life, so I didn't know if you had some kind of drama again." Luke's voice sounds far off and uninterested.

Feeling hurt Mia just takes a deep breath and says, "No, no drama to report. Just wanted to know how you were doing. Let's talk again soon, I love you."

"Kay, I love you too," Luke says before they each say goodbye and hang up.

Mia looks down at her phone, feeling defeated. First Leigh, and now Luke, each seeming frustrated with her for different reasons. Given how Luke is responding to her personal life, Mia can't even begin to wrap her head around how Leigh would act if she knew about Brett. Mia pulls up her text to Leigh to see that it's been delivered but is still marked as 'unread.' She sighs and clicks off the screen to her phone. Mia weighs whether or not she wants to call either of her parents, but comes down to the decision that she'd rather wallow and feel grumpy.

After letting herself sigh uselessly and lay around for an hour on the couch, Mia refocuses her attention to something more productive. She chooses to start reading a therapy skills manual one of her supervisors previously recommended, which she bought used and never bothered to look at before. Mia settles back onto the couch with her highlighter in hand. She peruses passages and folds down pages where she finds things relevant to current clients. Mia pauses her reading to eat some lunch and watch TV before diving back into the book. It's close to dinner time when her phone buzzes with a text message from Leigh.

Sorry just seeing this. Let's get dinner. Free?

Mia checks her phone again and hesitates for a moment. The last thing she wants is another conversation that makes her feel crappy, but she also wants to clear the air with Leigh. It already feels bad enough that she's keeping a secret from her, but to also have this rift feels lonely.

Sure, Mia texts back, **where and when?**

Leigh suggests their favorite Thai restaurant in the next thirty minutes and Mia confirms. She changes into a clean pair of jeans and a sweatshirt, and pulls on her sneakers and jacket. Before heading out the door she calls Renly into the kitchen and spoons out some cat food into his bowl.

Mia gets to the restaurant before Leigh and is seated by a hostess. She shrugs off her jacket and peers around at the mostly deserted place. The door opens and a quick blast of cold air floats in as Leigh hustles inside and throws herself into the seat opposite of Mia.

"It's like the one week it's actually cold here," Leigh says, removing her jacket.

Mia nods. "Yeah, maybe we'll get some snow."

"Ugh, I'd rather not. Earl is terrible about not closing even when the roads are a mess." Leigh says, while scanning the menu that was already laid out for her.

Mia briefly pictures being snowed in with Brett, and having a few quiet days together.

"I don't even know why I look at menus, I know what I'm getting here," Leigh says, interrupting Mia's thoughts. "You also ready?" Mia nods at Leigh's question and Leigh waves to the waitress that has been hovering. Both women order and the waitress takes their menus and leave.

"So," Mia says.

"So?" Leigh asks.

"I mean, are we okay?" Mia asks.

"Yeah, we can disagree about the Sasha and Danny stuff and be friends," Leigh answers. "I just worry about both of you, honestly. If Danny is willing to behave that way towards you, what is he also willing to do towards Sasha that we don't know about?"

Mia nods slowly while Leigh continues. "Like, if he's bold enough to threaten you from *outside* your front door, what could he be doing to Sasha *behind* closed doors? Like I said, I just worry."

"I follow, I guess…I guess I didn't think about that," Mia says, feeling admonished.

"I'm not trying to make you feel bad, Mia," Leigh says, noticing her friend's expression and tone, "I've just," Leigh sighs, "I've been there and have ignored the signs, and have ended up in a bad situation, so maybe I'm hyperaware to it, but I can't help but feel like I'm spotting some red flags with Danny."

Mia presses her lips together, hiding her sudden surprise, as she realizes her friend is sharing something new with her. "I had no idea that you've had some experience with this."

Leigh eyes her hands on the table and then back up at Mia. "Yeah, in college an ex-boyfriend got increasingly possessive until," Leigh takes a breath, "until it went too far. And at that point, I had let myself accept all those incremental steps to get there. So when he hit me," Leigh stops and shakes her head, tearing up. She wipes her eyes and then wipes her hands on her pants. "So when he hit me," she starts again, "I didn't even think it was wrong."

Mia reaches across the table and grabs Leigh's hands. "Leigh, I'm so sorry. I had no idea you've had to deal with something like that."

Leigh shrugs and looks down again. "How would you? I don't usually talk about it, cause it was a horrible time and I've worked hard to move forward. But what I am telling you, is that I just worry about what Danny is capable of, and that includes you and Sasha."

Mia gives her friend's hands a squeeze before letting go, "Of course, that makes sense. Thank you, for sharing with me. Everything."

Mia sits back in her chair as the waitress places their food in front of them and Leigh tries to smile at Mia.

"So like I said, think about telling Sasha." Leigh says seriously before starting in on her dinner.

Mia nods seriously, "I will. I will think about it." She starts to eat her own meal, thinking about how she could ever approach Sasha, and what kind of problems she could face with Danny if they did speak. She doesn't have to make a decision yet about what to do, but Leigh's words start to weigh heavily on her as she considers what she can possibly do.

"Anyway, yes, we're good," Leigh says between mouthfuls of food, sounding calmer. "How was the rest of your week last week?"

As Leigh changes the subject the two women fall into a discussion about their week, with Mia leaving out all details about Brett. After they've finished their meals and paid their bills, they've each bundled back up to head back out to their cars.

Mia grabs her friend in a hug before they leave, whispering to her, "Thank you again for sharing with me. You're an amazing woman and I'm lucky to know you." Leigh hugs her back and Mia feels her nod against her. "I'll see you this week, okay?" Mia confirms pulling out of the hug but still holding her friend by the arms.

"Yep, at least in class with Hot Prof," Leigh says smiling.

"Ew don't call him that," Mia says laughing and dropping her grip.

"You're so weird about that, at least admit he's attractive," Leigh teased.

"I mean, yes, he's very attractive, I just, I just feel weird talking about it, he's faculty. It's weird," Mia squirms.

"Whatever, I will at least see you in class which happens to be led by an insanely attractive faculty member." Leigh rolls her eyes.

"Uh huh, see you this week," Mia replies as the women part ways and she heads back home.

CHAPTER 58

Mia's following week sets what becomes her routine for the semester. She works out in the morning before heading to campus to either attend classes, work in one of the clinics she's seeing patients, address lab work in Dr. Thompson's lab , or manage her own research or homework. Mia actively avoids making eye contact with Brett during the class as much as she can, but tries to participate consistently in the discussions. She occasionally sees Leigh and sometimes Sasha too for lunch. Mia still thinks about what Leigh said to her, but finds herself struggling with telling Sasha more. She wants to make sure that Sasha is safe without garnering Danny's attention. In addition to worrying about her dilemma with Sasha, Mia is also trying to gently remind her advisor over email to review her latest thesis draft.

By the time Wednesday rolls around and Brett darts from the class once again, Mia turns to Leigh and Sasha and cheerily offers, "Lunch?"

Both women look at Mia, with Sasha nodding and Leigh saying "Yes" exuberantly.

"Kay," Mia says, while gathering her things, "dining hall? Sandwich shop?"

"I'm going to grab mine from my office, so whatever you two want," Leigh says.

"Let's do the panini place," Sasha says.

"Sounds good," Mia replies and the three women head towards Leigh's office so she can bring her own lunch. They pass by Brett's office as they walk towards the lab Leigh works in. Mia glances in to see Brett at his desk, seemingly working on his laptop. He glances up at the sound of the footsteps and smiles, and Mia smiles back with a quick wink before quickly directing her attention back to her friends.

After all three of them have their lunches, they settle down at an empty table. The women start to eat their lunches and Mia decides to gently assess the situation with Sasha.

"Are things any better with Danny?" she directs towards Sasha as casually as she can. Leigh seems to shoot an incredulous expression at Mia before turning her attention to Sasha.

Sasha shrugs while she chews, swallowing before saying,

"He's been a little weird and distant lately. Which I don't know if that's better than him being an asshole. I know he's really stressed right now with his dissertation proposal, not like that's an excuse, but I've just been giving him his space."

Mia and Leigh each nod as Sasha falls silent. "Has he, um, ever," Mia tries to find the words, "made you uncomfortable or anything?"

Sasha wrinkles her forehead, "What do you mean?"

"Um, just like, beyond saying dumb shit, anything else?" Mia prods clumsily.

Sasha's forehead crinkles more and she shakes her head, "Um, no? He just gets into a mood sometimes and talks without thinking. He knows to work on it."

Mia feels an internal pressure release, as though she received the pass she was looking for to not share more with Sasha. "Okay, just making sure. Like you know, if something happens, we're here for you."

Sasha looks back and forth between Mia and Leigh, who has maintained a poker face through the discussion. "Um, thanks," she says slowly and takes another bite of her lunch. "Is there a reason for this discussion?"

Leigh seems to flash another expression at Mia that she can't interpret. Before Mia can answer, Leigh shakes her head and directs to Sasha, "No, just checking in on you, that's all. Danny seemed to have a stick up his ass at the dinner and wanted to make sure you're okay."

"I'm fine, thanks for checking."

"Good," Leigh says, then turns to Mia to deliberately change the topic. "Speaking of proposals, how's your master's coming?"

Knowing she deserved the spotlighted attention after awkwardly trying to address Leigh's concerns about Sasha, Mia quickly answers, "Well I had to remind Jean today to read over my draft. So hopefully I'll get some comments from her soonish so that I can keep moving it along. I want to defend it before the semester ends and then turn it around quickly to propose my dissertation right away in the fall. But, you know, I feel like my hands are tied while I wait on her revisions."

Both Leigh and Sasha nod. Leigh has already defended her thesis and Sasha will be defending her master's in a couple of weeks. "She'll get back to you sooner rather than later," Leigh says reassuringly. "She doesn't want to look bad either."

"That's probably my saving grace with her," Mia snorts. The three then fall into a discussion about the pros and cons of their various advisors, equally praising and complaining about their experiences, passing the rest of the lunch easily.

CHAPTER 59

Any chance you'll need a ride back to your car tonight? Brett's text comes in Friday morning while Mia's showering after hitting her complex's gym. She's toweling off and figuring out what she wants to wear for the day when she sees the blinking light and checks her messages. She grins, thinking of the potential opportunity that Brett is inviting.

If you're willing, I'd love one. It'll be a chilly walk otherwise. She sends back. Brett replies with a thumbs up emoji accompanied by **Time?** and Mia lets him know to get to the clinic a little after eight in the evening, so that she has enough time to wrap up and write her progress notes for the day.

Mia turns back to her closet, now trying to decide on an outfit she'll know Brett will see. She moves past her dress slacks and sweaters and begins to push through her various dresses. Eventually she finds what she is searching for, a dark green shirt dress, that is long enough to be appropriate for meeting with patients, and that she can adjust the neckline of with a button or two. She pairs the dress with a cardigan and ankle boots and finishes getting ready in the bathroom by applying her makeup and brushing out her hair.

Mia arrives at her basement office, and after logging into her laptop, discovers her advisor has sent her back the revisions she's been waiting on. Mia immediately sets to work, reading Dr. Thompson's comments and beginning to tackle the necessary edits. Without any classes on her Fridays, she's able to focus on her writing and the lab management tasks she has left for the week. She eats lunch in her office, checks in with the undergraduate research assistants, and feels good about her overall progress by the time she leaves to grab a quick dinner before her later afternoon and evening patients.

Mia feels her body buzzing with excitement as each hour passes. The clock creeping closer to eight is the signal that she can switch back into her secret relationship, where she can burn off some stress, and maybe even talk about what she's been going through with her brother and Leigh. As Mia's last patient wraps up and leaves for the day, she rushes to complete her notes and check the building for other occupants. She tells her classmate that she usually walks with to head on without her, explaining that she has more notes to finish and doesn't want to hold her up. Mia waits a little more after her watch hits eight to check the occupancy of the building, which appears empty. She also glances out a front window and sees the parking lot is deserted too. Before heading outside she shimmies her panties off and stashes them in her bag, and then yanks her coat on. The front door automatically locks behind her as she gently sits on the cold bench by the entrance, waiting on Brett's arrival.

Mia jumps up from the bench as his car rolls in and comes to stop in front of the clinic. She runs over to the passenger side and lets herself in, automatically appreciating the warm flow of air from the vents. She barely registers the light scent of oranges that she's accustomed to following Brett everywhere.

"You must be freezing, were you out there long?" Brett asks, already guiding the car to where Mia's is parked.

"No, not at all, just don't have on heavy enough layers I guess," Mia answers. She's shaking her leg a bit, which Brett notices.

"You alright?" he asks.

"Yes, of course. How's your week been?" Mia smiles and stops bouncing her leg.

"Pretty good, got a revise resubmit on a paper and an acceptance contingent on a couple of edits, so I'm working on both of those. You?"

"A mix, we can talk more about it tomorrow though," Mia says somewhat impatiently, as she eagerly waits for Brett to reach her parking lot. He eventually pulls in, next to her car. A few other cars sit in the dark lot, but none are particularly close and Mia barely notices them. She glances over at Brett and smiles, smoothing the skirt part of her dress.

"Don't think I didn't notice," Brett says, nodding to her dress.

"Would you like to?" Mia asks, already shouldering off her jacket and cardigan. She unbuttons the top two buttons of her dress, revealing her cleavage.

As an answer, Brett pushes his seat back, making room for Mia to clamber over and climb on top of him. She straddles him in the driver's seat and he rests his hands on her legs, over her dress. Mia leans down and kisses him and drops a hand to his crotch, and begins to massage his penis through his pants. Brett grips at her legs and Mia feels his body respond under her hand. He pulls back from the kiss and begins moving his lips down her neck and to her breasts, unbuttoning her dress further to expose her. He gropes and kisses her breasts as Mia begins to rock against him. He lifts his face back up to Mia and they kiss again, her tongue moving against his steadily and with increasing need.

Mia breaks from the kiss, panting while Brett snakes his hands up underneath her dress. His eyes widen in surprise when he discovers she's already naked under the dress.

"I came prepared, did you?" Mia whispers with a slight giggle. Brett nods and Mia shifts back a bit as Brett frees his erection from his pants and takes a condom out of the console. After rolling it on, Mia moves back to steady herself above Brett's hard cock. She slowly lowers herself onto him, savoring the sensation of his erection expanding her. Brett moans as Mia slowly moves over him and pulls her in for a kiss. He tries to urge her faster, but Mia maintains her pace, her heart thudding through her slow fuck with Brett, her breath hot in the car. Brett reaches down between them and slowly circles her clit with a finger, his pace matching hers.

Mia moans at the feeling, and grips the headrest. She gasps when Brett leans in and begins to suck on her earlobe. Mia's pace only quickens as she urges the on the oncoming orgasm. Sensing her urgency, Brett's pressure on her clit intensifies and he pulls her in for another kiss. Mia moans into his mouth as she comes, her body quivering. Brett presses forward, finally reaching his own climax, and bringing his head to a rest on Mia's shoulder, panting and kissing her.

Mia takes a beat to take in the fogged up windows, the kind she's only used to seeing in dramatized renditions of car sex. She carefully extracts herself from Brett and settles back into the passenger seat. She fans herself a bit as Brett pulls himself together, removing the condom and stuffing it into the wrapper and adjusting himself back into his pants.

"So now you can cross that off your list," Brett says with a smile.

"Absolutely," Mia sighs.

"Anything else I can do to satisfy you?" he teases.

Mia thinks while she buttons her dress back up and pulls her cardigan back on.

"Honestly? I started back on the pill the other day…so maybe in a few weeks we can drop the condom? If you're comfortable with that?" Mia blurts.

Brett runs a hand through his hair and grins, "Yeah, I would definitely enjoy that."

Mia smiles and leans over, giving Brett a passionate kiss. "Good," she whispers into his ear, "cause I want to feel you and only you inside of me." She hears Brett's breath catch and kisses him again. Mia sits back in her seat and lets out a deep breath and closes her eyes. "And now I'm done."

Brett laughs, "Do I need to drive you home?"

Mia opens an eye to peek at him and smiles, "No. But I will see you tomorrow, right?"

"Yep," Brett nods.

"Good," Mia leans over and gives Brett one last quick peck before grabbing her things. "Thanks for the ride again," she winks and gets out from the car.

Brett waves to her and waits for her to get into her car and turn it on before driving away. Mia pulls down the visor and checks herself over in the mirror. She's flushed and her eyes are bright. Snapping the mirror back up she glances into the rearview mirror to back up and notices a car in the background. For a moment Mia thinks she catches someone in the driver's seat, but she blinks and it appears to be empty. Mia shakes her head and rolls her eyes at herself. *It's just dark and you're freaking yourself out.* However, Mia peals out of the parking lot and heads home without looking back.

CHAPTER 60

Despite having just seen him the night before, Mia wakes on Saturday eager for the evening to arrive and spend the night with Brett. She follows through with a new weekend routine of taking time to feel more awake before going for a run, showering, and settling down with some breakfast in front of the TV. After clearing her plates and cleaning up the mess she made in the kitchen, she heads into her office to work on the readings she has assigned for the week.

Close to lunch time, Mia hears her phone buzz and sees Brett has texted her.

Hate to do this, but have to cancel for tonight. Friend came to visit out of the blue.

Mia frowns at her phone after reading the message. She sighs, thinking through what to send back. She types out and sends, **That's too bad** accompanied by a sad emoji.

I'm sorry about this, we'll have to aim for next weekend.

Mia sighs loudly again, frustrated and annoyed at both Brett and his friend who she decides has no manners to just show up without asking first.

It's fine, she sends back, swallowing back her annoyance, **at least I saw you last night**. Mia knows she wasn't just hoping to sleep with Brett again, but that she also wanted to talk about what was going on with Luke and Leigh. She wants to feel the emotional support side of having a boyfriend, no matter how secret that boyfriend was.

I'll come over next weekend and make it up to you. Promise.

Given her now defunct plans, Mia pulls up Leigh's contact in her phone and texts her, **Drinks?**

Yes! How about that girls' night? I'll text Sasha? Leigh responds immediately.

Sounds good, Mia messages back. Drinking with Sasha was not on her shortlist of preferred activities, but at least it would mean getting out and taking her mind off of things.

I'll pick you up, I owe you a sober ride. Leigh sends back.

Even better, Mia thinks, now she can go and maybe let go

a little more than usual.

Mia downs a bowl of pasta for dinner, figuring she would benefit from having a particularly full stomach before going out to eat. Even though she's not hoping for anything romantic to spark at the bar, Mia has fun getting herself ready for the night. She picks a pair of tight jeans and black ankle boots, along with a low cut leopard blouse that hints at her curves. She applies her makeup and completes her look with red lipstick. She takes a quick picture of herself in the bathroom mirror, sending it to Brett along with the message **Gonna go have some fun without you tonight, will miss you!**

Mia checks out her window and sees Leigh has pulled into the parking lot at her building and grabs her purse and jacket and heads out the door. Mia's phone buzzes in her hand and she pulls up Brett's response.

Don't have too much fun, with a winking face. Mia shoves her phone back into her purse, deciding to put a pause on Brett for the rest of the night so that she can enjoy the time with her friends.

Inside Leigh's car and on their way to the bar where they planned to meet Sasha, Leigh clears her throat and Mia turns to her.

"So no awkward conversations with Sasha tonight, right?" Leigh starts by telling but ends up asking.

"Ah, no. And I know that lunch was weird, but I wanted to, I don't know, open the door to her if she needed it."

"Right," Leigh glances at Mia. "It just kind of came off as a little weird."

"I know, I could have been smoother about it. But I don't know if there's a more eloquent way to ask someone if their boyfriend is abusing them," Mia says lightly.

"There isn't. And talking around it doesn't always help either. If you're going to talk to her about it, be more direct next time," Leigh says seriously.

Mia nods, looking at her friend, "Yeah, okay."

Leigh seems to relax more and pulls into the parking lot of the bar, "Okay, good. Well let's go have a drink."

Despite her disappointment from earlier in the day, and Leigh's mild talking to, Mia finds herself laughing and having fun with the other women. Sasha ended up inviting a few other girls from the department to join them, so they've ended up creating a small crowd of their own at the bar. While she's been careful to not overdo it with the drinks, Mia is well aware that she's passed tipsy and verging on solidly drunk as the evening grows.

One of the girls has the brilliant idea to head to a dance bar more heavily populated by the undergraduate students, and Mia's group moves over to the new bar en masse. They easily make their way in, given that their IDs are real and far less questionable than the ones the bouncers usually see, and immediately land on the dance floor.

Mia bounces and sways on the dance floor, moving around her friends and swinging her head and hair from side to side. She feels the press of other bodies around her and begins to sweat from both the dancing and the density. One of her friends manages to push another drink into her hand and Mia knows this one has to be her last one if she wants to make it home without losing the contents of her stomach. A few more songs later, and starting to feel dizzy, Mia finds Leigh, who is also still dancing, to let her know she's ready to leave whenever Leigh is. Leigh nods her head and signals to stay for one more song. Mia motions to Leigh to indicate she'll be outside getting fresh air, and leaves the crowded bar.

Outside, Mia is able to take several deep, cooling, and steadying breaths of cold air. The sweat from dancing now starts to feel cold against her skin and she shivers. Mia quickly scans the area outside the bar, seeing that there's still a line of people trying to get in. She continues to gaze around her and sees Sasha off to the side. Mia walks over to her, concentrating on steadying her steps.

"Hey," she says, as she gets close to Sasha.

"Hey!" Sasha says brightly. She motions her head back to

the bar, "I had to get some fresh air. It is crazy packed in there."

Mia nods in agreement.

"I'm actually having Danny come and pick me up, since he's so close to here. I don't think I have the stamina everyone else has," Sasha laughs.

"Naw," Mia shakes her head, and stopping as it makes her dizzy, "Leigh and I are going soon too. These undergrads make me feel old." She gives Sasha a lopsided smile.

Sasha nods, but looks out to the road, scanning for Danny's car.

"Hey!" calls Leigh, who is now approaching them. She hooks an arm through Mia's. "You ready?"

"Um yeah, but let's wait to make sure Sasha gets picked up," Mia says.

"No worries about that, he's here," Sasha replies, walking towards a car that has pulled in. The window of the driver's side has rolled down and Danny leans out.

"Hey!" He calls out. Sasha hurries over and gets into the car. Danny peers at Leigh and Mia, as Leigh waves and the Mia tries to look elsewhere.

"Surprised to see you out," Danny says to them casually.

"I figured you'd be home with your boy."

Leigh calls back, "Girls' night, no boys allowed." Danny's eyes, however, are trained on Mia. She shifts and tugs on Leigh's arm. Leigh turns to her and nods, "Alright, let's go." Leigh turns back to Danny's car and shouts, "See ya!," before leading Mia back to her own.

Inside Leigh's car, Mia leans her head back and closes her eyes, focusing on her breathing and not the turns of the car. She knew that last drink was probably a bad idea.

"Are you going to be okay getting inside your place?" Leigh asks with concern.

Mia opens her eyes at her friend, realizing they've gotten back. "Ugh, yes. Thank you for driving. I'm going to go upstairs and chug water and lay down."

"Sounds like a good idea," Leigh replies and watches as Mia carefully gets out of the car and heads up to her apartment.

After letting herself in, Mia locks her door and shucks off her shoes. She fills a glass of water and drinks it slowly in her kitchen. She drinks another half glass of water before setting the glass down, grabbing her phone from her purse, and carefully walking back into her bedroom, shedding her clothes to the floor. Mia flops down on her bed and pulls up her text messages.

Hope you're having a good time!

A text from Brett that Mia didn't notice from a few hours earlier.

She texts him back, **I had lots of fun. Now I'm half naked in my bed and wouldn't mind company.**

Proof or it didn't happen. Brett texts back.

Mia holds the phone over herself and snaps a photo, barely checking it before sending it back. She then shifts and quickly removes her bra and takes another photo including her bare breasts and sends that one.

I want to make you come, she adds. She sees Brett typing and sighs, rolling over and pulling the covers over herself.

I really wish I could right now.

I'd let you fuck me raw right now. Mia replies.

I cannot tell you how tempting that is. Guessing you're drunk right now? Brett answers.

Maybe.

Then we'll revisit this offer when you can consciously make it. I'll see you this week. Goodnight gorgeous.

Mia's eyes are already half shut and she drops her phone to the floor. She focuses on her breathing, and not the false sensation of the bed moving beneath her, so that she can fall asleep.

CHAPTER 61

Mia rolls over and squints at her clock when she finally stirs awake. The sun is peeking through her blinds and she groans as some it catches her eyes. She's slept in, as she should have expected, and her mouth feels like it's been stuffed with cotton. She kicks her blankets off and reaches for her phone, which she had dropped to the floor the night before. She discovers it's dead, so after rummaging through her nightstand for a t-shirt that she pulls on, she plugs her phone in and drags herself out of bed.

Mia finds her various articles of clothing that she dropped throughout her apartment from the night before, and the half full water glass in the kitchen. She spills out the old water and refills her glass with fresh water from the tap, gulping down the glass. Mia pulls out her bottle of Advil, refilling her glass again, and takes two pills with another swig of water. She moves about her apartment, now collecting her clothes and throwing them into her laundry basket.

Mia tries to consider something to eat, and determines the only thing that will work is a simple frozen pizza, as if she were still in undergrad. She preheats the oven and pulls a pizza from the freezer, unwrapping it and gets it ready to pop into the oven once it beeps the ready signal.

She goes back to the bathroom and checks herself in the mirror, realizing she never washed her face, leaving her with smudged eyeliner and lipstick. She grabs a hair tie and pulls her hair back and gets to work scrubbing last night's residue off. She also brushes her teeth for good measure, trying to wash away the taste of old liquor. The oven beeps at her, and Mia goes back to the kitchen and pops the pizza in, setting the timer, and then goes to check on her phone, which is barely charged.

Mia knows she texted Brett last night, but cannot entirely recall what was said. Bracing herself, she pulls up their exchange. She claps a hand over her mouth, seeing that she sent a picture clearly showing her face and her tits. She normally tries to keep her sexts to a hint of a body part, such as covering her nipples, or at least covered in underwear, especially if she includes her face. *Too late now*, Mia thinks. *At least my makeup was not entirely smudged at that point*, she tries to console herself. She also sees her offer to Brett and double checks the calendar on her phone. The timing is about right to actually make good on that desire.

Mia drops her phone back down and heads back into her kitchen, waiting for the pizza to finish cooking. As soon as it's done, she takes it out, cuts it up, and plops down in front of her TV with several slices. After polishing off over half of the pie, Mia cleans up and puts the rest away in the refrigerator for leftovers. She grabs her phone from her room and sees a new text from Brett.

Alive?

Barely, she sends back.

What are your plans for today?

Avoid sunlight and loud noises, she texts only half-joking.

My friend is leaving this afternoon, if you'd like company later.

Mia purses her lips, even though she was disappointed the night before when Brett canceled at the last minute, now she's not particularly in the mood to see him. She'd rather spend the day being lazy and eating greasy food and just not giving a damn about anything.

Can't today, she sends back. **But we can aim for next Saturday's makeup date?**

Sounds good, feels like forever away though.

It appears I've sent you some material you can

console yourself with in the meantime ;), Mia replies.

Any more where that came from?

Mia smiles, **Be a good boy and maybe you'll get more this week.** Brett sends back emojis with a halo and fingers crossed. Mia tosses her phone aside and settles back onto the couch, figuring she'll eventually pull herself together to do something productive during the day.

CHAPTER 62

Mia never made anything useful out of her Sunday, and by the time she's on campus on Monday she's regretting having not tried harder. She rushes to finish her readings for Brett's seminar and takes a few notes so that she can make some coherent contributions. Mia arrives to the class just after Brett, catching the door as it starts to swing shut behind him.

"Sorry, didn't catch you behind me!" He says.

"Not a problem," Mia says, slightly out of breath from her haul up the flights of steps. "My office is in the basement, I should probably switch from a treadmill to a stair stepper," she jokes to explain her pant. Brett smiles and heads to the front of the seminar room. Mia forks off a different direction and sits next to Leigh, who has already seated next to Sasha.

"How was your Sunday?" Leigh asks with a smirk.

"Very hungover," Mia grumbles. Both Leigh and Sasha giggle.

"I'm glad we all got out and had fun, it's gotten so much harder to do so this year," Sasha says.

"Me too," Mia replies sincerely, "It was fun, even if I overdid it. Next time I'll DD and let Leigh be the messy one." She winks and the other women chuckle.

Brett gets the seminar underway, and Mia listens carefully to add her comments that she had jotted down earlier. For one of her insights Brett smiles and nods, and observes "That's an interesting thought, Mia," to which Mia feels herself begin to melt internally. Mia just lets a small smile poke through and ducks her head down. The class continues on around her, though Mia finds herself drifting. It eventually wraps up and Mia sees her friends off before heading back down to her office.

Back in the basement she meets with the undergraduate research assistant to direct her on the latest lab tasks and begins to tackle the IRB renewal that's due soon. Mia forces herself to focus and manages to turn in the documents by the end of the day. She finishes off her afternoon with two back to back clients and heads home.

Checking to make sure it's after five, Mia strips down to her underwear in her room and lays down on her bed. She places a hand with her fingers just reaching into the band of her panties and snaps a photo showing her torso and the suggestion. She sends it to Brett along with the message, **Good boys get rewarded**. Mia gets back up and throws on her pajamas, and goes back to her usual evening of dinner, work, and watching mindless TV.

The rest of her week follows similarly, with Mia hunkering down during working hours to be productive, and sending one suggestive photo to Brett each evening, with him always replying with appreciation. After her latest photo on Friday, Brett texts to confirm that they're on for Saturday and Mia assures him with an **Absolutely**.

Mia swings by a liquor store on the way to Brett's on Saturday and picks up a bottle of champagne. Once at his front door, she adjusts her tight jeans and the now clean leopard print top from last weekend. Underneath her clothes, her lacy panties are barely there and Mia's brought her vibrator and a toothbrush along in her purse. She knocks and Brett swings the door open.

"You have made this week very difficult for me," He says with a grin, pulling Mia into the house. He shuts the door behind Mia and gives her a long kiss. Brett notices the bottle in Mia's hand. "What's that for?" he asks.

"For a celebratory moment, but not just yet. I want my conversation first this time." Mia wrinkles her eyes with her smile.

"Oh, so I get teased all week," Brett murmurs, tracing a finger down Mia's arm, and leaning down to kiss and suck on her neck. Mia shivers and her nipples harden underneath her blouse. "And now I have to wait a little longer?" He slips a hand under the back of Mia's shirt and starts to fumble with her bra.

Mia sighs and giggles, before gently pushing Brett back and wagging a finger at him. "You have to keep being a good boy to get your reward."

"Alright, I guess I can wait a little longer," Brett grins and guides Mia to the couch. He sits down and pats the spot next to him. "Come talk to me."

Mia drops her purse and the champagne into the kitchen before she curls up into the spot next to him, tucking her legs under herself.

"How was your Saturday? With your friend?" She asks.

"It was good. I uh, obviously wasn't expecting him. So just showed him around town a little and then we just hung out here with some beers."

"Who was it again?" Mia asks.

"His name is Chris, I know him from college." Brett answers.

"Ah, okay," Mia nods.

"Was there more you wanted to talk about?" Brett asks.

"Ugh, yeah," Mia sighs. "I wanted to vent about what's been going on with my brother and Leigh…" she pauses, "but it's definitely hard to be focused on that stuff when we're finally together."

Brett takes that as an invitation to gently stroke her arm again, and leans back in to kiss along Mia's jawline.

"I guess I could focus better and actually talk after…" she breathes out.

"I'd be happy to help you release some of that tension," Brett whispers into her ear.

"Yes, but wait, first, the champagne," Mia pulls back from Brett and goes into the kitchen, while he watches her. "Do you have flutes?" She calls to him.

"Um, no, just wine glasses," he yells back.

"That'll do. Close your eyes!" Mia insists. Once she sees that Brett has closed his eyes with a smile, she pops open the champagne and pours it into two wine glasses she finds in the cupboard. Before heading back into the living room, she takes off her blouse and jeans and tip toes back to the couch. Mia stands in front of Brett and holds out a glass to him. "Okay, open."

Brett opens his eyes and spots the wine glasses before gazing up and down at Mia. He grins and takes the glass Mia has offered to him. She clinks her glass against his and they both take a sip.

"So what is the occasion? It can't be the papers I talked about last week?" Brett jokes.

"No," Mia says, settling down into a straddle over Brett.

"Does it have to do with your thesis?" Brett presses questioningly.

"Nope," Mia takes another sip, and she leans back, placing her wine glass on the coffee table. Brett takes another sip and hands his glass to her to put down, which she does.

"Are you going to elaborate then?" Brett grins, now resting his hands on Mia's hips.

"It's" Mia kisses one side of Brett's neck, "time," she kisses the other side, "to make good," she sucks on an earlobe, "on my offer," she whispers into his other ear. Brett's grip on her waist tightens a bit.

"Oh really?" he whispers, his eyes glowing.

Mia brushes her lips along Brett's jawline before passionately kissing him, urging his mouth open and thrusting her tongue in. "Mmhmm," she murmurs between kisses. Brett's hands slip from her waist to squeeze her ass. Mia arches her back, moving her breasts towards Brett's face, allowing him to press his lips against her cleavage. Mia rocks against Brett, encouraging his cock to harden.

"Do you want to fuck me?" She whispers into his ear.

"Absolutely," Brett whispers back.

"Then let's get you ready," Mia stands back up and steps back, allowing Brett to pull off his shirt, and shuck off his pants and boxers in one smooth motion. He grasps his cock, already at attention, slowly rubbing it up and down.

Mia winks at him and kneels between his legs. She replaces his hand with hers and winks at Brett while she begins to slowly pump. Brett closes his eyes and leans his head back in the couch. Mia licks his erection from stem to tip before wrapping her lips around him. She sucks and pumps, feeling Brett's hands twist into her hair, encouraging her on. He groans and stiffens. "Come up here," he gasps.

Mia lifts her head from his lap and stands up. Brett leans forward and tugs at the band of her panties. Mia pulls them the rest of the way off, before unclasping her bra and dropping to the floor. She climbs back on top of Brett, who has busied himself with her tits, fondling her and twirling her nipples between kissing and sucking on them.

Mia starts to lower herself onto Brett, but stops just as she senses his tip at her crevice. "I've been wanting this, since I've had a taste of it," she murmurs. She lowers herself further, luxuriating in the slow sensation of his skin against hers, stretching and filling her. “Fuck,” Mia moans. She arches her back once more, Brett landing kisses and nibbles across her chest as she carefully slides up and down on his cock.

“God this feels good,” Brett barely gasps out.” Mia moans again and Brett urges her to move faster with his hands on her hips. Mia responds, her ass now smacking against Brett’s thighs. Mia presses on at this pace a little longer before slowing again and climbing off of Brett.

“One second,” she says, and pads back into the kitchen, returning with her vibrator from her purse. Brett grins at her. Mia leans over the arm of the couch and starts the vibrator, gasping when she places it at her clit. She looks at Brett, who has returned to pumping his erection again. “Well, come over here and make me come,” Mia demands.

Brett grins and hops off the couch, and positions himself behind her. He starts to press himself into her bit by bit, Mia’s own body trying to urge him in faster, which he ignores. Brett starts to slowly thrust into her. “Faster,” Mia begs and Brett begins to pick up his pace. She increases the intensity on her vibrator, whimpering at the combined sensations.

“You’re fucking me so good,” Mia cries out with a thrust, “god, fuck me, Brett, fuck me with your thick cock.” She hears Brett grunt behind her, his thrusts coming harder and faster. Mia feels a sting on her ass as he slaps it and then caresses it. "Yes, Brett," she cries again, "Fuck me. God, come in me, come in me, Brett, please." Mia's voice rises as she begs, her own orgasm now on the brink of taking over her senses. Brett fucks Mia harder and lets out drawn out swear words as he orgasms. Mia feels her own legs shake and cries out once more as she feels her body go over the edge and her orgasm blossoms through her body.

"Holy fuck," Mia gasps, trying to catch her breath. Brett laughs from behind her and gives her ass another gentle slap. "Your cock is amazing, but without a condom…" she trails off.

"It's so much better, yeah," Brett finishes for her. Mia excuses herself to the bathroom and quickly cleans herself up. When she comes back to the living room she pulls her panties back on and Brett tosses her a t-shirt he already had downstairs.

"Thank you," she grins, pulling it over her head.

"That one's yours from here out," he says with a smile. He sits back down on the couch, back in his pants and shirt. Mia lays herself out on the couch, resting her feet in Brett's lap. He starts to rub her feet and Mia relaxes and sighs contentedly.

CHAPTER 63

Mia closes her eyes while Brett rubs her feet. She feels ready to fall into a deep content sleep when Brett interrupts her relaxation. "So how have your last few weeks been?" Brett asks.

"Ugh," Mia says. "Well, I had this, not a fight, but like, disagreement of sorts with Leigh. She uh," she hesitates, "wanted me to tell Danny's girlfriend about what happened."

Brett nods, his face serious.

Mia continues, "Because Sasha approached me after the department dinner to say she knows Danny and I have a history, and he was being a huge jerk to her that night, and I guess wanted to know if I had any insight? Or at least be more honest with each other going forward?"

"And you decided against that," Brett fills in.

"Kind of, but not? I've just decided that *going forward* if something comes up with Danny again, I'll say something to her. I just want to let sleeping dogs lie, you know? He's left me alone since that night." Mia chews her inner cheek.

"I see," Brett says quietly.

"I imagine you probably agree with Leigh, and anyway Leigh was upset with me that I didn't share more, and was worried that maybe there were things going on between Sasha and Danny that we didn't know about."

"What kind of things?" Brett says curiously.

Mia takes a deep breath, not feeling comfortable sharing Leigh's revelation to her. "Just that Leigh felt that there were some red flags with Danny," to which Brett snorts derisively, "and that she was concerned about Sasha's safety."

"Sure," Brett's earlier reaction gone from his face, his eyes now intent and serious on Mia. "Are you concerned about her well-being?"

"I mean, I was when Leigh said that! And I kind of asked Sasha, and let her know she could come talk to us, in a way that came out kind of weird, I guess." Mia notices some defensiveness creeping into her voice. Brett nods again, his face contemplative. Mia's teeth snap at the inside of her cheek again. "Anyway," she starts again, hoping to steer the conversation, "Leigh was upset with me but we've talked it out."

"Well that's good," Brett replies and goes silent.

"You agree with Leigh?" Mia asks quietly.

"That Danny is a walking red flag and you should probably report him to someone? Yes," Brett says decisively. He sees Mia's face, stricken with worry and shame. "I get why you don't want to though. Like I've said before, you should be careful and report him if anything comes up again," he says more gently.

"I know, I will," Mia promises.

"And your brother?" Brett asks.

"My brother?" Mia says confused, and then remembers she also mentioned Luke earlier to Brett. "Oh yeah, I spoke with Luke and he was annoyed that I hadn't called our parents and basically called me a magnet for drama. I felt like crap after we talked."

"Why haven't you called your parents?" Brett cocks his head to the side in question.

Mia shrugs and squirms. "I don't know. I've been busy?" She sighs, "Cause I'm a bad daughter? Cause talking to them is exhausting? All of the above?"

"Okay," Brett says without judgment.

"How often do you talk to your parents?" Mia asks curiously.

"Once a week. Sometimes it's brief, sometimes it's not, but we check in every week. Same with my sister." Brett answers.

"Oh." Mia feels a sense of shame again.

Brett squeezes her foot, "This isn't a competition and there's no right way to interact with your family."

"Uh huh."

Brett rolls his eyes at her, "Anyway, what makes you a magnet for drama?"

Mia sticks her tongue out at him. "Boys apparently. According to Luke I only seem to call when there's a boy problem? Which I don't think is true, but it made me feel like a terrible selfish sister. Did I tell you he's applying to law school here?" Brett shakes his head. "Well he is, and I told him how excited I'd be for him to be here, and he basically blew it off like I wouldn't make time for him even if he was here."

"But you would?"

"Yeah I would! I think it'd be kind of fun for us to both be adults in the same place. It's different than us being kids and having no control over anything. We'd like, *choose* to hang out with each other," Mia insists.

Brett smiles at her and nods, "I get that. My sister and I got closer after I finished college."

"See! That's what I'm talking about," Mia feels vindicated, that Brett understands her logic. "But overall, it just felt like a week where everyone was telling me I'm an awful person."

"Well I don't think you're an awful person," Brett gives Mia a smile and squeezes her leg.

Mia smiles back and pats Brett's hand, now resting on her calf, "Thank you."

"Though you did insinuate I'm trying to pad my CV…" Brett jokingly muses. Mia gives Brett a gentle kick to his thigh. "Ow," he says mockingly, "and you're violent."

"Oh shut up and have some more of your champagne," Mia says with a laugh. Brett pours more into each wine glass and clinks his to Mia's after handing it to her.

"Now what?" Brett asks after taking a sip.

"Now we enjoy the rest of this bottle, before you take me upstairs, we have sex, and go to bed," Mia lays out seriously.

"Not going to argue with that," Brett winks and follows through with the plan, ending with his arms wrapped around Mia as they each doze off under the covers of his bed.

CHAPTER 64

The next day Mia's returned to her place, showered and grocery shopped, and reluctantly picks up her phone to call each family member. She starts with Luke, knowing full well he won't answer at the time she's calling, and leaves a brief message.

"Hey Luke, it's Mia, just calling to catch up and say I miss you. Call me when you can!"

Mia follows the same steps for her dad, who also does not answer, before calling and reaching her mom.

"Hi there, sweetie," Valerie's voice floats over the phone when she answers. "How are you?"

"I'm good, just been busy, as usual. How have you been?"

"Pretty good. Been keeping quite busy actually. I started teaching a mindfulness meditation course down at the Y and my book club restarted. We're reading this new book, you might like it, wait, let me find it, so I can give you the author too…" Mia hears Valerie moving about and shuffling items on the other end of the line. "Ah, here it is, The Silent Patient by Alex Michaelides." Valerie sounds out the author's last name.

"What's it about?" Mia asks with some curiosity.

"Well I don't want to give anything away, but the main character is a psychotherapist, and he's treating a woman who's murdered her husband and then gone mute."

"Ah okay," Mia says with skepticism. She's always hesitant to read or watch things with a therapist protagonist, as they're always committing some ethical violation that drives her nuts.

Valerie seems to sense Mia's uncertainty, "Really, it's good. I don't think it'll annoy you."

Mia laughs, "Well, when I find some time, I will try it."

"Good," Valerie says, "anyway how has your semester been so far?"

"Decent, keeping pretty busy with the classes I'm in and clients. Plus trying to focus on my thesis, I really want to defend it this semester," Mia replies casually.

"Well I'm sure you'll get it done, you usually do," Valerie says reassuringly.

After a few more brief exchanges about Renly, the weather and the last time they each heard from Luke, Mia and her mother wish each other well and end their phone call.

Later that day Mia's phone buzzes with a text from Luke.

Sorry I missed your call. But guess who got an early admission to Earl Law? It's me! Can't talk right now, but let's talk sometime. Need to come up and find a place to live!

Mia's grinning reading the text. She's sends back multiple celebrating emojis and hearts, followed by **Congrats! I knew you'd get in! Can't wait to have you here!** She's excited to have Luke up here, and starts thinking about him meeting Brett. She sends one more text.

When will you come up to scope out a place?

Summer, after graduation, Luke replies, followed by a **got to go.**

Mia sends a thumbs up and sits back, content as her world feels like it's coming together.

Mia heads into the work week with renewed vigor after receiving more edits back from her advisor. She sets a meeting with Jean to review some of the comments, and gives Leigh a heads up, having the expectation she'll likely need a pick-me-up after.

By the time Mia's end of the week meeting with Dr. Thompson rolls around, she's reviewed all the revisions and comments, attended her week's worth of classes, seen five patients between the two clinics she works in, and has gotten a head start on next week's readings.

She heads into Dr. Thompson's office feeling fairly good about her progress on her thesis. Mia is expecting this meeting to go better than some of her previous ones. However, by the time the meeting has ended, Mia's head is swirling and she's holding back tears.

Phrases from Dr. Thompson churn in Mia's mind, like "How are you not asking these questions and want to be a clinician?" Or "I'm concerned you're not up to this task." Or what would become her favorite line, "Why does everyone always cry in here?" Instead of ducking into Leigh's office as originally planned, Mia makes a beeline for the stairwell and practically flies down the steps in a hurry to her own office. On the landing to the second floor she runs head on into Brett.

He looks at her, startled, and taking in her expression, with her red face, trembling mouth, and watery eyes. Brett opens his mouth as if to say something, but Mia shakes her head and waves her hand and quickly continues on her escape back to her office. She's eventually throws herself into her office and crumbles in her desk chair.

A soft rapping at her office door forces Mia to wipe her face and compose herself for the undergraduate research assistant. Instead of Amy, Mia sees Brett standing at the now open door.

"Hey," he says quietly, "you alright?"

Mia steps back and lets him into her office, closing the door behind him. She drops back in her chair, while Brett carefully sits in the empty desk chair across from her.

"Yeah. Just a typical meeting with Jean," Mia sniffs and grabs a tissue from the box on her desk to dab at her eyes and wipe her nose.

"You typically run out crying and almost knock down other people along the way?" Brett asks with a gentle smile.

"She was just extra hard on me today," Mia replies, ignoring Brett's humor. "It's like she had a shitty go of it when she was in grad school and she feels like everyone else has to be hazed the same way." Brett watches Mia, now quiet. "It's just very hot and cold with her." Mia's phone buzzes on the desk, but she ignores it. "I know she supports me and wants me to do well, but her delivery…" Mia shakes her head, "I just don't know how she ever saw patients. Maybe she used up all her empathy in grad school."

"Empathy is a finite resource?" Brett asks, again with a gentle smile.

"Yeah, and she'll be my case study for it," Mia jokes back, feeling calmer.

"It's hard to get those N equals one studies published," Brett replies. Mia laughs and tosses her tissues into the trashcan. "It sounds like she's tough to work with, but that you also trust her?" Brett asks more seriously. Mia nods. "That's a hard trade off, especially in grad school."

Mia nods again, "It's not easy when you're constantly fighting imposter syndrome and your advisor is basically like, *but you are an imposter.*"

Brett raises an eyebrow, "Did she say that?"

"Not those words exactly, but more of a questioning of me being in clinical," Mia shrugs and focuses on her breathing, so as not to start crying again.

Another loud knock sounds on Mia's office door. Mia looks at Brett, briefly alarmed at him being in her office with whoever is now outside the door. Brett is calm and nods at her to open the door while he gets up and moves to leave.

Brett opens the door, and Mia sees Leigh outside of her office, a surprised expression on her face upon seeing Brett.

"Oh, uh, hi, Dr. Dawson, I just came to see Mia," Leigh said.

"You can call me Brett, and I was just leaving, it seems like Mia could use a friend right now," he turns and faces Mia, "Sorry again about your meeting, let me know if I can help in some way."

"Thanks," Mia says, as Brett leaves and Leigh enters, pulling the door closed behind her.

"I texted you, cause I figured you'd be by my office already," Leigh starts and then tilts her head toward the door and the recently departed professor. "What was that about?"

"I practically knocked him over running back to my office from the meeting and he wanted to make sure I was okay," Mia shrugs.

"That was nice of him. I guess the meeting with Jean was that bad?" Leigh says compassionately.

"It was one definitely one of the worst ones we've had," Mia confirms. "I didn't want to bawl in your office around your lab mates, so I just kind of rushed down here."

Leigh nods, "Sure, I get it. Um, why don't we go get some fresh air, coffee or something?" Mia makes a face at the coffee suggestion. Leigh rolls her eyes comically, "Or hot chocolate whatever, let's just get out of this space for a few." Mia nods, and both women head out the building to follow through with Leigh's plan.

That evening, back in her apartment, Mia receives a text promptly at five, as if Brett had been waiting to be officially off their agreed upon clock.

How are you doing? He asks.

Mia pours a little more wine into her glass, her eyes red from crying more back at her home. She plops down on her couch, wine sloshing in the glass and glances at the text from Brett. While she had initially been upset over the meeting with Jean, she began to spiral at some point during her second glass of wine. Now in addition to feeling miserable about her thesis and graduate pursuits, she was feeling insecure about other things in her life, namely her relationships. Her relationships with her family members felt strained, and she is feeling guilty especially about Luke. She feels bad about the now resolved problems with Leigh, and now she was questioning her relationship with Brett. She could have used a hug from him today, but even in her office, he was still somewhat distant. He maintained a professional level of concern instead of a boyfriend level. *He could have been more concerned given that we've fucked,* Mia thinks with some derision.

It's all starting to feel a bit like what happened with Danny. *I'm being held at an arm's length and kept a secret,* Mia thinks with sadness. Mia gets into her third glass of wine, letting the self-pity party wash over her before she responds to Brett's text.

I've been better. Currently drowning my feelings.

Would you like company?

I'm a sad drunk right now, not a fun one. She sends back.

Would you like company anyway? Brett asks again.

Mia starts to feel annoyed, even though Brett is not the original source of her frustration. **I'm not really in the mood to fuck.**

The three dots on the text thread show Brett is typing, then stop, then start again. **I wasn't implying that when I asked. I'm just trying to be there for you, if you want me to.**

Mia feels chastised and embarrassed. **Sorry, clearly I'm just not in the best head space right now. You can come over if you want.**

I'll be there in 20.

Mia tosses her phone on the couch and kills the time by finishing her glass of wine and finding a random romantic comedy playing on TV. When she hears the knock on the door, she unsteadily gets up and opens it, to see Brett, dressed down in sweatpants and a sweatshirt, holding out a bottle of wine in one hand, and a pair of fuzzy socks in the other.

"In case you run out, and…I don't know, warm socks seem like a nice thing when you feel like shit," He says as he steps in and closes the door behind himself.

Mia gave him a strained smile, taking the items from him. "Thanks," she says, placing the wine on the counter and ripping the tags off the socks, before kicking her current ones off and putting the new ones on. "Oh, these are nice," she mutters and genuinely smiling at Brett, "thanks."

"I don't have to stay, I just wanted to check in on you," Brett says cautiously.

Mia shrugs with defeat and gestures to the couch, where Brett takes a seat. "I calmed down, but got back home and went through my notes and thought about the meeting and just felt like shit all over again. And when you texted, honestly I thought it was just for sex, which while enjoyable, as you can see I'm not entirely in the mood for." Mia gestures to herself, slightly slurring with wine stained teeth.

"Ouch," Brett says with a slight wince, "is that all you'd expect of me?"

Mia, her thoughts now unfiltered due to the wine, gives another defeated shrug as she flops back down on the couch, on the opposite end of Brett. "No." She looks down at her feet, "Maybe." She sighs, "I don't know. We don't do anything but-"

Brett cuts her off, "But go to each other's places and hook up, yeah."

"Yeah," Mia nods.

Brett nods slowly. "I get it, I know that's not what you want. I wish we could do more courtship stuff," Mia snorts at the term 'courtship,' as Brett continues, "but you know that has to wait until the semester ends. We can go on actual dates in just a couple of months, but yeah, it does require some patience until then."

Mia makes an exaggerated sigh and rolls her eyes, "I know, I know, am I not allowed to be frustrated in the mean time?"

Brett frowns, "Of course you can be. I am too."

Mia raises an eyebrow.

"I am!" Brett repeats. "I'd like to be able to share with my family that I'm seeing someone, or stop making excuses to colleagues and friends about my personal life or seemingly lack thereof."

Mia lets go of the breath she was holding, "Yeah, okay."

Brett reaches over to hold her hand, "I want to properly date you, Mia. I'm serious about that. We've just got to get through this weird period." He squeezes Mia's hand as a tear escapes from her eye.

"I just felt like you could have done more today," Mia whispered.

"Like what?" Brett asks, confused and concerned. "I can't exactly stroll into your advisor's office and yell at her for making you cry, even if we weren't sleeping together."

Mia shakes her head, "No, I don't expect that, I don't know, maybe a hug earlier could have been nice."

Brett pulls Mia to him and wraps her in a hug. He kisses the top of her head, "Sorry, I didn't even think to do that. I guess I just compartmentalize when I'm there, so that I don't do anything dumb, like give you a hug when I'm not supposed to."

Mia nods into Brett's shoulder. He gently strokes her hair with one hand. "Maybe, if that situation or something like it happens again, you could also let me know what you need?"

Mia nods into Brett's shoulder again, "Okay."

"What else can we do to make this seem like more?" Brett probes.

"Tell me a story from your childhood," Mia answers.

"So you can analyze me?" Brett teases.

"Ha ha, no, cause I want to learn more about you," Mia dryly responds.

"Hmm…alright, I have one. In elementary school I played on a recreational baseball team. And we had this one game, where I was playing shortstop, and a grounder slipped right between my legs and the other team scored two runs, and eventually ended up winning the game. And it felt like my team blamed me for it. I was miserable after it ended, so my dad took me out for ice cream to cheer me up. And then, cause he didn't want me to throw every game in the hopes for ice cream, he started taking me out after every game for ice cream. And that's how I ended up a little overweight when middle school rolled around. And standing out in *any* way in middle school - " Brett tells her.

"Is a nightmare," Mia interjects.

"Is a nightmare," Brett confirms. "And so that's why I blame baseball for my middle school years. How about you? A story from your childhood?"

"Hm, in middle school one day I tripped running in my neighborhood and fell funny, and broke my arm. I felt really dumb about how I broke it, so whenever anyone asked I would come up with these elaborate stories. Like, I was mountain climbing and a bear attacked us and flung me against a rock, breaking my arm. Or a car accident that my family barely survived, breaking my arm. Or, a fight with my mother's boyfriend, breaking my arm," Mia finishes the last sentence with a wince. "That last one got around to a teacher, and then CPS was called, and my parents were investigated, where I had to explain to that my mother didn't have a boyfriend, and I was just making stuff up. I got into huge trouble, understandably so."

"Yikes," Brett says with a grimace and then teases her, "So you were a sociopath in middle school? I was just a little overweight."

"Yeah, apparently I was acting out for attention, was the determination. So my parents sent me to a therapist, and she really helped, and it actually sort of created the interest to become one myself." Mia finished.

"So a happy ending?" Brett asks.

"Well, so long as I graduate, I guess so. Otherwise I'm a sociopath and a dropout," Mia jokes, and then pauses before continuing. "Let's do this more, I want to know more about you."

"That seems reasonable, I think we can do that," Brett smiles down at her.

Mia yawns, "Good. Welp, I'm ready to pass out now, and since I'm drunk and comfortable being rude, I'm gonna kick you out."

Brett laughs, and Mia untangles herself from him, getting up, and allowing Brett to stand too.

"Thank you for the wine and socks," she says, then adds, "and for the talking and listening."

"Anytime," Brett gives her a quick kiss and heads to the door to let himself out, "sleep well, drink plenty of water." Mia nods and locks the door after he's gone. Instead of cleaning up her glass and empty bottle, she heads straight to her bedroom, where she curls under her covers and lets the drunken sleep follow.

CHAPTER 65

Mia finds herself more comfortable with her routine as the semester wears on. She's taken a cue from Brett and works hard to compartmentalize her life. She focuses on classwork, her master's thesis, and clinical work during the week before spending the weekend nights with Brett. They've taken to sharing anecdotes each night they're together, allowing Mia to learn about Brett's fear of snakes, the first (and last) time he cussed at his parents, his favorite memory with his sister, and all the things he would get in trouble for during high school. Mia was careful about asking about college and graduate school, as she figured some of those memories and experiences may be more difficult to discuss given Brett's ex. In turn, Mia opened up and shared more about her parents' divorce, her obsession with rereading two of her favorite books on a yearly basis, what she wish she had done differently with her brother, and the revelations she's experienced from both being in and conducting therapy. While they don't go out, Mia finally feels like she and Brett are dating on some level. Mia notices her worry about their relationship melting away, and feels more carefree about their sexual connection. At times, she recognizes she lets her weekends get consumed by him, and quickly corrects course by making a point to spend time with Leigh or her cohort in general.

Mia even allows herself to start to feel hopeful about reaching the end of the semester. As she observes, her relationship with Brett is going well, and it's only a matter of weeks before they can complete whatever paperwork they need to and be out in the open. Additionally, despite her disastrous meeting with her advisor earlier in the semester, her final draft of her master's is almost complete and she has a date set to defend it. By focusing entirely on graduate work during the week, Mia's realized she's made the progress she aimed for. Without wanting to jinx the whole thing, she hesitantly acknowledges to herself that this is the first time, in a long time, where she feels content and competent.

Brett had spent the previous night at her apartment, as they had taken to alternating their homes each weekend they spent together. With the warming weather and extended daylight, he'd taken to arriving later and leaving earlier, as a precaution. Brett had already been long gone for the day, and Mia was shifting back into work mode, preparing slides for her master's defense in a couple of weeks.

Her phone buzzes next to her as she works on the PowerPoint, and initially Mia ignores it. Her phone buzzes several more times in quick succession, so Mia grabs her phone and swipes open the home screen to pull up her text messages.

I know who you're fucking. And I know it can get you kicked out. Danny's words sent a chill down her spine, but the photos that accompanied the text are what makes Mia nauseous. Danny had attached four pictures, one of Brett going into her apartment, another of him leaving, a grainy image of two people in a car, and a grainy image of the car's license plates, which were still readable. Mia knew the car picture had to have come from one of the nights that Brett gave her a ride back to her parked car. The poorly lit photo was clear enough to show a woman sitting on a man's lap, facing him in the driver's seat. Mia puts her phone down, runs to the bathroom, and throws up in the toilet.

After emptying her stomach, she splashes some water on her face and drinks some more from the faucet. Mia stares at herself in the mirror, her face ashen. She doesn't know what to do, does she respond to Danny? Alert Brett?

Mia heads back to her office, where she had left her phone. The notification light is blinking to indicate another message. Mia clicks her screen on and taps in her passcode to see the next message from Danny.

I'd be happy to keep my mouth shut. You just have to do something for me.

Mia feels a panic rising in her. **What do you want?** She texts back, not even bothering to deny his suspicions, given the pictures.

Let's meet to talk about it. I can be at your place in a few.

The last thing Mia wants, given this new development, is Danny alone with her in her home. She sends back to him, **No, we can meet at the bagel place in 10.**

Mia sets her phone down and quickly pulls on a jacket and grabs her purse. She stops for a moment, wondering if she should forward the initial message to Brett, or wait to find out what Danny wants. She'd rather handle the entire problem and then inform Brett once it's taken care of. Mia worries how Brett will respond knowing that Danny is causing her trouble again, and that she took her time in telling him. She promises herself that she will call Brett as soon as she's done talking with Danny, so that at least she'll have all the information she needs to share with Brett.

Mia leaves her apartment and makes the short drive to her nearby bagel place. She scans the restaurant and finds a mostly empty corner and takes a seat at a table, facing the door. Danny comes in not too long behind her, orders a cup of coffee at the counter, and casually makes his way to her once he's received it. He sits down, and smiles widely at Mia.

"Hey, how are you?" He asks, as though this was a normal encounter.

"What do you want?" Mia asks quietly.

"Well I thought we could start by catching up," Danny says innocently.

"Seriously Danny, what do you want?" Mia's earlier panic starts to feel more like agitation, especially as Danny now seems to be toying with her.

Danny sighs, "Fine, straight to business. So you are fucking your teacher?"

Mia's eyes widen and she glances around again, ensuring that no one is paying attention to them. Feeling reassured on that front, she answers, "You don't have proof of that."

Danny shrugs, "I do have proof of his comings and goings, and there are some more pictures of the two of you in his car. It's enough to cause you and him a problem."

"So you've been watching me? Following me?" Mia whispers in horror.

"Checking up on you, making sure you're doing well,"

Danny corrects. "Anyway, that's not what I wanted to discuss. As I texted, I'm happy to keep my mouth shut. I just need a few things from you."

"What could you possibly want?" Mia asks, feeling angry tears prick at her eyes.

"Well first, no more hanging out with Sasha. I don't want you around her or any friends we've shared."

Mia works to keep her facial expression neutral, "Is that it?"

Danny laughs, "No. I think I'm finally owed that break up fuck I never got."

Mia's unable to maintain her composure and a look of disgust passes across her face, "You're threatening me so that I fuck you?"

"I'm using creative means to enjoy your company again," Danny again puts his own spin on her words.

"No," Mia says flatly.

"I figured you'd say that. Which is why I have a letter drafted to the dean regarding your inappropriate relationship with your professor. With the pictures, it should be enough to start an investigation of some kind, probably get him fired. He'll have a tough time going somewhere else, and if you manage to stay, you'll have this hanging over you. None of the professors will respect you, want to work with you, be on your committees. This will follow you too," Danny replies evenly.

"I will tell the dean that you're threatening me, and that's why you shared that information," Mia responds through gritted teeth.

"And in the event you do that, I have numerous pictures of you that I'm happy to share on Reddit, including your name. After that, it'd be very easy for someone to figure out where you are or how to contact you," Danny smirked at the word "pictures," alerting Mia to exactly what kind of photos he was referring to. Photos that he had promised during their time together that he had deleted.

"What the fuck is wrong with you?" Mia whispers hoarsely, feeling drained.

"Nothing is wrong with me, Mia. I'm just treating you like the slut you are." Danny looks at her calmly.

Mia shakes her head, and feels a tear escape from her eye. She quickly wipes it away. "I can't believe you," she whispers.

"Believe me, I just think it's fair you throw some of that pussy back my way, and we can move on from this. I can see that this may be a lot to take in right now. So I'll give you till Friday to either let me come collect, or send my letter," Danny finishes his coffee and pushes back from the table to stand. "Don't do anything stupid though, cause as I said, I have plenty to fall back on." Danny flashes her a smile and says, "Talk to you soon," before turning and leaving.

Mia sits, momentarily stunned by this brief and painful exchange. After she sees Danny's car leave the parking lot, she gets up from the table and makes her way back to her car to go home.

CHAPTER 66

Mia sits on her couch, staring at her phone, trying to figure out how she is going to share any of this with Brett. She had agreed to tell him if Danny did anything else, and this threat could impact Brett too. As Mia thinks about it more, she realizes that with all of the photos Danny had, of Brett, of her and Brett, and of her nude, that Danny could continue to demand things of her indefinitely. Mia was going to be stuck, forever owing Danny, as she figures he won't just let this go, but rather continue to return to it over time. Mia's stomach has dropped at the thought of her entire life, her career plans, completely ruined.

Mia clicks the call option next to Brett's contact information in her phone. It rings twice before he answers.

"Hey gorgeous, how's it going?" He answers warmly.

Mia swallows and attempts to say calmly, "Not well. I have something to tell you."

Brett's tone changes instantly to concern, "What is it?"

"You're not going to like this, but I spoke this Danny earlier today," Mia says quietly.

"Okay…" Brett replies.

Mia continues, "He sent a text, with some pictures. Of you, of us. He knows." Her voice starts to crack at the end.

"How?" Brett's tone remains the same, and Mia wishes she could see his face.

"He's been following me, apparently," Mia answers. She takes a deep breath, "The bigger part of this is that he is threatening to tell the dean of students unless I sleep with him. He also said that if I shared what he was doing, that he'd upload photos of me to the internet. Private photos." Mia's voice rises a bit as she feels her panic return, "And I don't see him letting any of this go even if I give in and give him what he wants. He'll just keep doing it." A sob breaks free from Mia and she starts crying.

"Hey," Brett says quietly. "We can figure something out. I'll come over and we can talk about it."

"But what if he's watching me now?" Mia asks panicked.

"What's he going to do? Take another photo of me at your place? It doesn't matter at this point. I'm coming over," Brett says firmly.

"Okay," Mia whispers and hangs up.

Mia hadn't moved from the spot she was in during the phone call, still paralyzed with worry, when she heard the knock on her door. She shook herself out of her stupor and went to the door, opening it to Brett and letting him in.

Closing the door behind himself, he quickly wraps Mia in a hug, pulling her close to him and resting his chin on her head. Mia's paralysis breaks, and she sobs into Brett's chest. Brett strokes her hair and holds her until Mia pulls free of their embrace. She grabs tissues from the kitchen and tries to wipe her face and blow her nose. She notices now that Brett's face is serious and drawn, his body language both uncertain and tense as he still stands in the entryway.

Mia gestures to her couch for Brett to sit, and he almost collapses onto it. Mia sits next to him, her face red and tear streaked.

"I'm so sorry," she whispers. "If I had any idea that any of this was going to happen…"

Brett shakes his head, "There's nothing for you to be sorry for." He stares ahead as he says the words.

Mia is silent, unsure of what to say or do next.

"We just need to find a way to get ahold of what he has on you," Brett says.

"How?" Mia asks incredulously.

"I'm not entirely sure…maybe if you could get to his phone or computer somehow?" Brett puts forward hesitantly.

Mia gapes at him, her mouth open, "There's only one way he'd let me near his things like that, and I am not fucking him."

Brett shakes his head, "Right, of course."

"I can't believe you'd suggest that," Mia's voice is hurt and shocked.

Brett looks at her surprised, "I wasn't. I didn't know if there was a way to get to how he's saving those things that didn't involve sleeping with him."

Mia turns away briefly, concentrating her thoughts on her options. She begins to realize that there may be a way to get to Danny's blackmail material. Doing so would mean breaking their rules, but she wouldn't have to sleep with Danny and it could potentially save their asses. But could *she* be trusted?

"There's another option," Mia says quietly.

"Huh?" Brett asks.

"Someone else that could get rid of the photos," Mia continues.

Brett's face shows he's slightly alarmed. "What do you mean someone else?"

Mia takes a deep breath, "I could ask Sasha to do it."

"Sasha?" Brett asks confused.

"Sasha is dating Danny. She's already over at his place all the time. Maybe, I could ask her-" Mia is cut off from continuing.

"Does Sasha know about us?" Brett's face is a mixture of alarm and anger.

"Oh my god, no, of course not," Mia says quickly, "but," she continues carefully, "I could give her a vague idea of what's going on and see if she'll delete his evidence for me. I don't have to say it's you. Plus if she knew what Danny was doing, trying to force me into having sex with him, cheating on her, maybe she'd want to help."

Brett is already shaking his head, "All she'd have to do is look at the pictures and she'd know it's me. And then we're opening ourselves up to a new problem."

Mia, however, is feeling more certain in her idea and is shaking her head back at Brett. "No, I think we could trust her."

Brett says deeply concerned, "What makes you think that?"

"I- I don't know exactly. But she wanted me to be honest with her going forward. I think maybe she has an idea that something is up with Danny. Plus what would she even want with information on us? Nothing." Mia is feeling more reassured and confident in this idea, her voice reflecting her strength.

"She could use it against me for her grade," Brett offers.

Mia rolls her eyes, "I doubt she would. Besides, isn't she doing well enough already? All that's left is the final paper, and I'm sure she's already working on it."

Brett's arms are crossed and his face is dark. "I don't think it's a good idea."

"Well do you have any better ones that don't involve me debasing myself for Danny?" Mia shoots back, annoyed.

"Maybe Hank could do something," Brett muses, referring to his mentor.

"And how is that any better than enlisting Sasha? Plus, if Danny's advisor talks to him about this or disciplines him over it, Danny will post my nudes online!" Mia emphasizes the final words by slapping her hands onto the couch. "I'm trying to find a solution that works for both of us. Beside, how can *you* be sure that Hank won't report you?" Mia asks annoyed.

Brett gives a defeated shrug. "I don't, honestly."

Mia nods, "Exactly. Look, I've known Sasha longer than you've known Hank. I feel better relying on her. She doesn't know it yet, but she's impacted by all of this too. And I bet she'd have some feelings about Danny trying to force me into sleeping with him while he's still with her."

Brett sighs and drops his arms, and Mia starts to recognize that she's won this argument. "Fine, so what's your big plan?"

Mia bobs her head, "Approach her after class on Monday, briefly explain the situation to her, and ask for her help."

"Alright," Brett says as he reaches for Mia's hand and gives it a squeeze. "In the meantime, I'm going to clean up my job application materials, just in case."

Mia squeezes Brett's hand back and leans in and gives him a kiss. "I think we'll be okay," she says, hoping that saying it out loud will make it a reality.

CHAPTER 67

Mia is all nervous energy on Monday leading up to class. She knew she couldn't text or call Sasha in the event Danny was checking her phone, and that speaking to her after class is her only chance this week to make her request. Brett also seems unlike himself during class, more distant and less chatty with the graduate students. As class winds down and Leigh and Sasha both begin packing up, Mia turns to Sasha.

"Hey Sasha, do you mind doing a quick case consult with me? I'm feeling stuck regarding this one client and it'd be helpful to bounce some ideas off of you." Mia asks casually.

"Uh, sure, when?" Sasha answers.

"Is now okay? We could just head to my office?" Mia says.

"Yeah, sure," Sasha replies. Both women wave goodbye to Leigh, who indicates she's heading back to her own office. Mia feels Brett's eyes on her as she leaves the classroom, leading Sasha down to the building's basement.

Once inside her office, Mia shuts the door and Sasha takes a seat. Mia sits across from her and takes a deep breath. "I don't have a case consult," she confesses.

Sasha nods, "Yeah, considering we work in very different clinics, I was surprised you asked. What's going on?"

"Remember how we agreed to open and honest with each other?" Mia starts.

"Yes…" Sasha draws out.

"Well, I'm going to tell you a few things and I'm basically going to beg you for your help. And everything I'm about to tell you, I need you to keep to yourself." Mia says seriously, looking intently at Sasha.

Sasha shifts in her chair, "Uh, Mia, if this is something I shouldn't know about, don't tell me and ask me to keep it secret."

Mia gives her head a small shake, "Sasha, it affects you too."

"Is this about Danny?" Sasha asks, her face now showing concern.

"Yes," Mia says quietly.

Sasha sighs, "Ugh, fine. What is it?"

Mia speaks carefully and slowly, "Danny is trying to blackmail me into sleeping with him. I've been seeing someone that I technically should not be seeing, and Danny has proof of it. He's going to out us to the dean or put naked pictures of me online. I think he's been mad at me since New Year's. He tried to kiss me when he drove me home and I told him to leave me alone. And apparently since then he's been following me and…found out about my personal life."

Sasha's eyes are wide. "What the fuck?" She curses quietly, the first time Mia's heard her talk that way.

"I know this may be a lot to hear from me. He's also told me I can't talk to you or be around you or any of our mutual friends. And if he's doing this crazy shit to me, I worry what he could do to you." Mia's voice is steady and she maintains eye contact with Sasha.

"So why are you telling me all this?" Sasha blinks, her eyes starting to water.

"Because I need you to delete the evidence he has. It's on his phone for sure, it may even be on his computer. Pictures of me, pictures of the guy, some pictures of us together." Mia's lowered her voice as she describes the request.

"Mia, who are you seeing?" Sasha asks almost absently.

"Someone I'm not supposed to," Mia responds.

"A professor?" Sasha presses, to which Mia nods. "A psych professor?" Mia nods again. "Oh my god, Mia, who are you seeing?" Sasha seems shocked.

"Brett. Dr. Dawson. It started before I even knew who he was. And then when we figured out who we each were to each other, we tried to stop, but it was hard, and instead we've just sort of compartmentalized our relationship. All professional during the week, and dating on the weekend," Mia stumbles through her explanation, watching as Sasha's mouth drops more with each word. "And we're totally going to tell the dean and complete whatever paperwork as soon as the semester is over. We're not going to stay a secret," Mia adds quickly.

"Are you fucking serious?" Sasha's voice is almost squeaking, dropping another swear word in her shock.

"Yes," Mia whispers, "and so if Danny tells the dean, we could both be out." Mia leans forward and clasps her hands in front of her, "And this is why I am begging you to help me. You don't deserve to be treated this way, to have your boyfriend try to blackmail someone into sleeping with him. And I don't want to be kicked out of school or have private photos of me posted online."

Sasha leans back in her chair and rubs her face. "Oh my

god, Mia. This is…this is a lot of information."

"I know," Mia responds quietly.

"And he hit on you at New Year's?" Sasha asks, her voice muffled as she continues to rub her face.

"Yes," Mia affirms quietly.

"Ugh," Sasha groans. She lifts her head up to Mia.

"I know, it's a lot of information. And I wouldn't be asking you if I had any other way of dealing with this. And as we discussed, I felt that you should know what Danny is doing behind your back." Mia's voice is soft and she gives Sasha's knee a quick squeeze.

Sasha runs a hand through her long, dark hair. She removes her glasses and quickly cleans the lenses on her shirt, before placing them back on her face. "So you want me to find these photos and delete them?" She asks tiredly.

"Yes," Mia nods, "by Friday." Sasha slightly tilts her head to the side, as though to question the deadline. Mia continues to answer her silent question, "Danny told me I have until Friday to decide what to do with regard to…sleeping with him or getting turned in."

"How generous of him," Sasha mutters sarcastically. She slaps her hands down on her legs and looks back at Mia, "Yeah, I'll see what I can do. Though honestly, I really want to just have nothing to do with Danny at this point."

Mia gives a small smile, "Yeah, that makes sense. I won't ask you for anything else. If you can find anything and get rid of it, great, if you can't that's fine. I'll figure out something else."

"Okay. Uh, Mia?"

"Yeah?"

"Does Dr. Dawson know about this?"

Mia loses her smile, "Yeah, he's not thrilled about it either. But I told him that I trust you, and that you ought to know what Danny is up to, because it's all behind your back, and you don't deserve any of what he's doing."

Sasha nods solemnly. "You can trust me," Sasha pauses and adds, "Is this thing with Dr. Dawson, er, Brett, a good idea?"

Mia glances away with some embarrassment, "It obviously wasn't one of my best ideas once I knew who he was, but at that point, once I knew, I just didn't want to end it. And I'm happy with him. It'll be better once it's all out in the open, which will be soon."

Sasha takes a deep breath and nods slowly, but her eyes are narrowed as though she does not entirely agree with Mia.

"Alright. Well, I usually stay over at Danny's on Wednesdays, so I'll see what I can do then." Sasha says as she stands.

Mia jumps out of her chair and wraps Sasha into a hug. "Thank you," she whispers as she lets go, "and please, you can't say anything to anyone about any of this."

"Yeah, got it," Sasha says, gathering her things and starts heading towards the door before she stops. "Were you going to tell me about New Year's if this hadn't happened?" She asks.

Mia, ashamed, glances down and shakes her head. "I figured if he did anything again I would tell you. I just sort of chalked it up to the alcohol."

Sasha clenches her jaw and nods, "Okay. Well, I guess he did, huh?"

"I'm sorry, I should have," Mia says sincerely. "I was scared to. I didn't want you to get hurt, and I was scared of what Danny would do if I did tell you."

Sasha nods, "Well we have an idea now of how far he'll take things. I'll let you know after Wednesday."

Mia nods, "Thank you again, Sasha." Sasha nods and leaves Mia's office. Mia plops back down in her chair, feeling relieved that her plan was actionable, and now anxious about whether it will pan out.

CHAPTER 68

Mia texts Brett as soon as the clock hit five, letting him know that she's asked Sasha to help her. Instead of texting her back, Mia's phone rings and she can see it's Brett.

"Hey," she says as she answers the phone.

"How did it go?" Brett asks.

"I mean, it was a little weird and awkward and scary, but it's done now. She's going to see what she can do Wednesday night." Mia answers.

"And does she know? I mean, does she know it's me?" Brett's voice is steady over the phone, though Mia imagines he does not feel that way.

"Yes, she knows. She'd find out once she went searching

for the pictures. There was no sense in hiding that," Mia says calmly.

"How did she respond to that?" Brett presses.

"She was surprised. Who wouldn't be? Honestly, all around she handled the avalanche of information pretty well. She was pretty upset about Danny trying to cheat on her, understandably so. I feel like that was more of a concern to her than you and me," Mia starts to pace around her living room, prompting Renly to open one eye to stare at her.

Brett sighs over his end of the call. "This is just so…I don't know. Weird isn't the right word. Crazy? Fucked?"

Mia lets out a small laugh, feeling some tension from the day release, "Yeah, crazy and fucked both seem like appropriate descriptions."

"So, Wednesday? Why Wednesday?" Brett asks.

"Sasha says she's usually over at Danny's then, so she can see what she can find. She said she'd let me know."

"How am I going to run a class on Wednesday? I won't be able to look at her," Brett sounds worried.

Mia cringes to herself, having not given too much thought to Brett and Sasha's future interactions. "I don't know?"

Abruptly, Brett changes the line of the conversation. "You should come over Wednesday."

Mia feels thrown off by the request, as they have tried to avoid mixing up their weekdays and weekends. "How come?"

"Well, we know Danny will be occupied, and who knows what's going to happen after Wednesday," Brett says quietly.

Mia feels her breath catch. She realizes Brett is onto something. If Sasha cannot help her, then the only safe thing to do is for her and Brett to stop seeing each other. Neither of them can defend themselves against codes of conduct violations if they continue to purposely thwart them. Mia nods, then agrees, "Yes," to Brett. "So what now?" she asks after a brief pause.

"We wait," he says.

"Well, this sucks," Mia says lightly, and she hears Brett chuckle. After briefly exchanging supportive statements to one another, Mia bids Brett a good night and refocuses on classwork for the evening.

Tuesday passes uneventfully, and to Mia's surprise, Brett has canceled seminar on Wednesday, citing in an email to the class that he is unwell. Mia feels fairly certain his cancellation is more to do with a desire to avoid Sasha for the time being than any actual health problem. She figures she can follow up with him that evening. Additionally, Mia feels some relief herself about not having to face Sasha right now, knowing too well what Sasha will be likely finding that night. Despite having insisted that Sasha is trustworthy to Brett earlier, Mia is starting to have some doubts. What if Sasha tells the dean herself? What if Sasha tells Danny what Mia asked her to do? Mia's placed a lot of faith in Sasha, laying both her and Brett's individual and combined futures at Sasha's feet. Thinking about all of this, Mia's grateful to not have to face Sasha today.

With their seminar canceled, Leigh's already texted Mia to see if she'd like to grab lunch, but Mia declines. With all the thoughts running through her mind, she doesn't want Leigh to pick up on any weird vibes and ask about it. Instead, Mia chooses to hunker down as much as possible on Wednesday until she can head over to Brett's in the evening.

Given the burgeoning possibility that this evening may be their last together, Mia takes extra effort before leaving for Brett's place. She showers and dries her hair, and applies perfume and makeup. She rifles through her underwear drawer for something Brett hasn't seen recently and settles on the white lacy bra and panties set she wore in a picture for him months ago. Mia pulls a flowy, flowery dress over her head and slips her feet into heeled sandals, before layering with a jean jacket as the spring evening cools.

As Mia heads to her car in the parking lot, she scans it for the first time, wondering where Danny has parked in the past. She doesn't see his car in the lot, and while she knew he'd be home with Sasha, she still felt some relief to know that she wasn't being watched right now.

Mia arrives at Brett's home, and knocks on the door. He opens it to her, backlit by the light of his home, wearing pajama pants and a well-fitted shirt that clings to his chiseled chest.

"Come in," he says, stepping back to make way for her, "you look beautiful," he adds.

"Thanks," Mia says with a smile, and steps inside as Brett closes the door behind her. "So I assume you're not actually sick?" She throws down her purse on the kitchen table and makes herself comfortable on the couch. Brett stops in the kitchen to grab the two glasses of wine he's already poured. He hands one to Mia before sitting down next to her.

"Ah, no. I just couldn't. I know I'm going to have to face Sasha eventually, but I needed more time," Brett drinks his wine.

Mia nods and takes a sip of her own wine. A heavy silence lays between them and Mia shifts uncomfortably. She puts her wine down on the coffee table. "Why is this weird all of sudden?" She asks Brett.

He stares at her wordlessly, and places his own wine glass down before crossing the space between them. He pulls Mia close to him and kisses her passionately. Mia wraps her arms around his neck and returns his kiss.

Brett pulls away and strokes Mia's cheek while searching her face. "I don't know if we'll get to be together again after tonight," he whispers. Mia feels her heart thud and stomach drop. She moves her hands to stroke down Brett's back and pulls him to move onto her, as she lays back on the couch. Mia wraps her legs around Brett, her dress hitching up around her legs. Brett runs his hands up to Mia's thighs before planting his hands on the couch's armrest, on either side of Mia's face.

Mia locks into his eyes, which suddenly seem dark and hungry. Brett presses himself against her, and Mia feels that his passion has grown, as he is hard between her legs. Mia reaches down and pushes her hand past the flimsy elastic of his waistband and wraps her hand around Brett's erect cock. Brett quietly moans in Mia's ear as she slowly strokes the length of his erection. He buries his face in her neck, kissing and sucking on her soft skin. Mia lets go of him as Brett positions himself above her, lowering himself down with only his pajama pants and her panties between them. Mia feels the pressure between her legs and writhes against Brett's body, feeling her heart rate and breathing quicken. Brett reaches down and slips a hand between them, pulling at Mia's panties as he then deftly glides two fingers into her. He guides them in and out, and Mia moans as his fingers becomes slick. She grabs Brett by the neck and brings his face back down to hers. She kisses him, pressing her tongue against his, before giving his bottom lip a nibble.

Brett pulls his hand out of her underwear and breaks free of Mia's hold, leaning back. He grabs the side straps of Mia's panties with each hand and pulls them down and off, over each shoe. Brett pushes Mia's legs open again and bends forward. Mia closes her eyes and sighs at the sensation of Brett's mouth between her legs.

Mia moans and her body reacts involuntarily to Brett's tongue and fingers. Her back arches and she grabs at the couch as Brett's tongue flicks at her clitoris. Mia feels the exhilarating sensation, the telltale sign that her orgasm is incoming.

"Stop teasing me and fuck me already," she barely gasps out. Within seconds, Brett has removed his pants and shirt and positions himself between Mia's legs again. She feels the tip of his penis against her as Brett holds himself to her. "Please," she whispers, and Brett plunges in, Mia crying out as he does so.

Mia wraps her legs around Brett's waist, grabbing and squeezing his bare ass as he slowly pumps. After kissing her again, he returns to her neck, jawline, and cleavage, kissing and sucking every bare spot of skin.

"I'm going to miss how good you feel," Brett whispers,

finally breaking his silence. He nibbles on her earlobe and buries his face into her neck.

Mia's body rises to meet Brett's at their point of connection at every thrust. She tries to urge him on faster, but Brett maintains a steady pace. He runs a hand up her torso and gropes a breast through her dress. Brett suddenly pulls out of her and pulls Mia to stand. Holding her gaze, he removes her jacket and dress, and Mia unclasps and removes her bra. Brett cups one of her breasts as he leans down and kisses her, his other arm snaking around her waist, his thick erection firm against Mia's stomach. Mia breaks free and turns away from him, clambering onto the couch and kneeling as she braces herself against the back of the couch. Brett positions himself behind her, and leans down to kiss her neck and shoulders. He drops a hand to her clit, rubbing gently before moving his hand to her waist to steady himself as he enters Mia from behind.

Mia moans and grips the couch. She moves one hand to stimulate herself, panting as Brett begins to thrust faster. The sensation of a budding orgasm grows again in Mia.

"Yes," she moans, "yes, please, yes." Her words encourage Brett, who has moved his hand over Mia's to play with her clit. He kisses her neck and grazes her earlobe with his teeth as Mia's words become garbled, her moans louder, and her climax reached. Mia gasps as she comes, burying her face into the couch which muffles her ensuing cries of pleasure. In response, Brett moves his hands to Mia's breasts, groping her as he works to finish, pumping hard against her before he reaches his own climax, cussing quietly. Brett rests against Mia's back, steadying his breathing, before he kisses her shoulder and untangles himself from her. Mia lets herself fall sideways to lay on the couch facing up, her face blissful.

Brett dresses and the t-shirt he lends Mia is magically in his hands. Mia sits up, grabbing the shirt and pulling it over her head, before bending down to remove her shoes. She scans the floor until she spots her panties, quickly grabbing them and pulling them back on before curling back up on the couch.

Brett settles onto the couch next to her, draping an arm around her shoulders and gently stroking her arm. Mia rests her head against his chest and listens to his heart beat. She sighs and yawns.

"Tire you out?" Brett jokes.

Mia pulls back and looks at him seriously, "This whole thing is exhausting."

Brett's smile disappears and he nods, his face more severe. "Yeah, I know. On the one hand, I am terrified of Friday, but on another, at least we'll have some kind of conclusion."

"Hopefully that conclusion will be tonight," Mia says

quietly, acknowledging having placed all her hope in Sasha.

Brett shrugs in response, exhibiting his uncertainty, "Maybe."

Mia clasps his hand in hers, "What's your plan, if…if she can't help us?"

Brett stares ahead and then seems to shake his head before answering, "I don't know entirely. I don't know what the consequences will be. I'll obviously own up to it, and hopefully will only be placed on some kind of probation and not fired, but who knows?"

Mia squeezes Brett's hand, "I won't let you take all the blame on this. I've been an equal and eager participant in all of this."

Brett's body language seems to signal defeat, his shoulders hunched down, "I don't know if that will matter. I'm the one in the position of power. I should have been the one to end it."

"Brett," Mia says gently, "Neither of us wanted to stop seeing each other."

"Yes, and I kept pursuing you even after we knew, even after we agreed to stop. I should have known better." Brett chastises himself.

Mia's unsure of how to react to his self-admonishment,

They're both adults, who both made the decision to continue this relationship, despite knowing the risks. Brett catches onto Mia's silence and gives her a weak smile, "Sorry, I'm just worried about how this is all going to play out."

Mia nods, "Of course, me too."

"Let's just try to enjoy tonight," Brett says quietly, trying to alter the tone of the evening. Mia eagerly agrees, and snuggles up to him.

CHAPTER 69

Mia's awoken by the sound of her phone buzzing against the top of the night stand. She rubs her eyes, glancing over at Brett, still asleep beside her, and reaches out to grab her phone. Mia accidentally knocks it to the floor instead, and quietly curses as she pushes the covers off and swings her legs out of the bed. She crouches on the floor to find her phone in the dark. Clicking the screen on, she sees a missed call from Sasha. With an almost furtive glance behind her to ensure Bret is still sleeping, she quietly pads out of the room and shuts the door behind her. Mia makes her way downstairs in the dark and settles down on the couch where she and Brett were talking, kissing, and commiserating only hours earlier.

Just as Mia goes to call Sasha back, her phone begins to buzz again. Sasha.

Mia swipes to answer the call. "Hey," she says barely above a whisper.

"Hey," Sasha's voice comes back quiet as well. "I found your pictures," she says haltingly.

Mia holds her breath, unsure of what to say next.

"I found more than that too," Sasha whispers.

Mia freezes up, scared of what else Danny could have possibly had on her.

"Danny," Sasha's voice wavers, "Danny had videos. Of you. Of me. Of other girls. Some I recognize, some I don't. From the angle, and I didn't dare investigate it in case the camera is on, he's been recording the women he's having sex with. In his room." Mia can hear Sasha's voice breaks. "Mia, he's got all of these videos, and some were taken while we've been together."

Mia's heart races, thinking of the past time she'd willingly been with Danny, but never agreed to be recorded. At the same time, her heart breaks for Sasha, as she now confronts the depths of Danny's depravities.

"Oh Sasha," Mia says, "I'm so sorry. That, all of this, is awful. I had no idea he had been doing anything like that."

Sasha sniffles on the other end of the line. "I'm just so mad. And hurt. When you told me what he had done to you, I believed you, but had secretly hoped you were wrong about him. But..." Sasha's voice breaks again and she cries quietly, "but it is even worse than I could have imagined."

Mia listens to Sasha cry, searching for the right words to say. "Sasha, I'm so sorry," she repeats, "I cannot imagine how you are feeling right now. Do you want to meet up? Is there something I can do for you?"

"No," Sasha sputters on the other end. "Not right now. I went and deleted everything that had you in it. And Brett. Danny wasn't trying very hard to keep things hidden on his laptop. And I erased stuff from his phone too. So unless he's saved it anywhere else that I don't know about, it's gone."

Mia feels a wave of relief. "Thank you, Sasha," she says quietly. "But what are you going to do?"

Sasha sighs and seems to blow her nose. "I'm not entirely sure. I'm definitely breaking up with him. This is all just so disgusting. I don't know if I should try to find these other women and let them know? He saved every recording with the girl's first name, but not last, so I don't know how I'd find them. Should I delete them? Make copies so I have proof? Really, I have no idea what to do next."

"Well, what are you most comfortable with?" Mia asks gently.

"Aside from castration?" Sasha says sarcastically.

"Yes, aside from castration," Mia continues with a calm voice.

"Honestly, a taste of his own medicine. That if he dares say anything to anyone about you, I will find every girl from these videos and let her know. And have us all band together to let the university know. And file police reports."

Mia feels her stomach twist a bit. "Is there a way to leave me out of this? I know I asked you to do this for me, but if Danny knows I'm behind all of this, honestly, I don't know what he'd do."

"Well he doesn't have anything on you anymore," Sasha says.

"From his laptop or phone, as you said but if it's saved anywhere else…" Mia trails off.

"Yeah," Sasha replies slowly. "I'll think of something. I'm going to head home now, I don't want to be around him any more than I need to be."

"Sounds good," Mia says. "How about we meet tomorrow? Do you have time to come to my office?"

"Yeah, I'll swing by in the afternoon, before I head to the clinic, probably around three. Does that work?"

"Absolutely, I'll be there. And Sasha, thank you again." Mia says.

"You're welcome, Mia. I'll see you tomorrow." Sasha hangs up before Mia gets a chance to say goodbye. Mia sits, staring at her phone. She feels like a ragdoll, as though all the air and tension have left her body. With any luck, Sasha has gotten rid of all the evidence of her relationship with Brett and now Danny can no longer threaten her. Mia begins to feel guilty as she follows this train of thought, having not given as much thought to what Sasha is now going through and all of the now unnamed women that Danny has violated. Mia takes a deep breath to steady herself, and reminds herself that she cannot do anything about the women she doesn't know. She tells herself she can focus on Sasha tomorrow and makes a promise to do whatever she can to support Sasha going forward.

Mia quietly makes her way back upstairs and tries to get back in bed as silently as she can. As she sinks into the mattress, and pulls the covers over herself, she feels Brett snuggle up behind her, spooning her.

"Everything okay?" he murmurs sleepily into her ear.

"Yes. Sasha deleted what he has on us," Mia answers.

"That's good," Brett mumbles.

"There's more, though," Mia says.

"Whaddaya mean?" Brett's words slur together in his sleepy haze.

Mia explains what Sasha told her, about the videos and apparent cheating.

"Wow," Brett muses, seeming more alert. "That's all…awful."

Mia nods in the dark, "Yeah, I know. I don't know what Sasha is going to do next, but she agreed to find a way to leave me out of it." Mia feels Brett's lips on her cheek.

"Good. So…we're safe?" He asks carefully.

"For now, I think so," Mia answers. She feels Brett relaxing against her as she says the words. He hugs her tightly to him.

"Good," he whispers, sounding tired again.

"I knew Danny was a creep, but I guess I underestimated how much of a creep he is," Mia thinks out loud.

"I guess everyone's got secrets," Brett says quietly, nestling his face against Mia's hair. Mia nods against her pillow, and finally lets the exhaustion from the evening hit as she shuts her eyes and lets sleep take over.

CHAPTER 70

Mia left Brett's place early in the morning so that she could head home and change before heading onto campus. He is barely waking when she is already dressed as she lands quick kiss on his forehead before leaving. Mia showers and changes at home, noticing her mood to be considerably lighter. Despite the past few days, it's starting to feel as though everything is slowly falling into place. Her relationship with Brett remains a relative secret which will soon be out in the open. Danny no longer has any hold over her. She's on track to defend her master's thesis. Mia practically wants to knock on wood so as not to jinx her observations. Despite feeling silly, she does so against the doorframe of her apartment as she heads out to school.

Mia spends the morning continuing to revise her slides for her defense, while anxiously watching the time. She passes up lunch with Leigh, feeling her stomach becoming more unsettled as the day drags on. Mia's not sure why she is getting nervous about seeing Sasha this afternoon, but she does know that she's eager to start putting all of this behind her. However, she wants to make sure she supports Sasha in any way she can, given what Sasha has done for her and the harm it's caused her along the way.

Promptly at three in the afternoon, Mia hears a quiet knock on her office door and peers around her desk to see Sasha waiting outside her office.

"Hey, come in," Mia says as Sasha walks in and shuts the door behind herself. Sasha settles into the empty seat across from Mia. She seems tired and melts into the chair. "How are you?" Mia asks.

"Exhausted. I couldn't sleep when I got back home. And this morning I had it out with Danny, and that didn't feel great either."

"What happened with him?" Mia's curiosity taking hold of her.

Sasha takes a deep breath before sharing. "Well, I wanted to find a way to leave you out of it. I confronted him this morning, telling him I was looking for photos of him and me together, for an album I was making, and found all the other things."

Mia stares at her wide-eyed, "And what did he say?"

Sasha makes a sound of disgust, "At first he tried to deny it, and then he started crying saying he's got a problem. And I told him I didn't care, that he's disgusting and that I will find and alert every single girl he's taped, including you." She looks at Mia pointedly.

"Me?" Mia asks concerned.

"Yes, because even though I didn't mention the pictures specifically of you and Dr. Dawson, he'll figure out those are gone. But if you have evidence that he taped you without your consent, perhaps you'll have the upper hand now." At that, Sasha handed Mia a USB drive, which Mia assumes has her video on it, which Sasha confirms. "This is a copy of everything. You have one, and I have one. If Danny tries anything, anything, I told him both you and I have a copy of everything and will find and alert every single woman."

Mia stares at the tiny USB in her hand, "Sasha, I didn't want him to know any of my involvement," she says quietly.

"Well, I didn't want any of this to happen, but you pulled me into it, so this is how I choose to handle it. I hope you can understand that," Sasha says firmly.

Mia nods slowly, "Yeah, yes, okay. Thank you again, Sasha, for believing me and doing all of this." She makes eye contact with Sasha, hoping her gratitude is obvious.

"Anyway, I told him I'm done with him and to never contact me or any of my friends ever again," Sasha concludes.

"Wow, okay," Mia breathes out. The two women just sit and look at each other, both seemingly a lot for words. Mia opens her mouth to say something and stops, not sure of what to say or do next.

"Does Leigh know?" Sasha asks, breaking the silence.

"Leigh?" Mia says confused.

Sasha jerks her head, as if to motion upstairs, "About Dr. Dawson. And you."

Mia shakes her head quickly, "No. You know. My brother knows. That's it."

"But you're going to tell her?" Sasha presses.

Mia adjusts in her chair, "Yes. After this semester, we'll be open about it." Sasha raises an eyebrow. Mia shakes her head, "Not like gross, just, on paper official."

Sasha nods, "Alright. I just don't want to be walking around with this secret forever."

"Of course not," Mia says, "and I'm not expecting you to. Just a few more weeks."

Sasha nods again solemnly. "Good. I guess now we've

reached complete honesty with one another."

Mia feels a stab of guilt, knowing there's one last thing she should share with Sasha. At this point, knowing how hurt Sasha is from the events with Danny, Mia tries to weigh whether it's worth sharing another thing that can hurt her. In helping her tip the scales to a decision, Mia reminds herself how much she owes Sasha now, and how much she deserves the truth. Mia clears her throat, "There's one more thing. I hadn't told you. And you ought to know, and I'm pretty embarrassed by it."

Sasha waits for Mia to continue, uncertain and concerned.

Mia continues quietly, "While you were away during a weekend, last semester, Danny held a movie night. And he kissed me. And I briefly kissed him back, but quickly ended it and left."

Sasha's eyes widen and then narrow, "Alright."

Mia rushes on, "And obviously I should have told you about that too, but I was totally freaked out about that and my initial reaction. Because I would never, *never*, want to hurt you. And I would never help someone cheat. I'm not that kind of person."

Sasha nods slowly, her face stone. "Okay."

Mia takes a deep breath, "I am very sorry. For that, for this, for not being more honest with you, for not trusting you. I fucked up. In a lot of ways. And I'm really sorry." Sasha nods again, her face revealing nothing. "I owe you, Sasha. For all of this. Please know that I am here for you, for whatever. I do really hope that we can move forward from all of this."

Sasha seems to break from her own thoughts and blinks at Mia. "Yeah, let's move forward. And be honest."

Mia nods earnestly. Sasha pushes herself up to stand and glances hesitantly around Mia's office. Mia senses the awkwardness fill the air and stands up before she pulls Sasha into a hug. After a brief pause Sasha returns her hug. "I'm sorry," Mia says quietly again, and feels Sasha nod her head against her. The women break apart and Sasha grabs her things.

"I'll see you around," Sasha says with Mia nodding and saying goodbye before Sasha leaves the office. Mia practically flops into her chair once Sasha has left, feeling completely drained of energy and life from the exchange. Mia's completely unsure where her friendship with Sasha stands at this point. If Mia is being truthful with herself, she probably would not tolerate her own behavior if she was in Sasha's position. Mia can only hope that Sasha is truly willing to move forward and keep her secret for the time being.

Mia eyes the USB key, now sitting on her desk. She has no desire to look through it, and it would feel like a violation against the other women Danny's recorded. She trusts Sasha when she says everything is on it. It needs to go somewhere safe, and her office is not that place. Mia quickly zips it into a small compartment in her purse, and texts a reminder to herself to put it away in her apartment. Phone still in hand, Mia contemplates her next step. She likely needs to contact to Danny, to remind him herself to not report her, and she'd like to catch Brett up. Given that she's still trying her best to follow the rules she and Brett set, she pulls up Danny's contact information and sends a brief text, **Are you on campus?**

CHAPTER 71

Mia sits waiting on a bench outside the campus hospital. It's in a public enough space that should Danny try anything she could yell for help, but private enough that they won't be surrounded by people when they talk. She had thought carefully about the location once Danny texted her back and agreed to meet. A light spring breeze rustled the trees around her and Mia looks around, watching for Danny's approach. She sees him, his head ducked low and hands in his pockets, making his way toward their agreed upon spot. When he finally reaches her, he's scowling.

"So?" He starts, his voice dripping with irritation.

"I'm sure you know by now that Sasha has spoken with me," Mia says calmly.

Danny shrugs and then nods.

"So I know what you have been doing," Mia continues as Danny glares, "and I have evidence of it too." Danny rolls his eyes at her, still quiet. "And if you try to follow through with your earlier threats," Mia glares at Danny, trying to steel herself, "*any of those threats*, I will help each and everyone one of the girls that you recorded to press charges, including Sasha."

Danny rolls his eyes again at Mia. "Is that so?"

Mia nods, feeling more empowered, "Yes. Because what I did may not look great here at school, but you illegally recorded sex acts without these women knowing." Danny rolls his eyes and opens his mouth as if to counter her. Mia holds up a hand to stop him as she says, "And I'm sure it was without their consent, cause neither Sasha nor I gave you any permission to film us. What you did is illegal." Mia holds her head high, maintaining eye contact and nonverbally daring Danny to challenge her. Danny stares, his eyes flashing anger, before his own will seems to dissolve and his body goes slack.

"Whatever Mia," he mumbles.

Mia, emboldened by Danny's appearance of defeat, continues, "And this stands if you also post anything of me online too."

Danny snaps at her, "I don't have anything of you anymore. Sasha deleted it all. And she dumped me. Are you happy?"

Mia chooses to ignore his question and instead replies coldly, "You deserve much worse than just having Sasha dump you. Be happy that *that's* your only consequence." Mia gets up to leave, and pushes her way past Danny.

She hears him call after her, "You be careful now, I can always get evidence again." Mia continues walking away, but still feels anxious as she remembers that she's not in the clear just yet.

Danny's final threat continues to linger over Mia throughout the rest of her afternoon and into her evening. He's right, she acknowledges, until she and Brett have officially documented their relationship with the dean, Danny could still find a chance to photograph them together and blow up each of their lives. This means she and Brett have to lay low and practically keep away from one another until that time comes.

Mia grabs her phone, which had been charging in her kitchen, to text Brett.

Have a moment to talk?

In response her phone immediately begins to ring, with Brett's information flashing on her screen.

"Hey," Mia answers.

"Hi. What's going on? Did you see Sasha today?" Brett asks in quick succession.

"I did. She broke up with Danny this morning. She ah, made copies of his videos and gave me one. I guess as some kind of collateral or something against him? So I have that now," Mia says.

"Huh," Brett replies.

"Yeah, I feel kind of weird having it, and not just going ahead and finding these women, but for now it should keep Danny quiet about us," Mia says, she pauses briefly and continues, "and I saw him this afternoon. To make sure he knows to be quiet."

"How did that go?" Brett sounds concerned.

Mia shrugs, even though Brett can't see it, "As well as it could, I guess. He knows if he makes any move that I will help bring charges against him. I'm hoping it's enough for him to leave me alone. But," Mia takes a deep breath, "he did basically threaten me by saying he could very easily get more photos of me, of us."

"So he's still a problem?" Brett asks warily.

"In a way. I think if we can just be careful," Mia says, before thinking they *had* been careful, "even more careful. Maybe just really putting everything on pause for a few more weeks, until we file our paperwork, he won't get the chance to document anything."

Mia waits for Brett's response, feeling as though the

silence stretched on for forever. Eventually he breaks it, "Yeah, that makes sense I guess. So no seeing each other?"

"Beyond class, correct," Mia confirms. "But that'll pass quickly, the semester is almost over. We've got two weeks left of classes and then finals and then we can do what we need to do," she adds. "We can be open about our relationship," she says firmly.

"Yeah," Brett says slowly and then seems to snap back into the conversation, "yeah, that's a reasonable plan. We just have a few more in person classes left, and your final paper meeting. I think I can manage to behave." Brett's voice is light and teasing at the end. Mia had actually forgotten about meeting with Brett regarding her final paper for his class. However, as long as they're meeting during the day in his office with classes still in session, there's no reason that she can't also force herself to behave.

"So then that's our plan. Survive these last few weeks and then triumphantly fuck each other's brains out," Mia jokes.

"Sounds like a good plan to me," Brett laughs.

"How will you keep yourself occupied? I've got classes and my thesis defense," Mia says lightly.

"I'm the new assistant professor trying to earn tenure,"

Brett says lightly, "I'll be working on papers that need to get published. I can find ways to occupy my time."

Mia smiles, "Of course, the young hotshot professor still has to prove himself."

"I do, despite what you may think," Brett says seriously.

"Of course, I'm just teasing," Mia responds, feeling slightly defensive. She shakes it off, reminding herself that both she and Brett have had a trying few days. Though they didn't discuss it much, she imagines that the threats from Danny must have really shaken Brett, as it had the potential to jeopardize everything he had worked for the last few years. At the end of the day, Brett could have faced more severe consequences than her. Mia calms herself, thinking about this.

More calmly, Mia says "So I guess this is it until finals are over. Or at least, anything extracurricular until finals are over."

"I guess so," Brett replies and Mia thinks she detects some sadness in his tone.

"It'll be worth it," Mia encourages him.

"Absolutely. I guess until then, work hard and take care," Brett says warmly.

"You too. I…I can't wait," Mia says, biting her tongue to hold back from saying *I love you,* surprising herself. They hang up and Mia briefly stares at the phone in her hand. Does she love him? Is it just the rush of emotions associated with the craziness of the last few days? Or has she truly developed such a strong feeling towards Brett?

Mia realizes she's too tired to sort through these questions right now. Her body and brain are both crying out for rest after the week's events, and Mia feels better sorting through her thoughts and feelings before saying anything impulsively to Brett. She places her phone back down on the counter and looks around her apartment.

Despite Renly staring at her from her couch, her apartment seems emptier than usual. Mia rolls her eyes and chides herself for being overly dramatic. She's on an agreed upon mutual break that has nothing to do with breaking up and everything to do with their individual and combined preservation. Rather than allow herself to spiral into negative thoughts, Mia focuses her evening on her thesis defense presentation and mindless TV.

Eventually Mia checks her email one last time before bed, to see that Brett has emailed the seminar class their assigned one-on-one meetings. She scrolls through until she finds her time slot. Her stomach drops for a moment and her breathing quickens. One day after her thesis defense is her meeting with Brett. An early evening meeting on the Friday, when campus will practically be deserted. Mia's hand hovers over her keyboard, wondering whether it would be worth trying to switch with a classmate. Mia sits back in her desk chair and decides to wait on trying to change it. A smile begins to spread on her face as an idea starts to form. Before heading to bed, Mia checks around her apartment for the items she needs, and after confirming what she can be creative with, heads to bed, pleased with her idea.

CHAPTER 72

Mia keeps her head low as the spring semester winds down. She spends some lunches with Leigh and Sasha, and the weirdness between her and Sasha fades with each chance to be social. Mia noticed Leigh shooting her some glances that seemed to translate into *what the hell* at the beginning of these lunches, but those ended as the awkwardness subsided. When Leigh tried to address it more directly, Mia brushed her off, indicating it was nothing and everything was fine between her and Sasha. Eventually Leigh dropped it and the last two weeks of the semester felt shockingly normal.

In addition to her social life becoming tame, Mia completed the slides for her thesis defense and finally feels ready to present to her committee. She even received some rare compliments from her advisor, also indicating she's ready to defend. The unusual exchange could not have been more timely, and when Mia woke up on that Thursday she also had a text message from Brett.

They had chosen radio silence the last time they spoke, and aside from appropriate interactions during class, had no outside communication.

Good luck today! He had texted. Mia smiles, knowing that his text meant he had recalled when her defense was, even though they hadn't spoken in two weeks. She sends off a quick thank you text before getting ready for the day. She purposely scheduled her defense for the morning, so that she didn't feel anxious all day with the meeting hanging over her. Mia dons the one suit she owns that she initially got for graduate school interviews. It's a crisp black pantsuit with a violet blouse and simple gold necklace and matching stud earrings. She pulls on shiny heeled loafers and checks herself over in the bathroom mirror. She feels professional and confident, though knows she's going to feel neither of those in the minutes leading up to her defense.

On campus and in her office, Mia reviews her presentation once more. She practices her talking points and completes a mindfulness breathing exercise to help work through some of her nerves. A few minutes before she plans to head to her reserved conference room, Mia hears a knock at her office door and turns to see Leigh.

"Hey there!" Leigh says with a smile, leaning into the open doorway. "Just came by to wish you luck, and confirm a celebratory drink tonight."

Mia smiles back at her friend, "Thank you and absolutely.

Though calling it celebratory already may be a bit premature?"

Leigh rolls her eyes and clucks at Mia, "C'mon, you're gonna be fine and you will pass. Your advisor wouldn't let you schedule a defense if she thought you were going to humiliate her."

Mia lets out a nervous laugh, "True. Thank you for that vote of confidence."

"You've got this," Leigh encourages Mia again. "And I will see you later for drinks." Leigh leans in and gives Mia's arm a reassuring squeeze before leaving for her own office.

Mia takes a few more deep breaths, before packing up her laptop and grabbing her bag containing water and snacks for her committee, and makes her way to the conference room. She continues to practice steady breathing, trying to be mindful as she sets up her presentation and lays out the food and drink on the conference table. She smooths out her suit and stands waiting at the podium, smiling and ready for her committee members to arrive.

CHAPTER 73

As Mia's committee members file out of the room with their waters and snacks in hand, Dr. Thompson pulls her in for a brief hug.

"Congrats! That went well," Dr. Thompson smiles at Mia, and turns to gather up her things. "I think your committee also gave you some good ideas to follow up on for publishing this as a review."

Mia nods, still feeling warm and sweaty from her defense, but also relieved to have it done. "Yeah, I can start working on those suggestions and get a draft to you after finals."

Dr. Thompson waves a hand dismissively at Mia, "Whenever you get them to me. Also start thinking about turning this into your dissertation proposal. Perhaps you can pull that together over the summer so that I have a draft to review in the fall?"

Mia's unsurprised at the brief celebration turning immediately into planning for her next academic milestones. She simply nods again at Dr. Thompson, "Of course."

As Dr. Thompson heads out the door she says to Mia, "Congratulations again. If you need to touch base as you work on those projects, just send me an email. I'll be traveling a bit, but will get back to you as quickly as I can."

"Yes, of course, thank you again for your guidance!" Mia calls after Dr. Thompson, and is now left alone in the conference room. Mia breathes out a sigh of relief, feeling the weight of this milestone finally lifting from her shoulders. She starts to pack up the remaining refreshments and her laptop and notes.

The door creaks open to the conference room and Mia looks up to see Brett peering in.

"Just saw the department email and wanted say congratulations," he says with a grin.

"Thank you, Dr. Dawson," Mia says, blushing under his gaze.

"I hope you take some time to celebrate the accomplishment," he winks at her and then quickly glances behind him into the hallway.

"Oh, I will," Mia says with a smile.

"Good, well, I'll see you tomorrow then for your paper review," Brett says more seriously and then pops out of the room as quickly as he appeared in it.

Mia finishes gathering up her things and before heading back down to her office stops into the lab where Leigh works. She checks in Leigh's office to find it empty and runs into one of Leigh's labmates instead.

"Looking for Leigh?" Derek asks, familiar with Mia stopping in to talk to Leigh.

"Uh, yeah, is she around?" Mia asks, shifting the items in her arms.

Derek shakes his head, "Naw, she's running participants right now. We've been slammed lately with undergrads trying to get last minute subject credit." He shrugs, "I'll let her know you stopped in."

"Cool, thanks," Mia replies and leaves for her own office, where she carefully unloads her items. She pulls out her phone and sends a quick text to Leigh, confirming drinks for the evening. Next Mia studies the notes she took during the feedback and question portion of her defense, organizing them by the section associated with her paper and adding her own thoughts on how to address each committee member's suggestions. After attending her final statistics seminar, Mia packs up and heads home.

She purposely did not schedule any clients that day because of her anxiety over how her defense would go.

Mia allows herself to relax the rest of the afternoon and into the evening before heading out to meet up with Leigh for drinks. She brushes out her hair and smooths out her light spring dress, donning her jean jacket over it, along with strappy sandals. Leigh initially offered to give her a ride, but Mia chose to drive herself so that she doesn't overdo it that evening.

Mia gets to the bar first and stakes claim to one of the outdoor tables, taking advantage of the nice spring night. Leigh arrives soon after, followed by Sasha. As each woman arrives, they order a drink at the bar and return outside to join Mia. The three women joke and sip on their drinks, toasting to Mia's successful defense and commiserating about final papers.

"Have either of you had your meeting with Dr. Dawson yet?" Leigh asks, as she pushes aside an empty glass when the waiter returns with a new drink for her.

Sasha averts her eyes and shakes her head. "Nope, tomorrow morning. You?"

"Same," Leigh nods and then glances at Mia.

Mia clears her throat, "Tomorrow afternoon."

"Hmm," Leigh muses, "He really left all of this to the last

minute, huh?" Both Sasha and Mia look at Leigh questioningly. "Oh, cause he said he'd meet with everyone two weeks before the papers are due, and it's actually a little under two weeks after tomorrow. It's fine, it's just a quick turnaround, I guess." Leigh shrugs.

"Yeah I guess so," Mia agrees. Quick to change the subject away from Brett, she remarks to Leigh, "I dropped by your office and Derek said you've been swamped with participants?"

Leigh rolls her eyes. "Yes, all the undergrads trying to get last minute extra credit by participating in a study. On the one hand, it's great, we've gotten a lot of subjects. On the other, some of them are so difficult to schedule with and keep insisting on times that aren't available."

Mia and Sasha both nod sympathetically before Sasha pipes up. "Speaking of undergrads," she says while wiggling her eyebrows, "how's Jake?"

Leigh giggles, "He's good. We're good. Nothing too wild to report." Leigh's face becomes more serious and she asks Sasha, "But what about you? How have you been since breaking up with Danny?"

Sasha's face drops and Mia feels guilty about her own involvement in the matter. "I'm fine. I've had more time to focus on my final papers if there's an upside."

Leigh turns her attention onto Mia to lightly tease her.

"And now that you've defended, does this mean you're going to make time to date again?" Sasha tries to hide a slight knowing smile creeping across her face.

Mia narrows her eyes at Sasha before turning to Leigh and giving a noncommittal shrug. "Maybe? I don't know," she says.

"Would you be interested in being set up with someone?" Leigh pushes.

"Like one of Jake's friends?" Mia asks with disinterest.

Leigh rolls her eyes at Mia and takes another sip of her drink. "Firstly, he has several nice friends, so don't make that face. But no, not one of his friends. I was thinking maybe Derek? He's really nice and funny-"

Mia cuts Leigh off, "Ah, no. I think intradepartmental dating may not be the best idea for me."

Sasha coughs and both women turn to her. She waves at them to dismiss it, saying "Sorry, drink went down the wrong pipe." Mia narrows her eyes again at Sasha, who quickly looks away.

Mia continues to Leigh, "He's very nice. It's just…it's just a no for now."

"Okay," Leigh says lightly, unconcerned.

Mia changes the subject to talk about their summer plans

and funding, and after finishing her second drink, bids goodbye to her friends to head home. She felt slightly irritated with Sasha, who has managed to act normal in the last week and then be weird tonight. Mia observes that some of her frustration with Sasha is misdirected. She wishes she could tell Leigh everything that has been going on, and holding back from her best friend has left her feeling guilty. Once it's safe to do so, Leigh will be the first to know, she tells herself.

CHAPTER 74

Mia has been counting down the minutes to her meeting with Brett. While she was initially anxious about having their meeting so late on a Friday, she became more and more excited, given the idea she had brewing. She was distracted all day thinking about her plans, so it was fortunate for her that classes were done and she had no clients to meet with. Mia attempted to work on the final project for her statistics course, but kept getting sidetracked by daydreams.

Leigh texts Mia after her own meeting with Brett, to see if Mia would like to have lunch, and Mia passes, given the nervous butterflies she's feeling. Instead, she briefly texts back and forth with Leigh to see how her meeting went and plan a time to hang out over the weekend.

Mia's nerves are buzzing as the time inches closer and closer to five, her scheduled meeting with Brett. A few minutes before, she gets up from her desk and flattens out the maxi dress she's wearing, which is hiding the short skirt underneath it. She double checks her bag out of nervousness for the items she packed earlier, and then steadily makes her way to Brett's office.

The door to his office is still shut when she gets there, and Mia waits outside, correctly assuming the meeting before hers is wrapping up. A few minutes after five the door opens and one of the social psychology students steps out, waves at Mia, and heads down the hallway.

Mia steps into the open doorway and pulls the door closed behind her. With her back still against the door, she quietly pushes in the lock, hoping to ensure privacy. She smiles widely and then takes a seat across from Brett, who is sitting at his desk, the corners of his mouth slightly turned up.

"Ready to discuss your final paper?" He asks. Mia nods and grabs a hard copy of her paper from her bag, along with a pen. She listens carefully and takes notes as she and Brett go through her report, pausing to answer his questions or ask for clarification of his comments. As they reach the end of her essay, Brett observes, "This was a very thoughtful review. If you can take the time to address the areas of concern that I noted, I honestly think it'd be worth trying to publish."

Mia laughs, and referring back to their conversation months ago, says, "And you'd be second author?"

Brett smiles back at her and winks, "Well, without my input it may not be as publishable."

Mia smiles back and nods, "Uh huh, well first I will need to revise it and turn it back in, and then we can discuss where you think I should submit it."

"That's a great plan," Brett agrees. He hesitates for a moment, as though he wants to saying something, but is unsure. He smiles apologetically, "Well, I guess that's it for now."

A sly smile spreads over Mia's face. "Are you expecting any more students this evening?" Brett shakes his head. Mia's smile widens. "Good, then close your eyes."

"Mia," Brett begins to protest.

Mia shakes her head and shushes him, "Close your eyes and play along."

Brett seems nervous but closes his eyes. When he does so, Mia quickly stands and grabs what she needs from her bag. She pulls off her maxi dress and pulls on the items from her bag, before shoving her previously worn items back in. Mia straightens out the short black skirt, and tucks in the white button up blouse, which is strategically unbuttoned enough to show some cleavage. Her red lacy bra peeks through the fabric and underneath her skirt is the matching thong. Her high heeled black Mary Janes complete her outfit. She quickly runs her hands through her hair, as she notices Brett getting impatient and shifting around in his chair. She moves to stand by the door, and after a deep breath, says "Okay, you can open your eyes."

Brett does so, and sees Mia standing by the door to his office, dressed like a stereotypical school girl. His mouth forms an O in surprise, before he quickly catches himself. "Mia," he starts, "This isn't a good idea."

Mia waves him off with a smile. "The semester is over, campus is deserted, just play along." She goes to twirl a strand of hair in his finger and her face becomes more serious. "Dr. Dawson, thank you for meeting with me on such short notice." She sways her hips as she walks up to his desk. Brett is still skeptical, though his expression begins to soften into intrigue as she gets closer. "I was hoping to meet with you to discuss my grade for your class."

Brett is alarmed and hurriedly whispers, "Mia, I don't-" before she cuts him off with a finger to his lips to quiet him.

"Play along," she says with a wink. She takes her hand back and lazily runs it back and forth along his desk. She changes her posture and demeanor back into character. "As I was saying, Dr. Dawson, I was really hoping to discuss my grade with you." Mia moves between Brett and his desk. He pushes his chair back a bit to make room for her, gazing up at her.

"I really need an A, and my grade is so close," Mia braces her hands behind her on the desk, and pulls herself up to sit on Brett's desk, slightly parting her legs. She leans forward, while holding the edge of the desk. "Is there anything I can do? For extra credit?" Mia practically purrs the lines.

Brett lets out an excited breath, as his alarm and worry have disappeared, and his interest is piqued. "What were you thinking?" He asked huskily.

"Whatever you wanted me to do," Mia breathes, "I'd be happy to. Whatever it takes to fix my grade." Mia gently pushes herself off the desk to kneel in front of Brett in his chair.

Seeming to cringe at first, and then appearing to decide to go with it, Brett responds, "Well, Mia, I would need an oral argument for why you deserve a better grade."

Mia holds back a giggle at the corny line, and comes back at him with, "Dr. Dawson, I'd love to give you oral." At those words, Mia unbuckles Brett's belt before undoing the button on his trousers. She slowly unzips his pants and looks back up at Brett with a smile in her eyes. He's already hard, with his boxer briefs taut over his cock. Mia pulls his cock out of the fly and strokes him. She winks at Brett before wrapping her lips around his thick member.

Brett sighs and relaxes into his chair as Mia's mouth glides over his cock. Her hand follows suit with her mouth, pumping him, and slowly increasing her pace. Brett shudders and grasps at Mia's hair. As he begins to moan, Mia stops and stands up. Brett opens his eyes and gazes at her, his chest rising and falling rapidly. He pulls Mia towards him by the waist, and Mia clambers on top of his lap, straddling him. Brett reaches under her skirt to grab her by the ass and squeezes her cheeks. Mia leans down, brushing her cleavage against Brett's face. He drops his head down and kisses the tops of her breasts, as Mia starts to slowly writhe against Brett, the thin material of her lace thong the only thing separating them.

Brett's hands move to Mia's shirt, tugging and pulling until it's no longer tucked into her skirt. He starts to unbutton it, but fumbles in his eagerness, and Mia takes over. He watches as she slowly unbuttons and removes her blouse, dropping it to the ground, and revealing a lacy red balconette bra, barely containing her breasts. Brett buries his face in them, kissing her chest as his hands move over her.

Brett lifts his head back up and with one hand, pulls Mia's face down to his and kisses her passionately. He holds her close to him as she continues to rock against him. Mia pulls back and whispers into his ear, "Have I earned my A, Dr. Dawson?"

Brett pulls her back in, hungrily kissing her. "Not yet," he groans, his fingers now pulling at her thong. Mia untangles herself from him, getting off his lap and sliding back onto his desk. She parts her legs, leaving her short skirt to rest atop her thighs, baring her thong clad center. Mia rests her hands behind her on the desk, slightly leaning back.

"What else can I do to convince you, Dr. Dawson?" she asks as a strap from her bra loosens and falls down her shoulder. Brett pushes himself out of his chair and pulls his pants and boxers down before approaching Mia. He holds his cock in one hand, continuing to stroke himself as he considers Mia.

Mia wraps her legs around Brett when he's close enough, pulling him to her, allowing her to run her hands down his chest. "I have to tell you, Dr. Dawson, I've had a crush on you all semester, and I would do anything for that A," Mia murmurs. She pulls Brett's face to her and runs her lips along his jaw up to his earlobe, before giving it a nip.

Brett stares into her eyes, his own flaring with desire. "If you want that A, you will have to let me into that tight, wet pussy of yours."

"Tell me how you want me and you can have me," she whispers into his ear before kissing him hungrily.

Brett eagerly returns her kiss, his hands cupping her breasts and freeing her nipples from her flimsy bra. Brett rolls one of her nipples between her fingers while lowering his lips to her neck, kissing and sucking as he moves his mouth to her breasts. He takes one nipple into his mouth and sucks on it hard, causing Mia to gasp. She reflexively pulls him in closer, and feels the tip of Brett's penis press against her opening, her panties preventing his entry.

"Fuck me, Dr. Dawson," Mia breathes, her head thrown back. She gently lowers herself to lay on the desk, as Brett hitches her up to him, holding her thighs. Brett pushes her panties to the side and penetrates her immediately. Mia tries to hold back a gasp of pleasure. Brett steadily plunges into her over and over, and Mia caresses her breasts, moaning quietly. She takes one of Brett's hands and guides him to her clit, her hands over his as he stimulates it.

Brett's pace quickens and Mia's breasts jiggle with the force. Brett gropes her, rolling and pinching her nipples, as Mia keeps her own fingers on her clit, encouraging her pleasure to grow.

"Dr. Dawson," Mia gasps, "I'm going to come." Mia feels the oncoming explosion, ready to let it take over.

"Wait," Brett demands and pulls out of her, Mia gasping from the sudden emptiness. Brett pulls her to stand and turns her around. He pulls her panties off and tosses them to the side, before pushing her legs open and pushing back into her. Mia, filled again, moans with delight and bends forward, holding herself up with finger splayed on the desk. Brett grasps a breast with each hand, groping her as he continues to fuck her from behind. His pace and force quickens and his body slaps against hers, and Mia tries to quiet her cries from the pleasurable pain.

"Yes, oh my god, yes, fuck me harder Dr. Dawson," Mia whimpers, on the verge of orgasm. Brett does as she begs, burying himself into her quicker and harder as Mia's legs almost give out beneath her when her orgasm hits. She cries out as the sensation breaks through, begging Brett, "Come in me, Dr. Dawson, please, come in me."

Mia's words push Brett over the edge and he comes, spilling himself inside of her. He stops pumping after a beat and a visible shiver runs through his body. Brett pulls himself out of Mia once more, leaving Mia to notice the emptiness of his absence.

Mia watches him with a lazy smile as he pulls on his underwear and pants, thoroughly content and pleased with herself. She turns back around to sit on Brett's desk again. "So," she teases, "do I earn my A?"

Brett sits back in his office chair and smiles, resting a hand back on Mia's thigh. "Am I speaking to fantasy Mia or actual Mia?"

Mia laughs, "I guess the fantasy re-enactment is over. How would you grade me on that?"

Brett flicks at her skirt, "Well, it's not plaid," which Mia pouts at, "but otherwise no complaints." He grins at Mia,

"I guess this satisfies both of us." Mia raises a questioning eyebrow at him. "You know, teacher fantasy for me, a not actually private space for you," he explains.

"Oh, yeah. Well, it would be even more fun if I knew the building wasn't empty, but I'll take what I can get," Mia winks. She leans forward and gives Brett a peck on the mouth, and suddenly realizes she's still practically topless. Mia hops off the desk and starts to gather up her shirt and bag to change back. Her maxi dress is over her head and her shoes are switched when there's a loud rap at the door that startles both of them.

CHAPTER 75

Mia and Brett look at each other with alarm. She quickly pulls out her papers and rushes to sit across from Brett at his desk. They're both smoothing out their hair and clothes when Brett calls, "Come in." The door handle is jiggled, but doesn't open as neither of them had unlocked it from earlier. "Shit," Brett mutters and stands to unlock and open the door.

"It's locked," calls a familiar voice on the other side.

"Yep, sorry about that," Brett calls back as he quickly walks to the door, unlocks it and opens it. "Weird problem with my door, happens all the time," he says with a smile through the open doorway. Mia turns around to see Leigh, carrying her bags and clearly prepared to leave campus but with a new confused expression on her face.

"Hey!" Mia says warmly, acting as though everything is

normal, while her mind is racing. What could have Leigh possibly heard? How long was she there?

"Hey," Leigh says, her eyes narrowing. "I uh, I had a late participant and thought maybe you'd want to walk to our cars together. Your office light was on, but you weren't there, so I thought I'd stop by here, since you had your meeting."

Mia nods, her heart still racing, "Yeah, that's a great idea. We had just wrapped up. I just need to get my things from downstairs."

"Uh huh," Leigh says.

Brett continues to stand awkwardly at the door before finally clearing his throat. "Well great, good papers from both of you. I look forward to seeing the final products."

Mia shoves her papers back in her bag and rises from the chair. "Um, thank you again for the input, Dr. Dawson," she says as she heads out of the office. Brett nods and then wishes both women good luck with their finals before shutting the door as Mia walks out.

Mia looks at Leigh and smiles, "Let me just grab the rest of my things and we can head out."

Leigh's face is unreadable, "Alright. I'll meet you out in the front." Mia nods and rushes to the basement as Leigh moves more slowly to their agreed upon location. Mia's heart and mind are racing. How could she be some dumb and reckless? Mia tries to slow her breathing and calm herself down as she grabs what she needs from her office and locks up. It's going to be fine, she tells herself, it's Leigh.

She pulls all of her things together while in the basement, including her laptop and notebooks for her other classes. Finally she shimmies her skirt off from underneath her dress and shoves it towards the bottom of her bag, along with the heels she had threw in there earlier. In this process Mia realizes her panties are still somewhere on Brett's office floor. Did Leigh see them, she wonders, but quickly pushes the thought away as the underwear had to be behind the desk and Leigh didn't even step into the office. Mia takes a few deep breathes, in an attempt to slow her thoughts and heart rate. She instinctively smooths her hair and dress once more, then locks up her office on her way out. Mia exits through the front of the building, noticing her footsteps echoing, suggestive of an empty building.

Leigh waits at the bottom of the steps, her back to the front door. Mia reaches the bottom and announces a "Hey," before gently touching Leigh on the shoulder.

Leigh turns around, her eyes wide and her face seemingly uncertain. "Hey," she says back quietly. She seems to gently shake herself for a minute and then tilts her head in the direction they need to walk to their parking lot. Mia nods and they start their trek down campus.

Mia remains silent on the walk, still wondering if Leigh heard anything, when Leigh stops abruptly and clears her throat. “Mia,” she starts and takes a deep breath, “Mia did you just fuck Dr. Dawson for a good grade?”

Mia has to stifle a laugh from shock, though her heart rate picks back up. “Oh my god, no, Leigh. Why…why would you ask that?”

“Because I heard you ask about your grade. And…” Leigh screws up her face, getting ready to spit out the rest of her words, “and I could swear I heard some ah, suspicious noises before then.”

Mia’s breathing has practically stopped. She looks at Leigh, trying to figure out what Leigh is thinking. “It’s not what you think,” Mia starts to say.

“Oh. My. God. Mia!” Leigh’s voice starts to rise. “Are you fucking serious?”

Mia shakes her head, “Let me explain.”

Leigh’s eyes widen and she gets louder, “Let you explain? You gave me so much shit for hooking up with Jake, which happened *after* he wasn’t in my class anymore, and you’ve just fucked our professor? Oh my god, how long has this been going on?”

Mia whips her head around, ensuring that no one else is

around and can hear them. She motions with her hands to quiet down to Leigh, who now is livid. "Look, it's not what you think."

"Then what is it? Are you sleeping with him?"

Mia sighs, "Yes."

"Jesus fucking Christ, Mia," Leigh says exasperated.

"Let me explain," Mia begs again. Leigh closes her mouth and looks at Mia disbelievingly. "Okay, well, we met during winter break. I didn't know he was the new professor, he didn't know I was a grad student here. We had a date and clicked, and it was later that we found out."

"He's…he's the guy from winter break?" Leigh asks, incredulous. Mia nods. "When did you figure it out?"

Mia sighs again, "Right before the semester started. He was meeting with Dr. Thompson right before I met with her, ran into him in her office. Believe me, we were both shocked. And initially, we decided to call it quits, because obviously it was messy and complicated."

"And? Why did that change? Cause what I heard didn't sound like it was over," Leigh crosses her arms.

"We, we uh," Mia stutters, feeling caught off guard by her friend's anger. "We just didn't want to quit. In the end," she squeaks out. Leigh is slowly shaking her head. Trying to defend herself, Mia continues, "We compartmentalized. Professional during the week and dating during the weekend." Mia casts her eyes down, ashamed under Leigh's glare. "We're going to file paperwork with the dean. That was always the plan. Once the semester ended."

"And just now?" Leigh demands.

Mia glances back up at Leigh and says earnestly, "Was a one off. Seriously. It was just a silly thing I went for since it was the end of the semester."

Leigh shakes her head, "The grade talk?"

"A joke. Really," Mia insists. "Cause I was, ugh," Mia hates having to explain the rest and feels gross and pathetic having to do so, "I was acting out a fantasy for him. Pretending to be a school girl, you know?"

Leigh rolls her eyes, "I cannot believe you."

"That's the truth!" Mia exclaims.

"Oh, I get that. I cannot believe you've been doing this. You've had bad taste in guys before, but really, Mia," Leigh scolds.

Mia steps back in shock, wounded by Leigh's comment. "Leigh," she starts to say, but is at a loss for words.

"Does anyone else know about this?" Leigh almost barks

at Mia.

Mia weighs what she says next, opting for the truth, "Yes. Sasha, and unfortunately Danny."

Leigh makes a sound of disgust. She shakes her head again at Mia, "I can't believe you. And I can't believe those are the people you trusted." Mia opens her mouth to respond, but Leigh cuts her off. "No, I don't want to hear anything else." Leigh storms off, leaving Mia, shocked and hurt standing alone on campus.

CHAPTER 76

Mia stares at her phone. Her apartment has grown dark and her recently heated frozen dinner sits untouched in front of her. After Leigh walked off, Mia waited to give Leigh her space before finishing the trek to her car. She was surprised by Leigh's reaction and was frozen when Leigh left. Now that she's had some time to think about, to process what Leigh said about her, Mia's feeling a mix of emotions. She feels shocked by Leigh's anger, hurt from Leigh's assessment, and angry that she didn't get to continue to explain. She wants to reach out, to give the rest of her story, but doesn't know if Leigh is even open to hearing it. At this point, given how Leigh has reacted, Mia doesn't know if she's even willing to share more with Leigh. Would Leigh have any compassion for her after she learns why Danny knows? Or would Leigh throw it back in Mia's face regarding her "bad choices?" Without an answer to these worries, Mia is left it to stare at her phone and wonder what to do next.

Her trance is broken by her phone buzzing. Mia blinks and sees that Brett is calling. She lets it ring out, not ready to share with him what has happened. He didn't handle Sasha knowing very well, and she was fairly cool about it. Mia can't imagine how upset he'd be if he knew how Leigh reacted. Instead, Mia picks up her phone and calls Luke, hoping for less judgment and more support.

"What's up?" Luke answers.

"Drama," Mia says with regret, imagining Luke rolling his eyes at her answer.

"What's going on?" he asked calmly.

Mia takes a deep breath and launches into everything. She tells Luke about Danny, how she involved Sasha to help her, and Leigh's reaction to finding out about Brett. Mia glossed over exactly how Leigh found out, as it would be mortifying for her and figuring it would be gross for him. Luke is mostly silent on his end of the line, with the exception of an occasional "uh huh" to indicate he's still listening.

"And that's everything. Except of course that Leigh doesn't know what happened with Danny, and I wanted to explain to her why Danny knows, but she stormed off before I could. So, mess. Drama." Mia finishes up and waits for what feels like an eternity for Luke to respond.

Eventually she hears Luke breathe out and say, "Geez,

Mia…I don't know what to say. That's all…a lot."

Mia feels her emotions starting to surge and the urge to cry, stammering out a "Yeah."

"I'm sorry you're going through all of this. That stuff with Danny? Threatening you? Honestly, you should press charges. Or get a restraining order. Or something, cause he sounds dangerous," Luke sounds serious and concerned.

Mia shakes her head and says into the phone, "No, he could still report me. I just want to be done with him. I want nothing to do with him."

"Okay," Luke says skeptically. "And what are you going to do about Leigh?"

"I don't know. I'm hurt and I'm mad, and I don't know what to do," Mia answers. "She didn't give me a chance to explain myself and what she said about me…it feels awful."

Luke is quiet and Mia can imagine him silently agreeing with Leigh's words. She quietly asks, "You think so too? That I make bad decisions?"

Luke groans, "Don't put words into my mouth."

"But you do," Mia insists.

Luke sighs loudly. "You're smart, Mia, you are. But yes,

you make some less than stellar choices." He pauses and after a beat continues, "I'm not trying to pile on you. Brett seems like a nice enough guy, so I get why you wanted to stick it out. And you could have maybe, thought that through a little more?"

Mia feels crushed with her brother's reply. Does she truly not think when it comes to relationships? Is this mess entirely her own making? Defeated, she asks Luke, "So what am I supposed to do now?"

"I don't know, Mia," Luke says. "Find a way to talk with Leigh? Figure your shit out?"

"Break up with Brett?" she whispers.

"I'm not saying that," Luke hedges, "just figure yourself out. What do you want? What's the best way to go about that?"

Mia nods, "Yeah, you're right." She gives a small smile Luke can't see, "Maybe you should be the therapist."

"Pass," he says definitively.

"Thank you for listening. And for not being too hard on me," Mia says.

"Uh huh, anything else I can do?" Luke asks.

"No, just thank you. I love you," Mia says fondly.

"Love you too, now go figure out your shit."

"Aye aye captain," Mia responds and bids her brother goodbye.

CHAPTER 77

After hanging up with Luke, Mia's left with a choice to try Leigh or connect with Brett. She figures if she calls Leigh, she'll just be ignored. Talking to Brett will end up worrying him, and Mia would rather not have another person upset with her right now. With that thought in mind, Mia grabs an unopened bottle of wine and her keys and leaves her apartment for her car. On the drive to Leigh's apartment Mia repeats to herself that if she can explain, Leigh will understand. With all of the craziness that has happened to her recently, she wishes she had trusted her friend enough to open up and rely on her. Instead, Mia recognizes, she kept her own counsel and may have suffered for it.

Mia knocks on Leigh's apartment door, and sends a text as well.

It's me. Please open up.

Mia hears footsteps and the sound of the lock being undone before the door swings open. Leigh stands in the open doorway, her face blank once more.

"Thank you," Mia says weakly. She holds up the bottle of wine, "Could I come in and explain myself? I've brought wine."

Leigh sighs and steps back, making room for Mia to come in. She gestures Mia into the apartment, where Jake is already sitting on Leigh's couch.

"Oh, I uh, I'm sorry, I didn't know Jake was here," Mia directs to Leigh before saying hi to Jake, who nods back at her. His expression suggests Leigh has shared something with him about Mia, but Mia cannot quite read it.

Jake looks uncomfortably from Leigh to Mia and back again before clearing his throat. "I'll uh, I'll head home for the night." He bounds off the couch and gives Leigh a kiss and heads out the still open door, closing it behind him. Leigh locks it and then turns her attention back to Mia, arms crossed.

"Well?" she asks Mia skeptically.

"How about we have some wine, and I'll start," Mia suggests. Leigh shrugs and takes the bottle from Mia into the kitchen, where she uncorks it and pours it into two glasses. Mia follows her to the couch where they sit and

Leigh hands a glass over to Mia.

Mia takes a long sip. "Okay, the first thing I want to start with, is that I'm sorry. I'm sorry that I haven't told you anything that's been going on. There's been a lot. And I felt like I had to keep all of this a secret, and maybe I shouldn't have."

Leighs nods, "Correct. So…what is going on exactly?"

Mia takes a deep breath, "I have been sleeping with Brett. Since winter break." Leigh's face is pained but Mia presses on. "We had a brief break once I figured out he was going to be my teacher this semester. We were both horrified, embarrassed, and sad. I don't even know all the right words to use when we discovered our actual situation. I truly meant to cut things off with him. But somehow, I got sucked back into it." Mia pauses as Leigh continues to look at her questioningly. "And I guess a part of me didn't want to end things. I liked him. And I liked the…I don't know, thrill that came along with our relationship. Having a secret boyfriend? Sneaking around? I just liked it. And we agreed to make it through the semester and then file paperwork with the dean to acknowledge our relationship. Even though the sneaking around was fun, the goal the whole time was to make it safely to the end of the semester and have a relationship that other people could know about."

Leigh nods, though her expression is unchanged.

"And then, shit got complicated. Bad. Turns out Danny had been spying on me. Maybe spying isn't even the right word. Stalking? He had evidence of my relationship with Brett. He threatened me. He was going to turn us in if I didn't sleep with him. And if I reported anything he was doing to blackmail me, he was going to," Mia takes another deep breath, worried her friend will judge her more, "he was going to post private pictures of me online." Leigh's face slowly turns from stone to disbelief and then disgust.

"He did what?" she asks.

Mia nods, "He stalked me. Took photos. Threatened me. Threatened Brett. I was terrified and freaking out. The only thing I could think to do was ask Sasha for help. And even doing that felt dangerous, since I didn't know how she'd react and if *she'd* turn us in."

Leigh presses her lips together and nods slowly as Mia continues. "So I asked Sasha to find the evidence and get rid of it. And she did." Mia takes another swig from her glass. "And Sasha didn't just find pictures of me and of Brett and me. She founds videos. Danny had been secretly recording him having sex. At least we both assume it was secretly, because he had videos of Sasha and myself, neither of which we knew about. But not just us, other women too. Even while he was with Sasha."

Leigh's mouth has dropped open in shock. "What?" she says with disbelief.

"I know. It's insane. So Sasha made two copies of everything he had and then deleted all his originals. She has one copy, and I have another." Mia shudders, "It's our collateral against him. He stays quiet and we don't press charges or find these other women and help them press charges."

"Did you see who was on these recordings?" Leigh asks quietly.

Mia shakes her head, "No, I don't have any interest in looking at them. I just trust what Sasha says." Leigh nods again silently, so Mia finishes her mea culpa. "So that's everything. That's why Danny and Sasha know. I don't have a good excuse for why I hadn't told you about Brett. Maybe I should have, and had some of my decision making reflected back at me. But I didn't, and I regret that I didn't trust you enough. So that's where I'm at now. With a USB of sex tapes and a secret boyfriend, who won't be a secret much longer, and a best friend who hates me." Mia chokes on the last words, surprising herself.

"Jesus, Mia," Leigh eventually says. "What a fucking mess." Mia snorts and then bursts into tears. Mia places her glass down and covers her face. She feels Leigh's hand gently stroking her upper arm. "I'm not trying to make you cry, just…what's the word? Reflecting?" Mia laughs through her tears and nods, while wiping off her face.

"So…now what?" Leigh asks gently.

Mia sniffs and shrugs. "Well, I'm hoping to fix things with you."

Leigh nods slowly. "I'm sorry that I was quick to judge you, clearly you've been going through it. I still don't like the idea of you sleeping with one of our professors. I think it's asking for trouble. Another kind of trouble than what Danny brought."

Mia purses her lips and listens carefully. "I hear you, and I appreciate your concern for me. I have been trying to be thoughtful about this. I guess, I'm not asking you to like this relationship, but at least still be my friend? Support me?"

Leigh is hesitant. "I will support you, but I'm going to hold out on supporting the whole you and Brett thing." Leigh pauses briefly at calling their professor by his first name. "Give me some time, and I don't know, I guess I'll get to know him on a non-professor level? And maybe I'll get more comfortable with this whole thing."

Mia nods, satisfied enough with Leigh's answer. It's not a full-throated embrace, but Mia recognizes it may be the most she could get out of Leigh at this time. "Okay, well, I will take what I can get. Thank you for listening to me." Mia picks her glass back up and holds it out to Leigh. "To the end of the semester."

Leigh lifts her glass to meet Mia's and adds, "To dissertation proposals."

Mia rolls her eyes and jokes, "Ugh, and here I thought we were cool with each other." Leigh laughs and they clink their glasses, toasting to a renewed friendship.

CHAPTER 78

The last days of finals passed quickly and uneventfully for Mia, which is exactly what she had wanted. She turned in her final papers and terminated a number of her therapy cases, only planning to retain a few during the summer. Without classes during the next months, and funding from her advisor to work in the lab, Mia feels hopeful about focusing on her dissertation proposal and actually having time to breathe and relax. This sense of relief is what led her to convince Brett to take a weekend trip with her to the beach.

Brett was initially skeptical about the plans, as they still needed to file paperwork and the potential to run into people they knew. Mia was able to convince him by planning their trip to a beach less commonly visited by the students and faculty of Earl. She enlisted Leigh to check in on Renly while she was gone and created a to-do list for upon her return, including vague ideas for publishing her master's thesis and attempting a minimalist approach for her apartment.

As she was more familiar with the route, Mia picked up Brett and drove them out to the coast. As they cross over the sound into the small beach town, Mia feels all the stress and tension of the semester melt away. It was as though the incidents with Danny, the fight with Leigh, and the stress over her master's thesis never happened. Finally, with Brett beside her, it simply felt like she was spending time with her boyfriend without fear of discovery.

They checked into a recently renovated boutique hotel that Mia found, but Brett graciously paid for, and threw down their bags. They both quickly change into bathing suits and grab the beach towels Mia brought along.

Settling onto the beach, surrounded by blissfully ignorant strangers, Mia lays out in the sun and closes her eyes. Brett's propped up next to her, reading a book. She opens one eye and peeks at him, enjoying the view. She closes her eye again and sighs contentedly.

"Something you'd like to say?" Brett asks her.

Mia shakes her head, eyes still shut, but a smile crawling across her face. "No, just feel like a normal person for once. It's nice."

Brett laughs. "What's making you feel normal? Being on the beach?"

"No, just being out. In public. With you. No hiding or sneaking around or anything. It's nice." She rolls onto her side and props herself up with one arm, now looking at Brett. "Don't get me wrong, there was something thrilling about our secret, but it was also exhausting."

Brett puts his book down, nods and says, "Yeah. And terrifying? Whereas now, here, we can have an actual date."

"We're going to have a whole weekend of dates," Mia confirms with a smile.

After an afternoon in the sun and before heading to dinner Mia takes a quick shower after Brett completed his. She looks around in the shower and only sees a bar of soap, instead of his usual orange-y body wash. She scrubs herself down, relishing the feel of her skin clean from sunblock. Bret pops into the bathroom while she towels off.

"You didn't bring your usual soap," Mia observes.

"Huh?" Brett asks distractedly while rummaging through a toiletry bag.

"The stuff that makes you smell like oranges," Mia elaborates, "I love the scent. It makes you yummy." She winks at him and squeezes his butt as she passes him on her way out of the bathroom to get dressed.

Later that evening they devour a seafood feast at one of the local restaurants and then walk hand-in-hand on the beach at dusk before Brett and Mia end up back in their hotel room. Mia doesn't even bother with fancy lingerie, and just strips down to nothing. Her skin is already sun-kissed after their afternoon on the beach. Brett grins when he turns around to see her naked and quickly removes his own clothing. He starts to stroke himself, while quickly closing the space between them and pulling Mia in for a kiss.

Mia wraps her arms around Brett, holding him close, their bodies warm from the sun and the heat from this moment. Brett pushes the hair back from Mia's face and kisses her gently. Mia returns his kiss, their mouths moving in unison. Mia runs her hands down Brett's back and squeezes his butt with one hand, while slipping another between them, to grasp his hard cock and gently tug. Brett's kiss become more urgent, flicking his tongue into her mouth and pulling on Mia's lips with his teeth as he breaks away.

Mia steps back, breathless, and nods towards the bed. Brett quickly throws the blankets back and crawls in, and Mia follows. She curves her body against his, holding him close as he resumes kissing her. She rolls onto her back and Brett slides over her, propping himself up. Mia runs her hands over Brett's back and through his hair, clenching and releasing, while he rocks above her. She feels his erection press against her belly as he leans down and runs kisses along her neck, nibbling and sucking as he goes. Mia moans and her thoughts jumble, thinking that this can't be wrong when it feels this good.

"I need to feel you inside me," she whispers hoarsely. Brett gazes down at her and nods wordlessly. He licks the palm of his hand and rubs himself, before repositioning to enter her. Mia moans quietly as he slowly guides himself in.

Brett sighs in Mia's ear, "I need to be in you," leading Mia to shudder. She wraps her legs around him as Brett steadily moves above her. His lips travel from her mouth, to her jawline, to her earlobe, to her neck, and back all over again. Mia's nails dig into his back and her legs tighten around him.

Mia's breathing intensifies and Brett kisses her passionately. He breaks free from the kiss and rests his forehead against hers as his pace quickens. Mia holds on to Brett, her thoughts clouding her sensations. This feels different, she notices. She pushes back the urge to say the sudden thought rolling around her head, the words that change everything, the realization that she was now deeply emotional about their connection. She moves her face enough to kiss Brett, to occupy her mouth as her thoughts swirl. Mia pushes her thoughts aside, trying to refocus on the movements, sensations, and pleasures that come with the moment. She buries her face into Brett's shoulder and whispers, "Faster," to which he complies.

Mia bites down on his shoulder, causing Brett to gasp and she whispers again, "Come, please come."

Mia feels her own pleasure simmer to her breaking point and the release feels sweeter than previous times. She's thoroughly entranced in her moment that she barely registers when Brett reaches his own climax, collapsing on her after he's finished. She closes her eyes, feeling herself melting both physically and emotionally.

"You alright there?" she hears Brett ask.

Mia opens her eyes and smiles, "Yeah, I'm good. That was good."

Brett smiles back, "Well then, good." He lays beside her, his hand on his own chest, which Mia watches as it rises and falls with each breath. She contemplates saying it out loud, but hesitates, not sure if this moment is the moment.

Brett glances at her and notices her staring, "What's up?"

Mia shakes her head while smiling, "Nothing. It's nothing. Just nice to be here with you without all the stress and craziness that had been hanging over us. It's just, normal right now."

Brett nods beside her and props himself on his side to make eye contact with her. "Does that bore you?" he asks.

Mia shakes her head, "No, I'm relieved. Now we can go back, file whatever needs to be filed, and just be normal. Have a real date. In public."

"Mmhmm," Brett says with a smile. He leans down and gives her a quick peck on the cheek. "That will be nice," he says, as he swings himself out of the bed and pulls on his boxers.

Mia pulls on her panties and an oversized t-shirt to sleep in. They both crawl back into the bed and she snuggles up against Brett's chest, and he rests an arm around her. She opens her mouth as if to share her thoughts, but closes it again.

"Hmm?" Brett asks sleepily.

"Good night," Mia chooses to say.

"Night," Brett mumbles back and Mia closes her eyes and lets sleep take her.

CHAPTER 79

Mia reflects on the drive back home about the easy, pleasant, and relaxing weekend. Being out in public spaces with Brett felt like a confirmation of their relationship, that it could actually work and that they were actually a fit for one another. Mia managed to hold back on telling Brett fully how she was feeling, uncertain if he was in the same place, and scared to be the first to say it. To say *I love you.*

Instead, she just kept glancing over at Brett, with a goofy smile on her face. He didn't catch most of her glances, as he had fallen asleep in the passenger seat next to her. Eventually, after what must have been her thousandth peek, he blinked and saw her.

"Hey," he says as he stretches out as much as the car allows him.

"Hi, good nap?" Mia asks.

Brett nods and yawns, "Mmhmm." He opens his eyes at Mia, who's still grinning. "What is it?"

"Huh?" Mia asks, her eyes back on the road.

"That look on your face," Brett clarifies.

Mia glances at him briefly, smiling, and turns back to the road. "Nothing, just thinking what a nice weekend that was. I'm excited to have actual dates with you back home." Mia looks back at Brett again, and then adds, "Maybe even have you meet my friends."

Brett squints his eyes, "Haven't I met them? Like Leigh and Sasha?"

Mia rolls her eyes, though Brett can't see it. "In a school context. I'm talking about a more casual context."

"Ah, right," Brett says hesitantly.

Mia catches his tone and grips the wheel a little tighter. "No?"

"I'm not saying no. It's just that it'll be a little weird, right? Especially with Sasha?" Brett says quietly.

Mia chews the inside of her cheek. "Yeah, I guess. I mean we don't have to dive into hanging out with my friends." Mia feels her heart sink a little, but tries to reason with her emotions. It may still be too soon after all for that kind of interaction. Sasha knows more than Mia would have liked, and Leigh probably still needs more time to get comfortable with Mia and Brett together.

Brett nods, "Yeah, let's just give it some time. There are aspects of our relationship that just aren't in sync. Let's just get the private and public on the same page, and then find a way to do what you're asking for."

Mia nods in return, though feels confused. To her, part of the public syncing he's referring to means being able to spend time with her friends and him together. She sighs to herself, unsure of how to express this, but Brett interrupts her thoughts.

"Let's aim for growing us this summer. And once we see where we're at, we can then figure out friends and family and paperwork." Brett's last words hit Mia like a punch to her gut. She's shocked to hear him suggest delaying their notification to the dean. She glances at him briefly, wide-eyed and hurt. Brett sees her face and quickly says, "That doesn't sound right. What I should have said is I want more time between the semester ending and us telling the dean. So that it doesn't look like something started during the semester. I want it to look like we started dating in the summer. That's all. So that we're less likely to be accused of impropriety or whatever."

Mia feels uncertain, but nods, though her heart is still racing. She tries to give Brett a reassuring smile, but drives the rest of the way back to his home in silence.

Mia pulls into the guest spot by Brett's townhome and parks. "Mind if I come in to use the bathroom before I head home?"

"Of course not," Brett says, hopping out of the car and grabbing his bag from the backseat. Mia follows him up to his front door and waits while he finds the correct key to unlock it. As he puts the key into the lock, it suddenly swings open, causing Brett to step back in surprise and step on Mia's foot.

Mia cries out at the unexpected pain and before looking up. She sees a beautiful woman in the doorway, with long, bouncy brown hair and bright green eyes. She's wearing a short dress and is barefoot.

"Hi Brett! Tyrion is all settled in, he handled the drive well," she smiles widely at Brett, practically batting her eyelashes. Her eyes than land on Mia, finally noticing her. "And who's this?" she asks warily.

Mia pushes her way past Brett, who seems stunned into silence, to extend her hand to the stranger. "Mia, Brett's ah, girlfriend."

The brunette tosses her hair, sending a wave of a familiar orange scent, and regards Mia's hand. "It's nice to meet you Mia, I'm Emily Dawson, Brett's wife."

CHAPTER 80

Drunk and splayed out on her couch, Mia tries to work her way through what had just happened. She was speechless after Emily introduced herself. Mia had turned, briefly, to stare at Brett in shock, before she quickly made her way back to her car, bathroom trip forgotten. Brett had tried to catch her arm, tried to explain but she waved him off, pushed him off, and pulled out of his complex's parking lot like a bat out of hell.

Mia didn't even emotionally register what had happened until she got to her apartment's parking lot. She felt the surge of tears and quickly ran into her home, throwing her bag down in the entry way, before running to the kitchen sink and throwing up. She noticed with bitterness this being the second time a man has literally made her vomit in such a short time span. After drinking some water from the faucet to wash away the taste of bile, Mia sunk down onto her kitchen floor and starting sobbing. She cried without recognizing every emotion that was hitting her. As her tears slowed and she began to hiccup, she slowly started to sort through her thoughts.

He lied to her. She was hurt. He lied to her. She was angry. He lied to her. She was embarrassed. He lied to her. She was ashamed.

Mia couldn't help but wonder if their relationship was secretive now for dual reasons. Not just the complicated student-teacher piece, but the whole *he was married the whole time* piece. Mia attempts to wipe at her face with her sleeve, but gives up. She stands up and grabs some paper towels to wipe her eyes and blow her nose. The harshness of the towel makes her already raw feeling face burn more.

She stares blankly at the kitchen countertop. She risked everything that was important to her. Her education, her future career, her friendships, even her relationship with her brother was strained.

Mia automatically grabs an unopened bottle of wine and quickly works to uncork it. She pours a large amount into a mug and downs it with a few gulps. She pours another mug-full and takes it to the couch.

She can't tell anyone about this. Leigh and Luke will each say *I told you so* in some fashion. She can't face Sasha with another embarrassing fact about herself. Instead, Mia continues to sip from her mug of wine and polishes it off as she begins to cry her couch.

She's oblivious to her phone ringing in her bag, abandoned by her front door. As the heavy, drunken, fog washes over her, she reminds herself how only hours ago she was thinking about how she felt about Brett. How she was so excited for this next phase in their relationship. Mia cries quietly to herself, rolls over, and passes out.

When she wakes up, it's dark in her apartment and Renly has curled up at her feet. He looks as though something has disturbed him and his face is turned to Mia's apartment door. She blinks at him in the dark and then hears the knock, a repetition of what likely woke both her and the cat up.

Mia goes to check her phone, to see the time, and realizes she never took it out of her bag. She stumbles over to it, flipping on a light switch and blinking in the sudden, harsh light. She digs through her bag to pull her phone out, and sees it's nine in the evening. She also has five missed calls. All from Brett. There's a voicemail, but she swipes to delete it without listening. There's no point, there's no excuse, she decides.

A third knock on her door and Mia peers out the peephole. Brett.

"Go away," she calls through the door.

"I can explain," Brett says.

"Go away," Mia repeats.

"Emily is my ex. We're separated. We are divorcing. She's the…" Brett's voice trails off. "She's the one that cheated on me. We were married, and after that, I couldn't make it work. It's been over. Mia," his voice cracks. "Mia, I'm sorry."

Mia stares at the door silently.

"Please, Mia, let me in and I can explain. I'm sorry. I was scared to tell you. I was scared to tell you because I think I'm falling in love with you. I was worried it would scare you away." Brett's voice is unsteady on the other side of the door.

Mia feels the alcohol start to chip away at her resolve. She steels herself, and tries one last time, "Go away, Brett, please."

"I'm sorry Mia, I am. I fucked up. I'm sorry." Mia hears Brett's voice float once more through her door. It's finally silent and after a moment she checks the peephole again to see her front stoop empty. She breathes a momentary sigh of relief.

Mia practically drags herself and her luggage back to her bedroom. She grabs her bathroom supplies out of the bag and settles into a hot shower. She sits in the tub with her arms clasped around her legs. Hot water pelts her hair, as she's buried her face into her knees. Her tears mix with the shower. Her anger and hurt with Brett turn into frustration with herself.

She loves him and she hates herself for it.

ABOUT THE AUTHOR

Phoebe Thorpe lives in North Carolina with her partner and menagerie of pets. When she's not writing, she enjoys gardening, hiking, and spending time on the beach. Her time in graduate school was far less sexy than the contents of this book.

Made in the USA
Middletown, DE
25 September 2021

49038812R00305